Books by Hermann Hesse

STORIES OF
FIVE DECADES

Stories of
Five Decades

✺

HERMANN HESSE

Edited, and with an introduction, by
THEODORE ZIOLKOWSKI

Translated by
RALPH MANHEIM

With two stories translated by
Denver Lindley

Farrar, Straus and Giroux

NEW YORK

Contents

All the stories in this book were translated by Ralph Manheim, except for "Tragic" and "Dream Journeys," which were translated by Denver Lindley

The year of composition follows each title; in most cases, first publication in German also occurred that year

Introduction

IN 1921 Hermann Hesse's publisher urged him to prepare a selected edition of his works. But as Hesse read through the products of his past twenty-two years of literary activity, he came to the sobering conclusion that "there was nothing there to select." A realistic appraisal of his own abilities prevented him from invoking, even for purposes of comparison, the works of the grand masters of narrative: Cervantes, Dostoevsky, Balzac. Yet even when he considered such models as Turgenev or the nineteenth-century Swiss writer Gottfried Keller, Hesse realized that he was "by no stretch of the imagination a storyteller." For all his works, he belatedly saw, dealt not with the world but only with his own "secret dreams and wishes," his own "bitter anguish." "There was no doubt in my mind that, of all my stories, not a single one was good enough as a work of art to be worth mentioning."

Hesse's gloomy reassessment of 1921 anticipates his reflections on "the questionable art of storytelling" in the introduction to his late tale "The Interrupted Class." True storytelling, he argues, is possible only in societies in which the narrator can take for granted a common basis of language, values, and understanding between himself and his readers. But the fragmentation produced by the proliferation of beliefs and ideologies in the twentieth century has destroyed that common ground, isolating the author as merely one among countless alienated individuals in a pluralistic world. In his own efforts to use revered models of the past in order to come to grips with his essentially modern experience, Hesse had been, as he put it, a "deceiver deceived." As a result, he made up his mind henceforth to eschew "the good old tradition of storytelling" and to seek new modes of expression that, though less perfect and less beautiful, would provide a more honest reflection of the consciousness that he sought to render. These attempts, which produced his major novels beginning with *Demian* (1919), are the works with which most readers now identify Hesse.

Hesse's disenchantment with his early works and his determination to create a new style resulted directly from his experience with psychoanalysis in the years 1916 and 1917, during which he underwent some seventy sessions with Josef B. Lang, a disciple of Jung. The reevaluation of all his beliefs, sparked notably by the writings of Jung and Nietzsche, prompted him to turn frankly inward to the problems of his own consciousness. As a result, narratives that can be called "stories" in any conventional sense virtually disappear from his work. Instead, Hesse increasingly favored literary forms that enabled him to examine his own past and present, singling out for particular scrutiny those moments at which individual experience achieves the level of universal validity. "Fiction" begins to give way to essays that move from the private to the public, from the real to the symbolic, and to autobiographical reflections that turn out to be less an account of his life than an attempt to comprehend its meaning. And in his "fiction," from *Demian* to *The Glass Bead Game* (1943), "storytelling" in the traditional sense recedes in order to allow large mythic patterns to emerge. The forms that Hesse favored in the second half of his life—essay, autobiography, and mythic-symbolic narrative—constitute three different modes of access to the single problem that obsessed him: his own consciousness and its place in a timeless reality that transcends immediate temporal concerns.

Yet this seemingly abrupt change of direction *nel mezzo del cammin,* to cite one of Hesse's favorite poets, is no reason for us to reject the earlier works, as Hesse himself felt inclined to do in that moment of disillusionment in 1921. As we look back at them—with the benefit of hindsight, to be sure—we can see foreshadowed there not only the themes of alienation and introspection but even the style of mythic generalization that has attracted a new generation of readers to Hesse in the second half of the twentieth century. And in the 1941 introduction to a new edition of his first prose a somewhat mellower Hesse conceded that even such juvenalia as *An Hour beyond Midnight* (1899) and *The Posthumous Writings and Poems of Hermann Lauscher* (1901) are crucial documents for the history of his development.

Hesse's first published prose piece opens when a "shipwrecked dreamer" lays down his oars to greet the isle of his dreams. But his eye is suddenly caught by his reflection in the dark-green waters of the bay, and for two paragraphs, until he finally turns his attention back to the shore, he loses himself in the contemplation of his own image. The Narcissus pose was quite fashionable at the turn of the century, and it is hardly surprising to find the twenty-two-year-old Hesse adopting it in the prose sketches he published under the rather recherché title *An Hour beyond Midnight*. The dated tone of these misty lines and their conventional image seem quite remote from the style of Hesse's mature works. Yet, as we trace the development of Hesse's fiction, we shall be sent back repeatedly to that passage in which the young writer presented himself to the world, for it anticipates several characteristics of his subsequent oeuvre.

The style of Hesse's prose changes quite noticeably in the course of the fifty years from the early *poèmes en prose* to such late narratives as "The Interrupted Class" (1948). In the first decade of the century Hesse experimented with a variety of styles before he found the voice that is familiar to the readers of his major novels. The nine pieces of *An Hour beyond Midnight*, for instance, constitute a textbook case of *fin de siècle* aestheticism. In explicit imitation of Maeterlinck, Hesse created there a precious language of elegant archaisms and sonorous alliterations in order to do justice to what he called (in the 1941 introduction) "the dreamland of my poetic hours and days, which lay mysteriously somewhere between time and space." But within two years Hesse turned sharply away from the cult of *l'art pour l'art* and the otherworldly spirituality of his chief model, the Romantic poet Novalis. In *The Posthumous Writings and Poems of Hermann Lauscher* he exploited the ironic techniques of E. T. A. Hoffmann in order to distance himself from his own immediate past and what he had come to regard as its romantic excesses. In the person of Lauscher, as he noted in an expanded edition of 1907, Hesse wanted to "bury my own dreams." Using a fictional device that anticipates the framework of *Steppenwolf* (1927), Hesse introduces himself here in the guise of an editor who is publishing the works of his friend Lauscher "as documents of the curious soul of a modern aesthete and eccentric." Although Lauscher's poetic works, we are told, display the "carefully polished, precious form" that characterized Hesse's own first prose and poetry, the five pieces—ranging from Lauscher's recollections of his childhood to his "Diary, 1900"—are marked for the most part by a stridently contemporary style, evident in the student slang, the vulgarisms, and the strained imagery of "November Night."

After the success of his novel *Peter Camenzind* (1904), however, Hesse's style underwent yet another transformation as he moved away from the preciosity of his first prose vignettes and the radically anti-bourgeois shock tactics of *Hermann Lauscher* and settled upon the mellow tones of melancholy realism that dominated his works for the next decade. In a series of stories typified by "The Marble Works," "The Latin Scholar," and "The Cyclone," he depicted the life of shopkeepers, servant girls, and artisans in small-town Germany, explicitly modeling his narrative style on the stories of Gottfried Keller. Here Hesse seemed to be celebrating the very *gutbürgerlich* culture of the Wilhelmine era that he had previously so indignantly rejected. Appropriately enough, these tales, collected in volumes with such down-to-earth titles as *In This World* (1907), *Neighbors* (1908), and *Byways* (1912), assured his popularity with an audience content with the *status quo* and blithely closing its eyes to all the portents of the social revolution that was soon to erupt into World War I.

During these same years Hesse was also writing fiction of a strikingly different sort—stories that appeared in various newspapers and journals but were not collected until much later, when Hesse published them in such volumes as *Story Book* (1935) and *Dream Journeys* (1945). In "The City" (1910) Hesse sketches a pessimistic parable on the rise and fall of culture, which anticipates by almost ten years both Spengler and Hesse's own postwar cultural criticism. In his lyrical account of "The Wolf" (1907), an animal that is hounded to death by an insensitive mob of peasants, we encounter for the first time in Hesse's works the wolf motif that became increasingly obsessive until it generated the novel *Steppenwolf*. And nothing could be further from narrative realism than the fantasy about "A Man by the Name of Ziegler" (1908), who is driven mad when he comes to understand the language of animals. In such works as these we have a foretaste of the magically surreal style that characterizes the major novels of the twenties and thirties, as well as such later "stories" as "Inside and Outside," "An Evening with Dr. Faust," and "Edmund."

Yet in all these tales—from the perfumed aestheticism of the earliest prose poems through the realism and surrealism of the following decades down to the rarefied classicism of the stories collected in the volume *Late Prose* (1951)—we detect beneath the kaleidoscope of styles a consistent theme that is announced in the opening lines of "The Island Dream." For the image of narcissism betrays an introspective consciousness that has rejected the world outside for the sake of its own inner reality. The isle of beauty in that first volume, to which the young writer retreated from his humdrum existence as a book dealer in Tübingen, is nothing but a symbol for the realm of the imagination, where lovely ladies wander through fragrant groves or play Chopin in incense-laden, candle-lit chambers. Indeed, many of the early pieces are little more than aesthetic sublimations of those adolescent sex dreams in which a timid boy sees himself surrounded by choirs of adulating girls who cling to his every banal utterance with devoted attentiveness and who are perceptive enough to recognize genius in the proud youth scorned by the "real" world. But if we look behind the conventional pose and the dated exterior, we see in these vignettes the underlying theme of the alienated individual who rejects external reality for an inner realm of timelessness created by his own imagination. This is precisely the attitude that we encounter twenty-eight years later in the author of "Dream Journeys" (1927), who emphatically prefers the visions of his own fantasy to anything that mere "reality" has to offer. In a more radical form, the student Edmund (in the story of that title) does not flee from reality; instead, he forces the external world to conform to the reality of his vision when he strangles his skeptical teacher in accordance with the dictates of an Indic tantra.

But it is not only in the early escapist pieces and the late surreal stories that we find Hesse's characteristic tendency toward subordination of external reality to inner vision. It is also evident in many of the prewar stories, despite their ostensible "realism" after the fashion of Gottfried Keller. For all these schoolboys, students, missionaries, and apprentices turn out to be outsiders just as much as the magnificent wolf that, in the story of 1907, is struck down by the peasants. The action in these stories is never narrated for its own sake, as Hesse realized in 1921. Everything happens for the benefit of the hero, who is shocked out of childhood innocence into the consciousness of maturity by the events that he witnesses. The phenomenon of "The Cyclone," for all the beauty of the nature description, is important only to the extent that it reflects the violent sexuality to which the adolescent is exposed for the first time. By the same token, the characters of these stories seem to act or to be acted upon —e.g., the injury of Tina's fiancé in "The Latin Scholar" and Helene Lampart's death in "The Marble Works"— mainly so that the hero or narrator can gain insight into human nature and, ultimately, into his own consciousness. Storytelling for its own sake recedes, in other words, as external action is reduced to little more than material for the meditations of the hero on his road to self-awareness. Characteristically, in most of these stories the hero is not so much a participant in the action as, rather, a witness of it; and he often turns out to be a first-person narrator like the shipwrecked dreamer of the first prose piece—a Narcissus obsessed with the image of his own consciousness.

The tendency toward introspection is paralleled from first to last by a criticism of the world from which the author-hero is fleeing. In *Hermann Lauscher* this critique amounts to little more than the student's attempt to *épater le bourgeois*. In the parable in which society ladies flock to admire "Harry, the Steppenwolf" (1928), Hesse is lampooning an attitude that we recognize today as "radical chic." But even during the decade preceding World War I, Hesse's "wolf" frequently bit the hand that fed it —or, at least, bought its books. "Robert Aghion" (1913) can be read as a bitter attack on the arrogant colonializing mentality of Western man and the haughty complacency of Christianity. And "The Homecoming" (1909) belongs to that substantial genre of literature in which a man returning home after years abroad suddenly sees unmasked all the malice and pettiness of his own society. In many of these stories, by the way, Hesse portrays with considerable precision his own home town in southern Germany, Calw, which in its fictional form is called Gerbersau. In 1949 all of Hesse's early tales about provincial southern Germany were published in a two-volume edition

1972

entitled simply *Gerbersau.* It is probably safe to say that
the German public, in a mood of intense self-scrutiny
after two world wars, was able to perceive in those early
stories much of the social criticism that was not obvious
to their first readers.

If we now return to Hesse's first prose piece, "The
Island Dream," we note another characteristic that is anticipated there. After the narrator has beached his boat
on the sand and wandered for a time, he lies down to rest
in the shade of a cypress grove. Presently he is awakened
from his slumbers by the cheerful cries of some young
women who are tossing a golden ball in a nearby clearing.
When the ball happens to land near him, he picks it up
and reveals himself to the women, who, after recovering
from their fright, greet the young wanderer and invite
him to join them. By this point most readers will have
realized that Hesse is alluding here to the story of Odysseus and Nausicaä, who meet in precisely the same way;
and the remainder of Hesse's tale closely parallels Homer's
account of Odysseus' sojourn among the Phaeacians.
Now if we look at Hesse's other stories, we find that
many of them are similarly catalyzed by a literary source.
A second episode from *An Hour beyond Midnight,* "Incipit
vita nova," is sparked by Dante's work of that title. (A
similar use of Dante's *Vita Nuova* occurs some twenty
years later in the chapter of *Demian* entitled "Beatrice.")
The episode "November Night" in *Hermann Lauscher* is
prefigured by the scene in Auerbach's Cellar from Goethe's
Faust. "The Marble Works" is in part an updated version
of Gottfried Keller's well-known story concerning "A Rus-
tic Romeo and Juliet." The legend of "The Field Devil"
is based on the medieval Saints' Lives, while another story
relates an episode "From the Childhood of Saint Francis
of Assisi." In fact, almost every tale subsequently incor-
porated into the volume *Story Book* retells a legend or an
episode from history. Thus, "Chagrin d'Amour" uses a
fictional background borrowed from Wolfram von Eschen-

bach's epic *Parzival* as the setting for a plot suggested by a French folk song (recently revived by Joan Baez). Similarly, the inscription that precipitates the "magic" in the story "Inside and Outside" is taken from a poem by Goethe ("Epirrhema"). The action of "Edmund" is inspired by an Indic tantra. And the parable of "Harry, the Steppenwolf" amounts to a playful extension of Kafka—whose works Hesse was one of the first to admire—since the Steppenwolf occupies a menagerie cage recently vacated by a panther resembling the one that replaced Kafka's Hunger Artist.

To point out these sources is in no way to belittle Hesse's achievement. In the first place, he demonstrated his powers of creative imagination by "inventing" actions to accommodate the allusion (e.g., the tantra, or the French folk song, or the quotation from Goethe) that inspired the story. That is, his stories amount to more than the retelling of familiar tales in new words. (As an editor and anthologist, by the way, Hesse compiled a number of volumes during these years, ranging from his own translations of medieval and Renaissance tales to volumes of Romantic poetry and modern fiction.) In the second place, and more importantly: twentieth-century literature —from Joyce's *Ulysses* and Thomas Mann's *Doctor Faustus* to Eliot's *The Waste Land* and Brecht's *St. Joan of the Stockyards*—has made us increasingly conscious of the basic "literariness" of literature, which has come to be considered not so much an imitation of life in the Aristotelian sense as a playful manipulation of elements that already exist in an autonomous world of art. Precisely this kind of manipulation of existing forms occurs in Hesse's major novels. *Demian* is indebted, as many of the chapter headings and quotations suggest, to episodes in the Bible, from Genesis to Revelation. And *Siddhartha* (1922) gets its title as well as its basic outline from legends surrounding the life of Buddha. So the allusion, in "The Island Dream," to Odysseus among the Phaeacians anticipates the prefigurational techniques that Hesse, along with many of the other major writers of the century, was to develop with considerable sophistication.

The use of literary sources is related, moreover, to the tendency toward introspection. For the realm that Hesse opposes to everyday reality—in *An Hour beyond Midnight* as well as such later stories as "Dream Journeys"—is explicitly a realm of art. It became increasingly clear to Hesse, in the course of his life, that "eternity" is a frame of mind: the ability to perceive what Harry Haller, in *Steppenwolf*, calls "the golden trace" that gives life its meaning. Hesse was much more at home in that timeless spiritual realm than in the "real" world. He consistently resisted attempts to make of him a public figure, preferring to spend his days and hours in the relative isolation of a farmhouse on the shores of Lake Constance (1904–12), a villa in the suburbs of Bern (1912–19), and two different dwellings in the Swiss Alps above Lugano (1919–62). In his later years, behind a sign requesting "No Visitors Please," he devoted himself to his writing, to his painting, and to his books—notably, to the German literature of the period 1750 to 1850, in which he always claimed to feel spiritually most at home, and later to the world of Oriental culture that increasingly claimed his interest. From a writer of this sort, who by choice has shut himself off from the contemporary world, we would not reasonably expect a fertile invention of exciting fictional narratives set in the everyday reality of modern European society. But we would legitimately expect to encounter evidences of that cultural realm in which he preferred to spend his time—hence Saint Francis, Faust, the wisdom of India, and the many other references of that order. The Glass Bead Game, in the novel of that title, is Hesse's most brilliant image for the timeless realm of culture: for that institution has the sole function of enabling the men of Castalia to play with the cultural values of the past and present just as easily as one plays upon the various consoles of an organ. In those early stories, with their literary allusions and their rich associations of quotation 'and form, we sense the inchoate outlines of that cultural realm to which Hesse's introspective tendency ultimately led him.

Apart from literature and culture, the second principal source of Hesse's fiction is his own life. We have already noted that increasingly during the twenties Hesse turned to pure autobiography in the attempt to come to grips with his past. Up to that point, however, his stories represent the best reservoir of biographical information. "The Latin Scholar" describes the year when Hesse, before dropping out of school for good, was attending a *gymnasium* in a town near Calw. "The Cyclone" depicts the period when the youth was back in Calw, working as an apprentice in the local tower-clock workshop. The episodes of *Hermann Lauscher* provide a lightly fictionalized account of Hesse's life in Tübingen, where he worked as a bookseller by day while, at night, he sought refuge in an aesthetic realm "an hour beyond midnight." "Robert Aghion" combines Hesse's own firsthand observations during his voyage to Indonesia in 1911 with stories from the history of his family, several of whom had spent years as missionaries in India during the nineteenth century. But in all these stories, as well as the novels from these early years, biographical experience serves not as a starting point for the exploration of reality and other people; rather, it leads him inevitably back into his own consciousness for the encounter with himself. It was this realization, in 1921, that caused Hesse to reject these early works as failures, at least from the standpoint of traditional storytelling, and to say that they represented nothing more than his "secret dreams," his own "bitter anguish."

If we return for a final time to Hesse's earliest story, we can see a clear indication of the difference between his juvenalia and the works of his maturity. There, as the shipwrecked dreamer approaches the island of his dreams, his attention is distracted by his reflection in the wa-

ters of the bay. Almost fifty years later, a similar situation recurs in Hesse's recollection of "The Interrupted
Class." Sent on an errand by his teacher, the twelve-year-
old pauses on a bridge to watch the fish in the river
below; but as he looks into the water he falls into a state
of rapt contemplation in which he forgets all tempo-
rality until he is startled by the chiming of the church
clock, which summons him back to reality. This parallel
exemplifies the fact that to an astonishing degree Hesse's
works consist of varying configurations of the same limited group of images—in this case, an epiphany produced
by gazing into a body of water. But the image first occurs
in a fictional setting that represents an escapist flight
from reality. The shipwrecked dreamer, after all, has left
the world behind for an aesthetic realm where nothing
interferes with his rapturous contemplation of his own
reflection. The late variation of the image has an entirely
different context: for the autobiographical reminiscence
forces Hesse to come to grips with an episode from his
childhood that he had successfully repressed for many
years. The first image stands under the sign of Narcissus,
who is lost in worshipful contemplation of himself; the
second leads the author into a consideration of the individual's ethical responsibilities in the world into which he
has been thrust and with which he must somehow cope.
The first image represents the young Hesse, still trying to
express himself by means of literary forms appropriated
reverently from respected masters; the second reveals the
old Hesse, who has reverted frankly to autobiographical
reminiscence in an effort to understand his own consciousness, since "the questionable art of storytelling" has
unmasked itself as inadequate.

From all that has been said, it should be evident that
more than mere caprice dictated the choice of stories in
this volume. The contents pages reflect the fact that most
of Hesse's stories were written before World War I; those
that appeared thereafter moved ever closer to autobiog-

raphy, to the essay, and to the parable, tendencies that are apparent in such late narratives as "The Interrupted Class," "Dream Journeys," and "Harry, the Steppenwolf." *Stories of Five Decades* (none except "Inside and Outside," "Tragic," and "Dream Journeys" has ever before been available in English) provides a representative selection that displays the full range of Hesse's storytelling and the course of its development. It includes pieces from every major period and every important collection. And if some of his stories have been omitted for reasons of space, no aspect of his work is neglected. (Most of the omitted stories fall into one of two categories: realistic tales from the "Gerbersau" period, and the retelling of medieval and Renaissance stories and legends.) Since the boundary line between fiction on the one hand and pure autobiography or essay on the other becomes increasingly tenuous in Hesse's work, only one narrative from the last years is included here. Others may be found in Hesse's *My Belief: Essays on Life and Art,* to be published by Farrar, Straus and Giroux in the spring of 1973, and in the English-language edition of his *Autobiographical Writings.*

Hesse published most of his stories several times, first in various newspapers and magazines and subsequently in collections of his own works. Frequently the titles were altered, and sometimes the text itself was modified. The final titles are used in this edition and the translations follow the final revision, but the stories are arranged chronologically in the order in which they were first written. The selection thus offers a spectrum of Hesse's writing from 1899 to 1948 that can be duplicated only by an edition of his poetry, since in no other literary form —novel, essay, autobiographical reflection—did he span so many years. Here, within the covers of a single volume, one can follow Hesse's development from the aestheticism of his neoromantic youth to the classicism of his old age. And the reader who knows Hesse mainly through his major novels of the twenties and thirties will be surprised to encounter him here in a variety of earlier incarnations.

Yet the greatest surprise of all, surely, is to see how faithful Hesse remained to himself from start to finish and with what unremitting honesty he tested and discarded literary forms until he found the mode that was adequate for the expression of his own consciousness. Hesse's gloomy rejection of his early work in 1921 did not mark a radical break with his past but rather a turning point. Far from toning down the "secret dreams" that he detected in his prewar stories, Hesse transposed them from minor into major, proclaiming the realm of his imagination as his characteristic and principal theme.

Theodore Ziolkowski

STORIES OF
FIVE DECADES

The Island Dream

1899

A LONG-ARCHING WAVE lifted the rounded bow of my skiff and set it down on the shingle. Leaving the thwart, a shipwrecked dreamer held out his arms to the silent land. My frayed purple cloak fell in soft, humble folds from my hips down. My arms and neck were thin from rowing and fasting, my hair had grown long and was curling at the back of my neck. My reflection lay before me in the dark-green, still water of the bay, and I saw that in the course of my long journey everything about me had changed; I was browner, leaner, and more supple. Cruel hours had etched their dangers, defeats, and struggles into my cheeks. The sunless mornings when I had clung to my boat with my bruised limbs, the storms that had shown me the abysses of the sea had marked my cheeks and neck with their angular, furrowed script.

But my eyes shone clear, alert, and childlike in their wide hollows. Many nights they had watched, searching for the eternal stars and peering through the opalescent ocean darkness on the lookout for rising sails or land. For many days they had seen no dust, and only seldom, with smiling nostalgia, glimpsed the green of passing forests and the smoke of distant hidden cities. And now, large and radiant, they were smiling at me out of the smooth mirror.

They drank in the sight, of which they had so long been deprived, of the white stones, the brown earth, the grass, and the clumps of bushes. The air surrounding the bushes looked to me like a fine, whitish edge, for I had

long lost the habit of the air that lies over the green earth.
With diffident joy I breathed in the delicate full fragrance
of the meadow and of the bare ground and, at once firmly
and forbearingly, I set foot on the treasured realm of
terra firma.

A gentle land breeze brought me a smell of forest
plants and the faint perfume of distant gardens. In my
joy I stretched out both arms to it and with delight felt its
soft breath creeping over my hands and fingers and graz-
ing my temples that were accustomed to the biting sea
wind.

I pulled my gray boat up on the sand and passed my
right hand over the hard vault of the gunwale, which had
been worn smooth by my clutching hands. Then I made
my way inland till I came to a dense thicket which stood
before me like a circular wall and extended farther than
I could see. I skirted the green hedge, delighting in its
bluish shadow traversed by golden-green lights. I crossed
a meadow of soft grass which gradually grew taller and
grazed my knees with silken blossoms. The meadow lay
in the full sunlight, but on the edge, where I was walking, the high bushes cast an even band of shade.

A gentle weariness crept into my legs. When I had
gone some distance, I detected, on my left, a narrow
opening, a kind of gateway in the thicket. In the green
darkness I saw a path of seashells, and in the background
towering treetops. But the passage was barred by a plaited
garland. I stood there for a time, my eyes bathing in the
gentle twilight and delighting in the soft, graduated color.
From the bright green hedge to the half-visible secrets of
the innermost grove, the green dispersed into a thousand
shadows; eagerly my eyes followed the deepening darkness to the brown forest hues in the distance and returned with renewed pleasure to the yellowish light of the
sun-drenched meadow.

With joyful exuberance I removed the garland from
the rounded posts, so that the entrance lay open. I twined
the red and white garland round my neck and waist, as

though decking myself out for a summer festival. Then with cautious step I proceeded into the half-darkness. I came to a circular clearing, surrounded by a wall of saplings and bushes; both the clearing and the narrow path had been cut out of the forest by design. A brown and green light filtered through the overhanging treetops. In the circular clearing the ground had been strewn with white sand, and two narrow semicircular marble benches stood facing each other. I turned and followed the path leading into the grove. My head was heavy with the unaccustomed scent, and I heard the ringing of my quick-flowing blood.

After I had walked for some time, the heaviness in my legs increased and I longed for a place to rest. But then after a bend the path grew broader, and the forest walls on both sides receded, opening up a view of a large open space that appeared to be a garden. Any number of paths, wide and narrow, often bordered by bushes, twined round grass plots and flowerbeds, in which there were roses and other magnificent flowers of many colors, well tended and free of dead leaves. In the middle of the garden I saw groups of venerable trees, and behind them in the fading whiteness a marble building, a palace or temple.

I was drawn to a low bench shaded by cypresses. I sat down in the soft grass, crossed my hands behind my head, and leaned against the stone bench as I had often leaned against the thwart of my boat on quiet nights. High above me I saw the wide, marvelously blue sky and a few little fluffy, motionless clouds; then I shut my eyes and delighted in the red glow that shone through my lids. Then the god of sleep bent over me and unbound my weary limbs.

My soul spread its wings in a dream: images of yesterday and the day before filled me with new horror and grief. The sea lashed my boat with its waves and the angry sky sent storms. And the solitude for which I had so long yearned weighed upon me more heavily than the sky. And behind it the land with its noisy cities, from which I had torn myself away. A weary echo, a half-forgotten scent, a dimly remembered song of childhood—a shimmer of beauty and art cast in dirt and noise. Once again, as many times before, I saw anguished reflections of beauty's timid light, and trembled with her and suffered with her. Still further away, under bright, old-fashioned skies, lay the springtimes of my childhood, touching my heart with tender fragrance.

On unhurried wings my dream flew back over the tangled pathways of my life, back to the first sunrises, and hovered sadly over the first mountains I had climbed and over my father's house.

The sun had risen above the edges of the cypress wall and struck my slumbering eyes with hot light. I raised my head and woke to a new vision of the deep sky and the green gardens.

Bright voices sounded in my ears, and I heard that they were human voices, cries of exuberant joy. In those voices there was a pure metallic undertone, as deep as the sea, which I had never heard in human voices and which reminded me of the first untouched water of a fresh fountain, free from the knowledge of impurity, fraught with joy in life and in its own beauty. They carried the strong, sweet tone which, to our indescribable anguish, we seem to hear whenever our souls hold mournful converse with the generations of the golden ages of the past.

Cautiously parting the broad fronds, I glimpsed a group of slender young women playing with a gilded ball. Divided into two camps, they battled gracefully for possession of the glittering bauble that a laughing young girl kept tossing high in the air. They wore bright, loose-fitting robes, and most of them had their hair arranged in simple knots. I saw the pure lines of their necks and shoulders as they bent down or threw their heads back to follow the falling sphere with their eyes. I saw their delicately dimpled ankles through the white or golden bands of their sandals. I saw their supple slender bodies bent forward as they ran, and their shapely, slightly flushed arms rising from the soft folds of their robes.

Suddenly I heard a tremor in the boughs above me and the golden ball fell into the grass at my feet. I picked it up and my heart raced as though in the unexpected presence of a great danger or a great joy. Already the players were running toward my hiding place.

I broke through the thicket and stood like a ghost before the joyful throng, holding up the ball in my right hand. I threw it into the air, but they stepped aside as it fell and stood staring in amazement at the stranger. When I came closer, the throng parted, opening a broad passage before me. Looking up, I saw a tall woman facing me; she was the most beautiful of all, queen over the others.

I cast down my eyes and bowed low. A white robe flowed from her knees in long priestly folds, and there was such an air of purity and dignity about her that suddenly I felt small and full of shame. All the false pathways I had taken, all the sacrilege I had committed, everything ugly and sick in my inconstant life rose painfully to my mind, and all glitter and pride fell away from me. When she spoke in her pure voice, I knelt and bowed my head in shame and humility. Fuller and more beautiful than the voices of the other women, her voice had a lofty, noble tone that filled me with dread. "What brings you here, my friend, and how have you found your way to us?"

I looked up and I saw large eyes looking gravely down at me. "I have found my way to you through a hundred lonely days and nights on the hostile sea, through a hundred terrors and fearful night watches. My arms have grown thin from the hardship of my journey and my hands are bruised. The purple I am wearing is from your country and it was you who put it into my cradle. But my hands are sullied and my eyes have filled with disgust, I am tired and unworthy to wear the purple any longer; it is meant for happy hands and joyous eyes. I have come to give it back."

"Does the royal cloak mean so little to you?" the Queen asked, still standing motionless and looking at me gravely. "I know you well, you weary soul. I have hovered over your life, I told your childhood yearning of blue mountains and your boyhood piety of gods. Now and then I tried to show you images and symbols of beauty. Was it not you who destroyed the temple where I taught you to pray, and profaned the gardens of love whose gate I showed you? Was it not you who twisted the songs I taught you to sing into street songs and who, when I held out beakers of joy to you, abused them in drunkenness?"

"It was I. I went astray whenever you were far from me. I have often held out my arms to you in longing and cried out for you and conjured all that was noble in my earliest youth, but you did not hear me and the life that rolled past me was dead. Then my heart despaired and cursed its gods and fell from all its heights. Now I am tired of falling and rising again—take back your gift, put it on stronger shoulders, and let me become as others are."

The Queen looked aside. I ventured a quick glance at her face, which seemed deeply familiar to me, and saw the shadow of a smile. "I am surprised," she said, "that faintheartedness should have found the way to our island; it is a hard journey."

"Not faintheartedness, my Queen! What drove me from life was disgust with the smoke of the cities and the noisy pleasures of their temples. On my journey my yearning for the sight of you grew with each passing day. Toil and danger have hardened me, solitude has cleared my eyes of the vapors of the life I left behind. When I saw the gentle hills of your country rising slowly from bluer seas, my heart was made young again and learned a new and joyful pride. When I set foot upon your soil, I held out my arms in prayer to its wonders, I passed through your forest as a man reborn. Believe me, I drew the purple tighter round my shoulders, and my gait was not the gait of a penitent. I lay outstretched in the grass, behind the thicket, listening to the play of your women, and my heart beat deep. But my eyes could not withstand the sight of you; in the presence of your purity I was over-powered by all that was sick and unworthy in me."

"Stand up!" she said in a deep, kindly tone. "And don't press for an answer. Be my guest and try once again to live under my rule." I arose, looking about me uncertainly. But she who was the most beautiful of all took my left hand and led me to the women who were waiting. "Greet my friends," she said, "and see whether one or another of them is not known to you."

And then, as I went among the beautiful women, greeting them without constraint, a strange thing happened. From all sides familiar eyes looked at me; I encountered movements and glances I had known in other days, yet to my surprise I was unable to call these fair ones by name. Little by little I recognized a few of them, and soon it became clear to me that all the beautiful women I had ever known and admired were gathered there. But each was recognizable only by the particular traits which at one time had given her charm in my eyes, distinguishing her from all others and making her more beautiful. All those moments of my life which owed their goodness and grace to the sight of a woman's beauty lived here imperishably in perfect, magnificent images. None of these women could be ranked higher or lower than the rest; only the Queen miraculously combined all these particular beauties in the perfection of her form and face, whose dignity and loveliness, it seemed to me, were exalted above all images and all praise. And when her eyes met mine in quiet friendliness, they awakened within me the spring-time of my first love, with all its tremulous rapture and the tears I wept when I had lost it.

Night drew its black circle closer around the gardens; it came quickly and imperiously, as it does in the south. In quick succession hills, trees, and copses disappeared, until suddenly the bushes immediately surrounding us

veiled themselves in silence and vanished into the realm
of mysteries.

I sat at the Queen's feet in the spacious semicircle of
an open portico. The heavy columns stood out pure and
serene, like sentinels, against the veiled light of the distant sky. Two red fires burned in stone vessels at the
entrance; above us hung a silver lamp with four flames.
The heavy night air blew in from three sides, carrying
away the scent of the fragrant oil in slow waves. The sea,
which could not be heard in the palace or gardens in the
daytime, sang in grand muffled rhythms. —The women
had barely stopped singing, and there was still a faint
echo of festive melody in the air. They brought me a small
five-stringed lute and their eyes hung on my lips in ex-
pectancy. Closing my eyes, I sucked in the fragrance of
the night and felt its gentle breath in my hair. My heart
was full of mournful happiness and my voice trembled as
I began to sing. My fingers touched the fine strings—I
had not sung for a long time, and the rhythm and tone of
the words rose fresh and enchanting to my mind.

I sang of a summer in my boyhood, when for the first
time my eyes had dwelt on the form and gait of a young
woman. I sang of the evenings when the fragrance of the
lime trees mounted and, rowing wildly, I crossed the black
pond in my painful longing to visit every bench and path
and stairway where by day I had glimpsed the slender
beauty from a timid distance and of the days when my
love drove me on long overheated rides. I recalled the
full-flowering rose hedges and praised the shady walks
charged with the scent of jasmine.

Some of the women smiled and some looked at me
grave and wide-eyed. When I turned to the most beautiful of all, I saw wide bluish lids closed over her eyes; I
saw a charming mouth and fine cheeks in soft spring
colors and a smooth forehead smilingly shaded by curly
blond hair. I saw my first love, beautiful and enchanted
by memory and nostalgia, as she had sometimes appeared
to me in my favorite dreams. My heart was aflame, heavy

with songs and yearnings of another day. I touched the Queen's hand. "Do you remember, Loveliest One?"

She smiled and opened her eyes. "Tell me, were you not happier than others?" I nodded gently, unable to remove my eyes from the lips that were Elise's.

"But were you grateful?" Then I grew sad and had to bow my head again. She beckoned to one of the women, who filled a light goblet with white wine from a pitcher artfully fashioned of silver. She took the delicate goblet and held it out to me graciously. "Now you need rest. Drink and lie down. My hospitality will shelter your slumbers."

I drank and gave her my hand in gratitude for her kindness. A lovely handmaiden led me to a room in the spacious palace, lighted a hanging lamp, and left me. The room was of moderate size with high windows. In the middle a low, simple bed had been prepared. I lay down and saw a narrow frieze that ran around the walls a little above the floor, showing in low relief the virtues Wisdom, Moderation, Justice, and Courage, waiting on Beauty and offering up sacrifices to her. The figures soothed my agitated mind with their peace and simplicity and, turning to dream images, followed me into my slumbers.

Early in the morning, when I awoke refreshed and gay, I saw bent over me a smiling face wreathed in long, tender-colored hair. My heart recognized her loveliness and greeted her by the name she had borne in the days when her soft step had accompanied me for hours through grove and meadow. "Frau Gertrud!"

"Come," she said invitingly. "We will seek out the paths where we used to walk." Behind the palace and towering high over it, there was a grove of ancient plane trees, standing like friends in pairs and small groups. Frau Gertrud walked beside me on the winding path. The path and the grove were exactly like the path and the grove where we had roamed in times gone by. My heart was mellow and I listened with gentle melancholy to the breezes and the cries of the birds. My feet had wandered

through this same grass, my ears had heard these same breezes and bird calls, and whether yesterday or many forgotten years ago, I hardly knew.

"Do you remember it?" asked Frau Gertrud, setting her hand on the mottled trunk of a plane tree, which in those days, because it was the oldest and tallest, we had called "the father." I nodded in silence. "And do you remember this green and yellow, and these paths and copses?" Filled with a tired well-being, I nodded in silence.

"This is your late-summer dream," she said. "Your favorite! And all around you are the songs you sang of it, the days when it visited you on outspread wings, your memory and yearning."

I took Frau Gertrud's hand in mine, once again delighting in its aristocratic slenderness and whiteness, its pale, barely perceptible veins, and the delicate pink of the fingers. "Do you remember," Frau Gertrud asked, "that first day under the overhanging syringa?"

"I remember. I remember it all. How you comforted me and advised me, how you reminded me of my mother who was far away. I had been sick and gone astray, and you awakened all the piety and veneration that were left in me. You taught me once more to look for lost beauty and to be young again in the glorious moments when I glimpsed it."

"Once, my friend, you wanted to make a song of me and your happiness. Do you remember? Your days and nights were full of your burgeoning song. With diligent love you searched for everything rare and precious, for lights and tones that no artist had ever discovered, for words of love and words of veneration that no poet had ever spoken. Look around you. Here is your whole song, in unhoped-for perfection. Noble groups of trees and bushes, brown and golden lights, the songs of choice forest birds. And look at me as well! What was then small and nonessential and artificial in me has fallen away. What you see now is more beautiful than any reality, and more real than any reality. Listen to every gentle intonation of the

breeze, drink in all the many colors of the foliage with un-
clouded eye, see to it that all this becomes your very own.
When you are far away, you will wake at night and bitterly regret every sound and shadow that your inner eye
has lost. But then by a hundred pathways your song will
come to you, the joys of your first poems will seek you out,
the strange will blend with the strange, your work will
grow and take on life until one day in a blessed hour it
will leave the workshop and stand before you, finished,
pure, and melodious."

Frau Gertrud fell silent and again put her hand in
mine. We heard the cool, friendly sound of distant fountains. A large bird glided on motionless wings across a
patch of sky framed by the crowns of the plane trees.

The next day I awoke early, before the first birds had
begun to sing. A light rain had fallen during the night.
The ground was still damp and gave off a pungent smell.
Drops of clear water hung from the leaves. At every step
and breath I felt youth and health within me. The deep-
blue sky and the land in the distance looked fresh and
virginal. Not since my boyhood long ago, before intimations of love and tumultuous passion had come to torment
me, had the earth shown me this happy self-sufficient
face.

I took a crude untended path which became more and
more overgrown as I proceeded into the old forest. A
heavy wind blew through the crowns of the ancient oaks,
which high above the tangled underbrush embraced one
another, entwining their gnarled branches like a harmonious family of giants and reaching out for space and
light. On the black forest floor I saw clear traces of small
hooves cutting across the path, and once in the half-darkness of a nearby thicket I thought I saw a stag's head rise
slender and regal and look about. I peered and listened,
now and then holding my breath and standing still until
to my many times aroused and deceived senses the forest
was full of apparitions and silent wonders. A broad brook
flowed foaming and splashing down into a valley, which

suddenly came into view. In pools beneath arching waterfalls dark trout swam silently and vanished like lightning
when my shadow passed over their hiding place.

Following the joyous torrent, I suddenly found myself
in a familiar valley. At the end of it I came to a low hill;
there I left the brook, which turned the other way, and
soon I could hear it only faintly. I passed through a forest
of young beeches, which gradually thinned out and at
length ended altogether, opening up a view that reminded
me of home. A number of hills projected wooded spurs
into a broad meadowy valley. Before me, surrounded by
tall rushes, lay a dark pond, where I had spent many hours
as a boy. A few trees with gaunt branchless trunks and
high sparse crowns were wholly reflected in the brownish
surface. My first dreams of life had passed over my soul
amid the rushes on this shore and had been mirrored in
the motionless water. This gravely friendly solitude had
aroused my first, strangely tortuous poetic thoughts.

Shading my eyes with one hand, I took in the mild
colors and breathed the silence and peace which, it
seemed to me, I had left behind me long ago, at these beloved sites. The tips of the grasses and rushes moved
irregularly with a lifeless sound that made the silence
still more palpable. On the opposite shore the warm
damp ground gave forth a thin vapor, which joined the
more distant hills with the sky in a soft backdrop. Above
the crest of the nearest hill rose the narrow pointed
steeple of the monastery church. And soon, to be sure, a
pure sound of bells struck my ear. The long tones passed
over me in gentle waves.

Behind the hill, as I knew, stood the monastery where
I first learned to think of today and tomorrow, where for
the first time I tasted the bitter sweetness of knowledge
and the sweeter intimations of hidden beauty. There my
receptive mind became acquainted with all the great
names which preside, lofty and solemn, over my thoughts,
the names of Pericles, Socrates, and Phidias, and the
greater name of Homer.

In my mind's eye I clearly saw the vaulted halls and the Gothic windows of the cloisters. I very much wanted to taste the bitter pleasure of revisiting the place. But I stayed where I was; I was afraid of destroying my inner image; I was afraid of seeing others in the halls where in my dreams I was at home.

The sun shone on the tip of the steeple. The crest of the hill stood sharp and unsmiling between here and there, between me and those vanished twilights. Inwardly moved, I held out my hand in greeting. A part of me— and what a wealth of unresolved impulses and unfulfilled childhood dreams!—lay buried there.

A narrow wooden dock extended out into the pond. I set foot on the trembling boards and, as I had often done, leaned over the railing. My reflection lay still on the water. I looked for features that would remind me of the face which in those days had looked up at me from the same depths. Then I left the silent pond and walked slowly back through the woods.

In the garden I found the Queen and her women sitting in a circle. They were passing a bowl of fragrant golden-yellow fruit from hand to hand in a kind of game, and each of the women had to say a few words about the fruit before she could eat one. Still hidden by a row of olean-ders, I stopped for a moment just as a small dark-haired woman, behind whom I was standing, took the bowl in her hand. As she bent over the lovely bowl, carefully seek-ing out the ripest fruit, I saw the snow-white skin under the curls at the back of her neck. When she had chosen, she grasped the stem between two fingers, held the fruit up admiringly, and slowly lowered it to her avid lips. "Since the only one I would give sweets to is absent," she said, laughing, "I am too envious to let anyone else have this loveliest of fruits." Whereupon she took a good bite of the sweet flesh, while I stepped out from behind the branches.

The women who were sitting across from me and saw me first, burst into merry laughter. As each woman in

turn pointed me out to her neighbor, the laughter spread
until it reached the one who was sitting with her back to
me. Still holding the bowl in one hand, she looked round
the circle in surprise, and joined in the laughter without
knowing why. Then finally she stood up and turned
around and in doing so grazed me with the fruit she had
bitten into. She blushed with surprise and alarm, but then
she regained her composure, held the fruit up to my
mouth, and said heartily: "Here!"

"First your speech!" said the Queen gaily. And I replied: "I regard this most succulent of fruits as a visible
favor of fortune, which it would be fatal for me to reject.
Therefore let me have it and allow me to call the brave
girl who tasted it before me Fortuna. Tibi, Fortuna!" The
sweet morsel refreshed me to the marrow.

By then it was high noon and we retreated to the portico from the hot sun. Along with the fruit, there was
bread and honey, pitchers of milk, and an earthenware
jug of wine. We washed each other's hands in basins of
water and sat down happily to eat. Beside me sat Fortuna.
The others teased her and called her silly nicknames, but
she bore it bravely and joined in the chatter. But she fell
silent and listened, and so did I, when half in earnest one
of the women began to tell stories from my life, which
several others interrupted with laughter and more stories.
The Queen too took part.

"Do you remember," she asked me, "the story of Blondel when you were little? Poets are fortunate in being
able to remember more of their earliest life than others.
If you remember, do tell us about it."

Suddenly I saw this incident in my early boyhood,
which I had not thought of for years, standing before me
like a timid child. And I related it: "When I was very
little, not yet six, I somewhere, somehow heard of Blondel the troubadour. I'm sure I didn't understand the story
and I soon forgot it, but the tender, friendly-sounding
name of Blondel stuck in my memory. It had such a fine
melodious ring that I often said it softly to myself. To be

called by that name, I thought, would be the most wonderful thing in the world. And so I persuaded one of my little friends to call me Blondel in our games, and every time he did I was ever so pleased and flattered. But the little boy got used to my play name, and one day when he came over to call for me, he stood outside our gate and shouted up at the top of his lungs: "Blondel! Come on down, Blondel!" My father and mother and some visitors were in the room, and I was so ashamed and indignant at having my favorite secret shouted out loud that I didn't dare to go to the window. And the next time I saw my playmate I told him, much to his astonishment, that our friendship was at an end. Later, of course, we patched it up."

"That's the story," said the Queen. "But now, if you please, tell us where you were this morning. I was planning to show you the ocean in the morning light, but you were gone before sunrise."

"I woke up early with a desire to wander. I walked through a deep forest that lured me on with all sorts of shadows and secrets, until I came to a lovely and marvelous place. I stood by the side of a pond whose mirror-still surface still preserved the tenderest thoughts of my childhood with all their precious fragrance. Above a hill on the far side I saw the steeple of the monastery which years ago sheltered me and my dearest boyhood dreams."

"I know," said the Most Beautiful One, "those were your noblest and most reverent days. In those days I watched you taking melancholy walks through the woods, and shuffling through the fallen leaves in boyish sadness. I have never been closer to you than on those evenings when you picked up your fiddle or a book by an honored poet. I saw the shadows of later years approaching and I feared for you; yet I suspected that you would come to me some day with a new youth and a new sorrow. And the yearnings of those days made me go on loving you in your lost years."

As she said this, my whole youth stood before me in a single image, looking at me with the sad eyes of a mistreated child. But the Queen sent for a fiddle and, the meal ended, asked me to play. The women teased and cajoled me, and with a gracious gesture Fortuna handed me the bow. And so I took it and moved it softly and tentatively until my fingers had grown used to the hard frets. Then I abandoned myself with joy and played the passionate measures of a dark fantasia I had composed as a boy. And next, in response to a long look from Frau Gertrud, a Chopin nocturne, the beautiful, wind-swept nocturne whose measures move like the glints of the moonlit sea.

The Queen led me by forest paths to a castle surrounded by a garden, not far from the seashore. There she took me to a high wall with a painting on it. "My favorite picture," she said. With consummate art the painter had depicted a southern garden full of dark, shady copses; there were Greek columns and a surging fountain, against the rim of which a lyre was leaning. "Do you know this garden?"

"No. But the lyre is Ariosto's."

She smiled. "He still comes here now and then. He recites radiant flowing stanzas to me; we laugh and joke, and he lets me crown him with a garland."

At a sign from the Queen the painted wall suddenly vanished. A boundless horizon stretched out before us, and at our feet, dark green, lay the whole garden of the picture. A dark, slender man stepped slowly from a hidden path, picked up the lyre, and played, imitating the silvery note of the fountain. Then he strode down toward the darkening sea and vanished beyond the garden wall. The apparition passed me by like a couplet from the *Orlando*, slender, noble of form, and as mischievous as a girl's laughter. Then I myself, hand in hand with the Queen, went down to the seashore. The gently moving surface of the water lay blue and red and glittering-silver as far as the eye could see. For a long while our eyes rested with delight on the play of colors. Then the Most Beautiful One parted the branches of a hedge, revealing a white narrow stairway leading to the water. I found my boat tied up at the foot of it. The Queen broke off a branch of orange blossoms, tossed it into the boat, bade me gently go, and gave me her hand.

"Farewell," she said. "Leave-taking is an art that no one fully learns. I know you will come to me again for light, and one day you will come when you no longer need oars."

With a heavy gurgling sound a wave broke over the steps and, receding, carried my boat away with it. I held out both arms to the bright figure, until, waving, she vanished into Ariosto's garden paths. The night came quickly and cast its heavy cloak of darkness over my grief. From a thousand comforting eyes it looked gloriously down upon my slow voyage home.

Incipit vita nova

1899

I N MY LIFE as in the lives of most men there was a critical point of transformation from the universal to the particular, a place of terror and darkness, of confusion and loneliness, a day of unspeakable torpor and emptiness, whose evening brought forth new stars in the sky and new eyes within me.

Shivering, I passed among the ruins of the world of my youth, over shattered thoughts and twisted, quivering dreams, and everything I looked at dissolved into dust and ceased to live. I saw friends whom I was ashamed of knowing, thoughts I had thought only recently looked me in the face, and they had grown as alien and remote as if they had been a hundred years old and never been mine. Everything fell away from me, and soon there was a deadly emptiness and calm all about me. I had nothing more that was close to me, no loved ones or neighbors, and my life rose up in me with a shudder of disgust. Every measure was full to overflowing, every altar desecrated; there was no sweetness but sickened me, no summit I had not left behind me. Every shimmer of purity was spent, every intimation of beauty defaced and trampled under foot. I had nothing more to long for, nothing more to offer, nothing more to hate. Everything that was still sacred and unravished and harmonious within me had lost its eyes and voice. All the guardians of my life had fallen asleep. All the bridges had been severed and all horizons robbed of their blue.

When everything alluring and lovable had thus fallen away, when exhausted, infinitely poor and bereft, a spiritual derelict, I awoke to awareness of my misery, I cast down my eyes, arose with heavy limbs and, like a hunted criminal who leaves his house at night, without taking leave and without closing the doors behind him, departed from all the habits of my past.

Who has ever plumbed the depths of loneliness? Who can say that he knows the land of renunciation? My head reeled as I looked down into the abyss and found no end. I wandered through the land of renunciation until my knees crumpled with weariness, and still the road lay ahead in undiminished eternity.

A still, sad night arched over me, bringing comfort and sleep. Sleep and dreams came to me as friends to a home-comer and relieved me of a deadly burden as though lifting a pack from my shoulders.

Have you ever been lost at sea and seen a swimmer approaching from the land? Have you ever, recovering from deathly illness, taken a first draft of fresh garden air and felt the sweet surge of your reviving blood? Like such a rescued mariner and such a convalescent, I felt a swirling flood of gratitude, peace, light, and well-being that night, when it became clear to me that inscrutable beings were looking down at me with friendly eyes.

The sky looked different than ever before. The position and recurrence of the heavenly bodies entered into a fore-ordained pact of friendship with my innermost life, and the eternal established a clear and soothing bond between its laws and something within me. I felt that in my life resurrected from the desert a golden foundation had been laid, a power and a law, in accordance with which, as I felt to my glorious amazement, everything old and new within me would forever after be ordered in noble crystalline forms and conclude beneficent alliances with all the things and wonders of the world.

Incipit vita nova. I became a new man, still a miracle to myself, at once passive and active, receiving and giving, in possession of treasures, the most precious of which is perhaps still unknown to me.

To Frau Gertrud

1899

I<small>N THE MOST SECLUDED CHAMBER</small> of my castle, under the vaulting of the narrow window, you often sit, you, the friendliest among my dead. Your kindly, unfathomable presence has outlived the days when we held hands together, just as the rays of a star may shine down on us for centuries after the star has ceased to be.

I can no longer count how many times I have walked under the sky of the Vita Nuova. I cannot count how many times I have despaired of finding another incarnation of your image. No beauty, except for the beauty of that sweetest of poems, can be compared with yours. I often think that it must have been you who passed the enraptured Dante in the street and that you dwelt again on earth in the shadow of my youthful yearning. That I saw you with my own eyes, that I held your hand in mine, that your light step trod the ground beside mine—isn't all that a gift of the Transcendent, is it not a hand set on my forehead in blessing, a glance from transfigured eyes, a gate opened up to me into the land of eternal beauty?

In my dreams at night I often see your living form and see the white, finely articulated fingers of your aristocratic hands on the piano keys. Or I see you standing at nightfall, watching the sky pale and change color with eyes made profoundly radiant by a wonderful knowledge of beauty. Those eyes have awakened and guided innumerable artist's dreams in me. They are perhaps the most inestimable gift that was ever conferred on my life, for they are stars of beauty and truth, full of kindness and rigor, unerring, correcting and rewarding, vengeful enemies of everything unworthy, inessential, and fortuitous. They lay down laws, they examine and judge, they bestow superabundant happiness. What is success, what is prestige, what are fame and human praise without the favor and gracious glow of those incorruptible lights!

The day is loud and cruel, fit for children and soldiers, and all diurnal life is charged with unsufficiency. Is not every night that falls a homecoming, an open door, a place where the eternal becomes audible? You taught me to return home and open my ears to the voices of eternity. When the last gate was ready to open before you, you said to me: "Let the night be sacred to you; never banish its silence from your house. And never forget the stars, for they are the supreme symbols of eternity."

And another time you said: "Remember, even after I have been taken from you, to keep peace with women, for they are closest to all the mysteries." Since then I have never had such wordless conversations as with stars and women.

In the hour when we concluded our friendship, another, invisible and unfathomable, joined us, a spirit and tutelary god. I believe he made invisible signs of blessing over me and spoke these words: *Apparuit iam beatitudo vestra.* He has been with me ever since and has often been a comforter to me, a diviner of riddles, a third party to a happiness. Many times when my hand was ready for a hasty action, he thrust it back; many times when I had passed an object of beauty by, he made me stand still and look back; many times when I was about to tear an unripe fruit from its branch, he advised me: "Wait!"

Ever since then, everything harmonious and lovely, everything that has sweet voices and comforting meanings, everything that is rare, noble, and distinguished in its beauty, has had a visible aspect for me, and has somehow found a way to my senses. Rivers have spoken more clearly to me in the night, stars have been unable to rise or set without my knowledge.

This comforter of mine, this invisible third party, came

to me on a day when my heart had lost its rhythm and my
eyes seemed to have gone blind. He smoothed my forehead; now and then he came close to me and whispered
something in my ear, or pressed my hand as he passed by.
But you lay bedded in tea roses, at peace, transfigured,
friendly but unsmiling. You lay still, your hand did not
move, you were cold and white.

To me that time was a bottomless black night. I stood
in dense darkness, not knowing where I was, without far
or near, as though surrounded by spent lights. I stood
motionless, abysses opened around me on all sides; I felt
nothing but my folded hands, hard and cold, and believed
in no tomorrow. Then the comforter stood beside me, embraced me in firm arms and bent my head back. And in
the zenith of an invisible sky, amid the total darkness, I
saw a single bright, mild, steadfast star, of infinite beauty.
When I saw that star, I could not help thinking of an evening when I was walking in the woods with you. My arm
was around your waist. Suddenly I drew you close and
covered your face with quick, thirsty kisses. You were
frightened, you pushed me away, you seemed changed.
You said: "No, my darling. I was not given to you for em-
braces. The day is not far off when your hands and lips
will no longer reach me. But then a time will come when I
shall be nearer to you than today or ever before." And now
this nearness came to me with infinite sweetness and perfect understanding, a kiss without end. What are caresses
compared to this nameless union!

Long after your death, I was sometimes filled with this
great joy when my walks took me to places where we had
been together. Once when I was climbing through dark
woods in the Black Forest, I saw your bright form coming
down toward me. You came down the mountain waving
your hand in the old familiar way; you met me and you
were gone, and your presence filled me with deep sweetness.

But most often you appeared in the sky of my dreams

as on the day of my greatest darkness, full of spiritual beauty, the mild star of grace.

One evening, when music and loud talk had driven you to the farthermost garden paths, I found you walking back and forth, and gave you my arm. And you said: "When I am here no longer and when you yourself have grown more serene, perhaps this passing evening and others that have already passed will be more present and real to you than your own hand. Then somewhere, far from here perhaps, you will be awake in your room at midnight. And outside your windows the immediate world will fall away, and you will think you are seeing this path and the two of us strolling on it."

Today that evening lies before me; once again our soft voices mingle with the distant music, and I do not know whether that evening or this one is real and illumined by the moon of this earth.

November Night

A RECOLLECTION OF TÜBINGEN

1901

A BLACK, CLOUDY NOVEMBER NIGHT lay over Tübingen. A wet wind stormed and clattered through the narrow streets. Streetlamps flickered red and were reflected dimly on the wet cobbles. Black and gloomy, with two or three little red windows for eyes, the old castle crouched like a lazily dozing monster on its long hill, and tatters of cloud hovered round its steep gables. On the broad solemn avenues the old chestnut, lime, and plane trees stood gaunt and bare in the storm, like a steadfast woebegone army of old men. Fallen leaves swirled across the damp paths, the long meadows lay dead and gray, illumined here and there at the edges by the raw, jagged beam of a wind-blown streetlamp. From the nearby station the tired, long-drawn-out whistle of the last train to Reutlingen pierced the heavy air, and its hoarse, dying sound struck the keynote of the evening.

When the storm died down for a moment, the cool flow of the Neckar could be heard. Its banks lay shrouded in gray, mournful peace. Not the slightest trace remained of all the joyful summer festivals and their loud songs, any more than the broad, gloomy Stift preserved a trace of the many brilliant young men who had once dreamed and studied there, and awakened to themselves. Except perhaps for an occasional echo of poor Hölderlin's elegiac harp. Instead, the stern, industrious present burned in numerous study lamps distributed over the whole length of the building, and shone dull red through the low, broad windows. Innumerable compendia, dictionaries, and texts lay open before earnest young eyes, editions of Plato, Aristotle, Kant, Fichte, perhaps of Schopenhauer; Bibles in Hebrew, Greek, Latin, and German; at this very moment perhaps, behind these windows, a young philosophical genius was brooding over his first speculations, while at the same time a heavily armed apologist was laying the foundations of an impregnable fortress.

Coming from the lower Neckar bridge, two young men sauntered down the Platanenallee. They looked across the river at the Stift with a laugh that showed little respect for that citadel of the spirit which had once been so pregnant with the future. In gray loden capes, they plodded through the stormy autumn night, undismayed by the rain. "Is there any left?" the student Otto Aber asked his companion, the poet Hermann Lauscher, who in response extricated a pot-bellied bottle of Benedictine from his pocket and handed it to his friend.

"The last drop!" cried Aber, holding out the bottle in the direction of the Stift on the far side of the river. "Prosit, Stift!"

He emptied the bottle at one gulp.

"What will we do with the bottle?" Lauscher asked. "We could go to the guard post and make a present of it to the Tübingen police."

"Police be damned!" Aber laughed. "There!" He hurled the bottle across the Neckar and it smashed against one of the pillars of the Stift. "Now where do we go?"

"Where indeed?" said Lauscher thoughtfully. "At the Steinlach the wine is murder, at the Silberburg Georgette's not there any more, at the Kaiser you'll find Roigel drinking himself under the table, at the Sun it's too crowded, at the Lion—"

"That's it!" Aber cried out. "The Lion. I just remembered, Sabergrinder and Gloomy will be there tonight, healing their wounds after Thursday's dueling. Come on! We've got to go somewhere in this weather."

The student drew his long cape tighter and speeded his pace.

"What are you running for?" Lauscher called out. "The weather's plenty good enough for us. I'd rather be sloshing around in the rain than a scoundrel basking in the sun. If the Benedictine hadn't sung its swan song, I'd sooner do my drinking in the bosom of nature. Besides, Sabergrinder's a bore, and Gloomy will be weeping. —Think they're drinking Uhlbacher? If they are, count me out. The Uhlbacher at the Lion hates me. But what do you fellows know about wine!"

"Wine snob!" said Aber, laughing. "No, they've got a supply of Moselle, some bet they made ages ago. Or Winkler, or something of the kind. Anyway, something good. —Which reminds me: Why don't we start a club? The four or five of us are always sitting together anyway. We could recruit Appenzeller and a few more beer sponges; then we'd have sort of an exhibition of rejects."

"A club?" growled Lauscher, who at that time was far from anticipating the cénacle of a later day. "I'd rather be a hermit."

"But why not? We'd have an association of dropouts from all the fashionable fraternities and hopeless failures from every department. Gloomy would convert our collective sins into tears, we'd supply Sabergrinder with a twenty-four-hour fencing jacket, and he'd defend our honor with every weapon in the arsenal. I'd be the beer committee, you'd be the secretary and wine com—"

"Et cetera. That will do."

"Appenzeller would be just the man to convey the communications and demands of our club to the representatives of the fraternities. Nebuchadnezzar would be priceless as a censor morum. Kaisser has an uncle who's said to own some vineyards; Schnauzer is rich and stupid—"

"And then we'd rent a tavern and sing 'Old Heidelberg' and 'The Happy Vagabond' together twice a week. And haze freshmen and brandish sabers. No, thank you."

"Why not? We could make our headquarters at the

Schwarzwälder and blacklist all the decent places in our regulations. For instance: Anyone seen at the Ox or inside the university is liable to a fine of one mark. Anyone talking shop pays two pints—"

"No. Stop it. You're beginning to stink of regulations."

The friends had reached the old bridge. From the tavern of the Student Association loud choral singing was heard. The Neckar flowed furiously around the broad bridge piers, streetlamps cast restless reflections on the swift waters, the stately Platanenallee receded into the black night. The Horn of the Hours sounded from the cathedral tower; on the high far shore of the Neckar irregular wedges of light marked the picturesque row of houses reaching down to the Stift. While crossing the bridge, both friends fell silent. Perhaps the sight of the beautiful darkened city or the sound of the Neckar and the student songs awakened a memory of days not so long past, when the romantic beauty and atmosphere of this place had touched their hearts with joyful intimations, when they had crossed this bridge with the hope and all the vague sweet feelings of neophyte students.

They skirted the mill, climbed the steep street to the lumber market, passed the Stiftskirche, crossed the narrow Kirchgasse and the deserted market, passed the Sun, and arrived through mud and water at the back door of the Lion, whence three steep steps led directly down into the "back room." Before going in, they looked into the narrow room through one of the low windows and saw Sabergrinder and Gloomy sitting over their wine at the farthermost table.

"They're drinking Winkler," Aber announced triumphantly. "What did I tell you? For your unwarranted disrespect you'll have to pay a forfeit."

"Vulgarian! So I will," Lauscher grumbled and led the way through the narrow doorway. Aber followed, disgustedly turning a sign advertising Geroldstein Mineral Water to the wall. Mathilde, the daughter of the house, came hurrying in and took his coat.

Only then did the drinkers take note of the new arrivals.

"High time!" cried Sabergrinder. "Do you want to drink?
Do you want to take a bath? Do you want to drown your-
selves? There's no shortage of Winkler. I'll never make
that kind of a bet again as long as I live. Fifteen bottles.
That can get monotonous."

"I wouldn't worry," said Lauscher. "Mathilde, two glasses!" He inspected one of the bottles in the bucket and
poured. "Aber, my forfeit."

"Just drink."

"What do you say?" asked Sabergrinder.

"It's good," said Lauscher tersely. He threw his right
arm over the back of his chair, refilled his glass, and
drank it down in a long, steady draught.

"What's the trouble now?" asked Sabergrinder. "I've
seldom seen your skull looking so bony."

"I'll explain," said Aber. "Strong stuff doesn't agree
with him. That Benedictine—"

Lauscher let out a long whistle between his teeth. "Shut
up, Aber, my boy! Anyway, that's a stupid question, Sabergrinder." He started on a fresh glass. "The fact is, my
dear friends," he went on slowly and gravely, "that you're
all a bunch of swine, and I can't help wondering why I'm
always hanging around with you."

Gloomy laughed, and raised his glass to the poet.

"But what can I do? At least there's nothing wrong with
you except that you're boring; in other respects you're
good fellows."

"Hm . . . hm . . ."

"You don't like that, do you? But tell me this: What
intellectual baggage has any of you to show, except for
the usual crumbs from your freshman year? Has any of
you the slightest notion of humor, philosophy, or art?
Or—"

Aber laughed. "Look here," he protested. "Before shooting your mouth off any further, would you kindly give us
a sample of your own art, philosophy, and humor! I don't

find them in your sentimental poetry. If they exist, it must be somewhere else . . ."

"They exist all right. Poetry be damned. My sitting here, drinking your wine with you and contemplating your pathetic faces when I have gold, silver, palaces, fairy tales, and treasures inside me—that's my humor. What are you loafing and boozing away? An examination, a bit of family capital, some employment where you'd have worked your fingers to the bone and died of boredom? And why are you doing it? Because it's dawned on you that it's not worth living for such stuff. With me it's a different story. At every gulp I drink up a patch of blue poet's sky, a province of my imagination, a color from my palette, a string of my harp, a bit of art, a bit of fame, a bit of eternity. And why? Because it's not worth living for all that either. Because life isn't worth living altogether; a life without purpose is barren and a life with purpose is torment."

Gloomy laughed throughout Lauscher's speech. Aber took a long swallow and said good-naturedly, "Drink, Lauscher, and stop talking rot."

Then he turned to Gloomy. "Say," he asked, "what are you doing now? Does your old man know?"

"What?" Lauscher asked.

"Don't you know? He's stayed away from his exam for the third time. He's been expelled. Well, Gloomy, what are you going to do?"

"Do? I've signed up."

"I'll be damned! Signed up?"

"That's right."

"For what? Have they started an army of lunatics?"

"Some such thing. It seemed to me I'd wept enough tears in all these semesters of mine to buy me a free ticket to the Elysian Fields."

"Not bad," said Sabergrinder with a laugh. "It's not so cheap any more. You couldn't have got into hell, I know that much, because I once put in three terms of Protestant theology."

"But who on earth signed you up?" Lauscher asked.

"Aha! You'd like to meet him, wouldn't you! A gentleman, I'm telling you, a refined gentleman . . ."

"Idiot!" cried Lauscher. "I can imagine what you call a refined gentleman. Was he more refined than me?"

"Much more. A gentleman, I tell you. Anyway, we're wasting our breath. He's coming here tonight, he promised."

"Wha-at? You mean it? On your word?"

"On every word I've got. Prosit, Lauscher!"

"Prosit, Gloomy!"

Lauscher took a package of his vipers, long, thin black cigars, and offered them around. He lit one, blew clouds of smoke, flicked off the ash, took an occasional quick sip of wine, and fell into a dreamy lethargy. The others, too, devoted themselves in silence to their wine and cigars. A bluish cloud hovered over the table, the few other guests could be heard talking and laughing. The friends sat there drinking glass after glass, lost in thought and almost totally silent—they had spent many hours, whole evenings and nights together, silent and lost in thought, around such tables.

"All the same," said Aber after a long, long silence. "I'm curious about that recruiter of yours."

No answer. Mathilde opened two more bottles. Saber-grinder poured.

"Come to think of it," Aber began again, "come to think of it, my friends, what can any of us do at this point? Only two more semesters: my time is running out."

"With me it's money. I can't change horses any more."

"Neither can I," said Aber with a yawn. "My old man is fed up. America?"

Lauscher laughed. "Africa? Asia? Australia?" he mimicked. "You make me laugh with your troubles. How do you know you'll be alive in two semesters? Two semesters! Think of all that can happen in two semesters!"

"For instance?"

"For instance right now, with the careless way you're

lighting your cigar, suppose the flame gets too near your mouth, and all those alcohol fumes catch fire. A beautiful death! Or else—and I see it coming—you start your club, you build a clubhouse, and you put yourself in charge of the wine cellar—"

"Dammit!" cried Aber with enthusiasm. "Dammit! That's a wonderful idea!"

"Or else," Lauscher went on, "you could go—"

Breaking off in mid-sentence, he went white and stared at the open window across from him.

"Go on," cried Sabergrinder. "What's the matter!"

Lauscher pointed his finger at the window. "There!" he stammered. "Good God, we're not playing *Freischütz*."

All eyes followed the outstretched finger. In the window a tall, thin man with a pale face, a high forehead, and a goatee on his long chin stood peering insolently into the room out of bright, piercing, steel-gray eyes.

Only Sabergrinder was not frightened.

"Looks like he didn't know if he's supposed to be Kaspar or Samiel," he said with a laugh. "The impudence! Should I muss him up?"

The stranger disappeared from the window. A moment later the door opened; he stepped in, strode through the room, and sat down at the friends' table.

Sabergrinder was about to give the intruder a crude rebuff, but Gloomy laughed and held out his hand to the newcomer. "I beg your pardon, sir, I didn't recognize you before. May I introduce my friends?"

He introduced them with rather tipsy gestures, forgetting to give the stranger's name.

Again they sat for a long while drinking, silent and lethargic. At length Lauscher arose.

"I'm leaving. Would anyone care for a game of billiards?"

The friends were silent.

"I'll play if you like," said the stranger, rising. "We could all go over to the Whale. I just passed by, the billiard table is free."

All drained their glasses and followed the suggestion. Outside, a cold rain was falling and Kornhausgasse was a sea of mud. It was not far to the Whale. Gloomy led the way up the stairs. Under the gas flame at the entrance Aber stopped the stranger. "Just a moment, if you don't mind."

He glanced at the steps. The others were already at the top.

"Well?" asked the tall man.

"Gloomy has been talking about you," said Aber with embarrassment. "Are you conducting a membership drive?"

"That's it."

"I might . . . it's just possible that . . . in short, I wish I could have a talk with you."

"Flattered, I'm sure. I'm only here for the day, but you'll find out all about me from your friend tomorrow. I come to Tübingen about once every semester."

They followed the others into the smoky, disreputable café. Gloomy, who had already ordered champagne, dropped lazily down on a sofa. Lauscher was chalking his billiard cue. The stranger picked up another. He played brilliantly.

The game was soon over.

"You play very nicely," said the tall man to the poet. "If you get over your fear of the hazard shot, you may get to be very good. That shot is the beginning of the whole game. Watch me . . ."

He picked up his cue again and executed one of his dazzling shots. After touching the white ball, his ball rolled over to the red one in a strange, incredible arc. Lauscher was dumb with amazement.

Then they sat down with the others. Aber and Lauscher drank coffee; the others, champagne and sherry. Exuberant little Molly drank with them and sat down beside Gloomy on the sofa.

"What do you think of him?" the stranger asked Lauscher, with an almost imperceptible gesture in Gloomy's direction.

"A swine," Lauscher whispered. "A perfect swine. But a heart of gold."

"And that one?" The tall man indicated Sabergrinder with a movement of his chin.

"Not too dumb," Lauscher judged, "and he even has pretty good taste. But he's a hero of the saber. The Students' Association threw him out, and he'll never get over it."

"Hm. And the third?"

"Aber? The best of the three. But no backbone. He won't admit it, but he's scared of his finals."

"You speak rather unkindly of your friends."

"Why not? Different degrees of rot that phosphoresce in different ways."

"I like you."

"You don't say."

Lauscher stood up. "Come on!" he called out to Aber. "We're leaving."

With a smooth, ugly smile the stranger nodded to the departing friends. Sabergrinder had fallen asleep. Gloomy and Molly seemed to have forgotten that others were present.

Aber and Lauscher wandered about in the rain for half an hour, through the dark deserted streets. The Lion was closed and they weren't in the mood for the Schwarzwälder. The clock struck three.

At length Aber cried out impatiently, "I'm going home!"

"Not I!" Lauscher stopped still and looked around him. "Dead! How can these people sleep so much?"

"Come on. We'll do likewise."

"Sleep? No!" The poet turned around and looked into Aber's broad, rather bleary face. "Look here, Aber. Wouldn't you like to say 'To hell with it all'?"

"It wouldn't do any good. Let's go to the Schwarzwälder instead."

"Which amounts to the same thing. All right."

They went in and ordered kümmel. Little by little Aber was infected by his companion's gloom. Dull and disconsolate, they looked over their cigars with dead eyes. Three late stragglers were playing dice at one of the tables. The waitress was asleep at the counter, a solitary winter fly crawled along the gas pipe and seemed about to fall into the flame at any moment; the rain dripped down the windowpanes.

"Let's not get sentimental," said Aber an hour later. He tossed off his glass of kümmel; the two of them left the dismal café and descended the steep Judengasse. Passing by the Whale, they heard the waiter closing the doors. At the end of Schmiedtorgasse, near the old Ammer bridge, they stopped for a moment.

"Let's go left," said Aber with a yawn.

"It's nearer across the bridge," said Lauscher hoarsely, and they took the bridge.

On the other side, a man was lying head down on the stairs leading down to the Ammer.

"Hey," cried Aber, laughing. "There's a sound sleeper."

"Must be one of the holy brethren," said Lauscher, coming closer. "Won't he be surprised at his halo tomorrow!"

"Good God!" cried Aber. "It's Gloomy. Nobody else in all Europe has a frock coat like that."

They went down a few steps. Gloomy was lying face down on the stairs. They lifted him up, his whole face was smeared with blood.

"He's taken a bad fall," said Aber with a sigh. Something jangled against the stone. A revolver had fallen from Gloomy's stiff hand. And then the friends saw a small black wound in Gloomy's right temple. Lauscher lit a match.

"You stay here," said Aber faintly, "I'll go for the police."

"Let me attend to that," cried a sharp voice. The stranger was coming up the steps from Ammerweg. He touched his hat with a venomous, scornful smile and flashed cold insolent eyes at the friends. Frightened to the marrow, they ran off into the night.

When they woke up next day, they thought they had dreamed the whole thing. Lauscher's landlady knocked at his door and brought in his coffee.

"Just imagine, Herr Lauscher, it's so awful! A student killed himself last night!"

The Marble Works

1904

I T WAS ONE OF THOSE SUMMERS when the fine weather
is reckoned not in days but in weeks. The hay was in
before the end of June.

For some people there is nothing more wonderful than
such a summer, when the reeds in the dampest marsh
are seared and the heat penetrates your bones. When
their season comes, such people absorb amounts of
warmth and well-being unknown to others, and their
existence, for the most part none too industrious to begin
with, attains heights of benign idleness. I myself am one
of these people, and that is why I felt so uncommonly
happy that summer, though with radical interruptions
that I shall speak of later on.

I believe it was the most splendid June I have ever
experienced, and it's high time we had another like it.
The little flower garden in front of my father's house on
the village street was bursting with blooms and fragrance;
the dahlias that hid the broken-down fence grew tall and
dense; they had put out fat round buds, and already the
young petals, yellow and red and purple, were forcing
their way through the cracks in them. The honey-brown
gillyflowers shone so brilliantly, the scent they gave off
was so passionate, so riotous, they must have known that
the time was near when they would fade and make room
for the densely proliferating mignonette. Still and brooding stood the stiff balsamines on thick glassy stems, slender and dreamy the gladioli, bright red and smiling the
rank, neglected rose bushes. There was scarcely a hand's
breadth of earth to be seen, and the whole garden looked

like one big radiant bouquet crowded into a vase that was too small for it; the nasturtiums at the edges were choked by the roses, while in the middle the ostentatiously flaming Turk's cap made a shameless display of its great lush blossoms.

All this delighted me, but my cousin and the peasants hardly saw it. They begin to get some pleasure out of the garden only in the fall, when there is nothing left but late roses, immortelles, and asters. Now they were in the fields from dawn to dusk, and at night they fell into bed as heavily as toppled tin soldiers. And yet, every fall and every spring, they faithfully tend this garden, which brings in nothing and which they can scarcely look at in its finest season.

For two weeks there had been a hot blue sky, in the morning pure and smiling, in the afternoon framed in serried, low-lying, slowly expanding clouds. At night storms broke far and near, but every morning when I awoke—still with the thunder in my ears—the sky shone blue and sunny, already saturated with light and heat. Then, happy and without haste, I started on my particular kind of summer life: short walks on burning, thirsty paths, through high, warm-breathing grain fields, dotted with smiling poppies, cornflowers, sweet peas, cockles, and bindweed, long rests in the tall grass at the edge of the woods, above me the golden glints of beetles, the buzzing of the bees, and the motionless branches against the deep sky. Late in the afternoon I would saunter lazily homeward through the reddish golden dust that rose from the fields, through an air full of ripeness and tiredness amid the melancholy lowing of the cows. And at the end, long balmy hours, sitting alone under a maple or lime tree, or drinking yellow wine with a friend, chatting indolently into the warm night, until thunder was heard somewhere in the distance, the wind rose, the treetops shuddered with fright, and the first drops fell slowly and voluptuously, sinking softly and barely audibly into the dust.

"My goodness," said my good cousin, shaking his head in perplexity. "How can anyone be so lazy! I only hope your limbs don't fall off!"

"They're very well attached," I assured him. And it gave me pleasure to see how tired and sweaty he was. I knew I was within my rights; I had been through an examination and a long line of grueling months, during each day of which I had amply crucified and sacrificed my comfort.

Cousin Kilian was not the man to begrudge me my pleasure. He had deep respect for my learning; in his eyes it was a hallowed cloak around me, and it goes without saying that I let the folds fall in such a way as to conceal its numerous holes.

Never had I experienced such well-being. Slowly and silently I strolled through the fields and meadows, through grain and hay and tall pines; or I lay motionless, breathing like a snake in the delicious warmth, relishing the still, brooding hours.

And then the summer sounds! Those sounds I love so, that made me so deliciously sad: the song of the cicadas, which goes on without a break until past midnight, that sound in which you can lose yourself as completely as in the view of the sea—the glutted rustling of the grain—the muffled thunder that seems to lurk forever in the distance—in the evening the buzzing of the gnats and the poignant sound of scythes being whetted in the distance—at night the swelling warm wind and the wild clatter of sudden showers.

In those short, proud weeks everything blooms and breathes more fervently, lives more deeply and with a deeper fragrance, burns with a more intense and passionate flame. The rich scent of the lime trees fills whole valleys with its soft swell. How eagerly the motley field flowers live amid the tired ripening ears of grain, how they preen themselves, how feverishly they glow in the hasty moments until much too soon the sickle cuts them down!

I was twenty-four, well pleased with the world and

myself. My attitude toward life was that of a dilettante, hinging largely on aesthetic considerations. Nevertheless, when love came to me by none of my own choosing, it followed its course in accordance with the old traditional rules. But I would never have let anyone tell me that. After the indispensable doubts, hesitations, and what I then regarded as hard experiences, I had acquired a calm, objective view of things and adopted an optimistic philosophy. Moreover, I had passed my examination, I had plenty of pocket money and a two-month vacation in front of me.

There are probably such moments in every life: far ahead you see a clear road, no obstacles, not a cloud in the sky, no puddles. You look down comfortably from the heights and come to believe more and more that there is no such thing as luck and chance, that you have honestly earned what you have and a little more to spare, simply by being the man you are. And you will do well to enjoy this feeling while you have it, for on it is based the happiness of fairy-tale princes and the happiness of sparrows on a dung heap as well, and it never lasts very long.

Only the first two days of these wonderful vacation months had slipped through my fingers. With an easy, supple step I wandered up and down the valleys like a serene philosopher, a cigar in my mouth, a meadow pink in my hat, a pound of cherries and a good book in my pocket. I exchanged sage comments with the landowners, said friendly words to the peasants in the fields, accepted invitations to all the greater and lesser festivities, picnics and banquets, baptisms and bock beer evenings; occasionally in the late afternoon I had a drink with the parson, went trout fishing with factory owners and millers, conducted myself with restrained good cheer, and clucked inwardly when one of these sleek, experienced gentlemen treated me as an equal and made no reference to my youth. For in reality it was only on the surface that I was so absurdly young. It had been clear to me for quite some time that I had passed the age of childish folly and become a man; my newfound maturity was a constant source of delight to me. Life, I told myself, was a brisk and spirited horse, to be ridden boldly, but also with caution.

And there lay the earth in its summer beauty. The grain fields were turning yellow, the air was still full of the smell of hay, and the foliage was still alive with bright, strong colors. Children carried bread and cider out into the fields, the peasants were gay and always in a hurry, and in the evenings young girls trooped down the street, suddenly bursting into laughter for no reason, and spontaneously striking up their melancholy folk songs. From the heights of my new maturity I looked on benevolently, and approved the joy of the children, peasants, and young girls with all my heart, confident that I understood these people through and through.

In the cool wooded valley of the Sattelbach—a stream which every hundred yards lends its power to a mill— there was a marble-polishing works: sheds, polishing room, sluice, yard, dwelling house, and garden, all had a pleasantly substantial look, neither battered with age nor too new. Here blocks of marble were slowly and painstakingly sawed into slabs and disks, washed, and polished— clean, unhurried work that was a pleasure to watch. In that narrow, sinuous valley, amid firs and beeches and narrow strips of meadow, it was a charming surprise to come upon the yard full of great marble blocks, white, bluish gray, or colorfully veined, finished slabs of every size, odd scraps, and fine, glittering marble dust. The first time my curiosity led me there, I put a little piece of marble, polished on one side, in my pocket; I kept it for years and used it as a paperweight.

The owner of this marble works was a man named Lampart, who struck me as one of the oddest men in a region noted for its eccentrics. Widowed soon after his marriage, he was by nature unsociable, and his unusual occupation did not bring him into contact with the life of the community. He was thought to be very well off, but no one knew for sure, since there were no other marble polishers for miles around and no one had any idea how such a business operated or how much it brought in. What his eccentricity consisted in I had not yet found out. But eccentric he was, and this made it necessary to deal with Herr Lampart differently than with other people. Anyone who dropped in on him was given a friendly welcome, but the marble polisher was never known to return a call. When he turned up—a rare occurrence—at some village festivity or committee meeting, or joined in a hunting party, he was well received, but no one knew what to say to him, for in his encounters with people he was as imperturbably grave and indifferent as a hermit who would very shortly be going back to his woods.

If someone asked him how his business was getting along, he would reply, "Thank you, nothing to complain of," but he never asked a question in return. Someone would ask if he had been hurt by the last flood or the most recent drought. "Thank you," he would say, "not particularly." But he never went on to inquire, "And you?"

To judge by appearances, he had had and perhaps still had plenty of troubles, but was not inclined to share them with anyone.

That summer I got into the habit of calling on the marble polisher. Sometimes in the course of my wanderings I merely dropped into the yard, or stood in the cool, half-dark polishing room, where shining steel bands rose and fell rhythmically, grains of sand crunched and trickled, silent men stood working, and the water splashed and gurgled under the wooden floor. I watched the wheels and belts, sat down on a block of stone, moved a wooden roller back and forth with my foot or crunched grains and splinters of marble between my fingers, listened to the water, lit a cigar, enjoyed the cool stillness for a few minutes, and left. On such occasions I seldom met the owner. When I felt like it, and that was very often, I went to the sleepy-silent little dwelling house, scraped my boots in the doorway, and coughed until either Herr Lampart or his daughter came down, opened the door to the bright parlor, pulled up a chair, and brought me a glass of wine.

Then I sat down at the massive table, sipped the wine, and twiddled my thumbs. It always took me a long while to get a conversation started, for neither the master of the house nor his daughter, who were seldom present at the same time, ever took the first step, and in this house, with these people, no subject that I might have broached elsewhere seemed appropriate. Half an hour later, when a conversation was well under way, my wine glass, though I drank as slowly as possible, was usually empty. A second was not offered, I would never have asked for more, and I found it embarrassing to sit there in front of an empty glass. So I stood up, shook hands, and put on my hat.

As for the daughter, the only thing that struck me at first was that she strangely resembled her father. Like him she was tall, erect, and dark-haired; she had his steady black eyes, his straight, sharply chiseled nose, his quiet, well-shaped lips. She also had his gait, insofar as a woman can have a man's gait, and the same grave, pleasant voice. She held out her hand in the same way as her father, like him she waited for me to speak first, and requited polite questions with the same terse, matter-of-fact answers, in which I detected a note of surprise.

She had a kind of beauty that is often met with in the Alemannic border country. Its salient features are tallness of stature, a dark complexion, and an appearance of evenly distributed strength. At first I looked upon her as a lovely picture, but then I became more and more captivated by her assurance and maturity. It was then that I began to fall in love, and my love soon developed into a passion such as I had never known. It would soon have become visible if her restrained bearing and the cool, quiet atmosphere of the whole house had not struck me with a kind of paralysis and tamed me the moment I entered.

When I sat facing her or her father, my fire dwindled to a timid little flame, which I carefully concealed. And this room bore no resemblance to a stage where young knights of love can fall successfully to their knees, but seemed more like a place of resignation and restraint, where quiet forces prevail and an earnest bit of life is lived and suffered with seriousness. Nevertheless, behind this young girl's quiet, uneventful life I sensed a responsiveness and vitality which were held in check and seldom rose to the surface—and then only in a quick gesture or a sudden flashing glance, when a conversation aroused her.

I speculated a good deal about the true nature of this beautiful, rather austere young girl. Was she essentially passionate or essentially melancholy, or was she indeed imperturbable? In any event I was certain that what I saw was not her whole self. She seemed so independent, and so free in her judgments; yet her father had absolute power over her. I suspected that from her earliest childhood he, lovingly no doubt, had repressed her true and innermost nature and forced it, to her detriment, into other channels. When I saw them together, which was seldom, to be sure, I seemed to sense this perhaps unintentional tyrannical influence and I had a vague feeling that some day there would inevitably be a relentless and deadly struggle between them. When it occurred to me that this struggle might occur on my account, my heart pounded and I could not repress a shudder.

My acquaintance with Herr Lampart made no headway, but my friendship with Gustav Becker, the manager of the Rippach farm, throve all the more. We talked for hours, and only recently we had gone so far as to drink brotherhood. Despite my cousin's strong disapproval I was very proud of myself. Becker, who must have been about thirty-two, was well educated, shrewd, and experienced. Most often he listened to my fine speeches, my words of manly wisdom, with an ironic smile, but I was not offended, for I saw him honor much older and more dignified men with the same smile. He was entitled to his smile, for he was not only the sole manager, and perhaps future purchaser, of the largest farm in the region, but also a man far superior to most of those about him. He was spoken of with admiration as a damned clever fellow, but not very well liked. I suspected that he took so much interest in me because he felt that people avoided him.

True, he often drove me to despair. Without saying a word, merely by a cruelly expressive grin, he could make me doubt my own opinions on life and men, and sometimes he went so far as to say that philosophy of any kind was an absurdity.

One evening I was sitting in the garden of the Eagle with Becker over a glass of beer. We were quite alone and undisturbed, at a table facing the meadow. It was one of those dry, hot evenings, when the air is full of golden dust; the smell of the lime trees was almost overpowering, and the light seemed neither to increase nor diminish.

"You must know the marble polisher over in the Sattelbach valley?" I asked my friend.

He was filling his pipe. He nodded without looking up.

"Well," I said. "What kind of man is he, anyway?"

Becker laughed and slipped his pipe tamper into his vest pocket.

"He's a very intelligent man," he said. "Which is why he keeps his mouth shut. Why are you interested in him?"

"No reason. I was just wondering. He seems so strange."

"Intelligent people always do; there aren't very many."

"Is that all? Don't you know anything about him?"

"He has a beautiful daughter."

"I know. I wasn't thinking of that. Why does he never go to see anybody?"

"Why should he?"

"Oh, well. But it seems to me he must have had some bitter experience."

"Something romantic, you mean? The secluded mill in the valley. Marble. The silent hermit. Buried happiness. No, I'm sorry, there's nothing in it. He's a very good businessman."

"Are you so sure?"

"The man's no fool. He makes money."

Then he had to go. There was still work to be done. He paid for his beer and walked away through the mown meadow. He disappeared behind the first hummock and a moment later a long swathe of pipe smoke reached me —he was walking against the wind. The cows in the barn set up a slow contented mooing, the first evening idlers appeared in the village street, and when after a time I looked around me, the mountains were already bluish black and the sky had turned from red to a greenish blue, as though the first stars must appear at any moment.

My brief conversation with the farm manager had been rather a blow to my philosopher's pride. Since it was such a beautiful evening and my self-confidence was badly dented, I was suddenly overcome by my love for the marble polisher's daughter and at the same time by a feeling that the passions are not to be toyed with. I drank several more beers. When the stars were really out and one of those heart-rending folk songs came to me from the street, I left my wisdom and my hat on the bench, strolled out into the dark fields, and let my tears flow as they would.

But through my tears I saw the summer-night countryside. The fields stretched out endlessly, rising like a great soft wave on the horizon; to one side the forest lay sleeping, and behind me only a few flickering lights and an occasional soft, distant sound told me that the village was still there. Sky, fields, woods, and village, the many varied meadow scents, and now and then a belated chirping of crickets, all merged, surrounding me with warmth and speaking to me like a beautiful saddening and gladdening melody. Only the stars shone clear and unmoved in the darkening sky. A timid yet burning desire, a longing rose up in me; I couldn't have said whether it drove me onward to new and unknown joys and sorrows or back to my childhood home, to lean on the garden fence, to hear once more the voices of my dead parents and the barking of our dead dog, and to cry my eyes out.

Through no will of my own I went into the woods and made my way through parched branches and sultry darkness until suddenly I glimpsed a light open space. Then I stood for a long while amid the tall fir trees surmounting the narrow Sattelbach valley. Down below lay the Lampart house and the pale mounds of marble and the dark splashing of the weir. I stood there until I felt ashamed and took the shortest way home through the fields.

Next day Gustav Becker had my secret out of me.

"Don't beat about the bush," he said. "You're in love with the Lampart girl. That's all there is to it. It's not the end of the world. At your age you can expect these things to happen any number of times."

That was too much for my pride.

"Oh, no," I said. "You underestimate me. I've passed the age of boyhood crushes. I've thought the whole thing over and come to the conclusion that I'll never find anyone better to marry."

"Marry?" said Becker, laughing. "My boy, you're charming."

Then I grew angry in earnest, but I did not go away. Instead, I explained my thoughts and plans in the matter at great length.

"You forget the main point," he said with grave emphasis when I had finished. "The Lamparts aren't right for you. Those people are heavy caliber. Fall in love with anyone you please, but when you marry, it has to be someone you can handle and keep step with."

I made faces and wanted to interrupt him. But then suddenly he laughed and said, "If that's the way it is, son, get busy, and the best of luck."

For a while I discussed the matter with him whenever possible. Since he could seldom get away from his work, we had almost all our talks in the fields or in his barn. And the more I spoke, the clearer and simpler it all seemed to me.

But when I was sitting in the marble polisher's house, I felt dejected, for I saw how far I was from my goal. The

girl's manner was always the same, quietly friendly with
a trace of mannishness which delighted but also intimidated me. At times I felt that she was glad to see me and
secretly loved me; time and again she looked at me with
a self-forgetful attentiveness, as one looks at an object one
takes pleasure in. And she listened with grave interest to
my wise disquisitions, though underneath she seemed to
harbor a firmly contrary opinion.

Once she said: "Women, I myself at least, look at life
in a different way. We have to do a good many things, and
put up with things, that a man wouldn't. We aren't as
free . . ."

I said that each one of us has his fate in his own hands
and is in duty bound to make himself a life that is entirely his own work and belongs to him alone.

"Maybe a man can do that," she said. "I don't know.
But for us it's different. We too can make something out
of our lives, but for us it's not so much a question of acting on our own as of being reasonable about bearing what
can't be avoided."

And when I contradicted her again with a pretty little
speech, she grew more heated and said almost passionately: "Stick to your idea and leave me mine! It's no great
art to pick out the best things in life if you have your
choice. But who has a choice? If you're run over today or
tomorrow and lose your arms and legs, what will you do
with your castles in Spain? Then you'd be glad if you had
learned to accept your lot. But have it your way, find your
happiness and take it."

I had never seen her so agitated. But then she calmed
down and smiled strangely. When I stood up to take my
leave for that day, she did not detain me. I remembered
those words of hers, they kept running through my head,
often at the most inappropriate times. I meant to discuss
them with my friend at the Rippach Farm; but when I
saw Becker's cool eyes and the lurking mockery on his
lips, I lost all desire to. All in all, the more personal and
absorbing my conversations with Fräulein Lampart be-

came, the less I spoke about them to my friend. In any
event he seemed to have lost interest in the matter. He
merely asked me now and then if I was visiting the marble
works with proper regularity, teased me a bit, and dropped
the subject. That was his way.

Once to my surprise I ran into him at the Lampart her-
mitage. When I arrived, he was sitting in the parlor with
the usual glass of wine in front of him. When it was
empty, it gave me a certain satisfaction to see that he too
was not offered a second one. He soon rose to go, and
since Lampart was busy and his daughter was out, I
joined him.

"What brings you here?" I asked him, when we were on
the road. "You seem to know Lampart well."

"Pretty well."

"You have dealings with him?"

"Business dealings. Your lambkins wasn't there today,
was she? Your visit was very short."

"Oh, stop it!"

An easy friendship had developed between the girl and
myself, yet though I was more and more in love with her,
I had never knowingly given her any sign of it. But then
suddenly, very much to my surprise, her manner changed
in such a way that for a time I lost all hope. She was not
exactly reticent, but she seemed to be looking for a way
back to our former situation as strangers, trying to limit
our conversation to externals and generalities, and to stifle
the intimacy that had sprung up between us.

I mulled it over, roamed about in the woods and formed
dozens of absurd conjectures. I became more uncertain
than ever in my behavior toward her and slipped into a
pitiful state of anxiety and doubt that made a mockery of
my whole philosophy of happiness. By then more than
half my vacation had passed; I began to count the days
and to dwell with jealous despair on each one I had
wasted in aimless wanderings, as though that particular
day, now irrevocable, had been infinitely important.

Then came a day when to my mingled relief and alarm

it seemed to me that I had won; for a moment the gate to the garden of happiness stood open before me.

Passing by the marble works, I saw Helene among the tall dahlias in the garden. I went in, we exchanged greetings, and I helped her to fasten a fallen stalk to its stake. I stayed for a quarter of an hour at the most. My coming had surprised her, she was much more embarrassed and shy than usual, and in her shyness there was something that I took as an unmistakable sign. She loved me, I felt it through and through; suddenly I was happy and self-assured, I looked at her with tenderness, almost with pity. Mindful of her embarrassment, I pretended to notice nothing, and I felt like a hero when after a few minutes I gave her my hand and went my way, without even looking back. She loves me, I felt with my whole being, and tomorrow everything will be settled.

It was another glorious day. For a time, what with my anxiety and agitation, I had almost lost my feeling for the fine season and had gone about without eyes. Now once again the woods were full of quivering light, the brook was black, brown, and silver, the horizon was tender and luminous, the skirts of the peasant women laughed red and blue on the paths through the fields. I was so devoutly happy that I could not have shooed away a butterfly. At the upper edge of the woods, after a hot climb, I lay down. I looked over the fertile countryside to the round Staufen Mountain in the distance and, feeling deeply satisfied with the whole world and myself, basked in the noonday sun.

It was good that I enjoyed that day to the full, that I dreamed and sang it away.

When I called at the marble works next day, all the old coolness had returned. At the mere sight of the parlor and of Helene's quiet gravity, my assurance and sense of triumph evaporated. I sat there as dejected as a tramp on a doorstep, and went away like a wet dog, wretchedly sobered. Nothing had happened. Helene had been friendly. But of yesterday's feeling nothing remained.

That day my love became a grimly serious matter. I had had an intimation of happiness.

My longing devoured me like a desperate hunger, it was all up with my sleep and peace of mind. The world fell away from me and left me in solitude and silence, hearing nothing but the loud and soft cries of my passion. I dreamed that this tall, grave, beautiful girl had come to me and laid her head on my breast; and then, weeping and cursing, I held out my arms into the void. Day and night I circled around the marble works and hardly dared to enter.

It was no help to me when I listened without opposition to one of Becker's ironic, disabused sermons. It was no help that I wandered for hours through the searing heat and lay down in the cold forest brooks until my teeth chattered. Nor was it any help when I got into a fight in the village on Saturday night, and came away covered with bruises.

And the time seeped away like water. Only two more weeks of vacation. Only twelve days. Only ten. I went to the marble works twice during that time. Once I found only the father. I followed him to the polishing room and looked on dully as a new block of marble was fastened in place. Herr Lampart went out to the storeroom, and when he did not return right away, I left with the intention of never coming back.

But two days later I was there again. Helene welcomed me as usual, and I could not take my eyes off her. In my thoughtless bewilderment I trotted out all sorts of silly jokes and anecdotes that visibly irritated her.

"Why are you like this today?" she finally asked, giving me a look so open and lovely that my heart began to pound.

"How should I be?" I asked. And the devil made me attempt a laugh.

My unsuccessful laugh displeased her; she shrugged her shoulders and looked sad. For a moment it seemed to me that she was sad because she loved me and had tried to meet me halfway. For a moment I stood silent and downcast, but then the devil was back again and I relapsed into my clowning, making silly remarks, every word of which hurt me and must have annoyed her. And I was young and stupid enough to enjoy my suffering and my senseless clowning, as though looking on at a play. With childish defiance I broadened the gulf between us, instead of biting off my tongue or earnestly begging her forgiveness.

Then in my haste I swallowed some wine the wrong way, burst into a fit of coughing, and left the room and house more wretched than ever.

By then only a week was left of my vacation.

It was so beautiful a summer, everything had begun so happily, so full of promise. Now my joy was gone— what could I do in a week? I made up my mind to leave the next day.

But first I had to go to her house again. One last time I had to see her strong, noble beauty and say: I love you. Why did you toy with me?

First I went to the Rippach Farm to take my leave of Gustav Becker, whom I had been rather neglecting of late. He was standing in his big bare room writing letters on a tall, ridiculously narrow desk.

"I've come to say goodbye," I said. "I'll probably be leaving tomorrow. It's time I got down to work."

To my surprise Becker made no jokes. He patted me on the back, smiled almost pityingly, and said: "Well, my boy, then you'll just have to be going."

But when I was half through the doorway, he pulled me back into the room and said: "I'm really sorry. But this thing with the girl—I knew from the first that nothing would come of it. You've poured out words of wisdom from time to time—remember them now, and keep your head, even if it is spinning."

That was in the morning.

In the afternoon I was sitting in the moss on the slope,

directly above the Sattelbach, looking down at the brook and the marble works and the Lampart house. I stayed a long while, taking leave, dreaming and pondering, mostly about what Becker had said. I looked sorrowfully down into the narrow valley—a few rooftops, the glittering brook, and the white road raising dust in the breeze: I would not be coming back here for a long time, but the brook and the marble works and the people would go on day after day. One day perhaps Helene would cast off her resignation, her quiet acceptance of fate, respond to her inner drive and find fulfillment in a great happiness or a great sorrow. And perhaps, who knows, my own path would some day emerge from these gullies and tangled woodland valleys into a clear, wide land of peace? —Who knows?

I didn't believe it. For the first time a real passion held me in its grip, and no power within me seemed strong or noble enough to overcome it.

Perhaps, it occurred to me, I should leave without seeing Helene again. Yes, that would certainly be best. I nodded in the direction of her house and garden, decided not to see her again, and lay there until on toward evening, taking leave.

More dreaming than awake, I picked myself up and started down through the woods, often stumbling on the steep slope. I was jolted out of my dream when the marble scraps in the yard crunched under my feet and I found myself at the door that I had never meant to see or touch again. Now it was too late.

Without knowing how I had come in, I sat at the table in the half darkness. Helene sat across from me, her back to the window, silently looking into the room. It seemed to me that I had been sitting there in silence for hours. Then suddenly it came to me that this was the last time.

"Well," I said. "This is goodbye. My vacation is over."

"Really?"

And then again silence. I heard the workmen in the shed. A wagon drove slowly past, and I listened till it rounded the bend and the sound died away. I would gladly have listened to it for a long, long time. Then I tore myself out of my chair, determined to go.

I went over to the window. She too stood up and looked at me. Her eyes were steady and grave, and for a long time she did not avert them.

"Don't you remember that time in the garden?" I asked.

"Yes, I remember."

"Helene, that day I thought you loved me. And now I have to go."

She took my outstretched hand and drew me to the window.

"Let's have another look at you," she said, lifting up my head with one hand. She moved her eyes close to mine and her look was strangely rigid. Her face was so close to mine that I couldn't help myself; I pressed my lips to hers. She closed her eyes and returned the kiss. I put my arm around her, drew her close, and asked her: "Darling, why so late?"

"Don't talk," she said. "Now go away and come back in an hour. I've got to see about the workmen. Father isn't home yet."

I left the house and strolled down the valley through strange unknown places, amid dazzlingly bright cloud formations. As in a dream I heard the flowing of the brook and thought of remote irrelevant things—comical or touching little episodes from my childhood and other such scenes, which emerged in a dim outline from the clouds and vanished before I could fully recognize them. I sang as I walked along, but it was a common street song. And as I wandered through unknown places, I was suffused with a strange and delicious warmth and Helene's tall, strong figure stood before me. Then I came to myself and saw that I was far down the valley. Night was falling and I hurried joyfully back.

She was waiting. She led me through the house door and into the parlor. We sat down on the edge of the table, joined hands, and did not say a word. It was dark in the

room, and the air was balmy. One window was open; in
the upper part of it I could see the wooded hill and above
it a narrow strip of blue sky traversed by the sharp black
crowns of a few fir trees. We played with each other's
fingers and at every light touch a thrill of happiness ran
through me.

"Helene!"

"Yes?"

"Oh, Helene!"

Our fingers moved gently and after a time they lay still,
gently entwined. I looked at the pale strip of sky and when
I turned around I saw that she too was looking in that
direction. And through the darkness I saw the faint glow
of the sky reflected in two big tears that hung motionless
from her eyelids. I kissed them slowly away, surprised at
how cool and salty they tasted. Then she drew me to her,
gave me a long, vigorous kiss, and stood up.

"It's time. Now you must go."

When we were in the doorway, she suddenly kissed me
again with violent passion. And trembling so hard that I
too was shaken, she said in a choked, hardly audible
voice: "Go, go! Do you hear me, go now!" And when I was
outside: "Goodbye! Don't come back, don't come back!
Goodbye!"

Before I could say a word, she had closed the door. A
vague fear rose up in me, but it was outweighed by a great
feeling of happiness, which accompanied me like a beating of wings on my way home. Though I walked briskly,
I did not hear my footfalls. At home I started to undress,
but then settled down on the windowsill in my shirt
sleeves.

I wish I could have another night like that. The soft
breeze caressed me like a mother's hand, outside the little
window the darkening round chestnut trees whispered,
now and then a faint scent came blowing from the fields,
and in the distance summer lightning sent golden tremors
across the heavy sky. From time to time I heard faint
distant thunder; it was a strange sound, as though far

away the woods and mountains were stirring in their
sleep and muttering heavy, tired, dream-laden words. I
saw and heard all this like a king looking down from a
lofty tower of happiness; it belonged to me and existed
only as a setting for my profound joy. My whole being
breathed with delight, losing itself again and again in the
vast expanse of night over the sleeping countryside, graz-
ing the distant glitter of the clouds, touched as though
with loving hands by every single tree that rose from the
darkness and by the dim crest of every hill. It's nothing
when put into words, but it still lives undiminished within
me, and if there were a language for it, I could still describe exactly every wave of the fields rolling till it lost
itself in the darkness, every sound in the treetops, each
distant lightning streak, and the secret rhythm of the
thunder.

No, I cannot describe it. What is most beautiful and
inward and precious cannot be put into words. But I wish
that night would come again for me.

If I had not already taken leave of Becker, I would undoubtedly have gone to see him the following morning.
Instead I roamed about the village for a while, and then
wrote a long letter to Helene. I told her I would call that
evening and made all sorts of suggestions. I gave a serious
and detailed account of my circumstances and prospects,
and asked whether she thought it preferable that I should
speak to her father at once, or wait until I was sure of
the employment I had every reason to expect, so that at
least the immediate future would be secure. In the evening I went to see her. Again her father was absent, busy
with one of his suppliers, who had been spending the last
few days in the region.

I kissed my lovely sweetheart, drew her into the parlor,
and asked about my letter. Yes, she had received it. And
what did she think? She said nothing, but looked at me
imploringly. When I insisted, she put her hand over my
lips, kissed me on the forehead, and moaned softly but so
pitifully that I was utterly at a loss. In response to all my

tender questions she only shook her head, smiled a soft, delicate smile out of her misery, and threw her arms around me. And again we sat together in silent tenderness as we had the day before. She pressed close to me and buried her head in my shoulder. Unable to put a thought together, I slowly kissed her hair and forehead and cheek and neck, until my head was reeling. I jumped up.

"Well then, should I speak to your father tomorrow or not?"

"No," she said. "Please. You mustn't."

"Why not? Are you afraid?"

She shook her head.

"Then why not?"

"Hush," she said. "Hush. Don't talk about it. We still have fifteen minutes."

There we sat, silently enlaced. And as she pressed close to me, holding her breath and shuddering at every caress, her dejection and melancholy infected me. I tried to ward them off, I pleaded with her to have faith in me and our happiness.

"Oh yes," she said, nodding. "Don't talk about it. We're happy now."

She kissed me several times with strong silent passion; then she went limp and hung wearily in my arms. When it was time for me to go, she stroked my hair in the doorway and said in a faint voice: "Goodbye, darling. Don't come tomorrow. Don't ever come again. Please. You see that it makes me unhappy."

I went home with an agonizing conflict in my heart and spent half the night mulling it over. Why did she refuse to have faith and be happy? I was reminded of the words she had spoken several weeks before: "We women are not as free as you; we must learn to bear what is in store for us." What was in store for her?

In any event, I had to know. In the morning I sent her a note, and in the evening I waited in the marble shed until the machines had stopped and the workmen had gone.

Then after some time she came hesitantly across the yard.

"Why have you come? Let well enough alone. Father is at home."

"No," I said. "Now you must tell me what's on your heart, the whole story. I won't go away before you do."

Helene looked at me calmly. She was as pale as the marble slabs behind her.

"Don't torture me," she whispered painfully. "I can't tell you. I don't want to. All I can say is—go away. Go soon, today or tomorrow, and forget all this. I can't belong to you."

It was a balmy July evening, yet she was shivering. I have seldom felt such torment as in those moments. But I couldn't leave her like this.

"Tell me the whole story," I said. "I have to know."

She looked at me in a way that made me ache all over. But it would have been impossible for me to act any differently.

"Tell me," I said almost harshly. "Or I'll go over to your father this minute."

She drew herself up almost angrily. With her pallor and sadness, she was very beautiful in the failing light. She spoke without passion but more loudly than before.

"Very well. I'm not free, and you can't have me. There's someone else. Is that enough?"

"No," I said. "It's not enough. Do you love him? More than me?"

"Oh, darling," she cried out. "No, no, I don't love him. But I'm promised to him, and nothing can be done about it."

"Why not, if you don't love him?"

"I'd never even heard of you. I liked him; I didn't love him, but he was a good man and I didn't know any other. So I said yes, and that's how it is and that's how it has to be."

"It doesn't have to be, Helene. That kind of promise can be taken back."

"Maybe it can. But it's not because of him. It's because

of my father. I can't be disloyal to my father . . ."

"But I'll speak to him . . ."

"Silly child! Don't you understand anything?"

I looked at her. She was almost laughing.

"I've been sold, sold by my father with my consent. For money. We're to be married next winter."

She turned away, took a few steps, and came back.

"Darling," she said. "Be brave. You mustn't come here any more, you mustn't . . ."

"Just for money?" I couldn't help asking.

She shrugged. "What difference does it make? My father can't back down now. He's as much a prisoner as I am. You don't know him. If I fail him, something terrible will happen. So be a good boy, be reasonable."

And then in a sudden outburst: "Darling, try to understand; don't kill me! —I can still do as I will—now. But if you touch me once more—I won't be able to bear it . . . I can't kiss you again, or we'll all be lost."

For a moment nothing was said. The silence was so deep that I could hear her father moving about the house.

"I can't make any decision today," I said. "Won't you tell me . . . who it is?"

"The other one? No, it's best you don't know. Oh, don't come back—for my sake."

She went into the house and I looked after her. I meant to leave, but forgot, and sat down on the cool white stones. I listened to the brook, aware of nothing but a flowing away without end. It was as though my life and Helene's life and countless other lives were streaming past me, down through the gully into the darkness, indifferent and wordless as water. As water . . .

I came home late, dead tired. I slept. When I got up in the morning, I decided to pack my suitcase, but forgot, and after breakfast I strolled off into the woods. My thoughts refused to take form, they rose like bubbles in still water and burst, vanishing the moment they came to the surface.

Then it's all over, I thought from time to time, but the

thought evoked no image, it was mere words; I drew a
breath and nodded my head, but I was no wiser than before.

It was only in the course of the afternoon that my love
and my misery awoke within me, threatening to overwhelm me. But in that state I was still incapable of good,
clear thoughts, and instead of taking myself in hand and
waiting till I was able to think things over quietly, I let
myself be carried away and lay down not far from the
marble works, on the lookout until I saw Herr Lampart
leave the house, turn into the road leading down the
valley, and vanish in the direction of the village.

Then I went down.

When I stepped in, Helene let out a cry and looked at
me like a wounded animal.

"Why?" she moaned. "Why have you come back?"

I was bewildered and ashamed, and I have never felt
so woebegone. I still had my hand on the door, but I
hadn't the strength to leave. I went slowly in, and she gave
me a look of fear and pain. "Why? Oh darling, darling!"
In her face and movements she seemed to have grown
older and stronger and more mature. I felt almost like a
boy beside her.

"Well?" she asked finally and tried to smile.

"Say something," I begged her forlornly, "so I'll be able
to go."

A tremor ran over her face and I thought she was going
to burst into tears. But then unexpectedly she smiled, how
softly and sorrowfully I shall never be able to say, gave
herself a shake, and said in a faint whisper: "Come here.
Why are you standing there like a poker?" I stepped forward and took her in my arms. We held each other with
all our strength. While fear and anguish mingled with my
joy and I could scarcely hold back my sobs, she brightened
visibly, caressed me like a child, called me by fanciful pet
names, bit my hand, and invented little loving follies. A
deep-seated fear battled against my mounting passion, I
could find no words and held Helene close while she play-

fully fondled and caressed me. In the end she burst out laughing.

"Can't you cheer up, you icicle?" she cried out, pulling my mustache.

I asked her uneasily: "Now do you think everything will be all right? If it's true that you can't belong to me . . ."

She took my head in both hands, looked me full in the face, and said: "Yes, everything will be all right now."

"Then I can stay on and come back tomorrow and speak to your father?"

"Yes, silly boy, you can do all that. You can even come in a frock coat if you have one. Tomorrow is Sunday anyway."

"Oh, yes, I have one," I said, laughing. All at once I was so childishly happy that I took her around the waist and waltzed through the room with her. We landed by the table, I picked her up on my lap, she laid her forehead against my cheek, and I played with her dark, thick hair. At length she jumped up, stepped away, put her hair in order, threatened me with her finger, and said: "Father will be back any minute. How childish we are!"

I was given another kiss and still another and a sprig of mignonette from the window box. It was getting on toward evening and since it was Saturday I found plenty of company at the Eagle, drank a mug of beer, played a game of ninepins, and went home early. I took my frock coat out of the cupboard, hung it over the back of a chair, and looked at it with approval. It was as good as new, I had bought it for my examination and had seldom worn it since. The sleek black material aroused all manner of solemn, dignified thoughts in me. Instead of going to bed, I sat down and pondered what I would say to Helene's father next day. I visualized in every detail how I would approach him, modestly and yet with dignity, I imagined not only his objections and my answers, but even his thoughts and gestures, and my own. I spoke aloud like a preacher practicing his sermon, making the appropriate gestures, and even when I was in bed on the point of falling asleep, I declaimed a sentence or two from the next day's presumptive interview.

Then it was Sunday morning. Wanting to think it all over again at my ease, I lay in bed until the church bells rang. During the services, I put on my robe of state with at least as much care as before my examination, shaved, drank my morning milk, and listened to the throbbing of my heart. I waited impatiently until church was out; then, as soon as the bells had died down, I started slowly and solemnly through the hot, hazy morning and plodded down the Sattelbach road, avoiding the dusty places. For all my precautions, I got into something of a sweat in my frock coat and high collar.

When I reached the marble works, I was surprised and disgruntled to find a number of villagers standing in the yard waiting for something, talking in small groups that made me think of an auction.

But disinclined to ask anyone what was going on, I passed on to the house door with a sense of anguished amazement as in a weird and terrifying dream. In the hall I ran into my friend Becker and gave him a curt, shamefaced greeting. It embarrassed me to meet him here, because he must have thought I had left long ago. But he seemed to have other things on his mind. He was very pale, and he looked strained and tired.

"So you've come too?" he said rather sharply, with a shake of his head. "I'm afraid, my good friend, that your presence isn't needed here today."

"Isn't Herr Lampart here?" I countered.

"Oh, yes. Where else would he be?"

"And the young lady?"

He pointed at the parlor door.

"In there?"

Becker nodded, and I was just about to knock when the door opened and a man came out. I saw that several visitors were standing about inside, and that some of the furniture had been displaced.

Now I was alarmed. "Becker, good God, what has happened? What are these people here for? And why are you here?"

Becker turned around and gave me a strange look.

"You mean you don't know?" he asked in a changed voice.

"What? No."

He barred my way and looked into my face.

"In that case, son, go home," he said softly, almost gently, and laid his hand on my arm. I felt myself gagging and a nameless fear seized me.

Again Becker gave me a strange inquiring look. Then he asked softly: "Did you speak to her yesterday?" When I flushed, he coughed violently, but it sounded like a groan.

"What's happened to Helene? Where is she?" I cried in terror.

Becker paced back and forth and seemed to have forgotten me. I leaned against a banister post and felt myself hemmed in by strange, bloodless, mocking figures. Then Becker came back to me and said, "Come!" He climbed as far as the first bend in the stairs. There he sat down on a step and I sat down beside him, heedlessly rumpling my frock coat. For a moment the whole house was deathly still, then Becker began to speak.

"Take hold of yourself and grit your teeth, son. Helene Lampart is dead. We pulled her out of the brook this morning by the lower sluice. —Be still, don't talk. And don't collapse. You're not the only one this is hard on. Now's the time to show how manly you can be. She's lying down there in the parlor. She looks beautiful enough now, but when we fished her out—it was bad, bad . . ."

He stopped and shook his head.

"Be still! Don't say anything. There'll be time enough to talk later on. This affects me more than you. —No, forget it, I'll tell you all that tomorrow."

"No," I pleaded. "Tell me, Becker. I've got to know."

"All right. We can talk it over some other time, I'm at

your service. All I can tell you now is that I meant well by you, letting you come here all this time. You never know. —Well, I was engaged to Helene. Not yet officially, but . . ."

For a moment I thought I was going to stand up and hit Becker in the face with all my might. He seemed to read my thoughts.

"Don't!" he said, looking me calmly in the face. "As I've said, we can go into explanations another time."

We sat silent. Like racing ghosts the whole story of Helene and Becker and me flew by, quickly but clear of outline. Why hadn't I been told sooner, why hadn't I guessed it by myself? Everything would have been possible. One word, the merest hint, and I would have gone away in silence, and she wouldn't be lying in the parlor.

My anger had died down. I knew that Becker must have suspected the truth, and I knew what a weight he had to bear. He had felt so secure, he had left me free to play, and now he had the greater part of the guilt on his heart. I had to ask one more question.

"Becker, tell me—did you love her? Did you really love her?"

He tried to say something but his voice broke. He only nodded, twice, then a third time. When I saw him nod, when I saw how this tough, hard man's voice failed him, and how clearly the quivering muscles in his sleepless face spoke—then at last the full weight of the tragedy hit me.

After a long while, when I looked up through my drying tears, he stood before me and held out his hand. I took it and pressed it. Slowly he went down the steep stairs ahead of me and softly opened the door to the parlor, where Helene lay. And shaken with dread, I entered the room for the last time.

The Latin Scholar

1906

IN THE MIDDLE of the tight-huddled old town there is
an unbelievably big building with innumerable little
windows and sadly worn piers and stairways, a place both
venerable and absurd, and that is the impression it made
on Karl Bauer, a schoolboy of sixteen, who passed through
its portals every morning and afternoon with his school-
bag. Latin, so elegant, clear, and guileless, and the old
German poets were a pleasure to him; Greek, which he
found difficult, and algebra, which he liked no more in the
third year than he had in the first, were a torment. He
also took pleasure in some of the gray-bearded older
teachers and had his troubles with several of the younger
ones.

Not far from the schoolhouse stood a shop that had
been there for ages. The door was always open and people
were always going up and down the dark damp stairs.
The entrance was pitch-dark and smelled of alcohol, kero-
sene, and cheese. Karl found his way easily through the
darkness, for he lived on the top floor of the house, where
the shopkeeper's mother gave him board and lodging.
Here it was as bright and open as it was dark down below;
there was all the sunlight one could wish for and a view
over half the city. Those who lived on this top floor knew
almost every rooftop by name.

The shop was full of all sorts of good things, but very
few found their way up the narrow stairs, or if they did
Karl Bauer rarely saw them, for old Frau Kusterer's board
was meager and he always left the table hungry. But
otherwise he got along well enough with the family, and

his room was his castle. When he was in it, no one disturbed him, and he could do what he pleased, which was quite a lot. The two titmice in a cage were the least of it. He had also rigged up a sort of carpenter shop, he melted lead and tin in the stove and poured it into molds, and in the summer he kept slowworms and lizards in a crate— they always escaped after a short while through the spaces in the wire netting. In addition he had his violin, and when he wasn't reading or busy with his carpentry, he was sure to be playing it, at all hours of the day and night.

And so the young man had his daily pleasures; he was never bored, especially as he had plenty of books, which he borrowed wherever possible. He read a good deal, preferring, of course, some books to others; what he liked best was legends, fairy tales, and tragedies in verse.

Yet all this, splendid as it was, did not fill his belly. When his hunger became too much for him, he crept as stealthily as a weasel down the dark stairs to the stone passage on the ground floor, illumined only by a feeble strip of light from the shop. Here a remnant of good cheese might be lying on top of a tall empty crate, or an open barrel half-full of herring might be standing beside the door, and on lucky days, or when Karl on pretense of offering a helping hand ventured into the shop, a few handfuls of prunes or dried pears or something of the sort might find their way into his pockets.

These forays never troubled his conscience. He did not undertake them out of greed, but with the innocence of hunger or the feelings of a greathearted bandit, who knows no fear and looks danger calmly and proudly in the eye. It struck him as perfectly in keeping with the laws of the ethical world order that what the stingy mother saved on his board should be taken from the son's overflowing stores of treasure.

Along with the almighty school, these diverse habits, occupations, and hobbies might have sufficed to fill his time and thoughts. But they did not satisfy Karl Bauer. Partly in imitation of certain of his schoolmates, partly as a reaction to his reading, and partly in response to a profound inner need, he had recently set foot for the first time in that beautiful land so rich in mysterious promise —the land of love. And since he knew in advance that for the time being his doings and wooings could have no tangible results, he aimed high, devoting his attentions to the most beautiful girl in town. She came of a wealthy family and if only by the splendor of her attire far out-shone all the other girls of her age. The schoolboy passed by her house each day. When she came along, he took off his hat and bowed lower than he would have to the principal himself.

One evening in late autumn, when Karl had been not at all replenished by his bowl of thin café au lait, hunger sent him on one of his expeditions. He slipped inaudibly downstairs and reconnoitered the stone passage. After a brief search he caught sight of an earthenware dish, on which two winter pears of delectable size and color were leaning against a red-rimmed slice of Holland cheese.

The hungry boy could easily have guessed that this treat was intended for the master's table and that the maid had merely put it down for a moment; but he was so overjoyed at the unexpected sight that the idea of a benevolent turn of fate seemed much more plausible, and with a feeling of gratitude he began to transfer the offer-ing to his pockets.

But before he could finish and disappear, Babette, the maid, emerged from the cellar door on silent slippers and to her horror discovered the crime in the light of the can-dle she was holding. The young thief still had the cheese in his hand; he stood motionless, looking at the floor, while his whole world fell apart and sank into an abyss of shame. The two of them stood there in the candlelight. It seems safe to say that the intrepid young man would experience more painful moments in the course of his life, but certainly none more embarrassing.

"Goodness me!" said Babette finally, and there was a

sermon in the look she gave the contrite wrongdoer. He for his part had nothing to say.

"What a thing to do!" she went on. "Don't you know that's stealing?"

"Yes. I know."

"Then, heavens alive, why did you do it?"

"It was standing there, Babette, and I thought . . ."

"What did you think?"

"Well, I was so awfully hungry that . . ."

At these words she opened her eyes wide and stared at the poor fellow with infinite understanding, astonishment, and compassion.

"You're hungry? Don't they give you anything to eat up there?"

"Very little, Babette. Very little."

"My goodness. Never mind, it's all right. Keep what you've got in your pocket, and the cheese too. Keep it, there's plenty more in the house. But now I'd better go up, or somebody'll be coming."

In a strange mood Karl went back to his room, sat down, and thoughtfully devoured first the cheese and then the pears. After that his heart was lighter; he stretched, picked up his violin, and struck up a kind of psalm of thanksgiving. No sooner had he finished than someone knocked softly; when he opened, it was Babette, who had brought him a thick slice of bread, liberally buttered.

Though delighted, he attempted a polite refusal, but when she insisted he accepted without reluctance.

"You play the fiddle mighty well," she said admiringly. "I often listen. Don't you worry now, I'll see that you get enough to eat. I can easily bring you a little something in the evening, nobody needs to know. I'm blessed if I can see why she doesn't feed you better, your father certainly pays plenty for your board."

Again he tried shyly to decline with thanks, but she wouldn't hear of it and he willingly gave in. In the end they agreed that on days when he was especially hungry, he would whistle the song "Golden Evening Sun" on the stairs as he came in, and then she would bring him something to eat. If he whistled something else or nothing at all, then it would not be necessary. Contrite and thankful, he put his hand in her broad palm and she sealed their pact with a powerful squeeze.

From then on the Latin scholar basked in the sympathy and care of a kindly woman—for the first time since his childhood years at home, since his parents lived in the country and had sent him to boarding school at an early age. He was often reminded of his years at home, for Babette watched over him and spoiled him like a mother, which she could have been at her age. She was about forty, and in the main her character was stern and unyielding; but opportunity makes the thief, and now that she had so unexpectedly found in this boy a grateful friend and protégé, and a hungry mouth to feed, an almost bashful gentleness, a selfless tenderness began to emerge from beneath her hardened character.

Karl Bauer was the object of her tenderness, and it soon spoiled him, for boys of his age tend to accept whatever comes their way, even the rarest of fruits, almost as their due. In a few days he had completely forgotten the embarrassing encounter by the cellar door, and every evening he sang his "Golden Evening Sun" on the stairs as though he had never done otherwise.

For all his gratitude Karl's memory of Babette might not have lived on so indestructibly if her benevolence had been confined to edibles. Youth is hungry, but it is no less romantic, and a relationship with young people cannot be sustained indefinitely with cheese and ham, or even with wine and choice fruit from the cellar.

Not only was Babette highly respected and indispensable in the Kusterer household; throughout the neighborhood she enjoyed a reputation for perfect respectability. Wherever she was present, one could count on good cheer tempered by decorum. Of this the neighbor women were aware, and consequently they were glad to have their maids, especially the young ones, associate with her. Any-one she recommended was well received, and those whom she admitted to her intimate circle were in better hands than they would have been at the Servant Girls' Settle-ment or the Maidens' Association.

In the evening after work and on Sunday afternoons Babette was seldom alone. As a rule she was surrounded by a group of the younger servant girls; she helped them to pass the time and gave them all sorts of advice. There were games and songs, jokes and riddles; and any of the girls who had a fiancé or a brother was welcome to bring him along. To be sure, this happened none too often, be-cause when a girl became engaged she usually drifted away from the circle, and the young apprentices and hired men did not get along with Babette as well as the girls. She had no patience with flighty love affairs; any of her protégées who took such a turn despite Babette's earnest admonitions was excluded from the group.

The Latin scholar was admitted to this merry com-pany as a guest, and in it he quite possibly learned more than at school. He never forgot his first evening. The gath-ering was held in the back yard, the girls were sitting on doorsteps and empty crates; night was falling, and up above, a square cutout of evening sky was still bathed in a faint, soft-blue light. Babette was sitting on a keg near the arched cellar doorway, and Karl was standing shyly beside her, leaning against a doorpost, saying nothing, looking at the girls' faces in the failing light, and won-dering with some alarm what his schoolmates would think of his presence there if they heard about it.

Ah, those young girls' faces! He knew almost all of them by sight, but now, huddled together in the half-light, they were quite changed and he saw them as so many riddles. To this day he remembers the name and face of every last one of them, and a good many of their life stories. And what stories! What turns of fate, what earnestness, what courage, and what charm as well in the lives of those little housemaids!

One of them was Anna, who worked at the Green Tree; in her first position, as hardly more than a child, she had stolen and spent a month in jail. Now she had been honest and faithful for years and was regarded as a treasure. She had big brown eyes and a hard mouth; she sat there silently, looking at the schoolboy with cool curiosity. Her sweetheart, who had been untrue to her at the time of her trouble with the police, had married in the meantime. Now he was a widower and was running after her again, determined to have her. But she hardened herself and pretended to want nothing more to do with him, though in secret she loved him as much as ever.

Margret, who worked for the bookbinder, was always singing merrily, and there was sun in her curly reddish blond hair. She was neatly dressed at all times, always sporting something pretty and gay, a blue ribbon or a sprig of flowers. But she never spent any money, she sent every pfennig to her stepfather, who drank it up and never thanked her. Later on she had a hard life, made a foolish marriage and had all sorts of trouble and bad luck, but even then she went about lightly, and kept herself trim and pretty; her smile, though less frequent, was all the more lovely.

And so it was with almost all of them. How little pleasure or money or friendly treatment they had, and how much work and worry and vexation! And how they struggled through and kept their heads up, all of them with few exceptions staunch and courageous fighters! And how they laughed in their few free hours and managed to be gay over nothing, with a joke and a song, with a handful of walnuts and a snippet of red ribbon! And how pleasurably they shuddered when a cruel horror story was told them, and how when sad songs were sung they joined in, and sighed as great tears welled up in their eyes.

One or two, to be sure, were unpleasant, forever grumbling and finding fault, avid gossips, though Babette cut them short when necessary. But they too had their troubles. Gret of Bischofseck was an especially unfortunate soul. Life was hard on her, and so was her own virtue; not even the Maidens' Association was pious and strict enough for her. Whenever a crude word fell on her ear, she heaved a deep sigh, bit her lips, and said in little more than a whisper: "The righteous are doomed to suffer." She suffered year in, year out, but throve on it, and when she counted over her stockingful of saved talers, emotion brought the tears to her eyes. Twice she could have married a master artisan, but both times she declined, because one was a flibbertigibbet, while the other was himself so righteous and noble that with him she would have had to forgo the pleasure of sighing and not being understood.

They all sat in the corner of the dark yard, telling each other their news and waiting to see what amusement the evening would bring. At first the learned young man found their words and gestures none too intelligent or refined, but soon, as his embarrassment wore off, he felt freer in his mind and he began to see these girls huddled together in the darkness as an unusual, strangely beautiful picture.

"Well, this is our Latin scholar," said Babette. She was going to tell them the pitiful story of his hunger, but he tugged imploringly at her sleeve, and she kindly spared him.

"You must learn an awful lot," said reddish blond Margret, the bookbinder's maid. And she went on: "What do you expect to be?"

"I haven't really made up my mind. Maybe a doctor."

That inspired respect and all looked at him attentively.

"But then you'll have to grow a mustache first," said Lene, who worked for the pharmacist, and they all laughed, some with a quiet giggle, others uproariously. Then they found a dozen ways of teasing him, and without Babette's help he would have had a hard time defending himself. Finally they asked him to tell a story. For all his reading, all he could think of was the fairy tale "He Who Set Out to Learn Fear"; but he had hardly begun when they cried out laughingly, "We know that one," and Gret of Bischofseck said disparagingly, "That's for children." Feeling very foolish, he stopped, and Babette promised for him: "He'll tell you something else next time; he has so many books in his room." That was all right with him and he resolved that next time they would be more than satisfied.

By then the last shimmer of blue had gone out of the sky and a star was hovering in the smooth blackness.

"And now you must all go home," said Babette. They stood up, shook to smooth out their skirts, fussed at their pigtails, nodded to one another, and went off, some through the little back gate, others through the hallway and the house door.

Karl Bauer also said good night and went up to his room with uncertain feelings, contented, yet not contented. For despite his youthful arrogance and all the foolishness that goes with being a Latin scholar, he had noticed that these new friends lived a different life from his and that nearly all of them, chained as they were to their daily chores, were moved by forces, and knew of things, which to him were as strange as a fairy tale. Not without a certain intellectual priggishness, he decided to look as deeply as possible into the interesting poetry of these naïve lives, the primitive soul of the common people, the world of street ballads and soldiers' songs. But at the same time he felt that in certain respects this world was uncomfortably superior to his own, and feared that it might somehow tyrannize and overpower him.

For the present, however, there was no danger of such an eventuality. The evening gatherings grew shorter, for it was getting on toward winter, and though the weather was still mild, the first snow was expected any day. Nevertheless, Karl found occasion to tell his story. It was the tale of Zundelheiner and Zundelfrieder, which he had found in Hebbel's *Treasure Chest,* and it met with no small applause. He left out the moral at the end, but Babette, who felt the need of a moral, contributed one to the best of her ability. The girls, all except Gret, praised the storyteller beyond his deserts, took turns in repeating the main episodes, and begged him to tell another such story soon. He promised he would, but the very next day the weather turned so cold that sitting in the open was out of the question. And then, with the approach of Christmas, he turned to other thoughts and other joys.

Every evening he worked on a tobacco box that he was carving for his father and on a Latin couplet to go with it. But the verses refused to take on the air of classical nobility without which a Latin distich cannot stand up, and in the end he simply wrote "With best wishes" in large ornate letters on the cover, cut along the lines with his penknife, and polished the box with pumice and wax. Then he went happily off on his vacation.

January was cold and clear, and Karl went skating whenever he had an hour to spare. One day at the rink he lost his bit of imaginary love for the fair damsel of good family. His school friends courted her with all sorts of chivalrous little favors, and he could see that she treated them all with the same cool, rather arch politeness and coquetry. Screwing up his courage, he asked her, with pounding heart but not too much blushing or stammering, to skate with him. She put her little left hand, gloved in soft leather, in his raw right hand. As they skated together, she hardly bothered to conceal her amusement at his awkward attempts at romantic conversation. Finally, with an offhand thank-you and a toss of her head, she left him to join her girl friends, some of whom squinted slyly in his direction. A moment later he heard her laughing as maliciously as only a spoiled pretty girl can laugh.

That was too much for him; indignantly he discarded his passion, which had not been genuine to begin with, and from then on made a point of snubbing the "imp," as he now called her, both at the skating rink and on the street.

He tried to express and perhaps even to enhance his joy at being released from this vapid, unworthy courtship by sallying forth in the evening in quest of adventure with a few of his more daring friends. They needled the policemen, tapped on people's windowpanes, pulled at bell ropes, jammed electric bells with slivers cut from matchsticks, molested chained watchdogs till they were foaming at the mouth, and frightened lone women in deserted streets by whistling and setting off firecrackers.

For a while Karl Bauer thoroughly enjoyed these expeditions in the wintry twilight; sheer animal spirits mingled with a feverish lust for adventure made him wild and brave, and gave him delicious heartthrobs, which he admitted to no one but savored like a kind of drunkenness. Afterward in his room he played the fiddle until late into the night or read exciting books, feeling like a robber knight who had returned after a raid, wiped his sword and hung it on the wall, and was now enjoying the peace of a bright fire.

But when on these evening forays the same little tricks kept repeating themselves and the real adventures to which he had secretly looked forward refused to materialize, the pleasure began to wear off, and little by little he withdrew from the obstreperous little band. But one evening when he had halfheartedly joined in for the last time, an adventure of sorts came his way.

Four of them were roaming about on Brühelgasse, playing with little canes and contemplating shameful deeds. One sported a tin pince-nez, and all four were wearing their hats or caps at a rakish angle on the backs of their heads. After a while, a hurrying servant girl overtook them and quickly passed them by. She was carrying a large basket, from which a long strip of black ribbon protruded, now fluttering gaily in the air, now dragging along the ground.

Playfully, with nothing particular in mind, Karl Bauer

picked up the ribbon and held it fast. The girl continued unsuspectingly on her way and the boys burst into triumphant laughter. The girl—young and blond and beautiful —glared lightnings at the laughing boys, slapped Bauer in the face, quickly gathered up her ribbon, and hurried away.

The laughter was now directed at the chastised Bauer, but he had fallen silent and at the next street corner he curtly took his leave.

A strange feeling had taken hold of him. He had only seen the girl's face for a moment in the half-light, but he had the impression that she was very lovely. Though the slap in the face had left him smarting with shame, it had given him more pleasure than pain. But then, at the thought that he had played an idiotic trick on this dear creature, that she would be angry with him and take him for a stupid practical joker, he felt thoroughly ashamed of himself and suffered torments of remorse.

He went slowly home. He did not whistle on the steep stairs but climbed up to his room in dejected silence. For half an hour he sat in the cold darkness, pressing his forehead against the windowpane. Then he took out his fiddle and played mellow old songs from his childhood, including some that he had neither sung nor played for four or five years. He thought of his sister and of the garden at home, of the chestnut tree and the red nasturtiums on the veranda, and of his mother. He went to bed tired and confused, and when he could not fall asleep the bold adventurer and hero of the streets began to cry very softly. He cried until he dozed off.

The companions of Karl's evening forays now began to regard him as a coward and deserter, for he no longer took part in their expeditions. Instead he read *Don Carlos*, the poems of Emanuel Geibel, and Biernatzki's *Hallig* and started a diary. And from then on he seldom appealed to the good Babette's benevolence.

It occurred to her that there must be something wrong

with the young man, and since she had made it her business to watch over him she appeared one day at his door
to see what was going on. She did not come empty-handed;
she brought a good chunk of Lyons sausage and insisted
on Karl's eating it before her eyes.

"Oh, Babette," he said. "Let me be. I'm not hungry
right now."

In her opinion, however, young people ought to be able
to eat at any time, and she kept at him until he complied. She had heard how overworked the youngsters
were at the Latin school, and could not suspect that her
protégé was far from burning the midnight oil over his
studies. She interpreted his conspicuous loss of appetite
as the beginning of an illness, gave him a serious talking-
to, inquired into the details of his health, and in the end
offered him a reliable laxative. At that Karl could not help
laughing. He assured her that he was in perfect health
and that his lack of appetite was due to a mood; he was a
little out of sorts. This she understood.

"I hardly ever hear you whistling any more," she ex-
claimed. "And there hasn't been a death in your family.
Look here. You wouldn't be in love?"

Karl couldn't help blushing a little, but he rejected this
suspicion with indignation and maintained that all he
needed was a bit of distraction; he was bored.

"In that case I know just the thing for you," cried Babette with enthusiasm. "Tomorrow little Lies from the
lower town is getting married. She's been engaged for
ages to a laborer. You'd think she could have made a better match, but he's a good man and money alone doesn't
make anybody happy. Well, you'll come to the wedding,
Lies knows you, and we'll all be glad if you come, and
show that you're not too proud. Anna from the Green
Tree and Gret from Bischofseck will be there, and so will
I; there won't be many more. Who'd pay for it? It will be
what they call a quiet wedding, no big banquet or dancing or that sort of thing. They can be gay without it."

"But I haven't been invited," said Karl doubtfully, since the prospect held no great attraction for him. But Babette only laughed.

"Don't you worry, I'll take care of that. It will only be an hour or two in the evening. And look—I've got a wonderful idea. You'll bring your fiddle. —Why not? Don't give me any silly excuses. You will, won't you? That will be entertainment, and they'll all be grateful to you."

It was not too long before the young man consented.

Late the following afternoon Babette called for him; flushed with festive joy, she was wearing the well-preserved party dress of her younger days, which impeded her movements and made her too warm. Nevertheless she would not let Karl change, but only asked him to put on a clean collar, and party dress or not, she gave his shoes a good brushing then and there, without his having to take them off. Then they set out for the house in one of the poorer sections where the young couple had rented an apartment consisting of parlor, bedroom, and kitchen. Karl took his fiddle along.

They walked slowly and cautiously, for a thaw had set in the day before, and they wanted to arrive with clean shoes. Holding her enormous umbrella wedged under her arm, Babette used both hands to hold up her reddish brown skirt. This was not at all to Karl's liking and altogether he was rather ashamed to be seen with her.

Seven or eight people were sitting round the neatly set white-pine table in the newlyweds' whitewashed living room. In addition to the couple, there were two of the bridegroom's fellow workers and two or three girls, cousins or friends of the bride. They had had roast pork and salad for dinner, and now there was a cake on the table and two big jugs of beer on the floor. When Babette and Karl came in, all arose, the master of the house made two awkward bows, and the bride, who was the talker in the family, took charge of the greetings and introductions. Each of the guests shook hands with the new arrivals.

"Have some cake," said the hostess. And without a word the husband brought out two more glasses and poured beer.

The lamps had not yet been lit and Karl recognized no one except for Gret from Bischofseck. At a sign from Babette he slipped a coin wrapped in paper into the hostess's hand with a few words of congratulation. Then a chair was moved up for him and he sat down behind his beer glass.

Suddenly he was face to face with his neighbor and to his dismay recognized the young servant girl who had slapped his face on Brühelgasse. But she did not seem to know him; in any case, she seemed quite unruffled, and when the host proposed that all should clink glasses, she held out her glass to him with a friendly smile. Somewhat reassured, Karl now ventured to look her full in the face. Since their encounter he had often thought of this face which he had seen for the barest instant, and now he was surprised at how different she was from the image he had been carrying about with him. Her features were softer and more delicate, and she was slimmer. But she was no less pretty and charming, and he had the impression that she was hardly older than himself.

While the others, especially Babette and Anna, carried on a lively conversation, Karl could think of nothing to say; toying with his beer glass, he sat silent, unable to take his eyes off the blond girl. He was almost frightened at the thought of how often he had yearned to kiss these lips, for the more he looked at her, the more presumptuous and difficult, not to say impossible, his project seemed.

He sat there silent and dejected. But then Babette asked him to play something on his violin. After hemming and hawing a little, he removed the fiddle from its case, plucked at the strings, tuned it, and played a popular song. Though he had chosen too high a key, the whole company joined in.

With that the ice was broken and merriment took over.

A brand-new standing lamp was exhibited, filled with oil, and lit, song after song was sung, a fresh jug of beer was brought in, and when Karl Bauer began to play one of the few dances he knew, three couples sprang to the floor and revolved, amid laughter, about the much-too-small room.

At about nine o'clock the guests took their leave. The blond girl started out with Karl and Babette, and he ventured to strike up a conversation with her.

"Who do you work for?" he asked her shyly.

"For Kolderer, the merchant, on the corner of Salzgasse."

"I see."

"Yes."

"I see. You . . ."

Then there was a long pause. But finally he screwed up his courage and started in again.

"Have you been here long?"

"Six months."

"I keep thinking I've seen you before."

"I've never seen you."

"Couldn't it have been one evening on Brühelgasse?"

"Not that I know of. My goodness, I can't stop to look at everybody that passes me in the street."

He was happily relieved that she had not recognized the culprit; he had already made up his mind to ask her forgiveness.

At the corner of her street she stopped to say goodbye. She gave Babette her hand, and to Karl she said: "Goodbye, Herr Student. And many thanks."

"For what?"

"For the music, it was lovely. Good night to both of you."

Just as she was turning away, Karl held out his hand and for an instant she gave him hers. Then she was gone.

When he bade Babette good night on the stair landing, she asked him: "Well, was it nice?"

"It was nice, it was wonderful," he said happily, glad that it was dark, for he felt the blood rising to his face.

The days grew longer. Little by little the weather turned warmer and the sky bluer; even in dark ditches and the sheltered corners of the back yards the old gray ice melted, and on bright afternoons there was a whiff of spring in the air.

Babette resumed her evening gatherings and as often as the weather permitted sat chatting with her friends and protégées outside the cellar door. But Karl stayed away and spent his time wandering about in a dream cloud of lovesickness. He had let the vivarium in his room perish and had also given up his carving and carpentry. Instead, he acquired a pair of immoderately large and heavy dumbbells, and when his fiddle didn't help, he strode up and down his room brandishing them.

Three or four times he had seen the blond girl on the street and each time he had found her more beautiful and more adorable. But he had not spoken to her again and he saw no prospect of ever doing so.

Then, as he was leaving the house one Sunday afternoon, the first Sunday in March, he heard the voices of the housemaids gathered in the yard. His curiosity was aroused; the gate was ajar and he looked through the opening. He saw Gret, and merry Margret from the bookbindery, and behind them a blond head, which in that moment was slightly upraised. And Karl recognized the girl, the blond Tina. He was so blissfully startled that he had to catch his breath and pull himself together before he could open the gate and join the company.

Margret held out her hand to him and laughed. "We were beginning to think the young gentleman was too proud." Babette shook a menacing forefinger but moved over to make room for him and bade him be seated. The women went on with their conversations and as soon as possible Karl left his place. For a while he paced back and forth; then he stopped beside Tina.

"Ah," he said softly. "So here you are."

"Why wouldn't I be? I thought you'd turn up one of these days. But I guess you're always busy with your schoolwork."

"Oh, it's not as bad as all that. I can manage. If I'd known you were here, I'd have come every time."

"Oh, you and your compliments."

"But it's the truth. It was so nice that time at the wedding."

"Yes, it was very nice."

"Because you were there, that's why."

"You mustn't say such things; anyway you're joking."

"Not at all. Don't be angry with me."

"Why should I be angry?"

"I was beginning to think I'd never see you again."

"Really? And what would you have done then?"

"I . . . I don't know what I'd have done. Maybe I'd have jumped in the river."

"Goodness, your poor skin. It might have got wet."

"Yes. And you'd just have laughed."

"Of course not. But the way you talk, it's making me dizzy. You'd better watch out, I might believe you."

"I wish you would, I mean every word of it."

At this point his protestations were drowned out by Gret's harsh voice. In shrill plaintive tones she was telling a long, grim story about some wicked masters who had starved and mistreated their maid, and when she fell sick dismissed her on the spot. And no sooner had she finished than the others started up in vehement chorus, until Babette quieted them. In the heat of the discussion Tina's neighbor had thrown her arm around her waist, and Karl realized that for the moment he would be unable to talk to her.

He found no further opportunity to approach her, but he waited obstinately until, almost two hours later, Margret gave the signal for departure. Night was falling and there was a chill in the air. He said a brief goodbye and hurried away.

Fifteen minutes later, when Tina had taken leave of her last companion not far from her house and was quite alone, the Latin scholar suddenly stepped out from behind a maple tree with a polite, bashful greeting. He had given her a start, and she looked at him almost angrily.

"What are you doing here?"

Then she noticed how frightened and pale he looked, and her voice and expression became appreciably gentler.

"Well, what's on your mind?"

He replied in a stammer and very little of what he said was intelligible. Nevertheless she caught his meaning, and she realized that he was in earnest. Seeing the youngster so helplessly at her mercy, she felt sorry for him, though this in no way diminished her pride and pleasure at her conquest.

"You mustn't do these silly things," she said in a kindly tone. And when she heard the repressed tears in his voice, she added: "We'll talk about it another time, now I have to go home. Try and calm down. *Auf Wiedersehen!*"

With that she nodded and hurriedly left him. Slowly, slowly he walked away as the twilight deepened and turned to dark night. He wandered through streets and squares, past houses, walls, gardens, and gently flowing fountains. He went out into the fields on the outskirts and back into town again, through the arch of the town hall to the upper marketplace, but everything he saw had been changed into an unknown fairy-tale landscape. He loved a girl and he had told her so, and she had answered kindly and said *auf Wiedersehen!*

For a long time he wandered about aimlessly, and when he began to feel cold he thrust his hands into his trouser pockets. When on turning into his street he looked up and saw where he was, he awoke from his dream and despite the late hour began to whistle loudly and piercingly. The sound echoed through the dark street and stopped only when he had reached the dark entrance to the Widow Kusterer's house.

Tina wondered what all this would lead to; she gave the matter a good deal more thought than the lovesick boy, whose feverish expectations and sweet agitation made it impossible for him to think. The more she reflected on what had happened, the less fault she could find with the handsome youngster; and besides, it gave her a delightful new feeling to know that such a refined and well-educated, but unspoiled young fellow was in love with her. Still, she did not for a moment contemplate a love affair, which could only create difficulties if not serious trouble for her, and could certainly lead to nothing substantial.

On the other hand, she rebelled at the thought of hurting the boy with a harsh answer or none at all. She would have liked best to lecture him jokingly, with sisterly or motherly kindness. At that age girls are more poised, and know themselves better, than boys; and in particular a servant girl, who earns her own living, is a good deal wiser than any student or schoolboy, especially if the schoolboy is in love and surrenders his will to her judgment.

For two days the poor girl wavered. She kept telling herself that a stern rebuff was in order, but she hadn't the heart, for though she was not in love with the boy, she liked him and felt sorry for him.

In the end she did what most people do in such situations: she weighed the pros and cons until they were equally worn out and was left with the same uncertainty she had started out with. And when it came time to take action, she forgot all her deliberations and surrendered to the impulse of the moment, just as Karl Bauer did.

On the third evening she was sent on a late errand and met him not far from her house. He greeted her humbly and seemed rather dejected. The young people stood face to face, neither knowing exactly what to say. For fear of their being seen together, Tina stepped into a dark open doorway, and Karl timidly followed her. Nearby some horses were pawing the ground in their stable, and somewhere in one of the gardens or back yards a beginner was trying to play a tin flute.

"Would you listen to that piping!" said Tina under her breath, with a forced laugh.

"Tina!"

"Yes?"

"Oh, Tina . . ."

The boy was apprehensive; he could not foresee what she would say, but he had the impression that she was not irreconcilably angry.

"You're so sweet," he said very softly and was instantly horrified at his boldness.

For a moment she hesitated, pondering her reply. Feeling empty and giddy, he took her hand. He took it so shyly, his grip was so timidly loose and his manner so imploring that she could not bring herself to give him the reprimand he deserved. Instead she smiled and stroked the poor fellow's hair with her free left hand.

"Then you're not angry with me?"

"No, silly boy," she said with a friendly laugh. "But now I have to go, they're waiting for me at home. And I have to buy sausage."

"Couldn't I go with you?"

"No. You must be out of your mind. You leave first and go home; we mustn't be seen together."

"All right. Good night, Tina."

"Good night. Now run along."

He had had various questions and favors to ask of her, but he forgot them and went away happy, with a light easy step, as though the cobbled city street were a soft lawn, his eyes blind and turned inward, as though he had come from a dazzlingly luminous place. He had hardly spoken to her, but he had spoken tenderly and her answer had been friendly, he had held her hand, and she had stroked his hair. That seemed more than enough, and years later, whenever he thought of that evening, happiness and kindly gratitude invaded his soul like a flood of light.

As for Tina, when she thought about the incident afterward, it was quite beyond her how such a thing could have happened. Yet she felt that Karl had known happiness that evening and was grateful to her for it. She remembered his childlike timidity and all in all she could not see that any great harm had been done. Still, intelligent as she was, she felt that from then on she was responsible for the romantic young man, and undertook to guide him as gently and surely as possible to a more reasonable state of mind. For not too long ago she herself had learned to her sorrow that a first love, however precious and holy, is only a makeshift and a detour. Now she hoped to help the youngster recover without hurting him unnecessarily.

They did not see each other again until the following Sunday at Babette's. Tina greeted the Latin scholar amiably, smiled at him once or twice from her place, and drew him into conversation several times. Otherwise her attitude toward him seemed unchanged. But for him every one of her smiles was a priceless gift and every glance a flame that filled him with light and warmth.

One afternoon some days later Tina finally got around to speaking plainly. After school he had wandered into her neighborhood again and was on the lookout for her. That displeased her. She led him through the little garden into a woodshed behind the house, where it smelled of sawdust and dry beech logs, and took him to task. She forbade him, most particularly, to follow her and hang about waiting for her, and told him very plainly how a young admirer in his position ought to behave.

"You always see me at Babette's. When I leave you can come along if you like, but only as far as the others do, not the whole way. You mustn't walk alone with me, and if you don't pull yourself together and watch yourself in front of the others, everything will go smash. People are always watching, and where they see smoke they cry fire."

"Yes, but if I'm your sweetheart," said Karl rather plaintively. She laughed.

"My sweetheart! What kind of nonsense is that? Tell that to Babette or to your father at home or your teacher! I like you and I don't want to be hard on you, but before you can be my sweetheart you've got to be your own master and make your own living, and that won't be for a long time. In the meantime you're just a lovesick schoolboy, and if I didn't like you, I wouldn't even talk to you about it. And there's no point in hanging your head, that won't change anything."

"But what can I do? Don't you care for me?"

"Poor thing. That has nothing to do with it. Just be sensible and don't go wanting things you can't have at your age. Let's just be good friends and wait. It will take time, but then everything will turn out all right."

"Do you think so? But look, there was something I wanted to say . . ."

"What?"

"Well, you see . . ."

"Speak up!"

"Wouldn't you give me a kiss some time?"

She saw him blush, she saw his look of anxious entreaty and his winning boyish lips, and for a moment she thought it might almost be permissible to do as he asked. But then, calling herself to order, she sternly shook her blond head.

"A kiss? What for?"

"Just like that. Don't be angry."

"I'm not angry. But you mustn't be bold. We'll see later on. You hardly know me and here you want to kiss me! It's no good playing with these things. So be reasonable. I'll see you Sunday. Could you bring your fiddle?"

"Gladly."

She let him go and looked after him, as thoughtfully

and a little morosely he walked away. He was really a decent lad, she told herself; she mustn't hurt him too much.

Though Tina's admonitions were a bitter pill for Karl, he complied with them and felt none the worse for it. True, his conception of a love affair had been rather different and at first he was somewhat disappointed, but soon he discovered the ancient truth that it is more blessed to give than to receive, and that loving gives more happiness than being loved. The knowledge that he had no need to conceal his love or feel ashamed of it and that his love, though for the present unrewarded, was acknowledged gave him a feeling of happiness and freedom and raised him from the narrow sphere of his previous insignificant existence into the higher world of grandiose sentiments and ideals.

From then on he played a few pieces on his violin at each of the housemaids' gatherings.

"It's only for you, Tina," he said afterward, "because there's nothing else I can give you or do for you."

Spring was coming, and one day it was there, with yellow starwort on tender green meadows, with the deep föhn-blue of distant wooded mountains, with soft veils of young foliage in the branches and returning flights of birds. The housewives set out pots of hyacinth and geranium on their green-painted windowsills. After the noonday meal the men sat on doorsteps in their shirt sleeves and in the evening played ninepins in the open. The young people became dreamy and restless, and fell in love.

One Sunday, when the river valley was already green under a soft, smiling blue sky, Tina set out with a girl friend to visit the Emanuelsburg, an ancient ruin in the woods, an hour's walk from town. Just outside the city they passed a garden café, where music was playing and couples were waltzing on the grass. They resisted the temptation, but their pace became slow and hesitant.

When at a bend in the road the receding music surged up sweetly in their ears, their pace became still slower and they finally stopped altogether. They leaned against a fence and listened. After a while, when they felt strong enough to walk again, the joy and yearning of the music were too much for them and they retraced their steps.

"The good old Emanuelsburg won't run away," said the girl friend. That set their minds at rest, and blushing, with downcast eyes, they went into the garden, where, seen through a network of branches and brown resinous chestnut blossoms, the sky was bluer and more smiling than ever. It was a glorious afternoon, and toward evening when Tina started back to town, she was not alone, but respectfully escorted by a sturdy, good-looking young man.

This time Tina had found what she wanted. He was a carpenter's apprentice, who before long would be a master carpenter and able to get married. He spoke allusively and haltingly of his love, and clearly and fluently of his circumstances and prospects. It turned out that he had already, unbeknownst to her, seen Tina several times and set his heart on her, and that he was not out for the amusement of a passing flirtation. In the next week she saw him every day and they came to an understanding. After that they considered themselves engaged, and were so regarded by their friends.

Tina's first dreamlike excitement was followed by a quiet, almost solemn happiness, which for a while made her forget everything, including poor Karl Bauer, who all this time had waited for her in vain.

When she remembered the neglected schoolboy, she felt so sorry for him that her first thought was not to tell him right away. But then it struck her that this would be wrong, and the more she thought about it the more difficult the situation seemed. She dreaded the prospect of breaking the news to the unsuspecting youngster, yet she knew that this was the only way to set things right. In any case, she had to do something before Karl heard of her engagement from others. She didn't want him to think ill of her. She felt, without clearly knowing it, that she had given the boy a foretaste and intimation of love and that if he thought he had been betrayed it would harm him and poison the experience for him. She had never imagined that her involvement with him would become such a worry to her.

In the end she took her perplexity to Babette, who to be sure was not the most competent authority in matters of love. But she knew that Babette was fond of her Latin scholar and concerned over his well-being, and she preferred to be scolded by her than to leave the lovesick youngster to his own resources.

The scolding was forthcoming. After listening to the girl's confession in attentive silence, Babette stamped angrily on the floor.

"Don't try to make it sound pretty," she cried indignantly. "You simply led him around by the nose and had your godless fun at his expense, that's all there is to it."

"Hard words won't help, Babette. If I'd wanted to amuse myself, I wouldn't have come running to you now. It hasn't been so easy for me."

"I see. And now what? Who's going to clean up the mess you've made? Me? And any way you look at it, it's the poor boy who's going to suffer."

"I know it. And I'm really sorry for him. But now listen to me. I think I'll talk to him myself and tell him everything. I'm not trying to make things easy for myself. I only wanted you to know, so you could keep an eye on him if he's too unhappy. —Will you . . . ?"

"What else can I do? You little fool, maybe this will teach you a lesson. About vanity and playing God, I mean. It wouldn't hurt you."

The outcome of this conference was that Babette arranged a meeting in the yard that same day without Karl guessing that she knew anything. It was late in the afternoon, there was a faint golden glow in the little patch of sky over the yard. But in the doorway it was dark and there the two young people were able to talk without being seen.

"Karl," the girl began. "There's something I have to tell you. I've come to say goodbye. Everything has an end, you know."

"But what . . . why? . . ."

"Because I have a fiancé now . . ."

"A . . ."

"Keep calm and listen to me. It's like this. You were fond of me, and I didn't want to send you away just like that. But remember, I told you not to think of yourself as my sweetheart. Didn't I?"

Karl was silent.

"Didn't I?"

"Well, yes."

"And now we've got to stop and you mustn't take it so hard, there are plenty of girls, I'm not the only one, and I'm not the right girl for you, what with your studies— you'll probably get to be a doctor, and you'll be a fine gentleman."

"Oh, Tina, don't say that."

"But that's the way it is. And another thing I wanted to say is that the first time in love is never right. At that age people never know what they want. Nothing comes of it. Later on, everything looks different and we see that it wasn't right."

Karl wanted to answer, he had any number of objections, but in his misery he couldn't utter a word.

"Did you want to say something?" Tina asked.

"Oh, Tina, you just don't know . . ."

"What, Karl?"

"Oh, nothing. Oh, Tina, what am I going to do?"

"Don't do anything. Just keep calm. You feel bad now, but it won't last. And then you'll be glad it turned out like this."

"How . . . how can you say . . . ?"

"I'm only saying what's true, and you'll see that I'm right even if you don't believe it now. I'm sorry, Karl. I'm really sorry."

"Are you? . . . Oh, Tina, I won't argue, maybe you're right . . . but having it all stop so suddenly . . ."

He could say no more. She put her hand on his quivering shoulder and waited in silence until his sobbing had died down.

Then she said resolutely: "Now listen to me. You must promise me to be reasonable."

"I don't want to be reasonable. I wish I were dead. I'd rather be dead than—"

"Karl, that's wicked. Look, you once asked me for a kiss —do you remember?"

"Yes."

"Well, if you'll be good—look, I don't want you to think badly of me. I want so much for us to part like friends. If you'll be good, I'll give you the kiss now. All right?"

He only nodded and looked at her in bewilderment. She came close to him and gave him the kiss, a quiet kiss without desire, purely given and purely received. At the same time she took his hand and pressed it gently. Then she went quickly into the house and out through the hallway.

Karl Bauer heard her steps resounding and dying away; he heard her leave the house and go down the front steps to the street. He heard, but he was thinking of other things.

He thought of a winter evening when a blond girl had given him a slap in the face, and he thought of an evening in early spring when a girl's hand had stroked his hair in the shadow of a doorway, when the world was enchanted and the streets of the town were strange, blissfully beautiful places. He remembered tunes he had once played on his fiddle, and the wedding in the poor neighborhood, with its beer and cake. Beer and cake, it struck him, was a ridiculous combination, but the thought di-

verted him for only a moment, for he had lost his sweetheart, he had been betrayed and forsaken. True, she had
given him a kiss—a kiss . . . Oh, Tina!

Wearily he sat down on one of the many empty crates
in the yard. The little square of sky above him turned
red and turned silvery, then the light faded and for a long
time the sky was dead and dark. Hours later when it was
lit by the moon, Karl Bauer was still sitting on his crate,
and his shortened shadow lay black and ungainly before
him on the uneven paving stones.

Young Bauer had only caught fleeting glimpses of the
land of love, but they had sufficed to make life seem dismal and worthless without the consolation of a woman's
love. He lived through empty, melancholy days, as indifferent to the events and duties of everyday life as if he
were no longer a part of it. His Greek teacher remon-
strated with the inattentive dreamer to no avail; the tasty
morsels brought to him by the faithful Babette meant
nothing to him, and her well-meant words of comfort fell
on deaf ears.

It took a severe reprimand by the principal and the dis-
grace of being kept after school to make him see the light
and start working again. He realized how foolish and
bothersome it would be if he were left behind in his next-
to-last school year, and in the lengthening spring evenings
he began to study until his head swam. That was the beginning of his recovery.

He still went occasionally to Salzgasse where Tina
lived. He could not understand why he never ran into her.
But there was a very good reason. Soon after her last talk
with Karl, she had gone back home to attend to her trous-
seau. He thought she was still there and avoiding him,
and he could not bear to ask anyone, not even Babette,
for news of her. After these useless trips he came home
angry or sad as the case might be, and played the fiddle
furiously or stood staring out his little window at the rooftops.

Still, he was on the mend, and Babette had a good deal

to do with it. Often, when she saw he was having a bad day, she came up in the evening and knocked at his door. And without letting on that she knew the reason for his unhappiness or so much as mentioning Tina, she sat with him for a long time and gave him comfort. She brought him half a bottle of cider or wine, told him amusing little anecdotes, and asked him to play a tune on his fiddle or to read her a story. The evening passed peacefully, and when Babette left him late in the night, Karl felt better and was able to sleep without bad dreams. Before she went, the old maid always thanked him for the lovely evening.

Little by little, the lovesick youngster recovered his old spirits. He was unaware that Tina often asked about him in her letters to Babette. He had grown a little more manly and mature. Once he had caught up on his schoolwork, he began to lead pretty much the same life as a year before, except that he did not start collecting lizards again or keeping birds in his room. The conversations of the boys in the graduating class, who were preparing for their final examinations, were full of alluring references to the splendors of academic life, and he delighted in the thought that he was approaching this paradise. He found himself looking forward with impatience to summer vacation. Only then did Babette tell him that Tina had left town ages ago. Though his wound still quivered and smarted a little, it was well on its way to healing.

Even if nothing more had happened, Karl would have preserved tender and grateful thoughts of his first love; he would certainly not have forgotten it. But there followed a brief epilogue, which he forgot even less.

A week before school was out, his joyful anticipation of summer vacation had driven the last of his grief from his resilient mind. He set about burning old copybooks and packing. The prospect of walks in the woods, of bathing in the river and boating, of blueberries and early apples and days of unconstrained idleness made him happier than he had been in a long while, and he strolled gaily through the hot streets. He had not thought of Tina for several days.

He was all the more startled when one afternoon on the way home from gymnastics class he ran into her on Salzgasse. He stopped, held out his hand with embarrassment, and uttered a subdued greeting. But despite his confusion, he soon noticed her worried, dejected look.

"Well, Tina," he asked timidly, "how are things?"

"Bad," she said. "Would you come a little way with me?"

He turned around and walked along slowly beside her. He could not help recalling her old reluctance to be seen with him. Oh, well, he thought, it's because she's engaged now. And just to be saying something, he asked her how her fiancé was getting along. She winced so pitifully under the question that he too was sick at heart.

"Haven't you heard?" she said faintly. "He's in the hospital, they don't know if he'll live. —He fell from a scaffolding yesterday, and he's still unconscious."

They walked on in silence. Karl would have liked to express his sympathy but he searched in vain for words. It seemed like an anguished dream to be walking in the street beside her, feeling sorry for her.

"Where are you going now?" he asked finally, when he could no longer bear the silence.

"I'm going back to see him. They sent me away this morning, they said it was too much for me."

He accompanied her to the hospital, a large, silent building surrounded by tall trees and fenced-in grounds, and went in with her, up the broad stairway and through the immaculate corridors. The medicinal smell frightened and oppressed him.

They came to a numbered door and Tina went in alone. He waited outside in the corridor. He had never been in a hospital before, and he shuddered at the thought of the fears and sufferings hidden behind the light-gray doors. He hardly dared to move. Then Tina appeared.

"They say he's a little better, they think he may wake

up today. Goodbye, Karl, I'll be staying. Thank you."

She slipped into the room and closed the door on which Karl for the hundredth time unthinkingly read the number seventeen. His happiness had left him, but what he felt now was no longer the ache of lost love, it was embedded in a much wider and larger feeling. He saw his own despair reduced to absurdity by this disaster that had so unexpectedly crossed his path. And all at once it came to him that his own little sorrow did not amount to much, that it was not a cruel exception, and that those whom he had regarded as fortunate were also subject to inexorable fate.

But he was to learn even more, something even more precious and more important. In the following days, he went to see Tina at the hospital as often as he could, and when the patient was well enough, he was allowed into the room from time to time. And then he learned something that was quite new to him.

He learned that inexorable fate is not the highest and ultimate power, and that weak, frightened, bowed human beings can get the better of it. It was not yet known whether the patient could be saved for anything more than the wretched, helpless existence of a lifelong invalid and cripple. But Karl Bauer saw the unfortunate couple enjoy the fullness of their love despite their fears; he saw the tired, careworn girl radiate light and joy, and saw the broken man's pale face, despite his pain, transfigured by a glow of tender gratitude.

He stayed on for several days after summer vacation had begun, until Tina herself made him leave.

He bade her goodbye in the corridor outside the sickroom, and this was a different leave-taking, better than the one in the Kusterers' yard. He only took her hand and thanked her without a word, and she nodded to him through her tears. With all his heart he wished her well, and for himself he could wish for nothing better than that one day he would love and be loved as blessedly as this poor girl and her betrothed.

The Wolf

1907

NEVER HAD THERE BEEN so cruelly cold and long a winter in the French mountains. For weeks the air had been clear, crisp, and cold. By day the great slanting snowfields lay dull-white and endless under the glaring blue sky; by night the moon passed over them, a small, clear, angry, frosty moon, and on the snow its yellowish glare turned a dull blue that seemed the very essence of coldness. The roads and trails were deserted, especially the higher ones, and the people sat lazy and grumbling in the village huts. At night the windows glowed smoky red in the blue moonlight, and before long they were dark.

It was a hard time for the animals of the region. Many of the smaller ones, and birds as well, froze to death, and their gaunt corpses fell prey to the hawks and wolves. But they too suffered cruelly from cold and hunger. There were only a few wolf families in the region, and their distress led them to band more closely together. By day they went out singly. Here and there one of them would dart through the snow, lean, hungry, and alert, as soundless and furtive as a ghost, his narrow shadow gliding beside him in the whiteness. He would turn his pointed muzzle into the wind and sniff, and from time to time let out a dry, tortured howl. But at night they would all go out together and the villages would be surrounded by their plaintive howling. Cattle and poultry were carefully shut up, and guns lay in readiness behind sturdy shutters. Only seldom were the wolves able to pounce on a dog or other small prey, and two of the pack had already been shot.

The cold went on and on. Often the wolves huddled together for warmth and lay still and brooding, listening woefully to the dead countryside around them, until one of them, tortured by hunger, suddenly jumped up with a blood-curdling roar. Then all the others turned their muzzles toward him and trembled; and all together burst into a terrible, menacing, dismal howl.

Finally a small part of the pack decided to move. Early in the morning they left their holes, gathered together, and sniffed anxiously and excitedly at the frosty air. Then they started off at a quick, even trot. Those who were staying behind looked after them with wide glassy eyes, trotted a few steps in their wake, stopped, stood still for a moment in indecision, and went slowly back to their empty dens.

At noon the traveling party split in two. Three of the wolves turned eastward toward the Swiss Jura, the others continued southward. The three were fine strong animals, but dreadfully emaciated. Their indrawn light-colored bellies were as narrow as straps, their ribs stood out pitifully on their chests, their mouths were dry and their eyes distended and desperate. They went deep into the Jura. The second day they killed a sheep, the third a dog and a foal. On all sides the infuriated country people began to hunt them. Fear of the unaccustomed intruders spread through the towns and villages of the region. The mail sleighs went out armed, no one went from one village to another without a gun. After such good pickings, the three wolves felt at once contented and uncertain in the strange surroundings. Becoming more foolhardy than they had ever been at home, they broke into a cow barn in broad daylight. The warm little building was filled with the bellowing of cows, the crashing of wooden bars, the thudding of hooves, and the hot, hungry breath of the wolves. But this time people stepped in. A price had been set on the wolves, and that redoubled the peasants' courage. They killed one with a gunshot through the neck, the second with an ax. The third escaped and ran until he fell half-dead in the snow. He was the youngest and most beautiful of the wolves, a proud beast, strong and graceful. For a long time he lay panting. Blood-red circles whirled before his eyes, and at times a painful, wheezing moan escaped him. A hurled ax had struck him in the back. But he recovered and managed to stand up. Only then did he see how far he had run. Far and wide there were neither people nor houses. Ahead of him lay an enormous, snow-covered mountain, the Chasseral. He decided to go around it. Tortured by thirst, he took a few bites of the frozen hard snow crust.

On the other side of the mountain he spied a village. It was getting on toward nightfall. He waited in a dense clump of fir trees. Then he crept cautiously past the garden fences, following the smell of warm barns. There was no one in the street. Hungrily but fearfully, he peered between the houses. A shot rang out. He threw his head back and was about to run when a second shot came. He was hit. On one side his whitish belly was spotted with blood, which fell steadily in big drops. In spite of his wound he broke into a bounding run and managed to reach the wooded mountain. There he stopped for a moment to listen, and heard voices and steps in the distance. Terror-stricken, he looked up at the mountainside. It was steep, densely wooded, and hard to climb. But he had no choice. Panting, he made his way up the steep wall, while below him a confusion of curses, commands, and lantern lights skirted the mountain. Trembling, the wounded wolf climbed through the woods in the half-light, while slowly the brown blood trickled down his flank.

The cold had let up. The sky in the west was hazy, giving promise of snow.

At last the exhausted beast reached the top. He was at the edge of a large, slightly inclined snowfield not far from Mont Crosin, high above the village from which he had escaped. He felt no hunger, but a dull persistent pain from his wound. A low sick bark came from his drooping jaws, his heart beat heavily and painfully; the hand of death weighed on it like a heavy load. A lone fir tree with spreading branches lured him; there he sat down and stared forlornly into the snow-gray night. Half an hour passed. Then a red, strangely muted light fell on the snow. With a groan the wolf stood up and turned his beautiful head toward the light. It was the moon, which, gigantic and blood-red, had risen in the southeast and was slowly climbing higher in the misty sky. For many weeks it had not been so big and red. Sadly, the dying wolf's eyes clung to the hazy disk, and again a faint howl rattled painfully through the night.

Then came lights and steps. Peasants in thick coats, hunters and boys in fur caps and clumsy leggings came tramping through the snow. A triumphant cry went up. They had sighted the dying wolf, two shots were quickly fired. Both missed. Then they saw that he was already dying and fell upon him with sticks and clubs. He felt nothing more.

Having broken his bones, they dragged him down to Saint-Immer. They laughed, they boasted, they sang, they cursed; they were looking forward to brandy and coffee. None of them saw the beauty of the snow-covered forest, or the radiance of the high plateau, or the red moon which hovered over the Chasseral, and whose faint light shimmered on their rifle barrels, on the crystalline snow, and on the blurred eyes of the dead wolf.

Walter Kömpff

1908

THERE IS LITTLE to be said of old Hugo Kömpff except that he was a genuine product of Gerbersau, in the better sense. The large, solidly built old house on the marketplace and the shop, which though dark and hardly high enough for a man to stand up in was generally regarded as a gold mine, had come down to him from his father and grandfather, and he ran the business as they had run it. His only break with custom was to marry a girl from out of town. Her name was Cornelia and she was a pastor's daughter, a beautiful and sedate young lady without a penny to her name. Tongues wagged for a while, and even after the surprise had died down people still continued to find the woman rather odd, but they more or less got used to her. Kömpff's married life was quiet and withdrawn, the times were prosperous, and he carried on the obscure, day-to-day existence of his forefathers. Good-natured, respected, and an excellent businessman to boot, he had everything that in Gerbersau made for happiness and well-being. A son was born in due time and baptized Walter. Walter had the features and the build of the Kömpffs, but his eyes, instead of being gray-blue, were brown like his mother's. Of course no one had ever seen a Kömpff with brown eyes, but after some thought the father found himself unable to regard this as a calamity, and nothing else about the boy seemed abnormal. Life went its slow, natural course and business prospered. True, the wife never became exactly what the townspeople were accustomed to, but there was no harm in that. The little boy grew and throve and went to school, where he was always at the head of his class. Only one thing was lacking to the shopkeeper's happiness: he was not yet a member of the town council, but that could not be long in coming; then he would be at the height of his achievement, everything would be the same as with his father and grandfather.

But this was not to be. In a radical break with the Kömpff tradition, the master of the house lay down to die at the early age of forty-four. He was carried off slowly and had time to make all the necessary arrangements. One day the dark, attractive woman sat by his bedside. They talked about the various things that would have to be done, and about what the future might bring. It goes without saying that their boy, Walter, was foremost in their discussion. Neither was surprised to find that on this point they were not at all of the same opinion. A quiet but relentless argument ensued, though if anyone had knocked at the door, he would have noticed no sign of a quarrel.

From the first day of their marriage, the wife had insisted on good manners and soft-spokenness even on bad days. On several occasions when one of his suggestions or decisions had met with her gentle but firm opposition, the husband had flown into a rage. But at the first harsh word, she had looked at him in such a way that he quickly subsided and, if unable to subdue his anger, took it away with him to the shop or out into the street. As a rule nothing more was said, and the wife had her way. And now they still observed moderation and decorum, though he was close to death and his last and most fervent wish encountered her firm opposition. But the look on the sick man's face showed that he was controlling himself with difficulty, that he might lose his composure at any moment and give vent to his rage or despair.

"I've accepted a good many things, Cornelia," he said, "and undoubtedly you've sometimes been right, but this time it's different, you must see that. What I've said is what I've been thinking for years, it's my firm decision and I insist on it. You know it's not a whim, I'm on the point of death. It's part of my testament, and I think you ought to accept it with good grace."

"We're wasting words," she said. "You're asking me for something I can't give. I'm sorry, I just can't."

"Cornelia, it's the last request of a dying man. Have you thought of that?"

"I have. But what I'm thinking even more is that you're asking me to decide the child's whole life. I have no right to do that, and neither have you."

"Why not? It's done every day. If I had kept my health I would have made what I saw fit out of Walter. Now at least I want to make sure that when I'm gone he'll still have an aim in life and do what's best for him."

"You're forgetting that he belongs to both of us. If you had your health, we would both have guided him, we would have waited to see what really seemed to be best for him."

The dying man scowled, but said nothing. He closed his eyes and cast about for a peaceful, friendly way of getting what he wanted. But he could think of none, and since he was in pain and could not be sure that he would still be conscious the next day, he finally decided what to do.

"Please bring him here to me," he said calmly.

"Walter?"

"Yes, right away."

Frau Cornelia went slowly as far as the door. Then she turned around.

"Please don't do it," she said imploringly.

"What?"

"What you're meaning to do, Hugo. I'm sure it's not right."

He had closed his eyes again and only said wearily: "Bring him here."

She went to the large light front room, where Walter was sitting over his homework. He was between twelve and thirteen, a sensitive, good-natured boy. At the moment, to be sure, he was frightened and off balance, for it had not been kept secret from him that his father was dying, and it was with distress, fighting down a deep reluctance, that he followed his mother to the sickroom, where his father bade him sit down on the edge of the bed beside him.

The sick man stroked the boy's warm little hand and looked at him kindly.

"I have something important to say to you, Walter. You're old enough, so listen carefully and try to understand. My father and my grandfather died in this room, in this same bed, but they were both much older than I am, they both had grown-up sons, who were ready to take over the house and shop. And that, I hope you realize, is important. You see, your great-grandfather and then your grandfather and then your father all worked here for many years, and we all had our worries, because we wanted the business to be in good shape when we passed it on to our sons. And now I'm dying, and I don't even know what will become of the house and shop, and who's going to take over when I'm gone. You see how it is. Well, what do you think?"

Saddened and confused, the boy looked down, powerless to speak or even to think. The seriousness, the hushed solemnity of this strange moment in the darkening room surrounded him like sultry weather. On the verge of tears, he swallowed, but was too embarrassed and unhappy to speak.

"You see what I mean," his father went on, again stroking his hand. "It would make me very happy to know for sure that when you grow up you'll carry on our old family business. If you'd promise me to take over, it would be a great load off my mind, I'd be able to die at peace. Your mother thinks—"

"Yes, Walter," Frau Cornelia broke in. "You've heard what your father had to say. And now it's entirely up to you. Think it over carefully. If you think it might be better for you not to go into business, you must say so; no one is going to force you."

For a time all three were silent.

"If you like," said Frau Cornelia, "you can go back to the other room and think it over. I'll call you in a little while." The sick man gave Walter a long, questioning look. The boy stood up; he could think of nothing to say. He sensed that his mother did not want the same thing as his father, who, he thought, had not asked so very much of him. He was about to turn away and leave the room, when his father tried to take his hand again, but was unable to reach it. Walter turned back. He saw the question and the plea and the shadow of fear in the dying man's eyes, and it suddenly came to him, with compassion and dread, that it was in his power to hurt or relieve his dying father. The unaccustomed responsibility weighed on him like a sense of guilt; he hesitated, and then with a sudden impulse he gave his father his hand and said softly amid welling tears, "Yes, I promise."

His mother took him back to the good room. Here too it was beginning to grow dark; she lit the lamp, kissed the boy on his forehead, and tried to comfort him. Then she went back to the sick man, who had sunk exhausted on his pillows and fallen into a light sleep. She sat down in an armchair by the window and with tired eyes looked out across the yard and the steep irregular roofs at the evening sky. She was still in her prime and still beautiful, except that the pale skin around her temples seemed to have grown tired.

A nap would have done her good, but though she sat quite motionless, she did not fall asleep. She was thinking. It was her nature to live such crucial episodes in their entirety, to the very end, whether she wished to or not. And now, despite her weariness, she clung fast to the eerie, overwrought, quiet intensity of these hours, in which everything was important and serious and fraught with unforeseeable consequences. She had to think of the boy and comfort him in her thoughts, she had to listen to the breathing of her husband, who lay dozing and still alive, though he had actually ceased to be a part of life. But most of all she had to think of this past hour.

This had been her last battle with her husband, and she had lost, though she knew she was in the right. All these years she had understood her husband and seen into his heart, in love and in conflict; thanks to her, they had led a quiet, dignified life together. She loved him, she still loved him, yet she had always been alone. She had known his soul, but for all his love he had not understood hers and had gone his accustomed ways. With his heart and mind he had always lived on the surface, and when matters arose in which her whole being forbade her to obey him, he had smilingly given in, but without understanding her.

And now the worst had happened. She had never been able to talk seriously to him about the child; what could she have said? For he had no insight into the heart of the matter. He was convinced that the boy had inherited his mother's brown eyes, but had everything else from him. But she had always known that the child had her soul, and that in this soul there was something that unconsciously and with uncomprehending sorrow opposed the father's spirit and character. True, he had a good deal from his father, he resembled him in almost everything. But the innermost fiber, the true being that mysteriously shapes a man's destiny—this life spark he had inherited from her, and anyone who could have seen into the innermost mirror of his heart, into the sensitive, gently flowing sources of his most intimate being, would have found his mother's soul reflected in it.

Cautiously Frau Kömpff arose and went to the bed; she bent down over the sleeper and looked at him. If only she could have another day, a few hours in which to look at him properly. He had never fully understood her, but he was not to blame for that, and the very narrowness of this strong, straightforward man, who had so often given in to her without really knowing why, struck her as chivalrous and lovable. Not without a faint pang, she had seen through him even at the time of their engagement.

Later on, in his business dealings and among his friends, he had become a little coarser, more commonplace and philistine than she would have liked, but the substance of his honorable, steadfast character had remained unchanged, and there had been nothing to regret in the life they led together. But she had expected to guide the boy in such a way as to leave him free to follow his native bent. And now perhaps she was losing the child along with his father.

The sick man slept until late into the night. Then he awoke in pain, and toward morning it was plain to see that his last strength was dwindling fast. Only for a brief moment was he able to speak clearly.

"Cornelia," he said. "He's given me his promise, hasn't he?"

"Yes, he's given you his promise."

"Then I can set my mind at rest?"

"Yes, you can set your mind at rest."

"I'm glad. —Cornelia, you're not angry with me?"

"Why should I be angry?"

"About Walter."

"No, not at all."

"Really?"

"Really. And you're not angry with me?"

"No, no! Oh, Cornelia! And thank you."

Still holding his hand, she stood up. His pain came over him and he moaned softly, hour after hour. By morning he was exhausted and lay still with half-open eyes.

He did not die until twenty hours later.

The beautiful Cornelia now wore black dresses and the boy a band of black crape on his arm. They continued to live in the house, but the shop was leased. Herr Leipolt, the lessee, was a tiny, unctuously polite little man. The father had appointed a friend as the boy's legal guardian, a good-natured man who seldom showed his face in the house and was rather afraid of the grave, stern-looking widow, but who was known to have a good head for business. All in all the arrangements were as satisfactory as could have been hoped for, and life ran on smoothly enough in the Kömpff household.

Only the servant problem, which had always been troublesome, was now worse than ever. On one occasion the widow was obliged to do the cooking and housework herself for three whole weeks. She paid no less wages than anyone else, she never scrimped on the servants' food or on New Year's presents, and yet she seldom kept a maid very long. For though in many ways she was almost too friendly, though she never uttered a harsh word, she was incredibly severe about certain trifles. Not so long ago she had dismissed a competent, hard-working girl, with whom she had been extremely pleased at first, because of an insignificant lie. The girl wept and pleaded, but in vain. To Frau Kömpff the slightest subterfuge or falsehood was more intolerable than a dozen broken dishes or burnt soups.

Then it so happened that Lisa Holder returned home to Gerbersau. After years of domestic employment, she had saved a tidy sum. Her chief reason for returning was a foreman at the blanket factory, whom she had gone with long ago but who had not written to her for ages. She came too late, her faithless lover was married. This was such a blow to her that she decided to leave without delay. But then she chanced to meet Frau Kömpff, who comforted her and persuaded her to stay on. She was to remain with the household for a good thirty years.

For a few months she did her work quietly and conscientiously. Her obedience left nothing to be desired, but now and then she ventured to disregard a piece of advice or very gently to find fault with an order. Since she spoke intelligently, respectfully, and always with perfect frankness, Frau Cornelia listened to her, sometimes justifying herself and sometimes showing a willingness to take correction. Little by little the maid, though never failing to recognize the authority of her mistress, became a trusted collaborator, sharing in the responsibilities of the household. And the relationship between the two women did not stop there. One evening as they were sitting at the table in the lamplight and Lisa was busy with her needlework, it came about quite naturally that she told Frau Cornelia the whole story of her highly respectable but not very happy past. Whereupon Frau Kömpff conceived so much respect and sympathy for the aging maid that, responding to her open-heartedness, she imparted some of her own strictly guarded memories. And soon they fell into the habit of exchanging their thoughts and opinions.

Imperceptibly the maid took on a good many of the mistress's ideas. Especially in religious matters—not by conversion, but unconsciously, through habit and friendship. Frau Kömpff was none too orthodox in her views; she attached far more importance to the Bible and to her inborn feeling than to Church dogma. She made every effort to keep her daily life in harmony with her worship of God and the laws of her own feeling. Without evading the self-evident realities and demands of the day, she preserved deep within her a silent realm to which words and events were not admitted, a place in which to rest or, in uncertain situations, to recover her balance.

Inevitably little Walter was influenced by the two women and the manner of their life together. But at first school took up too much of his attention to leave much room for other conversation or instruction. Moreover, his mother preferred not to interfere with him, and the surer she became of his innermost nature, the less it troubled her to see so many of his father's traits cropping up in the boy. Especially in appearance he came to resemble him more and more.

Yet, though at first no one saw anything very unusual, the boy did have a strange nature. Just as his brown eyes seemed out of place in his Kömpff-family face, so in his character maternal and paternal traits seemed unable to blend. For the present even his mother rarely noticed this.

Walter was now in the last years of his childhood, a period of sudden impulses and strange transitions, of sudden shifts from sensitive timidity to uproarious wildness. Even so, it was startling how quickly his states of agitation could come and go, and how easily his mood could change. Like his father, he felt the need to adapt himself to the prevailing tone of his environment; he was a good friend and classmate, and well liked by his teachers. But along with this he seemed to have other strong impulses. At times he seemed to throw off a mask and to remember his true self. He would slip away from some wild game and either withdraw to the solitude of his attic room or turn to his mother with quiet, unaccustomed tenderness. If she softened and responded to his caresses, he was overcome by unboylike emotion and sometimes burst into tears. On one occasion he had joined his class in playing some vengeful little trick on the teacher. First he had boasted loudly of the exploit, but then he suddenly felt so contrite that he had gone to the teacher of his own free will and apologized.

All this was understandable and didn't amount to much. Such behavior betokened a certain weakness, but also a good heart; in any case it was harmless. Until he was fifteen, mother, maid, and son lived in quiet contentment. Herr Leipolt showed a certain interest in Walter, trying to win his friendship by frequent gifts from the shop, little things that are supposed to appeal to boys. But Walter disliked the overpolite merchant and kept out of his way as much as possible.

At the end of his last school year, his mother had a talk with him, wishing to find out if her son had made up his mind, if he was really willing to become a merchant. She felt that he might prefer to go on with his studies. But the boy raised no objection, it struck him as only natural that he should become an apprentice in the shop. It was her duty to be pleased and pleased she was, yet in a way she was disappointed. At this point, however, Walter put up resistance of an extremely unexpected kind; he stubbornly

refused to serve his apprenticeship in his own house under
Herr Leipolt, which would have been the simplest solution
for all concerned and had long been taken for granted by
both his mother and his guardian. Not displeased at perceiving something of her own nature in this obstinate
stand, the mother gave in, and an apprentice's post was
found in another shop.

Walter embarked on his new activity with his usual
pride and zeal. He came home full of stories about his day
and was quick to adopt certain gestures and turns of
phrase current in the Gerbersau business world, which
his mother noted with an affectionate smile. But this
happy beginning was short-lived.

After a time the apprentice, who at first had been permitted only to look on and perform menial tasks, was
called upon to wait on customers. At the start this made
him very happy and proud, but it soon led to a serious
conflict. For after his first few sales his employer told
him to be more careful in weighing out the merchandise.
Unaware of having done anything wrong, Walter asked
for an explanation.

"Didn't you learn that from your father?" said the
merchant.

"Learn what?" asked Walter in surprise. "No, I don't
understand."

The merchant now showed him how in weighing salt,
coffee, sugar, and so on one must make a show of favor-
ing the customer by adding a little more at the end,
whereas actually the weight remained slightly short. This,
he explained, was necessary because there was next to
no profit in such articles as sugar. And besides, no one
noticed.

Walter was dumbfounded.

"But that's dishonest," he stammered.

The merchant gave him a stern lecture, but Walter was
so overwhelmed that he hardly listened. Then suddenly
he remembered the merchant's question. Red in the face

with anger, he interrupted: "Anyway, my father never did that, never!"

His employer was taken aback by his impudence, but wisely repressing his anger he shrugged his shoulders and said: "Don't tell me that, you little whippersnapper. Every merchant with a grain of sense does it."

But the boy was already at the door. Angry and miserable, he went home, where the incident and his lamentations left his mother aghast. She knew how deeply he had respected his employer and how contrary it was to his nature to call attention to himself and make scenes. But on this occasion she understood Walter very well; despite her momentary worry, she was glad his conscience had proved stronger than custom and policy. First she herself went to see the merchant and tried to mollify him; then she consulted Walter's guardian, who found the boy's rebellion ridiculous and was utterly at a loss to see how his mother could say he had been right. He too went to the merchant and spoke to him. Then he suggested to Walter's mother that the boy should be left alone for a few days, which was done. But after three days, four days, seven days, the boy was still adamant; he would never go back to that shop. And if it was true that a merchant had to steal, he didn't want to be one.

In a small town higher up the valley Walter's guardian had a friend who kept a small shop. He was known to be a pietist, for which reason the guardian held him in low esteem. In his perplexity he wrote to this man, who soon replied that though he ordinarily did not keep an apprentice he was willing to take the boy on trial. And so Walter was taken to Deltingen and entrusted to this man.

His name was Leckle and he was known in the town as "the Thumbsucker," because in his thoughtful moments he tended to suck ideas and decisions from his left thumb. He was indeed extremely pious and belonged to a small sect. But he was an excellent merchant, did a thriving business, and despite his shabby dress was believed to be very well off. He took Walter into his house, where the boy did not fare badly, for though the Thumbsucker was something of a crank, Frau Leckle was a kindly soul bubbling with unnecessary sympathy, and was at pains, whenever she could do so in secret, to spoil the young apprentice with love pats, goodies, and words of comfort.

Leckle's shop was run on principles of economy and exactitude, but not at the expense of the customer, whose sugar and coffee were weighed out in full measure. Walter Kömpff began to think that even as a merchant a man could keep his honesty, and since he was not without skill in his work, he seldom received a reprimand from his strict master. Yet shopkeeping was not the only thing he learned in Deltingen. The Thumbsucker took him regularly to his prayer meetings, which often enough were held in his own house. Peasants, tailors, bakers, and shoemakers sat together, sometimes with and sometimes without their womenfolk, and tried to appease the hunger of their spirits with prayers, lay sermons, and Bible texts, which they interpreted collectively. There is a strong streak of pietism in that region, and by and large it is the more high-minded who are attracted to it.

All in all, though the biblical exegesis sometimes got on his nerves, Walter was not by nature averse to such gatherings and his frame of mind was often one of true devotion. But in addition to being very young he was a Kömpff of Gerbersau. Little by little he began to find the meetings a bit ridiculous, and he often had occasion to hear other young men making fun of them. His suspicions were aroused and he withdrew as much as possible. If attendance at the prayer meetings attracted attention and even made people laugh, then it was not for him, for in spite of his contrary impulses he was profoundly attached to middle-class ways. Nevertheless, the prayer meetings and the spirit of the Leckle household were to leave their mark on him.

In the end he became so accustomed to his life in Deltingen that he dreaded to leave, and despite his guardian's remonstrances stayed on with the Thumbsucker for two whole years after his term of apprenticeship had expired. Then finally his guardian managed to convince him that he must see something more of the world and its commerce if he was to run his own business later on. And so Walter reluctantly went abroad after completing his military service. Without this hard schooling it seems unlikely that he would have stuck it out very long. Even so, he had no easy time of it. He had no difficulty in obtaining what passed for good positions, for wherever he went he brought excellent references. But it cost him a severe inner struggle to keep his chin up and not to run away. True, he worked mostly in the offices of large business firms and no one expected him to give short weight, but though he encountered no demonstrable dishonesty, all this bustle and struggle for money struck him as insufferably crude and cruel and dull, all the more so as he no longer came into contact with men of the Thumbsucker's type and knew of no way to satisfy the vague demands of his imagination.

However, he struggled through and in the end wearily resigned himself to the thought that this was how things had to be, that his father had had it no better, and that whatever happened was by God's will. A secret yearning, which he himself did not understand, for the freedom of a life that was its own clear meaning and satisfaction never left him, but it lost its intensity and came to resemble the faint sorrow with which, as he outgrows his youth, a man with deeper aspirations resigns himself to the inadequacy of life.

Strange to say, it was only with the greatest difficulty that he let himself be persuaded to return to Gerbersau. Though he was aware that he stood to lose by leaving the family business in the hands of a lessee any longer than necessary, he had no desire to go home. As the time drew near, he was seized with a mounting dread. Once he was installed in his own house and shop, he told himself, escape would be impossible. He was horrified at the thought of doing business on his own, for it seemed to him that business made people wicked. True, he knew a number of merchants, big and small, whose honesty and noble sentiments were an honor to their profession and whom he looked up to as models; but these were all men of strong, incisive character, to whom respect and success seemed to come of their own accord, and Kömpff knew himself well enough to realize that he was totally lacking in such strength and single-mindedness.

He put off his return for almost a year. After that there was no help for it; Leipolt's lease, which had once been extended, had again expired, and further absence would have involved considerable loss.

He was no longer so very young when in the first days of winter he arrived home and took possession of his father's house. He looked almost exactly like his father at the time of his marriage. In Gerbersau he was welcomed with the respect due him as the heir to a good-sized fortune returned home to take charge of his business, and fell into his role more easily than he had expected. His father's friends received him with benevolence and made a point of bringing him together with their sons. His former schoolmates shook hands with him, wished him luck, and took him along to the Stag and the Anchor. Wherever he went, he found that the memory and example of his father not only opened all doors to him, but also mapped out a program from which it was impossible to deviate. Still, he was surprised now and then to observe that he was held in exactly the same esteem as his father, for he felt sure that his father had been a very different kind of man.

Since Herr Leipolt would soon be leaving, Kömpff was kept very busy familiarizing himself with the books and the inventory, settling his account with Leipolt, and introducing himself to the wholesalers and customers. He often sat up at night over the books and was secretly glad to have found so much work waiting for him, because for the present it drove his more deep-seated worries from his mind and enabled him without attracting attention to evade his mother's questions. He felt that a long, serious talk was a necessity to both of them but he was glad to put it off as long as possible. Otherwise he showed her a sincere, though somewhat embarrassed tenderness, for it had once more become clear to him that she was the only being on earth who was really congenial to him, who understood him and loved him in the right way.

When at length Leipolt was gone and everything was running smoothly, Walter began to spend most of his evenings and an occasional half hour during the day with his mother, talking and listening. And then, quite unsought and unbidden, a time came when Frau Cornelia looked into her son's heart and once again as in his boyhood saw his rather diffident soul open before her. It gave her a strange feeling to find her old premonition confirmed: despite all appearances her son was not a Kömpff and had not become a merchant; inwardly still a child, he merely played the role that had been forced on him; he let himself be driven, but his heart was not in it. He could reckon, keep books, buy and sell as well as the next man, but these were acquired, superficial skills. And now he had two fears, either that he might play his role badly and dishonor his father's name, or that he might in the end sink into it, become wicked, and lose his soul for money.

The next few years passed quietly. Herr Kömpff soon noticed that the respectful welcome he had received in his native town was in part due to his bachelor status. That in spite of many temptations he grew older and older without marrying was—as he himself felt with an uneasy conscience—a radical break with the traditional rules of his town and family. But there was nothing he could do about it. More and more he was overcome by a dread of important decisions. And how could this man, who with his restless heart and lack of self-confidence often felt like a child, have dealt with a wife, not to speak of children? Sometimes as he watched his contemporaries at their tables in the notables' room of one of the inns, as he ob-

served their manner and the way they took themselves
and each other seriously, he could not help wondering
whether at heart they really were as sure of themselves,
as settled in their manhood, as they seemed to be. And if
so, why did they take him seriously, why did they fail to
notice that he was entirely unlike them?

But no one noticed—no customer in the shop, no colleague or friend in the market or at the inn; only his
mother, who had every reason to know him through and
through, for the overgrown child spent half his time with
her, lamenting and seeking advice. She comforted him
and, without trying to, dominated him. Lisa Holder played
a modest role in their relationship. When these three
curious beings met in the evenings, they spoke of unusual
things. The merchant's always troubled conscience gave
rise to more and more questions and ideas, which they
discussed, taking counsel of their experience and of the
Bible. The center of all the questions was the unfortunate
fact that Herr Kömpff was not happy and would have
liked to be happy.

Ah, if only he had married, said Lisa with a sigh. Oh,
no, he proved to her, if he had married it would have been
even worse, and he adduced any number of reasons. But,
she suggested, if he had gone on with his studies, or had
become a clerk or an artisan, then this or that might have
happened. And he proved that in that case he would probably have been in real trouble. They experimented with
other trades—carpenter, schoolteacher, pastor, doctor;
the result was no better.

"But even if that had been the right thing," he concluded sadly, "it didn't turn out that way and I'm a merchant like my father."

Now and then Frau Cornelia spoke to him of his father.
He was always glad to listen. Ah yes, if I had been a man
like him! he thought, and occasionally said. Then they
would read a chapter in the Bible, or some novel they had
borrowed from the town library. And the mother drew her
conclusions from their reading, and said: "It's plain that

very few people find what's right for them in life. Everyone has his share of trouble and suffering, even if he
doesn't show it. God must know what it's all good for, and
in the meantime we just have to bear it and have patience."

Meanwhile Walter Kömpff carried on his business, reckoned, wrote letters, made an occasional call, and went to
church, all in a punctual, orderly fashion as tradition
demanded. In the course of the years his routine lulled
him a little, but not entirely; his face still had a look of
astonished, anxious thoughtfulness.

At first his mother had been somewhat alarmed at his
ways. She had rather expected him to become even more
dissatisfied than he was, but at the same time more manly
and resolute. Still she was moved by his trusting attach-
ment to her and the way he shared all his thoughts with
her. Then as time passed she grew accustomed to things
as they were and ceased to be greatly troubled by his aimless, tormented life.

By now Walter Kömpff was almost forty; he had not
married and he had changed very little. The townspeople
attached little importance to his aloofness; they merely
set him down as a crotchety bachelor.

He was resigned to his life and it never occurred to him
that there might still be a change in it.

The change came suddenly. Frau Cornelia had aged
slowly and almost imperceptibly. Then in the course of a
brief illness her hair turned white. She recovered, fell sick
again, and died—quickly and quietly. Her son and Lisa
stood by the deathbed after the pastor left.

"Leave me, Lisa," said Herr Kömpff.

"Oh, dear Herr . . ."

"Please leave me."

She left the room and sat bewildered in the kitchen.
After a while she knocked, received no answer, and went
away. She returned an hour later and knocked in vain.
She knocked again.

"Herr Kömpff! Oh, Herr Kömpff!"

"Lisa, be still," came his voice from within.

"What about supper?"

"Be still, Lisa. Go ahead and eat."

"What about you?"

"No. That will do now. Good night."

"But can't I come in any more?"

"Tomorrow, Lisa."

She had to give in. But at five in the morning, after a tormented, sleepless night, she was back at the door again.

"Herr Kömpff!"

"Yes, what is it?"

"Should I make coffee now?"

"If you want to."

"And then can I come in?"

"Yes, Lisa."

She boiled the water, measured two spoonfuls of ground coffee and chicory, let the water drip through, set cups on the table, and poured the coffee. Then she went back to the door.

He opened and let her in. She kneeled down by the bedside, looked at the dead woman, and smoothed the shroud. Then she turned around toward her master, wondering how to speak to him. When she looked at him, she scarcely knew him. His face was pale and drawn, and he had strange wide eyes, as though to look one through and through, which was not his way.

"Oh, Herr Kömpff, you're not well . . ."

"I'm perfectly well. We can drink our coffee now."

And they did so without exchanging a word.

All day he sat alone in the room. A few callers came. He received them very calmly and soon coolly dismissed them. None was permitted to see the dead woman. That night he prepared to sit up again, but fell asleep in his chair and did not wake until almost morning. Only then did it occur to him that he must dress in black. He himself took his swallowtail coat out of the chest. At the funeral, which was held in the afternoon, he shed no tears and seemed very calm. Lisa, her face red with weeping, was all the more agitated as in her wide best dress she led the procession of women. Blinking through her tears, she kept casting glances at her master over her wet handkerchief; she was worried about him. She felt that his cold, calm demeanor was not real and that his defiant aloofness, his solitude, must be consuming him.

But her efforts to shake him out of his rigidity were in vain. He sat at home by the window and went restlessly from room to room. A notice on the door announced that the shop would be closed for three days. But it remained closed on the fourth and fifth day as well, until some of his friends earnestly admonished him.

After that Kömpff stood behind his counter, weighed, reckoned, and took money, but his soul was absent. He ceased to accept invitations from his friends or to appear at the Stag, and no one interfered, because after all he was in mourning. His mind was empty and lifeless. How was he to live? A deadly bewilderment held him as in a vise; he could neither stand nor fall, but felt himself hovering in the void, with no ground under his feet.

After a time he was seized with restlessness; he felt that something must happen, not outside, but within himself, something that would set him free. Then people began to notice that something was wrong, and soon Walter Kömpff became the best-known and most talked-about man in Gerbersau.

It seems that at that time, when he sensed that his destiny was coming to a head, the strange merchant felt an intense need of solitude and a distrust of himself that commanded him to free himself from accustomed influences and to create an exclusive atmosphere of his own. In any event, he began to avoid all company and even tried to send the faithful Lisa away.

"Maybe that will make it easier for me to forget my poor mother," he said, and offered Lisa a considerable sum of money to go in peace. But the aging servant only

laughed; her place was in the household, she said, and
there she would stay. She well knew that he had no desire to forget his mother, that he conjured up her memory
hour after hour and would not have forgone the slightest
object that reminded him of her. And perhaps even then
Lisa had some intimation of her master's state of mind.
In any event she did not leave him, but cared like a
mother for his orphaned household.

It cannot have been easy for her, in those days, to put
up with his eccentricities. Walter Kömpff began to feel
that he had been his mother's child too long. The storms
that now assailed him had been in him for years; he had
gratefully let his mother conjure and appease them. But
now it seemed to him that it would have been better if
he had come to grief long ago and made a fresh start,
rather than now, when he had lost the vigor of youth and
was fettered and paralyzed by years of habit. His soul
longed as passionately as ever for freedom and a balanced
existence, but his mind was that of a merchant. His whole
life was a narrow and smooth inclined plane and he knew
of no way to stop his inexorable descent and find new
pathways leading upward.

In his distress he attended a few of the Pietists' evening gatherings. Here he gained some intimation of so-
lace and light, yet he secretly doubted the sincerity of
these men who spent whole evenings in paltry attempts
at an untheological interpretation of the Bible, disclosed
the obstinate pride of the self-educated, and seldom arrived at any agreement among themselves. Somewhere,
he thought, there must be a source of trust and divine
happiness, a possibility of returning to childlike simplicity
in the arms of God; but it was not here. All these people,
it seemed to him, had at some time accepted a compro-
mise; in their lives they had come to observe a dividing
line between the spiritual and the worldly. Kömpff himself had done just that all his life, and that is what had
made him tired and sad and deprived him of all consolation.

He dreamed of a life whose every impulse would be dedicated to God, a life illumined by perfect trust. In all his actions, however trifling, he wished to be at harmony with himself and with God. And he was well aware that ledger and till could never give him this sweet, holy feeling. Sometimes in his parish paper he read about great lay preachers and great spiritual awakenings in America, Sweden, or Scotland, about meetings at which hundreds of people, struck by the lightning of insight, vowed to live a new life in the truth of the spirit from that day onward. He read such reports avidly, with the feeling that God Himself sometimes descended to earth and walked among men, here and there, in various countries, but never here, never in his vicinity.

According to Lisa, he looked pitiful in those days. His kindly, rather childlike face became lean and sharp, the wrinkles deeper and harder. He had always been smooth-shaven, but now he let his beard grow—a thin, unkempt, colorless blond beard that made little boys jeer at him. He also neglected his clothes, and if not for the distressed servant's obstinate care, he would have become an utter laughingstock. As a rule he wore his old grease-stained shop coat at table and even in the evening when he took his long walks, from which he often did not return home until on toward midnight.

The one thing he did not neglect was the shop itself. It was his last bond with former days and the old traditional life; he continued to keep his books meticulously and to spend the whole day behind the counter. His work brought him no joy, though business was good. But it was a necessity for him to work, to tie his conscience and his energy to a prescribed, unvarying duty; he was well aware that if he gave up his accustomed activity he would lose his last prop and succumb hopelessly to the powers which he honored but also feared.

In small towns there is always some beggar or good-for-nothing, an old drunkard or jailbird, a public scandal and object of derision who, in return for the meager assistance accorded him by the community, plays the role of bogeyman and despised outcast. In those days this figure was one Alois Beckeler, known as the Cackler, an outlandish old reprobate and worldly-wise tramp, who after long years on the road had foundered in Gerbersau. Whenever he had something to eat or drink, he assumed an air of grandeur and expounded a waggish philosophy of idleness in the taverns, called himself the Duke of Emptypurse and Crown Prince of Fools' Paradise, expressed his pity for all those who lived by the sweat of their brow, and always found a few listeners, who took him under their protection and treated him to beer.

One evening as Walter Kömpff was taking one of his long, lonely, desolate walks, he came upon the Cackler, who had just slept off a little afternoon spree and was lying in the street.

In the half-darkness Kömpff almost stepped on him. At first he was frightened. But he soon recognized the tramp and called out to him reproachfully: "Ho, Beckeler, what are you doing here?"

The old man sat up, blinked merrily, and replied: "What about you, Kömpff? What are you doing here?"

Kömpff was vexed at the tramp's tone and at his failure to address him as "Herr."

"Can't you be more polite, Beckeler?" he asked.

"No, Kömpff," the old man grinned. "I'm sorry, I can't."

"Why not?"

"Because nobody gives me anything to be polite about and only death is free. Did the honorable Herr von Kömpff ever make me a present or do anything for me? Oh no, the wealthy Herr von Kömpff never did anything of the sort. He's too high and mighty to worry his head about a poor devil. Am I right or am I wrong?"

"I don't have to tell you why. What do you do with the alms you get? You drink it up. I don't spend my money on drink, either for myself or anyone else."

"I see. Well, good night and sweet dreams, brother."

"Brother?"

"Aren't all men brothers, Kömpff? Eh? Do you think the Savior died for you and not for me?"

"Don't say such things. It's no joking matter."

"Was I joking?"

Kömpff mulled it over. The tramp's words merged with his own troubled thoughts and aroused him strangely.

"Very well," he said in a friendly tone. "Just get up, I'll give you something."

"Fancy that!"

"Yes, but you must promise not to drink it up. Well?"

Beckeler shrugged his shoulders. He was in one of his communicative moods. "I can give you my promise easily enough, but keeping it is another story. Money that I can't spend as I please is as good as no money at all."

"What I say is for your own good. You can believe me."

The drunkard laughed. "I'm sixty-four years old. Do you really think you know what's good for me better than I do?"

Kömpff had already taken out his purse. Now he stood there at a loss. He had never been quick to find words and in the presence of this outlaw, who called him brother and scorned his benevolence, he felt helpless and inferior. Quickly, with a feeling almost of fear, he took out a taler and handed it to Beckeler.

"Here."

Astonished, Alois Beckeler took the large coin, held it up to his eyes, and shook his shaggy head. Then humbly, with elaborate eloquence, he poured forth thanks. Shamed and saddened at the obsequiousness and self-abasement to which a bit of money had driven the philosopher, Kömpff hurried away.

Nevertheless he was relieved and felt that he had done something extraordinary. Giving Beckeler a taler to drink up was for him an adventurous deed, at least as daring and astonishing as if he himself had spent the money on dissipation. That evening he returned home earlier and happier than he had done for weeks.

A prosperous period now began for the Cackler. Every few days Walter Kömpff gave him a coin, sometimes a mark, sometimes a fifty-pfennig piece; there was no end to his well-being. Once as he was passing the Kömpff shop, the merchant called him in and gave him a dozen good cigars. Lisa, who happened to be there, intervened.

"You're not going to give this tramp your expensive cigars!"

"Never mind," said Kömpff. "Why shouldn't he get something out of life?"

The old good-for-nothing was not the only receiver of gifts. More and more the lonely, troubled man was carried away by an impulse to give and give pleasure. In the shop he gave poor women double weight or declined to take their money; on market day he gave the teamsters overgenerous tips, and when peasant women came to the shop he often slipped an extra package of chicory or a handful of raisins into their baskets.

This could not go on for long without attracting attention. The first to notice was Lisa, who poured out bitter reproaches which, though they had no practical effect, shamed and tormented him, so that he gradually learned to conceal his extravagance from her. This made the faithful soul suspicious and she began to spy on him. All of which put a severe strain on their domestic peace.

Apart from Lisa and the Cackler, it was the children who noticed the merchant's odd generosity. They would come running in with a pfennig, asking for sugar lumps, licorice, or carob beans, and be given as much as they wanted. And while Lisa kept silent for shame and the Cackler out of policy, the children did not, but soon spread the news of Kömpff's openhandedness all over town.

The strange part of it was that he himself feared this generosity and fought against it. When he checked his books in the evening after throwing away money all day, he would be aghast at his reckless, unbusinesslike behavior. He would anxiously reckon his losses, scrimp on orders, and cast about for cheap sources of merchandise. But the next day he would again be overcome by the joy of giving. Sometimes he scolded the children and chased them out of the shop, sometimes he would overwhelm them with goodies. He was hard only on himself; he economized on his household and clothing, gave up his afternoon coffee, and when the wine keg in his cellar was empty he did not have it refilled.

The consequences were not long in coming. Fellow merchants complained by word of mouth and in angry letters that he was luring their customers away with his senseless generosity. Scandalized by the change that had come over him, substantial townspeople as well as his peasant customers began to stay away from his shop, and when they could not avoid meeting him, made no attempt to conceal their distrust. The parents of several children to whom he had given sweets and fireworks expressed their annoyance in no uncertain terms. His standing among the town notables, which had not been brilliant in recent years, fell rapidly, and his dubious popularity with the poor and lowly was hardly a compensation. Though he took none of these changes too much to heart, Kömpff felt that he was slipping irresistibly into a realm of uncertainty. More and more often, acquaintances greeted him with a gesture of mockery or pity, people laughed behind his back on the street, and substantial citizens avoided his company. The old gentlemen, friends of his father, who had come to him a few times with reproaches, advice, and offers of help, soon turned away in anger. More and more of the townspeople decided that Walter Kömpff was not right in the head and that he would soon be ripe for the madhouse.

It was all up with his shopkeeping; of that the tormented man was fully aware. But before closing the shop for good, he indulged in one more act of unwise generosity that made him many enemies.

One Monday he ran an advertisement in the weekly

paper, announcing that from that day on he would sell all his merchandise at cost price.

For a whole day his shop was busier than ever. The leading families stayed away, but everyone else came to take advantage of the obviously demented merchant. All day the scales were in motion and the doorbell rang itself hoarse. Baskets and sacks full of articles bought for a song were carried away. Lisa was beside herself. Since her master refused to listen and had sent her out of the shop, she posted herself in the doorway and gave the customers a piece of her mind as they came out. The customers answered back, but the angry old woman stood her ground, determined to make all those who were not utterly thickskinned think twice about their bargains.

"Wouldn't you like us to give you another two pfennigs?" she asked one, and to another she said: "At least you haven't taken the counter. That's very kind of you."

But two hours before closing time the mayor appeared, accompanied by the bailiff, and ordered Kömpff to shut down. He offered no resistance and closed the shutters at once. The next day he was summoned to the town hall, where, after explaining that he had decided to give up the business, he was dismissed with much headshaking.

Now he was rid of the shop. He had his business struck from the commercial register, since he wished neither to sell nor to rent. What remained of his stock he gave away indiscriminately to the poor. Lisa fought for every single article, and seized coffee, sugar, and everything she could find room for, for household use.

A distant relative petitioned that Walter Kömpff should be declared irresponsible and his affairs put in the hands of a trustee, but after lengthy deliberations the authorities decided against it, partly because there were no minor heirs and partly because after giving up his business Kömpff seemed harmless.

No one seemed to concern himself with the poor man. People talked about him for miles around, for the most part with contempt and disapproval, though sometimes with commiseration. But no one called to see how he was getting along. Only his still-outstanding bills turned up with unusual rapidity, for his creditors feared that a clumsy attempt at bankruptcy might be at the bottom of the whole affair. But Kömpff wound up his books in orderly fashion, had them notarized, and paid all his debts. To be sure, this hasty conclusion of his affairs made heavy demands not only on his purse but on his strength as well. When he had finished he felt wretched and on the point of collapse.

In those hard days, when after a period of frenzied work he suddenly found himself idle and left to his own resources, only one man came to him with words of advice. That was the Thumbsucker, Kömpff's former master from Deltingen. The pious merchant, whom Walter had several times visited after taking over the shop but had not seen for years, had grown old and gray, and his journey to Gerbersau was an act of heroism.

He wore a long brown swallowtail coat and carried an enormous blue and yellow handkerchief with a design figuring landscapes, houses, and animals.

"May I come in?" he asked as he stepped into the living room, where Kömpff was sitting weary and bewildered, leafing through his big Bible. Then he sat down, set his hat and handkerchief on the table, drew his coattails up over his knees, and looked inquiringly into his old apprentice's pale, uncertain face.

"I hear you've retired."

"Yes, I've given up the business."

"Hm. And may I ask what you mean to do now? You're still a young man, comparatively speaking."

"I wish I knew. All I know is that I was never a real merchant, that's why I gave it up. Now I want to see if I can still make something of myself."

"If you don't mind my speaking my mind, I believe it's too late."

"Can it ever be too late to do the right thing?"

"Not if you know what's right. But to give up the trade

you've learned just like that, without knowing what you're going to do, that's wrong. Ah, if you'd only done it as a young man!"

"It took me a long time to make the decision."

"So it seems. It seems to me that life is too short for such slow decisions. Look here, I know you a little, and I know you've had a hard time of it, that you've never really found your niche in life. There are quite a few such people. You went into business for your father's sake, didn't you? Now you've bungled your life, and even so you haven't done what your father wanted."

"What should I have done?"

"What should you have done? Grit your teeth and keep going. You thought your life was a mistake, and maybe it was, but are you on the right track now? You cast off the lot you had taken on yourself. That was cowardly and unwise. You were unhappy, but your unhappiness was decent and did you honor. You threw it away, not for the sake of something better, but only because you were tired. Am I right?"

"Maybe you are."

"Good. That is why I've come. You haven't kept faith, I tell you. But I wouldn't have dragged my old bones all this way just to find fault with you. What I have to say to you is: repair the damage as soon as you possibly can."

"How can I?"

"Here in Gerbersau you can't make a new start, I see that. But somewhere else—why not? Open another shop, it doesn't have to be a big one, and be an honor to your father's name again. You won't find anything overnight, but if you like I'll help you look. Do you want me to?"

"Many thanks, Herr Leckle. I'll think it over."

The Thumbsucker accepted neither food nor drink and took the next train home.

Kömpff felt grateful to him but could not accept his advice. Sometimes in his unaccustomed idleness, which he found hard to bear, the former merchant took melancholy walks about town. Whenever he did so, he was surprised and dismayed to see how artisans and shopkeepers, workmen and servants went about their business, how each had his place and his standing and his aim, while he alone went about aimlessly, with no justification for his existence.

He consulted a doctor about his insomnia. Horrified at Kömpff's inactivity, the doctor advised him to buy a piece of land and take up gardening. The suggestion appealed to him. He purchased a small property on the outskirts, bought implements, and began to spade and hoe with a will. When he was tired and drenched with sweat, he felt easier in his troubled mind. But in the long evenings and when the weather was bad, he sat home reading the Bible and inconclusively pondering the unfathomable order of the world and his own wretched life. He felt that giving up his business had brought him no closer to God, and in moments of despair it seemed to him that God was unattainably remote, looking down on his folly with scornful wrath.

Often when he was gardening he had a visitor and onlooker. This was Alois Beckeler. It tickled the old good-for-nothing to see such a wealthy man wearing himself out with toil, while he, a beggar, looked on and did nothing. When Kömpff stopped to rest, they talked of everything under the sun. At such times, Beckeler gave himself lofty airs or was obsequiously polite by turns, according to the circumstances.

"Wouldn't you care to help?" Kömpff might ask.

"No, sir, I'd rather not. You see, it's not good for me. Work deadens my mind."

"Not mine, Beckeler."

"Of course not. Do you know why? Because you work for your pleasure. It's gentleman's work and it doesn't hurt. Besides, you're in the prime of life and I'm seventy. At that age a man has earned his rest."

"You told me not so long ago that you were sixty-four, not seventy."

"Did I say sixty-four? Yes, I suppose I did, I was in a

fog. I always feel younger when I've had plenty to drink."

"Then you're really seventy?"

"Or pretty near it. I've never counted."

"What amazes me is that you can't stop drinking. Doesn't it weigh on your conscience?"

"No. My conscience is hale and hearty, it can take a lot. If there were nothing else wrong with me but my conscience, I wouldn't be surprised if I lived another seventy years."

There were also days when Kömpff was gloomy and uncommunicative. The Cackler had a keen nose for his moods; the moment he spied him he could tell how things stood with the crazy amateur gardener. On such occasions he did not go near him, but stood outside the fence for about half an hour—a silent duty call, as it were. Quietly amused, he would lean on the garden fence contemplating his strange patron, who sighed as he hoed, spaded, hauled water, or planted saplings. Then he spat, thrust his hands into his trouser pockets, and grinning happily went his way.

Lisa had a hard time of it. She was all alone in the cheerless house, cooking, washing, and cleaning. At first she had reacted to the change in her master with a cross face and harsh words. Then she changed her mind and decided to hold her peace for a while and let the ill-advised man do as he pleased until he got sick of it and started listening to her again. This had been going on for several weeks.

What infuriated her most was his friendship with the Cackler, whom she had never forgiven for those fine cigars. On toward fall, during a rainy spell when Kömpff was unable to garden, her hour came. Her master was gloomier than ever.

One evening she came into the good room with her sewing basket and sat down at the table. The master of the house had lit the lamp and was going over his monthly accounts.

"What is it, Lisa?" he asked in astonishment.

"I'd like to sit here and mend. The days are shorter now and I need the lamplight."

"You may, you may."

"Oh, I may! In the old days, when your mother, God rest her soul, was still living, I always had my place here, unasked."

"Of course."

"Of course, certain things have changed. People are pointing their fingers at me."

"Lisa, what do you mean?"

"Do you want me to tell you something?"

"Go ahead."

"Very well. The Cackler—do you know what he's been doing? He's been lolling around in the taverns, running you down."

"Me? What does he say?"

"He imitates the way you work in the garden, and makes fun of you, and repeats your conversations."

"Is that true, Lisa?"

"Is it true! You won't catch me lying, not me. That's what the Cackler's been doing, and there are people who sit there laughing and egging him on, and buying him beer to make him talk about you."

Kömpff had listened attentively. Then he pushed the lamp away as far as his arm could reach, and when Lisa looked up expecting an answer, she saw to her consternation that he had tears in his eyes.

She knew that her master was sick, but she would not have thought him capable of such unresisting weakness. Suddenly she saw how old and wretched he looked. She turned back to her mending, not daring to look up again, and he sat there with the tears running down his cheeks and through his thin beard. Lisa herself had to swallow down her emotion. Up until then she had thought her master overworked, moody, and odd. Now she saw that he was helpless, disturbed in his mind and sick at heart.

That evening the two of them said nothing more. After a while Kömpff went back to his accounts; Lisa knitted and mended, fiddled once or twice with the lamp wick, and left the room early with a gentle good night.

Now that she knew how miserable and helpless he was, her jealousy and bitterness left her. She was glad to be able to care for him and treat him kindly; she came to regard him as a child, ministered to his needs, and no longer took anything he did amiss.

One day when the weather was good and Walter had gone back to his spading and hoeing, Alois Beckeler appeared with a joyful greeting, and took up his position at the edge of the garden.

"Grüss Gott," said Kömpff. "What do you want?"

"Nothing, just paying a visit. I haven't seen you out here in a long time."

"Is there anything else you want of me?"

"No. But what do you mean? I've always been coming here."

"Well, there's no need for you to come again."

"But Herr Kömpff, what makes you say that?"

"We'd better not talk about it. Just go away, Beckeler, and leave me in peace."

The Cackler put on an offended look.

"All right, I'll go if I'm not good enough for you any more. I suppose it says in the Bible that this is the way to treat an old friend."

Kömpff was dejected.

"Don't talk like that, Beckeler," he said in a friendly tone. "Let's part without bitterness. It's always better that way. Here."

He gave him a taler. Beckeler looked at it with surprise and put it in his pocket.

"Well, thank you, and no hard feelings. Many thanks. So goodbye, Herr Kömpff, goodbye."

With that he went away, more cheerful than ever. A few days later he came back. This time, receiving a sharp dismissal and no present, he went off angrily and shouted back across the fence: "You fine gentleman, you! Do you know where you belong? You belong in Tübingen. That's where the madhouse is, in case you didn't know."

The Cackler was not mistaken. In his months of solitude Kömpff had sunk deeper and deeper into the morass of his self-tormenting speculations and had worn himself down with fruitless soul-searching. Now with the onset of winter his only wholesome work and distraction, his gardening, came to an end, and there was no escape from the dismal narrow circle of his sick thoughts. From then on, he sank quickly, though his illness progressed by fits and starts, and played tricks on him.

His idleness and solitude led him to rummage through his past life and consume himself with remorse over the supposed sins of former years. He would accuse himself in despair of not having kept his word to his father. He came across passages in the Bible that seemed to have been written expressly for him and made him feel like a criminal.

In these days of torment he was gentle with Lisa, as docile as a guilty child. He would implore her forgiveness for trifles. She was frightened. She felt that his reason was giving way, but dared speak of it to no one.

For a time Kömpff stayed entirely at home. Toward Christmas he grew restless and began to talk at length about his mother and the old times. Then his restlessness drove him out of doors, where his behavior became stranger than ever. For he no longer felt natural in the presence of people, he noticed that he attracted attention, that they talked about him and pointed at him, that children ran after him and dignified citizens avoided him.

He began to feel unsure of himself. He would doff his hat with exaggerated humility to passersby. To others he would hold out his hand and beg earnestly for forgiveness, without saying what for. And when he saw that a little boy was making fun of him by imitating his way of walking, he gave him his ivory-handled cane.

Dropping in on a former friend and customer who had broken with him after his first follies in the shop, he said he was sorry, very, very sorry, and begged the man to forgive him and think kindly of him again.

One evening shortly before New Year's, he went—for the first time in many years—to the Stag and sat down at the notables' table. He had come early, he was the first guest in the room. Little by little the others arrived. Each one looked at him with astonishment and gave him an embarrassed nod. Soon several tables were occupied, but no one went to Kömpff's table, though that was their customary place. After a while he paid for his wine that he had not touched, bade them a sad good evening, and went home.

A profound sense of guilt made him submissive to everyone he met. Even to Alois Beckeler he took off his hat, and when mischievous children jostled him, he said, "Excuse me." A good many people felt sorry for him, but he was the fool and laughingstock of the town.

At the behest of the town fathers, Kömpff was examined by a doctor, who diagnosed incipient madness, but declared him harmless and recommended that he be permitted to stay at home and lead his customary life.

After this examination the poor man grew suspicious. In the end it was found necessary to put his affairs in the hands of a trustee, a measure which he had desperately resisted. From then on his illness took a new form.

"Lisa," he said one day to his housekeeper. "Lisa, I've been an ass. But now I know where I'm at."

"What? All of a sudden?" she asked anxiously, for his tone frightened her.

"Listen to me, Lisa, you can learn something. Yes, I've been an ass. All my life I've worn myself out and missed out on my chance of happiness, looking for something that doesn't exist."

"I don't understand."

"Suppose a man has heard of a glorious city far away. He yearns to go there, however far it may be. Finally he drops everything, gives away all he has, says goodbye to all his good friends, and sets out. He goes on and on, for days and months, through thick and thin, as long as his strength holds out. And then, when he has gone so far that he can no longer return, it dawns on him that the glorious city in the distance is a lie and a fairy tale. The city doesn't exist and never did."

"That's a sad story. But no one would do such a thing."

"Oh, yes, Lisa, that's just what I did. You can say what you like, Lisa, that's the kind of man I was. And have been all my life."

"That's not possible! Where is this city?"

"There is no such city, that was only a parable. I've always stayed right here. But I had such a yearning, and for the sake of it I dropped everything and lost everything. I had a yearning for God—yes, Lisa, God. I wanted to find Him, I ran after Him, and now I've come so far that I can't go back—do you understand? I can never go back. And it was all a lie."

"What? What was a lie?"

"God. He's nowhere, there is no God."

"Herr Kömpff! Don't say such things! You mustn't. That's a deadly sin."

"Let me speak. —No, be still. Or have *you* run after Him all your life? Have you read the Bible night after night? Have you prayed God a thousand times on your knees to hear you, to accept your sacrifice and give you just a little light and peace in return? Have you? And have you lost your friends in order to come closer to God, and given up your work and your honor, in order to see God? —That's exactly what I have done, all that and much more, and if God had existed and had even as much heart and sense of justice as old Beckeler, He would have looked at me."

"He wanted to test you."

"He's done that, oh yes, he's done that. He ought to have seen that I wanted nothing from Him. And He saw nothing. He didn't test me, I tested Him, and I found out that He is a myth."

This thought never left him. It came almost as a comfort to him that he had found an explanation for his bungled life. Yet he was not at all sure of his new insight. Whenever he denied the existence of God, he was seized with hope as well as fear that the Nonexistent One would enter his room and prove that He was everywhere. And occasionally Kömpff went so far as to blaspheme in the hope that God might answer, very much as a child shouts bowwow outside a wall in order to find out whether or not there is a dog inside.

That was the last development in his life. His God had become an idol, whom he provoked and cursed in order to force an answer. With that the meaning of his existence was lost; iridescent bubbles and dream figures still flashed through his soul, but the living seeds were gone. His light had burned down, and it went out quickly and sadly.

Late one night Lisa heard him speaking and pacing back and forth. Then there was quiet in his bedroom. In the morning she knocked and knocked, but there was no answer. At length she opened the door and tiptoed into the room. Suddenly she screamed and fled in terror. Her master had hanged himself with a trunk strap.

For a time the townspeople talked a good deal about his death. But few of them had any intimation of what his destiny had been. And few realized how close we all of us are to the darkness in whose shadow Walter Kömpff had lost himself.

The Field Devil

1908

IN THE DAYS when paganism was dying in Egypt and gradually giving way to the new religion, when Christian communities were springing up in every town and village, the devils retreated to the Theban desert. This desert was as yet uninhabited except for wild beasts and venomous reptiles, for though the pious penitents and hermits had cut themselves off from all contact with the world, most of them were still living in hovels or barns on the outskirts of the towns and villages and had not yet ventured out into its desolate, perilous wastes. Consequently there was plenty of room for the host of demons fleeing before the onslaught of the saints. The accursed host included not only devils of every rank but all manner of pagan creatures, unicorns and centaurs, dryads and satyrs, or field devils, as they now came to be called. For the Devil had been given power over all these creatures, and it was believed that partly because of their heathen origin and partly because of their animal form they had been rejected by God and had no part in salvation.

But by no means all of these animal-men and fallen pagan idols were evil; some of them served the Devil reluctantly. Others obeyed him gladly and in their rage took on a distinctly diabolical character; for they could not see why they had been forcibly removed from their former harmless, unmolested existence and thrust among the despised, the persecuted, and the wicked. To judge by the life of the holy father Anthony, as recorded by Athanasius and the desert monk Paul, the centaurs were evil but the satyrs or field devils, or some of them at least, were peaceful and gentle. In any event it is written that in the course of his miraculous journey through the desert to visit Father Paul, Saint Anthony met both a centaur and a field devil. The centaur, it appears, was rude and ill-tempered, whereas the satyr spoke to the saint and asked for his blessing. The present legend concerns this same satyr or field devil.

With many of his kind, the field devil had followed the march of the evil spirits into the desert, and now he was wandering about in those inhospitable wastes. Since he had formerly lived in a fertile, wooded region, associating only with his fellow satyrs and a few charming dryads, he was sorely grieved at finding himself in this barren wilderness, condemned to the company of devils and evil spirits.

By day he broke away from the others and wandered alone over the rocks and sandy deserts, dreaming of the sunny scenes of his carefree past, or dozing away the hours under an occasional solitary palm tree. In the evening he usually sat beside a little stream in a dark rocky gully, playing sad, nostalgic songs of his own composition on a reed flute. Other satyrs listened from afar to his mournful tunes and thought sorrowfully of the old days. Some of them sighed and lamented, some whistled and shrieked and danced wildly about in the hope of forgetting their loss. But when the true devils saw the little field devil sitting there alone, playing his flute, they made fun of him, mimicked him, and teased him in a thousand ways.

After much solitary thinking about the causes of his unhappiness, about the paradisiac joy of former days and his present wretched, despised existence in the desert, he began, little by little, to speak of these things with his brothers. Soon the more serious-minded of the field devils formed a little group and set out to investigate the reasons for their downfall and to consider the possibility of a return to their earlier, happy condition.

They all knew they had been relegated to the Devil's host because a new God ruled the world. Concerning this new God they knew little, but they knew a good deal about the character and rule of their prince, the Devil. And what they knew of him was not to their liking. True, he was powerful and versed in all sorts of magic; indeed, they too were under his spell, but his rule was harsh and cruel.

Then it occurred to them that this mighty Devil had himself been driven into the desert. Consequently, the new God must be far more powerful. The poor field devils concluded that they would probably be better off under God's rule than under Lucifer's, and became curious to know more about this God. They decided to find out all they could about Him, and if they liked what they found out, make their way to Him.

And so the disheartened little group of field devils led by the flute player were buoyed by a faint, furtive hope. They did not yet know how great was the Supreme Devil's power. But they were soon to find out.

For just then the pious hermits were beginning to take their first steps into the hitherto untrodden Theban desert. Some years before, Father Paul had come this way alone. The holy legend relates that he had lived the life of a penitent for many years in a small cave, with no other sustenance than the water of a spring, the fruits of a palm tree, and half a loaf of bread that was brought to him each day by a raven.

One day the field devil caught sight of this Paul of Thebes, and since he felt a certain timid affection for humans, he began to observe the hermit whenever possible. He found the man's behavior very strange. For Paul lived in utter poverty and solitude. He ate and drank no more than a bird, he clothed himself with the leaves of a palm tree, slept on the ground in a narrow cave, and not content with his sufferings from the heat, cold, and dampness, he mortified himself with special exercises, knelt for hours on the hard rock, and spent whole days in fasting and prayer, during which he would abstain even from what wretched food he had.

All this struck the curious field devil as most extraordinary, and at first he regarded the hermit as a madman. But soon he noticed that though this Paul led a miserable, comfortless life, there was a curious warmth and fervor and inward joy in his voice when he prayed, and round the man's head and drawn, emaciated face he saw a holy, blissful light.

Day after day the field devil observed the holy penitent, and at length he came to the conclusion that this hermit was a happy man and that streams of unearthly joy came to him from some unknown source. And since the hermit was forever calling God by name and singing His praises, the field devil decided that Paul must be a servant and friend of this new God, and that it would be a good idea to go over to His side.

And so one day he took courage, stepped out from behind the rock, and approached the aged hermit. The hermit warded him off, crying: *Apage, apage!* and threatened him in a loud voice, but the field devil uttered a humble greeting and said softly: "Hermit, I have come to thee because I love thee! If thou art a servant of God, tell me something about thy God and teach me, that I may serve Him too."

At this speech Paul was seized with doubt, but in his loving-kindness he cried out: "Know that God is love. And blessed is he who serves Him and gives up his life to Him. But thou seemest to be an impure spirit, so I cannot give thee God's blessing. Demon, get thee hence!"

The field devil went sadly away, bearing the penitent's words with him. He would gladly have given his life to become like this servant of God. The words "love" and "blessing," though their meaning was obscure to him, aroused delicious intimations in his heart and inspired him with a yearning no less poignant than his homesickness for the lost past. After a few troubled days he remembered his friends, who like him were weary of serving the Devil, and went to see them. He told them the whole story, and they talked it over and sighed. They could think of nothing to do.

Just then a second penitent went to the desert and settled in a desolate spot. An army of loathsome reptiles fled at his coming. This was Saint Anthony. But furious at the intrusion and fearing for his power over the desert, the Devil summoned up his powers to drive him away. Everyone knows by what artifices he tried to seduce the holy man, then to frighten him. He appeared to him first as a lewd and beautiful woman, then as a brother and fellow penitent; he offered him choice foods and laid gold and silver in his path.

When all this proved ineffectual, he resorted to his terrors. He beat the saint black and blue, he appeared to him in hideous forms, he led a procession of devils, evil spirits, satyrs, and centaurs, of ferocious wolves, panthers, lions, and hyenas through the saint's cave. The tender-hearted field devil was obliged to join in the procession, but when he approached the suffering saint it was with kindly gestures, and when his companions teased the holy man, pulled his beard, and abused him, he silently begged forgiveness with contrite glances. But Anthony failed to notice him, or regarded him as an artifice of the Evil One. He resisted all temptations and for many years lived a life of solitude and holiness.

When he was ninety years of age, God made it known to him that there was a still older and worthier penitent living in this same desert, and Anthony set out in quest of him forthwith, though he did not know the way. He wandered through the desert, and in his yearning for God the field devil followed him, secretly helping him to find the right way. At length, after much hesitation, the field devil showed himself, greeting the penitent humbly. After telling the saint how he and his brothers yearned for God, he asked him to bless them. But then, seeing that Anthony distrusted him, he vanished amid loud laments, as one can read in all the old accounts of the Church Fathers.

Anthony pursued his journey and found Father Paul. He humbled himself before him and stayed on as his guest. Paul died at the age of a hundred and thirteen, and Anthony was a witness as two lions appeared, roaring sorrowfully, and dug a grave for the saint with their claws. Thereupon Anthony returned to his former dwelling place.

The field devil had observed all these events from a distance. His innocent heart was sorely grieved that the holy fathers had both rebuffed him and left him without consolation. Since he preferred to die rather than go on serving the Evil One, and since he had carefully observed the ways of the departed saint and imprinted them on his memory, he went to live in Paul's wretched cave. He put on the saint's shirt of palm leaves, sustained himself on water and dates, knelt for hours on the hard stones in a painful position, and did his best to imitate him in all ways.

But his heart grew sadder and sadder. He could see that God did not accept him as he had accepted Paul, for the raven who had brought Paul his daily bread had stopped coming, though when Saint Anthony was visiting the old man, he had brought double portions. There was indeed a book of Gospels in the cave, but the field devil could not read. At certain moments, when he had knelt and cried out God's name to the point of exhaustion, he gained a faint, secret intimation of God and His beatitude, but full knowledge was beyond his powers.

And so, remembering Paul's words—it is blessed to die for God—he decided to die. Never had he seen one of his people die, and the thought of death was bitter and terrible to him. But he persevered in his decision. He stopped eating and drinking and spent day and night on his knees, calling out the name of God.

And he died. He died kneeling, as he had seen Father Paul die. A few moments before his death he was amazed to see the raven come flying with a loaf of bread such as he had brought the saint. And he was filled with a profound joy and the certainty that God had accepted his sacrifice and elected him to beatitude.

Shortly after his death some more pious pilgrims came to that part of the desert with the intention of settling there. They saw the corpse in penitent's dress kneeling against the rock, and decided to give the deceased a Christian burial. Intoning prayers, they dug a small pit, for the body was small of stature.

But when they picked up the body to lower it into the pit, they saw that two little horns were hidden beneath the tangled hair and two goat's feet under the garment of leaves. And they cried aloud, stricken with horror at what they took to be a mockery on the part of the Evil One. Praying loudly, they left the body lying and fled.

Chagrin d'Amour

1908

FOR QUITE SOME TIME the cream of chivalry had been
camped in magnificent tents before the walls of Kanvoleis, the chief city of the land of Valois. Each day the
warriors returned to the tournament, whose prize was to
be the fair Queen Herzeloyde, daughter of the Grail-king
Frimutel and virgin-widow of King Kastis. The contestants
included great lords, King Pendragon of Britain, King
Lot of the Orkneys, the King of Aragon, the Duke of
Brabant, and illustrious counts, knights, and heroes such
as Morholt and Riwalin, whose names are listed in the
second canto of Wolfram's *Parzival*. Some had been
drawn by hopes of martial renown, others by the young
Queen's beautiful blue eyes, but most by her rich and fertile lands, her cities and castles.

Along with the many great lords and famous heroes, the
tournament had attracted a throng of nameless knights,
adventurers, highwaymen, and poor devils. Some lacked
so much as a tent of their own; they spent their nights
where they could, often out in the open with no other
shelter but their cloaks. They let their horses graze in the
meadows round about, and ate and drank, invited or uninvited, at other people's tables. Those who had any intention of taking part in the tournament set their hopes
on luck. Their prospects were indeed meager, for their
horses were wretched and even the bravest of men cannot get very far in a tournament with a pitiful nag. Consequently many of them came with no thought of contest-
ing; they wished merely to be there, to join in the general
merriment or draw profit from it. They were all in high

spirits. Each day brought feasts and banquets, sometimes in the Queen's castle, sometimes in the tents of the rich and powerful lords, and many a poor knight was glad that the decision was so long delayed. They rode about the country, hunted, chatted, drank, and gamed; they watched the combats, occasionally took part in one, cared for injured horses, marveled at the sumptuous display of the great, missed nothing, and thoroughly enjoyed themselves.

Among the poor and inglorious warriors there was one named Marcel, stepson of a petty baron in the south, a handsome, rather emaciated soldier of fortune with unimpressive armor and a feeble old nag by the name of Melissa. Like all the rest, he had come to satisfy his curiosity, to try his luck, and to share a little in the general bustle and merrymaking. Among his fellow adventurers, but among some of the respected knights as well, Marcel had attained a certain fame, not as a knight but as a singer and troubadour, for he composed verses and sang them very nicely to the lute. He felt at his ease amid the hubbub, which reminded him of a great fair, and he had no greater desire than that this merry encampment with all its festivities should continue a long, long while. One evening the Duke of Brabant, who admired him for his songs, invited him to attend a banquet that the Queen was giving for the most distinguished among the knights. Marcel went with him to the castle in the city. The hall was grandly lighted, and dishes and beakers offered ample refreshment. But the poor lad came away with a heavy heart. He had seen Queen Herzeloyde, he had heard her clear lilting voice and drunk in her sweet glances. And now his heart beat with love for the noble lady, who seemed as gentle and modest as any young girl and yet was so unattainably far above him.

Like any knight, he could fight for her, of course. He was free to try his luck in the lists. But neither his horse nor his armor was in very good condition, and he could hardly call himself a great hero. To be sure, he knew no fear and was willing to risk his life at any time in combat for the adored Queen. But his strength was not to be measured with that of Marholt or of King Lot, not to mention Riwalin and other heroes. Of that he was well aware. Nevertheless, he was resolved to try his luck. He fed his horse Melissa bread and fine hay, which he was obliged to beg, fortified himself by eating and sleeping regularly, and carefully scoured and polished his rather ungainly armor. One morning a few days later he rode into the lists. A Spanish knight accepted his challenge and they charged with their long lances. Marcel and his nag were thrown to the ground. Blood flowed from his mouth and he ached in every limb, but he rose unaided and led his trembling mount to a secluded brook, where he washed and spent the rest of the day in sorrow and humiliation.

Torches were being lighted for the night when he returned to the encampment. The Duke of Brabant called out to him. "Well, my friend," he said good-naturedly, "the fortunes of war have gone against you. Next time, if you should wish to try again, take one of my chargers, and if you win, you may keep him for your own. But now let us make merry; sing us one of your fine songs."

The little knight was in no mood for singing and merrymaking. But for the sake of the promised horse he complied. He went to the Duke's tent, drank a beaker of red wine, and took the proffered lute. He sang one song and then another; comrades and lords praised him and drank his health.

"God bless you, troubadour!" cried the Duke in high spirits. "Forget about breaking lances, come to my court with me, you will know happy days."

"You are very kind," said Marcel softly. "But you have promised me a good horse, and before I think of anything else, I want to enter the lists just once more. What good to me are pretty songs and happy days, when other knights are fighting for glory and love?"

"Do you hope to win the Queen?" asked one of the knights, laughing.

Marcel flared up. "I hope what you all hope for, even if I am only a poor knight. And if I cannot win her, at least I can fight and bleed for her, and suffer pain and defeat for her. Rather would I die for her than live in cowardly comfort. And if any man sees fit to scoff at me for that, sir knight, for that man my sword was tempered."

The Duke bade them hold their peace, and soon the company dispersed for the night. As the troubadour was leaving, the Duke beckoned him to stay. Looking him straight in the eye, he said kindly: "You're a spirited lad. But must you shed your blood for a dream? You know you can never become King of Valois or have Queen Herzeloyde for your lady. What good will it do for you to unsaddle a petty knight or two? To achieve your end you would still have to defeat the kings and Riwalin and myself and all the heroes. Therefore I say: If you are determined to fight, start with me, and if you lose, then forget your dream, come with me, and be my minstrel, as I have already suggested."

Marcel blushed, but replied without hesitation: "Thank you, noble Duke, tomorrow I will joust with you." He went away and saw to his mare. Melissa whinnied affectionately, ate bread out of his hand, and rested her head on his shoulder.

"Ah, Melissa," Marcel said softly, stroking her head. "You love me. But it would have been better if we had died in the woods before coming to this encampment. Sleep well, Melissa."

Early next morning he rode into the city of Kanvoleis and traded Melissa for a new helmet and new boots. As he was leaving, the mare craned her neck after him, but he went on without looking back. One of the Duke's squires brought him a roan stallion, a powerful young beast, and an hour later the Duke himself faced him in single combat. Many had come to look on, since a noble lord was fighting. In the first passage, neither gained the upper hand, for the Duke was sparing the lad. But then the thought of this youngster's folly made him angry, and he charged so violently that Marcel was thrown backward; his foot caught in the stirrup and the roan stallion dragged him off the field.

As the adventurer's wounds and bruises were being cared for in one of the tents set aside for the Duke's servants, city and camp resounded with the report that Gachmuret, the world-famous hero, had arrived. He rode into the city with pomp and circumstance, his name preceding him like a bright star. The great knights frowned, but the petty poor ones cheered him, and the fair Herzeloyde blushed as she watched him pass. The next day Gachmuret rode nonchalantly into the lists and began to challenge and joust. One after another he thrust the great knights from their saddles. The camp spoke of no one else; he was the victor, the Queen's hand and country were his. The news came to the ears of Marcel on his sickbed. He heard that Herzeloyde was lost to him, he heard the praises of Gachmuret. Silently he turned his face to the tent wall and longed to die. But that was not all he heard. The Duke came to see him with a gift of raiment, and he too spoke of the victor. Marcel learned that Queen Herzeloyde was red and pale with love for Gachmuret. And he also learned that this Gachmuret not only wore the colors of Queen Anflise of France, but had also left behind him a black Moorish princess in the land of the heathen, and that she had been his wife. When the Duke had gone, Marcel raised himself with difficulty from his couch, dressed, and despite his pain went into the city to see Gachmuret, the victor. And he saw him, a mighty brown warrior, a burly giant with powerful limbs. To Marcel he looked like a butcher. Marcel managed to creep into the castle and mingle unnoticed with the guests. He saw the gentle, maidenly Queen flushed with happiness, and he saw her offer the foreign hero her lips. But toward the end of the banquet the Duke, his protector, recognized him and called him to his side.

"Permit me," said the Duke to the Queen, "to present

this young knight. His name is Marcel; he is a troubadour and has often given us great joy with his art. If you so desire, he will sing us a song."

Herzeloyde nodded amiably to the Duke and to the knight as well, smiled, and sent for a lute. The young knight was pale, he bowed very low and took the lute hesitantly. But then he quickly ran his fingers over the strings and, looking straight at the Queen, sang a song which he had composed long before at home. But as a refrain he added after each stanza two simple, sad lines, which came straight from his wounded heart. And these two lines, which were heard for the first time that night in the castle, were soon sung far and wide. They ran:

> *Plaisir d'amour ne dure qu'un moment,*
> *Chagrin d'amour dure toute la vie.*

When he had finished his song, Marcel left the castle; the glow of candlelight from the windows followed him on his way. He did not go back to the tents, but left the city in the opposite direction. Casting away his knighthood, he led the life of a homeless troubadour from then on.

The festive sounds are silent and the tents have moldered away; the Duke of Brabant, the hero Gachmuret, and the fair Queen have been dead for hundreds of years; no one speaks of Kanvoleis or of the tournament for the hand of Queen Herzeloyde. Nothing has remained but their names, which sound strange and antiquated to our ears, and the young knight's verses. They are still sung.

A Man by the Name
of Ziegler
1908

THERE WAS ONCE A YOUNG MAN by the name of Ziegler, who lived on Brauergasse. He was one of those
people we see every day on the street, whose faces we
can never really remember, because they all have the
same face: a collective face.

Ziegler was everything and did everything that such
people always are and do. He was not stupid, but neither
was he gifted; he loved money and pleasure, liked to dress
well, and was as cowardly as most people: his life and
activities were governed less by desires and strivings than
by prohibitions, by the fear of punishment. Still, he had
a number of good qualities and all in all he was a gratify-
ingly normal young man, whose own person was most interesting and important to him. Like every other man, he
regarded himself as an individual, though in reality he
was only a specimen, and like other men he regarded himself and his life as the center of the world. He was far
removed from all doubts, and when facts contradicted his
opinions, he shut his eyes disapprovingly.

As a modern man, he had unlimited respect not only
for money, but also for a second power: science. He could
not have said exactly what science was, he had in mind
something on the order of statistics and perhaps a bit of
bacteriology, and he knew how much money and honor
the state accorded to science. He especially admired cancer research, for his father had died of cancer, and Ziegler

firmly believed that science, which had developed so re-
markably since then, would not let the same thing happen
to him.

Outwardly Ziegler distinguished himself by his tendency to dress somewhat beyond his means, always in the
fashion of the year. For since he could not afford the
fashions of the month or season, it goes without saying
that he despised them as foolish affectation. He was a
great believer in independence of character and often
spoke harshly, among friends and in safe places, of his
employers and of the government. I am probably dwelling too long on this portrait. But Ziegler was a charming
young fellow, and he has been a great loss to us. For he
met with a strange and premature end, which set all his
plans and justified hopes at naught.

One Sunday soon after his arrival in our town, he decided on a day's recreation. He had not yet made any real
friends and had not yet been able to make up his mind
to join a club. Perhaps this was his undoing. It is not good
for man to be alone.

He could think of nothing else to do but go sightseeing.
After conscientious inquiry and mature reflection he decided on the historical museum and the zoo. The museum
was free of charge on Sunday mornings, and the zoo could
be visited in the afternoon for a moderate fee.

Wearing his new suit with cloth buttons—he was very
fond of it—he set out for the historical museum. He was
carrying his thin, elegant, red-lacquered walking cane,
which lent him dignity and distinction, but which to his
profound displeasure he was obliged to part with at the
entrance.

There were all sorts of things to be seen in the lofty
rooms, and in his heart the pious visitor sang the praises
of almighty science, which here again, as Ziegler observed
in reading the meticulous inscriptions on the showcases,
proved that it could be counted on. Thanks to these inscriptions, old bric-a-brac, such as rusty keys, broken and

tarnished necklaces, and so on, became amazingly interesting. It was marvelous how science looked into everything, understood everything and found a name for it—
oh, yes, it would definitely get rid of cancer very soon,
maybe it would even abolish death.

In the second room he found a glass case in which he
was reflected so clearly that he was able to stop for a moment and check up, carefully and to his entire satisfaction, on his coat, trousers, and the knot of his tie. Pleasantly reassured, he passed on and devoted his attention to
the products of some early wood-carvers. Competent men,
though shockingly naïve, he reflected benevolently. He
also contemplated an old grandfather clock with ivory
figures which danced the minuet when it struck the hour,
and it too met with his patient approval. Then he began
to feel rather bored; he yawned and looked more and more
frequently at his watch, which he was not ashamed of
showing, for it was solid gold, inherited from his father.

As he saw to his regret, he still had a long way to go
until lunchtime, and so he entered another room. Here his
curiosity revived. It contained objects of medieval superstition, books of magic, amulets, trappings of witchcraft,
and in one corner a whole alchemist's workshop, complete
with forge, mortars, pot-bellied flasks, dried-out pig's blad-
ders, bellows, and so on. This corner was roped off, and
there was a sign forbidding the public to touch the objects.
But one never reads such signs very attentively, and Ziegler was alone in the room.

Unthinkingly he stretched out his arm over the rope
and touched a few of the weird things. He had heard and
read about the Middle Ages and their comical supersti-
tions; it was beyond him how the people of those days
could have bothered with such childish nonsense, and he
failed to see why such absurdities as witchcraft had not
simply been prohibited. Alchemy, on the other hand, was
pardonable, since the useful science of chemistry had developed from it. Good Lord, to think that these gold-
makers' crucibles and all this magic hocus-pocus may

have been necessary, because without them there would be no aspirin or gas bombs today!

Absentmindedly he picked up a small dark-colored pellet, rather like a pill, rolled the dry, weightless little thing between his fingers, and was about to put it down again when he heard steps behind him. He turned around. A visitor had entered the room. Ziegler was embarrassed at having the pellet in his hand, for actually he had read the sign. So he closed his hand, put it in his pocket, and left.

He did not think of the pellet again until he was on the street. He took it out and decided to throw it away. But first he raised it to his nose and sniffed it. It had a faint resinous smell that he found rather pleasing, so he put it back in his pocket.

Then he went to a restaurant, ordered, leafed through a few newspapers, toyed with his tie, and cast respectful or haughty glances at the guests around him, depending on how they were dressed. But when his meal was rather long in coming, he took out the alchemist's pill that he had involuntarily stolen, and smelled it. Then he scratched it with his fingernail, and finally, naïvely giving in to a child-like impulse, he put it in his mouth. It did not taste bad and dissolved quickly; he washed it down with a sip of beer. And then his meal arrived.

At two o'clock the young man jumped off the street car, went to the zoo, and bought a Sunday ticket.

Smiling amiably, he went to the primate house and planted himself in front of the big cage where the chimpanzees were kept. A large chimpanzee blinked at him, gave him a good-natured nod, and said in a deep voice: "How goes it, brother?"

Repelled and strangely frightened, Ziegler turned away. As he was hurrying off, he heard the ape scolding: "What's he got to be so proud about! The stupid bastard!"

He went to see the long-tailed monkeys. They were dancing merrily. "Give us some sugar, old buddy!" they cried. And when he had no sugar, they grew angry, mimicked him, called him a cheapskate, and bared their teeth.

That was more than he could stand; he fled in consternation and made for the deer, whom he expected to behave better.

A large stately elk stood close to the bars, looking him over. And suddenly Ziegler was stricken with horror. For since swallowing the magic pill, he understood the language of the animals. And the elk spoke with his eyes, two big brown eyes. His silent gaze expressed dignity, resignation, sadness, and with regard to the visitor a lofty and solemn contempt, a terrible contempt. In the language of these silent, majestic eyes, Ziegler read, he, with his hat and cane, his gold watch and his Sunday suit, was no better than vermin, an absurd and repulsive bug.

From the elk he fled to the ibex, from the ibex to the chamois, the llama, and the gnu, to the wild boars and bears. They did not all insult him, but without exception they despised him. He listened to them and learned from their conversations what they thought of people in general. And what they thought was most distressing. Most of all, they were surprised that these ugly, stinking, undignified bipeds with their foppish disguises should be allowed to run around loose.

He heard a puma talking to her cub, a conversation full of dignity and practical wisdom, such as one seldom hears among humans. He heard a beautiful panther expressing his opinions of this riffraff, the Sunday visitors, in succinct, well-turned, aristocratic phrases. He looked the blond lion in the eye and learned of the wonderful immensity of the wilderness, where there are no cages and no human beings. He saw a kestrel perched proud and forlorn, congealed in melancholy, on a dead branch and saw the jays bearing their imprisonment with dignity, resignation, and humor.

Dejected and wrenched out of all his habits of thought, Ziegler turned back to his fellow men in his despair. He looked for eyes that would understand his terror and misery; he listened to conversations in the hope of hearing something comforting, something understandable and soothing; he observed the gestures of the visitors in the hope of finding nobility and quiet, natural dignity.

But he was disappointed. He heard voices and words, he saw movements, gestures, and glances, but since he now saw everything as through the eyes of an animal, he found nothing but a degenerate, dissembling mob of bestial fops, who seemed to be an unbeautiful mixture of all the animal species.

In despair Ziegler wandered about. He felt hopelessly ashamed of himself. He had long since thrown his red-lacquered cane into the bushes and his gloves after it. But when he threw away his hat, took off his shoes and his tie, and shaken with sobs pressed against the bars of the elk's cage, a crowd collected, the guards seized him, and he was taken away to an insane asylum.

The Homecoming

1909

THE PEOPLE OF GERBERSAU are not averse to travel, and it is traditional for the young men to see a bit of the world and foreign ways before establishing themselves, marrying, and submitting to the rule of local custom. But after a short period abroad most of them tend to recognize the advantages of home and to go back. Rarely does one of them stay away until the years of mature manhood, not to say for good. Nevertheless, it happens now and then, and such a man becomes a reluctantly recognized, but much discussed celebrity in Gerbersau.

A case in point was August Schlotterbeck, the only son of Schlotterbeck the tanner, of Waldwiese. Like other young men he left town as a traveling apprentice—in the merchant's trade, for he had not been strong as a boy and had been thought unfit to become a tanner. Later, to be sure, it turned out that his delicate health had been a mere caprice of his years of growth, and that he was an exceedingly sturdy young fellow. But he had already chosen his profession, he relished his clerk's coat and looked upon tanners, not excepting his father, with a certain commiseration. And either because this detracted from old Schlotterbeck's paternal affection or because for want of other sons he saw that there was no possible way of keeping the old-established tannery in the family, he began in his later years to take it easy and neglect the business. The upshot of it was that he passed the business on to his son in such a state of indebtedness that August was glad to sell it to a young tanner for a song.

This may have been why August spent more time than necessary abroad, where he prospered and finally abandoned all thought of returning home. Then, having passed the age of thirty without finding an occasion either to set himself up in business or to marry, he was seized with a belated desire to see more of the world. For the last few years he had been working for good wages in a factory town in eastern Switzerland. To broaden his knowledge and avoid sinking into a rut, he now gave up his position and went to Scotland. Though he had no great liking for Scotland or the city of Glasgow, where he had found work, he became accustomed during his stay there to a free cosmopolitan existence, and lost his sense of kinship with his home town, or extended it to the whole world. Since there was nothing to hold him, he was only too glad to accept the offer of a factory managership in Chicago, and was soon as much, or as little, at home in America as in his previous stopping places. He had long since lost the identifying marks of a Gerbersau man, and when he ran into a fellow townsman, as occurred every few years, he treated him with the same polite affability as he did everyone else. Word got back to Gerbersau that Schlotterbeck had grown wealthy and powerful, but also haughty and American.

After some years he thought he had learned enough and saved enough in Chicago. When his only friend, a German established in southern Russia, returned home, Schlotterbeck followed him. In Russia he soon opened a small factory which prospered and acquired a good reputation. He married his friend's daughter and thought he was settled for the rest of his life. But the future did not fall in with his expectations. His wife remained childless. This was a cruel disappointment and seriously detracted from the peace and fulfillment of his marriage. Then she died, and in spite of everything her death came as a blow to him and made him, for all his vigorous health, a little older and more thoughtful. After a few more years, business began to fall off alarmingly as a result of political unrest. When his friend and father-in-law died, leaving him alone, it was all up with his peace and his sedentary life. It suddenly came to him that one place is not as good as another after all, not, at least, for a man whose best years are drawing to an end. He thought more and more of ways to secure contentment in his old age, and since business had lost its appeal for him and much of his old resiliency and enthusiasm for travel had left him, the aging manufacturer's hope and yearning began, to his own surprise, to revolve more and more explicitly around his home country and the town of Gerbersau, to which he had seldom given a thought in the last ten years, and then without emotion.

One day he decided with the calm dispatch characteristic of his younger years to sell his factory, which by then brought in next to nothing, and to leave Russia. He sold the business, then his house and furnishings, transferred his liquid assets to various south German banks, and made his way to Germany via Venice and Vienna.

At the first border station he drank his first Bavarian beer in years, with a sense of quiet well-being, but when the names of the cities began to take on a more homelike ring and the dialect of his fellow travelers became more and more suggestive of Gerbersau, the cosmopolitan was seized with a wild agitation. He was surprised at his emotion as the conductor called out the stations and as he discerned the familiar, almost kindred features of the people boarding his carriage. At last the train wound its way down the last stretch, and deep in the hollow, first small, then larger and nearer and more real from loop to loop, lay the little city by the river, at the foot of the pine-clad mountains. The traveler felt a heavy weight on his heart. The thought that this world—the river and the town-hall tower, the streets and gardens—was still there came to him as a kind of reproach for having so long neglected and forgotten it and banished it from his heart.

But his agitation was short-lived. At the station Herr Schlotterbeck picked up his light-brown suitcase and left

the train with the manner of a man traveling on business
who welcomes the opportunity to revisit a place familiar
to him from former days. At the station the presence of
runners from three hotels gave him an impression of
progress and development, and since one of them had the
name of the old "Gasthaus zum Schwan," which Schlotterbeck remembered, inscribed on his cap, he gave the
man his bag and proceeded into town by himself on foot.

As he strode slowly along, the stranger attracted a
glance or two, but paid no heed. Recovering his traveler's
curiosity of former years, he looked about the old town
attentively; the greetings and questions and recognition
scenes could wait. First he strolled down the somewhat
changed Bahnhofstrasse to the river, on whose green surface geese were swimming about as they had always done,
and to which as in times gone by the houses turned their
untended backs and tiny back gardens. Then he crossed
the upper footbridge and passed through unchanged
shabby narrow streets to the site of the old Schlotterbeck
tannery. But he looked in vain for the tall gabled house and
the large grass plot with the tanning pits. The house had
vanished and the garden and grass plot had been built
over. Rather dejected and disgruntled, he turned away
and went on to the marketplace, which he found in its
old condition except that it seemed to have grown smaller.
The stately town hall also seemed less imposing than he
remembered.

The homecomer had seen enough for the present and
found his way without difficulty to the Swan, where he
ordered a good dinner and prepared himself for the first
recognition scene. But the old owners were no longer
there and he was treated exactly like a welcome but
strange guest. Only then did he discover that his pronun-
ciation and manner of speaking, which all through the
years he had thought to be good Swabian and virtually
unchanged, sounded foreign to the ears of the local people, so much so that the waitress had some difficulty in
understanding him. It also attracted notice that he sent

back his salad and called for another which he himself prepared, and that instead of the sweet pastry that is always served for dessert in Gerbersau he ordered compote and ate a whole jar of it. And when after his meal he pulled up another chair and rested his feet on it, both the personnel and his fellow guests were filled with consternation. Scandalized by these strange manners, a guest at the next table stood up and wiped off his chair with his handkerchief, saying: "I'd forgotten to wipe it. Why, somebody may have put his filthy boots on it!" There was soft laughter, but Schlotterbeck merely turned his head toward the man and quickly back again. Then he folded his hands and devoted himself to his digestion.

An hour later he arose and went for another stroll about town. He looked curiously through the windows of various shops and workshops to see if any of the very old people, who had been old people even in his boyhood, were still there. He found none. Only a teacher, in whose class he had daubed his first alphabet, passed him in the street. The man must have been at least in his late seventies, and had no doubt retired long since; yet, still easily recognizable by the cast of his nose and even by his movements, he walked reasonably erect and seemed contented enough. Schlotterbeck would have liked to speak to him, but he was still deterred by a certain dread of all the exclamations and handshaking that would follow. He went on, greeting no one, scrutinized by many but recognized by none, thus spending his first day in his native town as an unknown stranger.

But despite the absence of human welcome, the town spoke all the more clearly and warmly to its returned child. Though there were new developments on all sides, the town itself in its general aspect had neither aged nor changed, and smiled at the new arrival with motherly tenderness. He felt happy and sheltered; his travels and adventures and the years spent abroad merged and shrank strangely, as though all that had been a mere diversion, a slight detour. He had done business and made money here and there; he had taken a wife and lost her; he had known well-being and suffering in foreign countries. But this was the only place where he belonged, where he was at home; and though he was looked upon as a stranger and even as a foreigner, he himself felt perfectly at home, akin to these people, streets, and houses.

He was pleased with the innovations in the town. He reflected that here too human effort and human needs had expanded, though moderately; both the gasworks and the new school building met with his approval. The population seemed to be in good shape—he had developed an eye for such things in the course of his travels—though no longer so markedly indigenous as in the old days when the grandchildren of immigrants had still been regarded as foreigners. The more imposing shops still appeared to be owned by natives, the influx of outside blood was clearly noticeable only among the workers. He therefore presumed that the life of the middle classes was very much as it had been and thought it likely that a home-comer, even after a long absence, would soon be able to find his place and make himself at home.

In short, the man was charmed by his native city, which he had not uselessly transfigured by nostalgia and memory during his years abroad. It breathed an enchantment which he did not resist. When he returned to the hotel early in the evening, he was in a good humor and did not regret his journey. He decided to stay awhile, to wait and see, and then if his contentment lasted, to settle down.

He found it very strange to be going about as though masked among old friends, schoolmates, and relatives. But the world traveler's pleasantly expectant incognito soon came to an end. After dinner the landlord of the Swan brought him the register and politely asked him to fill it out—not so much because this was absolutely necessary as because he was sick of racking his brains as to the stranger's origin and status. The guest took the thick book and spent a few moments reading over the names of former guests. Then he took the pen which the landlord had dipped for him and wrote with a firm legible hand, conscientiously filling in all the columns. The landlord thanked him, strewed sand on the page, and vanished with the book as with a prize, in his haste to satisfy his curiosity unobserved. He read: Schlotterbeck, August—coming from Russia; purpose of trip: business. Though the man's origin and story were unknown to him, the name Schlotterbeck seemed to suggest a native of Gerbersau. Returning to the dining room, he addressed the stranger respectfully and struck up a conversation. Beginning with the prosperity and growth of the town, he went on to the improved roads and new railroad connections, touched on local politics, offered his opinion of the dividend paid the previous year by the Associated Woolen Mills, and after fifteen minutes came out with an innocent question: did the gentleman have relatives in town? Schlotterbeck replied nonchalantly that he did, but he made no inquiries about them and showed so little curiosity that the conversation soon died down and the landlord had no choice but to withdraw. Disregarding the conversations at the surrounding tables, the guest read the paper and soon retired to his bedroom.

In the meantime the entry in the hotel register and the conversation with the landlord were quietly taking effect, and while August Schlotterbeck in unsuspecting contentment was settling in his good bed made up in the native manner, while he was enjoying his first slumbers and first dreams since his return to his native land, the rumor of his arrival was making a number of people unusually talkative and depriving one person of his sleep. This was August's cousin and closest living relative, the merchant Lukas Pfrommer on Spitalgasse. He was actually a bookbinder; for long years he had mended the schoolchildren's ravaged primers, bound *House and Garden* every six months for the wife of the justice of the peace, made copybooks, framed wall mottoes, rescued imperiled woodcuts with backing, and supplied offices with gray and green folders, portfolios, and cardboard binders. Over the years he had saved a little, in any case he had been free from worry. Then the times had changed, nearly all the small artisans had opened some sort of shop, while the larger ones became manufacturers. Pfrommer, too, had pierced the front wall of his little house, put in a shop window, taken his savings out of the bank, and opened a stationery and notions shop. His wife had tended the shop, neglecting her household and children, while he himself had kept on working in his bindery. But the shop had become the main thing, at least as far as the townspeople were concerned, and though it did not bring in more than his craft, it cost more and gave him more worry. In short, Pfrommer had become a merchant. In the course of time he grew accustomed to this more respected and imposing status; he put on a proper coat instead of his green apron when he went out, and learned to operate with credit and mortgages. Though he managed to keep up an honorable position, he had a much harder time of it than before. The stocks of no longer salable New Year's cards, albums, vignettes, shopworn cigars, and of knickknacks that had lost their luster from being too long exposed in the shopwindow, accumulated and figured not infrequently in his dreams. And his wife, who had formerly been a cheerful and affable little woman, had little by little been transformed into a worrier, whose sweet shop-counter smile had become permanent and inappropriate to her aging features.

At about nine the previous evening, as Schlotterbeck's cousin was sitting by the lamp with his paper, the landlord of the Swan had dropped in. Though very much surprised, Pfrommer had received him hospitably, but the landlord had declined to sit down. No, he must hurry back to his guests, among whom, he regretted to say, he had not often had the pleasure of numbering Herr Pfrommer of late. Nevertheless, he thought it a point of honor and no more than natural that neighbors and fellow citizens should do each other small favors, for which reason he had come to inform Pfrommer in all confidence of the arrival at his hotel of a stranger with distinguished manners, who gave his name as Schlotterbeck and claimed to have come from Russia. Lukas Pfrommer had jumped up and roused his wife, who had already gone to bed. Puffing and blowing, he had called for his boots, cane, and Sunday hat, and even, for all his haste, stopped to wash his hands. Then he had rushed to the Swan in the landlord's wake. But he had found that his cousin was no longer in the public room and did not dare to knock at his door, for he could not help seeing that if his cousin had taken the long trip on his account he would already have called on him. Agitated and rather disappointed, he had taken a pint of Heilbronner at sixty pfennigs out of consideration for the landlord, listened in on the conversation of a group of habitués, and taken good care not to reveal what he had come for.

In the morning Schlotterbeck had no sooner come down for his coffee than an elderly man of small stature, who had apparently been waiting for some time over a glass of kirsch, approached his table awkwardly and offered him a timid greeting. Schlotterbeck said good morning and went on spreading butter and honey on his bread; his visitor stood watching him, cleared his throat, but said nothing. Only when Schlotterbeck turned to him with a questioning look did he step closer to the table with a second greeting and start to explain himself.

"My name is Lukas Pfrommer," he said with an expectant look at the man from Russia.

"Ah," said Schlotterbeck casually. "Are you a bookbinder by any chance?"

"Yes. Merchant and bookbinder, on Spitalgasse. Are you . . ."

Schlotterbeck realized that his identity was known and made no further attempt at concealment.

"Then you're my cousin," he said simply. "Have you had your breakfast?"

"So it's you!" cried Pfrommer triumphantly. "I'd hardly have known you."

With sudden joy he held out his hand to his cousin and it was only after venting his emotion in an assortment of gestures that he was able to sit down at the table.

"My Lord!" he cried. "Who would have thought we'd see you again? From Russia! On business?"

"Yes. Have a cigarette. Now tell me, what brings you here?"

Ah, any number of things had brought the bookbinder, but for the present he did not mention them. He merely said that once he had heard the rumor of his cousin's arrival there had been no holding him. Now, thank goodness, he had seen him and welcomed him. He would have regretted it to his dying day if anyone had got ahead of him. Was his cousin well? And how was his dear family?

"Thank you. My wife died years ago."

Pfrommer was taken aback. "No, it's not possible!" he cried with deep regret. "And we knew nothing, we couldn't even write you a letter of condolence. My heartfelt sympathy, cousin."

"Never mind. That was long ago. And how are things with you? You've become a merchant?"

"More or less. I try to keep my head above water and set something aside for the children. Incidentally, I carry good cigars. —And you? How is the factory doing?"

"I've given it up."

"Really? But why?"

"Business had fallen off. What with the famine and the uprisings."

"Ah yes, Russia! I was always rather surprised at your going into business in Russia. The despotism, the nihilists —and the bureaucracy must be frightful. I've tried to keep informed, you see, knowing I had a relative there. Pobedonostsev . . ."

"Oh, yes, he's still alive. But I'm sure you know more about politics than I do."

"Hardly. I read a thing or two in the paper, but . . . Well, what line of business are you in now? Did you lose a lot?"

"Yes, quite a lot."

"You say that so calmly. Sorry to hear it, cousin. We had no idea."

Schlotterbeck smiled a little.

"Oh yes," he said thoughtfully, "when things were at their worst, I thought of appealing to you people here. But then I managed without it. Who could be expected to sink money into the bankruptcy of a distant cousin he hardly remembers?"

"Good Lord! Bankruptcy, you say?"

"Well, it could have happened. But as I say, I found help in another quarter . . ."

"You shouldn't have. See here, we're poor devils and we need what little we have. But it was wrong of you to think we'd leave you in the lurch."

"Don't take it to heart; it's better this way. But how's your wife?"

"Well, thank you. What a fool I am! In my excitement I almost forgot I was supposed to invite you for dinner. You'll come?"

"Yes. Thank you. I picked up a few little things for the children on my way here. Why don't you take them home with you? And give your wife my regards."

With that he got rid of him. The bookbinder went off happily with the little package, and since the contents proved to be quite splendid, his estimate of his cousin's business affairs rose again. Schlotterbeck, meanwhile, was glad to be free of the talkative fellow. He went to the town hall to submit his passport and apply for a residence permit for an indeterminate time.

There was no need of his visit to the town hall to make it known that Schlotterbeck had returned. The news spread by a mysterious grapevine; at every step someone spoke to him, or cast him a friendly glance, or tipped his hat to him. A good deal was already known of him, and his wealth assumed regal proportions in the local gossip. Some, as they hastily passed the story on, confused Chicago with San Francisco and Russia with Turkey, but the fortune amassed in some unknown business remained a firm article of faith. In the next few days Gerbersau was alive with versions in which the fortune, according to the temperament and imagination of the narrator, ranged from a million to ten millions, and the branch of business from munitions to the slave trade. People remembered the long-deceased tanner and the story of his son's boyhood; there were some who recalled him as an apprentice, as a schoolboy, or as a candidate for confirmation, and a manufacturer's deceased wife was mentioned as his unhappy boyhood love.

He himself, since he was not interested, heard little of all this. The day he went to his cousin's for dinner, he had found the family's hopes in him as a wealthy relative so thinly masked that he had conceived an invincible loathing for his cousin's wife and children. His cousin lamented copiously, and to keep the peace Schlotterbeck had agreed to a modest loan, but immediately afterward he had grown very cool and taciturn, and had politely declined all further invitations for the time being. His cousin's wife had been disappointed and offended, but before witnesses the Pfrommers continued to speak respectfully of their cousin.

Schlotterbeck stayed on at the Swan for another few days. Then he found lodgings that suited him. Above the city, not far from the woods, a new road had been built, originally for the sole use of some quarries situated higher up. But an architect with an eye to the future possibilities of this beautiful though inaccessible quarter had built three little houses faced with white stucco and brown woodwork at the beginning of the new road, where land was still to be had for next to nothing. From here one could look down over the old town and beyond it to the river winding its way between meadows and the red rocky heights across the valley. On the other side, it was only a step to the pine forest. One of the speculator's three houses was finished but unoccupied, one had been bought three years before by a retired bailiff, and the third was still under construction. The bailiff had died. The inactive life had disagreed with him and he had soon succumbed to an old ailment against which he had held his own for many years with the help of hard work and good humor. At present the bailiff's widow, a brisk, tidy little woman, of whom we shall hear more, was living in the house with an elderly sister-in-law.

Schlotterbeck settled in the middle house, some hundred yards distant from the other two. He rented the ground floor, consisting of three rooms and a kitchen. Having no desire to take his meals up there all by himself, he bought and rented only a bed, tables, chair, and a sofa, left the kitchen empty, and arranged for a woman to come in twice a day to do the housekeeping. He made his own coffee in the morning on an alcohol burner as he had done during his long years as a bachelor, and had his noonday and evening meals in town. Setting up his little household kept him pleasantly busy for a time, his trunks arrived from Russia, and their contents soon filled his empty clothes cupboards. Every day he received and read a few newspapers, including two foreign ones; he wrote many letters and from time to time paid calls in town, some on relatives and old friends, some on businessmen, especially factory owners. For he was looking unhurriedly but with keen interest for an opportunity to start a business. Little by little he established a certain contact with the society of his native town. He was invited to various houses, to social clubs, and to the notables' tables at the inns and taverns. He participated in this social life with the friendly good manners of a widely traveled man, making no firm commitments and quite unaware of how much he was criticized behind his back.

Despite his clear-sightedness August Schlotterbeck was under a misapprehension about himself. Though he felt a trifle superior to his fellow townspeople, he nevertheless regarded himself as a product of Gerbersau, who in all

essential respects would easily fit into the life of the town.
And that was not quite true. He failed to see how very
much he differed from his fellow citizens in his language
and mode of life, in his ideas and habits. His fellow citizens were all the more aware of it, and even though
Schlotterbeck's reputation lay secure in the shadow of
his bank balance, quite a few comments were made about
him that he would not have liked to hear. Various things
that he did unsuspectingly, out of old habit, provoked criticism and disapproval; his speech was thought to be too
free, his vocabulary too foreign, his opinions American,
and his easy manner toward everyone arrogant and crude.
He spoke to his housekeeper very much as he did to the
mayor; after an invitation to dinner he neglected to pay a
"bread-and-butter call" within the week; and though when
in male company he abstained from the usual off-color
jokes, he said certain things that seemed natural to him
quite candidly and openly in the presence of ladies. Especially in official circles, which formed the top of the social
pyramid and set the tone, in the area between chief district magistrate and head postmaster, he made no con-
quests. This small, anxiously guarded world of bureau-
cratic potentates and their wives, full of mutual respect
and regard, in which each member knew his fellows' circumstances down to the last thread and all lived in glass
houses, was none too pleased with the returned world
traveler, all the less so as it could hope for no advantage
from his legendary wealth. And in America Schlotterbeck
had learned to regard officials as mere employees, who
work for money like everyone else, while in Russia he had
come to know them as an unsavory clique, from whom
nothing could be obtained except with money. With no
one to advise him, he found it hard to appreciate the sanc-
tity of these men's titles and all their sensitive dignity, to
display jealousy in the right quarter, not to confuse secre-
taries with undersecretaries, and in his social relations
with them to find the tone appropriate to each individual
and group. As an outsider he was unacquainted with their

intricate family histories, so that through no fault of his own he was only too likely to speak of the noose in the house of the hanged man. Under cover of perfect politeness and the most affable smiles his little misdemeanors were neatly totted up till they amounted to a sizable sum of grievances, of which he was quite unaware, and those in a position to do so looked on with malicious glee. Still other innocent misdeeds which Schlotterbeck committed with a clear conscience were taken amiss. If a man's shoes appealed to him, he would make no bones about asking their price. Then there was the lawyer's wife, who employed every possible artifice to conceal the fact that in atonement for heaven knows what sins of her ancestors the forefinger was missing from her left hand. With sincere sympathy Schlotterbeck asked her when and where she had lost her finger. The man who for so many years had done business and taken care of himself in foreign lands had no way of knowing that one does not ask a magistrate how much his trousers had cost. He had learned to be polite in conversation with all sorts of people, he had learned that certain peoples do not eat pork or squab, that in a region inhabited by Russians, Armenians, and Turks it is best not to claim exclusive truth for any one religion; but he had so far fallen away from his Gerbersau beginnings as to be quite unaware that in the center of Europe there are whole castes and social groups which regard it as crude to speak openly of life and death, eating and drinking, money and health.

All in all it was a matter of indifference to him whether or not people were pleased with him, since he made far fewer demands on others than they did on him. He was asked to contribute to all manner of good causes, and always gave what he thought fit. People thanked him politely and soon came back with new requests, but here again they were only moderately pleased, having received silver when they expected gold or banknotes.

Several times a day on his way to town, Herr Schlotterbeck passed the neat little house belonging to Frau Entriss, the bailiff's widow, who led a quiet life in the company of her slightly feebleminded sister-in-law.

The well-preserved woman, who had not turned her back on life, might have spent very pleasant days in the enjoyment of her freedom and small income. She was prevented from doing so by her own character and by the reputation she had acquired in the course of her years in Gerbersau. She came from Baden and on her arrival, if only out of regard for her husband, who was well liked in the town, she had been received with friendly expectation. But in time people began to think ill of her, chiefly because of her exaggerated frugality, which gossip transformed into pernicious greed. And once they had taken a dislike to her, one thing was added to another, and she came to be regarded not only as a skinflint and penny pincher, but as a shrew as well. The bailiff himself was not a man to have spoken ill of his own wife, but it remained no secret that the cheerful and sociable man sought his pleasure and recreation not so much at home with his wife as drinking beer at the White Horse or the Swan. Not that he became a drunkard, there were no drunkards among the respected citizens of Gerbersau. But he did fall into the habit of spending a good part of his free time in the taprooms and of dropping in for an occasional mug of beer in the daytime. In spite of his poor health he went on living in this manner until the authorities as well as his doctor put pressure on him to retire from his exacting office. But after his retirement his health had grown worse rather than better, and now all agreed that his wife had poisoned his home life and had been responsible from the start for the good man's downfall. Left alone with her sister-in-law, she found neither woman to comfort her nor man to protect her, though there was a bit of money in addition to the mortgage-free house.

But her solitude did not seem to weigh unduly on the unloved widow. Her house, bankbook, and garden were in perfect order, and that kept her busy, for her sister-in-law,

who was not quite right in the head, spent her days looking on, muttering, rubbing her nose, or leafing through an
old picture album. To make sure the gossip would not
die down after her husband's death, the townspeople had
taken it into their heads that the widow scrimped on the
poor creature's keep and held her in dire imprisonment.
It was bruited about that the deranged sister-in-law went
hungry and was made to do heavy work, in short that her
days were numbered, which after all was to Frau Entriss's
interest and undoubtedly what she was aiming at. When
these rumors became more and more blatant, the authorities felt called upon to intervene. One day the mayor, accompanied by the public health commissioner, turned up
at the astonished woman's house, lectured her on her responsibility, announced that they had come to see where
her sister-in-law lived and slept, what she ate, and what
work she did, pointing out that should anything be found
unsatisfactory the patient would be sent to a state hospital, naturally at Frau Entriss's expense. Frau Entriss replied very calmly that they could investigate whatever
they pleased, that her sister-in-law was quite harmless,
that if they wished to have her cared for elsewhere she
had no objection, but that the township would have to de-
fray the costs and she doubted whether the poor thing
would be any better off. The investigation showed that
the sick woman wanted for nothing. When asked in a
kindly tone whether she would like to live somewhere
else, where she would be made very comfortable, she was
stricken with fear and clung imploringly to her sister-in-
law. The health commissioner found her well fed and detected no sign of hard work. Then the two men took an
embarrassed leave.

As for Frau Entriss's avarice, divergent opinions are
possible. It is easy to find fault with a defenseless woman's
character and mode of life. Undoubtedly she was thrifty.
She had such profound respect not only for money but for
any possession however small that it was hard for her to
spend anything, and impossible for her to throw anything

away or let it go to waste. Every penny of the money her husband had spent at the taverns in his day still galled her like an unatonable wrong, and this may well have been what undermined the harmony of their marriage. She had tried desperately to compensate through hard work and exact accounts for what her husband had so frivolously squandered. And now that he was dead, now that not a single taler was spent in vain and a part of her income could be converted each year into capital, the good house-keeper was at last comfortably well off. Not that she ever indulged in superfluities; if anything, she saved more than ever, but the knowledge that her savings were bearing fruit and gradually accruing gave her a contentment which she was resolved never to risk again.

Frau Entriss experienced a very special joy and satis-faction when she managed to give value to something worthless, to find or take possession of something useful, to make use of something that had been thrown away, or to derive some advantage from a despised object. This passion was not directed solely toward profit; in this con-nection, on the contrary, her thoughts and desires went beyond the narrow sphere of necessity and rose to the realm of the aesthetic. She was not disinclined to beauty and luxury, she too liked pretty and pleasant things, only they must not cost money. Accordingly, her dress was modest, but trim and tidy, and ever since she had moved into this house and owned a bit of land, her need for beauty had found a rewarding outlet. She had become an enthusiastic gardener.

Every time August Schlotterbeck passed his neighbor's fence, he looked with pleasure and a tinge of envy at the widow's splendid little garden. Neatly laid out vegetable patches were attractively framed in borders of chives, strawberries, and flowers; roses, stock, wallflowers, and mignonette seemed to betoken a modest happiness.

It had not been easy to obtain such results on this slop-ing sandy soil. Frau Entriss's passion had done, and was still doing, wonders. With her own hands she brought black soil and leaves from the woods; in the evenings she followed in the traces of the heavy quarry wagons, gathering little shovelfuls of precious horse droppings. Behind her house she carefully laid potato peelings and other kitchen waste on a heap, which would decay and serve to enrich the ground the following spring. From the woods she also brought wild roses and slips of lily of the valley and snowdrop, which during the winter she would carefully tend in the house and cellar. The yearning for beauty that lies hidden in every human soul, the pleasure she took in tilling a fallow field and making use of what could be had for nothing, and perhaps unconsciously a vestige of unfulfilled womanhood made her into an excellent garden-mother.

Several times each day, Herr Schlotterbeck, who knew nothing of his neighbor, cast appreciative glances at the perfectly weeded garden, feasted his eyes on the joyful green of the vegetables, the tender red of the roses, the gay colors of the bindweed; and when there was a light breeze and a handful of garden fragrance followed him on his way, he felt more and more grateful at having such a neighbor. For there were times when in spite of himself he suspected that his native soil was not making it exactly easy for him to take root, and when he felt rather lonely and cheated.

When he inquired of acquaintances about the owner of the garden, he was told the story of the late bailiff and heard quite a few harsh opinions of his widow, so that for a time the sight of the peaceful little house in the garden filled him with astonishment that such loveliness should be the dwelling place of so abject a soul.

Then one morning he caught sight of her for the first time, behind her low fence, and spoke to her. Until then, she had always slipped away into the house when she saw him coming in the distance. This time, bending over her plants, she had been too deep in her work to hear him, and suddenly there he stood at the fence, politely holding his hat in hand and saying good morning. She returned his greeting. In no hurry to go his way, he asked: "Working so bright and early?"

"A little," she said, and encouraged he went on: "What a beautiful garden you have!"

To this she made no answer but resumed her weeding, and he watched her in surprise. After the talk he had heard he had expected her to look like a Fury, and now to his pleasant surprise she was not in the least forbidding. Her face, though a trifle severe and reserved, was fresh and open, and her figure was by no means unattractive.

"Well, I'll be getting on," he said amiably. "Goodbye, neighbor."

She looked up and nodded as he waved his hat, watched him take three or four paces, and went on with her work without troubling herself any further about him. But he thought about her for some time. He found it amazing that this woman should be such a monster, and decided to keep an eye on her. He saw her in town making her scant purchases quickly and without wasting words; he saw her tending her garden and hanging out her washing, and noted that she received no visitors. With respect and a certain emotion he spied on the hardworking woman's modest, solitary life. Nor did her rather shamefaced evening forays for horse droppings, for which she was so frowned upon, remain hidden from him. But though he could not help smiling, he saw nothing to find fault with. It seemed to him that she was rather withdrawn, but brave and decent, and thought it a pity that so much care and attention should be devoted to such insignificant purposes. For the first time, his suspicions aroused by her case, he began to distrust the judgment of the townspeople, and to doubt a number of things that he had hitherto taken on faith.

Meanwhile he met his neighbor now and then and exchanged a few words with her. He now addressed her by name; she too knew who he was and called him Herr Schlotterbeck. Before going out, he tended to wait until he saw her in the open; as he passed by, he would strike up a little chat about the weather and the prospects for the garden, taking pleasure in her frank, intelligent answers.

One evening while sitting at the Eagle with an acquaintance, he brought the conversation around to her. He told the man that he had been struck by the well-tended garden, that he had watched the woman's quiet life and failed to understand how she could have acquired so unsavory a reputation. The man listened politely and replied: "Look. You didn't know her husband. A fine fellow, the life of the party, a good friend, and a heart of gold. And she did him in, neither more nor less."

"What did he die of?"

"Kidney trouble. But he'd had that for years and had always borne up under it. But then he retired. You'd have expected his wife to make things nice for him at home, but he began to dread the place. Sometimes he even went out to lunch because of her wretched cooking. Maybe he was a bit unsteady, but if he drank too much at the end it was all her fault. She's a fiend, that's all there is to it. For instance, she has a sister-in-law living with her, a poor sick creature who's been out of her mind for years. Well, the way she was starving her and mistreating her, the authorities had to step in and investigate."

Schlotterbeck didn't quite believe this story, but wherever he inquired he found it confirmed. He was surprised and dismayed to have been so mistaken about the woman. But whenever he saw her and exchanged a few words with her, all his suspicions vanished. Finally he took the bull by the horns and went to the mayor for reliable information. He was given a friendly reception, but when he asked about Frau Entriss—was she really under suspicion of mistreating her sister-in-law, was she really under investigation?—the mayor replied coldly: "It's nice of you to take an interest in your neighbor, but is it really any concern of yours? I believe you can trust us to do the right thing. Or have you a complaint to make?"

At this Schlotterbeck went cold with rage, as had occasionally happened to him in America. He stood up, quietly closed the door, sat down again and said: "Mr. Mayor, you know what people have been saying about Frau Entriss, and you've been to her house, so you must know how much truth there is in it. You've given me all the answer I need, it's all lies and malicious gossip. Or am I wrong? —I thought not. Why do you stand for it?"

At first the mayor took fright, but he quickly regained his composure. "My dear Herr Schlotterbeck," he said with a shrug. "I have other things to worry about. Here and there people may have been making false statements about the woman, but it's up to her to defend herself. She can bring suit."

"Very well," said Schlotterbeck. "That's all I wanted to know. In other words you give me your assurance that to the best of your knowledge Frau Entriss's sister-in-law has been receiving proper treatment?"

"When it comes to that, yes, Herr Schlotterbeck. But if I may give you a bit of advice, don't interfere. You don't know the people here, you'll only make yourself disliked by meddling in their affairs."

"Thank you, Mr. Mayor. I'll think about it. But in the meantime, if I hear anybody saying such things about that woman I'll call him a slanderer to his face and cite you as my witness."

"Better not. You won't be helping the woman and you'll only be making trouble for yourself. I'm warning you, because I'd be sorry if—"

"I see. Thank you."

The first consequence of Schlotterbeck's call on the mayor was a visit from his cousin Pfrommer. It had long been common knowledge that Schlotterbeck was taking a strange interest in the wicked widow, and Pfrommer was terrified lest his crazy cousin do something foolish in his old age. If the worst came to the worst and he married the woman, Pfrommer's children would never see a penny of all his millions. Cautiously Pfrommer admired the attractive situation of Schlotterbeck's house, led slowly up to his neighbor, and gave it to be understood that he knew plenty about Frau Entriss if his cousin was interested. But Schlotterbeck made an evasive gesture, offered the book-binder a glass of excellent brandy, and never let him come to the purpose of his visit.

That same afternoon he spied his neighbor in her garden and went over to see her. For the first time he had a long heart-to-heart talk with her. Though unaccustomed to conversation, she spoke intelligently and without affectation, showing feminine adaptability and, he would have said, charm.

From then on such conversations were repeated daily, always over the rail fence, for when he asked leave to come into the house or even the garden, her reply was a resolute no.

"It won't do," she said with a smile. "We're neither of us young any more, but these Gerbersau people are always glad of something to gossip about and before you knew it there would be no end of stupid talk. They have it in for me to begin with, and they take you for some kind of freak, you know."

Yes, he knew it now, in the second month of his stay, and his pleasure in Gerbersau and his fellow townsmen had fallen off considerably. It amused him that they should vastly overestimate his fortune, and the anxious attentions of his cousin Pfrommer and of other anglers rather tickled him, but this did not compensate him for the disappointment he was beginning to feel. In his heart he had already abandoned all desire to settle there for good. Perhaps he would simply have left and resumed his wanderings of former years, a prospect that did not frighten him. But now a fine thorn held him fast, he felt that he could not go away without hurting himself and leaving a little piece of himself behind.

And so he stayed on, and often passed by the little white and brown house next door. Now that he knew Frau Entriss better and she had told him certain things, her life was no longer such a mystery to him. In particular, he was able to form a clear enough picture of the late bailiff, whose widow spoke of him without a word of reproach but who must have been a fool not to have detected the precious core beneath this woman's dry severity, and brought it to light. Herr Schlotterbeck was convinced that under proper conditions, with an understanding man, she would become a pearl.

The more he knew her, the clearer it became to him that she could not possibly be understood in Gerbersau. For he felt that he had now gained a better insight into the Gerbersau character, though he liked it no more for that. In any case he recognized that he himself did not share, or no longer shared, this character, and that he was no more able than Frau Entriss to give the best of himself in this town. But these thoughts were no more than playful paraphrases of his silent longing to remarry and to make his thus far solitary life fruitful and immortal.

The summer was at its height. In the midst of the blazing sandy countryside the widow's garden spread its fragrance triumphantly far beyond its low fence—especially in the evening when at the edge of the nearby woods the birds sang the praises of the glorious day, when the hum of the factories ceased for the night and the soft flow of the river rose up through the silence. On such an evening August Schlotterbeck went to the house next door and not only stepped uninvited into the garden but opened the door as well. A thin, frightened bell announced his presence, and the lady of the house addressed him with surprise bordering on displeasure. He insisted, however, that this time he simply had to come in. She led him into the good room, where he looked around, finding the place rather bare and unadorned, but neat and brightened by the evening sun. She quickly took off her apron, sat down in a chair by the window, and bade him be seated.

Herr Schlotterbeck embarked on a long, eloquent speech. With dry simplicity he told the story of his whole life, not excluding his first brief marriage, then with somewhat more warmth described his return to Gerbersau and his first acquaintance with her, recalling certain talks in which they had understood each other so well. And now he had come, she knew perfectly well why, and he hoped she was not too surprised.

"I'm not a millionaire, as the people here seem to think, but there is a little something. Aside from that, it seems to me that we're both young and healthy and that the time hasn't come yet for us to give up and shut ourselves off from life. Why should a woman like you be sitting all alone, contenting herself with her little garden, instead of starting out again in the hope of finding the true happiness that passed her by before?"

Both hands lying quietly in her lap, Frau Entriss had listened attentively to her suitor, who gradually warmed to his subject and from time to time held out his right hand as though inviting her to take it and hold it fast. But she did nothing of the sort; she sat very still, drinking in his words without fully realizing that someone had actually come to show her love and kindness. Since she neither answered him nor looked up from the strange dream state she was in, Schlotterbeck, after a pause, went on talking. Tenderly and hopefully he told her how, if she consented, they might lead a peaceful, industrious life in some other place free from unpleasant memories, how they might have a larger garden and in general spend a little more freely, though it went without saying that they would set something aside year after year. Soothed by the sight of her, slightly and pleasantly dazzled by the red and yellow sunset, he spoke very gently, in hardly more than a whisper, content that she at least was listening to him. And she listened in silence, her mind benumbed by weariness. She was not fully aware that this was a proposal, involving a lifelong decision, and the thought neither excited nor pained her, for it never occurred to her for a moment to take it seriously. But the minutes slipped by so lightly, as though borne by music, that she listened spellbound, incapable of any decision, not even so trifling a decision as to shake her head and stand up.

Schlotterbeck paused again and looked at her questioningly. She was still sitting there with downcast eyes and a delicate flush on her cheeks, as though listening to music. He misunderstood her state of mind, interpreting it in a manner favorable to himself, but he himself was in the same absorbed, dreamlike state; he too heard the strange moments whirring as on melodious wings through the room and through his mind.

It seemed to both of them later that they had sat for a long while as though under a spell, but only a few minutes had elapsed, for the sun was still close to the edge of the mountain when they were awakened from the stillness.

The unexpected visit had alarmed the invalid in the next room and this long, barely audible conversation filled her with dark forebodings. She felt that something unusual and menacing must be going on, and little by little, unable to think of anything but herself, she was overcome by fear that the man had come to take her away. The visit of the gentlemen from the town hall had aroused her suspicions and since then every little incident in the house had rekindled her terror of being forcibly removed.

For a time she struggled with her fears; then she came running into the room sobbing desperately, threw herself at her sister-in-law's feet, and clasped her knees, weeping and moaning convulsively. Schlotterbeck started up in fright and Frau Entriss, wrenched out of her enchantment, awoke to sober reality, suddenly ashamed and dismayed at having so lost herself.

She jumped to her feet, drawing the kneeling woman with her, stroked her hair, and murmured soft comforting words as to a sobbing child.

"No, no, dear heart, don't cry. There, you won't cry any more, will you? Come, child, come, everything's all right now, there's going to be something nice for supper. Did you think the man was going to take you away? Silly thing, nobody's going to take you away; no, no, you must believe me, no one's going to hurt you. Don't cry any more, silly thing, don't cry!"

Embarrassed but moved, August Schlotterbeck saw that the sick woman was crying more quietly, with a certain childlike pleasure. She rocked her head, her plaints became softer and softer, and suddenly, though the tears were still flowing, she screwed up her despairing face into an idiotic, infantile smile. Feeling that his presence was not needed, the visitor gave a little cough and said: "I'm sorry, Frau Entriss. I hope she feels better soon. I'll come again tomorrow if I may."

Only in that moment was it all borne in on her: how he had proposed and she had listened and let him go on, though with no thought of accepting. She was surprised at herself; why, she may have seemed to be playing with him. It was clear to her that she mustn't let him leave with such an idea of her. "No, don't go," she said. "It's over now. I must talk to you." Her voice was calm and her face showed no sign of emotion; the glow of the sun and the glow of her sweet agitation had died away, and she looked with cool composure but also with a furtive note of sorrow at the suitor, who, this time without relinquishing his hat, sat down again.

She settled her sister-in-law in a chair and returned to her former place. "We have to keep her here," she said in an undertone, "or she'll get upset again. —I let you speak before, Herr Schlotterbeck, I myself don't know why, I was a little tired. I hope you didn't misinterpret that. Because I made up my mind long ago not to change my life. I'm almost forty and you must be over fifty; sensible people don't marry at our age. You know I like you and that I'm grateful to have you as a friendly neighbor. We can continue on those terms if you like. But let's content ourselves with that, or we're likely to regret it."

Herr Schlotterbeck's expression was dismayed but

friendly. Under other circumstances, he thought, he would leave it at that and go. But the glow he had seen in her face only a few minutes before had remained in his memory like a gravely beautiful late-summer bloom and reinforced his longing. If not for that glow, he would have gone his way, sadly but with no thorn in his heart; as it was, he felt that happiness had alighted on his finger like a trusting bird and he had merely failed to grasp it at the right moment. And when one has been so close to capturing a bird, one does not let it fly away without nourishing a stubborn hope of a better opportunity. Besides, despite his dismay that she should slip away from him after his little speech had brought that gentle glow to her cheeks, he loved her much more than he had an hour before. Then he had thought he was aiming at a pleasant and beneficial marriage of reason, but now, after this last hour in the evening sun, he was really in love.

"Frau Entriss," he said resolutely. "You've had a fright, and my proposal may have come as too much of a surprise. I love you, and since it's only your reason that resists, I can't accept defeat like a peddler who is told to try his luck next door. On the contrary, I am determined to go on with this war and to besiege you to the best of my ability. We shall see who is the stronger."

She had not been prepared for this tone; it sounded warm and flattering to her woman's heart and, though she would not have admitted it, cheered her like a first blackbird's call in February. But she was not a woman to be guided by vague stirrings; she was determined to resist the onslaught and to preserve the freedom that had grown so dear to her.

She said: "You frighten me, neighbor. I know men stay young longer than we women, and I'm sorry you won't content yourself with my answer. I can't make myself young again and act as if I were in love; it wouldn't come from the heart. I've become accustomed to my life as it is, and come to love it; I have my freedom and no worries. And besides, there's my sister-in-law, poor thing, who needs me, I won't ever leave her, I've promised her and I'll keep my promise. —But why am I talking so much when there's nothing to say? I can't do it and I don't want to. If you wish me well, leave me in peace, don't threaten me with your sieges. If you like, we'll forget what happened today and remain good neighbors. If not, I won't be able to see you again."

Schlotterbeck stood up, but did not leave. He paced the floor in agitation as though he were in his own house, trying to find a solution. She watched him for a while, somewhat amused, somewhat moved, and somewhat offended, until she had had enough. Then she cried out: "Don't be a fool, neighbor. We want to eat our supper, and it must be time for yours too."

But by then he had made his decision. Picking up his hat, which he had put down in his excitement, he bowed and said: "Very well, I'll go now, Frau Entriss. I'll bid you goodbye and I won't bother you for a while. You mustn't think I'm a brute. But I'll come again, let's say in four, five weeks, and all I ask of you is to think it over in the meantime. I'm leaving town; when I come back, it will be only to hear your answer. Then if you say no, I promise to let well enough alone, and you won't have me as your neighbor any more. There's nothing but you to keep me in Gerbersau. So goodbye, till we meet again!"

He laid his hand on the door handle, cast a glance back into the room, which was answered only by the sister-in-law, and stepped out into the evening. Faint sounds rose up to him from the town, and he shook his fist at it. He was convinced that the town alone was to blame for Frau Entriss's obstinacy, and he resolved to leave it forever as soon as possible, either with her or without her.

Slowly he walked the few yards to his house, not without looking back from time to time. A small cloud, a mere puff of vapor hovered in the darkening distance, glowing softly pink and gold as it greeted the first star. At the sight he felt the delicious excitement of the last hour pass over him once more; he shook his aging head and smiled at the impulses of his heart. Then he went into his lonely house and began that same evening to prepare for a journey.

By the following afternoon he was ready. He gave the keys to his housekeeper, entrusted his suitcase to a porter, breathed a sigh of relief, and started for the railway station without venturing so much as a glance at Frau Entriss's garden or windows as he passed. She saw him, though, as he went off with the porter. She felt sorry for him and with all her heart she wished him a pleasant and restful journey.

Quiet days began for Frau Entriss. Her modest life slipped back into the old solitude, no one came to see her any more, and no one looked over her garden fence. The townspeople knew she had employed all her arts to ensnare the rich man from Russia, and rubbed their hands at the news of his departure, which had become known to all that very same day. As was her way, she ignored all this and went calmly about her duties and customary tasks. She felt sorry about what had happened with Herr Schlotterbeck. But she could not feel she had been to blame in any way, and over the years she had become so accustomed to living alone that she was not gravely upset at his going away. She gathered flower seeds from the fading beds, watered the garden morning and evening, picked berries and made preserves, all with industrious contentment. And then suddenly she had her hands full with her sister-in-law.

Since that evening she had been quiet enough, but she seemed more than ever to be beset by anxiety, a kind of persecution mania fraught with dreams of abduction and violence. The hot stormy summer made matters worse; she could no longer bear to be alone and Frau Entriss was scarcely able to leave the house for the half hour it took her to do her marketing. The poor creature felt secure only in the presence of her guardian, whom she tormented with her moaning and hand-wringing and looks of groundless terror. Finally Frau Entriss was obliged to call in a doctor, who took to coming every few days, in-spiring the sick woman with new fear. His visits led the townspeople to redouble their talk of mistreatment and official intervention.

In the meantime August Schlotterbeck had gone to Wildbad, which he found both too hot and too lively for his taste. He soon packed up and went on to Freudenstadt, which he remembered from his younger days and which was more to his liking. There he fell in with a Swabian manufacturer with whom he was able to discuss the indus-trial and commercial matters in which he was experienced. Every day they took long walks together in the cool woods. The man's name was Viktor Trefz. He owned an old-es-tablished leather-goods factory in eastern Germany and like Schlotterbeck he had traveled widely. Schlotterbeck possessed a thorough knowledge of the leather industry and for a man living in retirement was surprisingly well informed about the world market. They were soon on terms of courteous familiarity. Schlotterbeck acquainted the manufacturer with his history and situation in some detail, and it seemed to both of them that their friendship might one day extend itself to business relations.

So it happened that Schlotterbeck found all the recrea-tion he had hoped for, and that he sometimes forgot his unfinished business with the widow in Gerbersau for half a day at a time. As a lifelong merchant he was stimulated and cheered by his conversations with his experienced colleague and by the prospect of a collaboration. The needs of the heart, which had never held an exaggerated place in his life, receded into the background. Only when he was alone, especially at night before going to sleep, was he haunted and aroused by the image of Frau Ent-riss. But even then the matter no longer seemed to him so very important. As he thought of that evening in his neighbor's little house, he finally came to the conclusion that she had not been entirely wrong. He saw that his thoughts of marriage had sprung in good part from his solitude and idleness.

On one of their walks Herr Trefz invited him to visit him that fall and take a look at his plant. Not a word had been said about a business connection, but both knew how things stood and were well aware that the visit might easily lead to a partnership and expansion of the business. Schlotterbeck accepted with thanks and gave his friend the name of his bank, in case he wished to make inquiries.

"Never mind about that," said Trefz. "We can go into the details later on if you're interested."

August Schlotterbeck felt that he had begun to live again. That night he went to bed happy and fell asleep without having once thought of his widow. He did not suspect that she was having a very bad time of it and could have used his help. Under the doctor's observation the sister-in-law had become more anxious and unsettled than ever and life in the little house had become a nightmare. Sometimes she squealed like a stuck pig, sometimes she would run up and down the stairs and through the rooms, wailing and groaning, and sometimes she would shut herself up in her room to whimper and pray and resist imaginary assailants. The poor creature now had to be watched constantly, and the frightened doctor urged Frau Entriss to have her taken away and cared for in an institution. The widow held out as long as she could. Over the years she had become accustomed to the melancholy old maid's presence, she had hopes that the present crisis would pass, and she dreaded the expense. She was perfectly willing to cook, wash, and care for the unhappy woman and to put up with her moods as long as she lived; but she was terrified at the thought that this ruined life might devour her savings year after year. Frau Entriss was a strong woman, but under her fears and burdens she was beginning to age and waste away.

Of all this Schlotterbeck knew nothing. He thought the widow was living happily in her little house, quite content perhaps to be rid of her troublesome suitor for a while.

But this was no longer true. To be sure, Herr Schlotterbeck's absence had not made her heart grow fonder or transfigured his image with tenderness; but now in her distress she would have been very glad of a friend and adviser. Indeed, it seemed likely that if things should go badly with her sister-in-law, she would come to take a kindlier view of the wealthy man's proposal.

In the meantime the talk about Schlotterbeck's departure and its presumptive significance and duration had died down, since for the moment all tongues were busy with the widow Entriss. While beneath the fir trees of Freudenstadt the two business friends improved their understanding and spoke more and more openly of future common undertakings, bookbinder Pfrommer in his house on Spitalgasse sat for two long evenings over a letter to his cousin, whose welfare and future he took very much to heart. A few days later the amazed August Schlotterbeck held this letter, written on the best gilt-edged paper, in his hands, and slowly read it through twice. It ran:

Dear Cousin Schlotterbeck:
Herr Schwarzmantel, the registrar, who returned recently from a tour of the Black Forest, informs us that he saw you in Freudenstadt and that you are well and living at the Linden. We were glad to hear it and wish you a good rest in those beautiful surroundings. When possible, a summer cure is always beneficial. I myself was once in Herrenalb for a few days after an illness and it did me no end of good. Once again I wish you an excellent stay, confident that you are happy in our good old Black Forest with its murmuring fir trees.

Dear Cousin, we all miss you very much, and when you come home again after a good rest, I am sure you will like it very much in Gerbersau. A man has only one home, and though the world may be full of beautiful things, it is only at home that he can be really happy. You have made yourself extremely well liked in our town and everybody is looking forward to your return.

It is a good thing that you went away when you did, for terrible things have been happening again in your neighborhood. I don't know whether you have already heard. The Entriss woman has finally had to let her sick sister-in-law go. She had been treating her so badly that the poor creature could bear it no longer. Day and night she cried out for help until finally the health commissioner was called in. She was found to be in a dreadful condition, but Frau Entriss insisted on keeping her at all costs, you can imagine why. But now they have put a spoke in her wheel and taken her sister-in-law away. Maybe she will have to answer for her misdeeds in another world. The sister-in-law has been sent to the madhouse in Zwiefalten, and the Entriss woman has to pay plenty for her. Which serves her right for scrimping on the poor thing!

You should have seen it when they took her away, it was pitiful. They took a carriage, the Entriss woman, the health commissioner, the warder from Zwiefalten, and the patient were in it. She started right in and screamed so hard that a big crowd ran after them all the way to the station. On the way home the people shouted all sorts of things at the Entriss woman and a little boy threw a stone at her.

Dear Cousin, if there is anything I can do for you here, I shall be very glad to. You were away from home for thirty years, but that doesn't matter. As you know, I regard no service as too great for a kinsman. My wife sends her regards.

I wish you good weather for your holiday. Up there in Freudenstadt it must be cooler than down in this narrow valley. We have been having very hot weather and lots of storms. The Bayrischer Hof was struck by lightning the day before yesterday, but there was no fire.

If you need anything, I am entirely at your disposal.

Your faithful friend and cousin,
Lukas Pfrommer.

Herr Schlotterbeck read the letter through attentively, put it in his pocket, took it out again, translated it from Gerbersau into German, and tried to form a picture of the events related. He was seized with shame and anger; he saw the poor woman mocked and persecuted, he saw her sitting alone, fighting back the tears with no one to comfort her. The more he thought about it and the more clearly he visualized and understood what had happened, the less inclined he was to laugh at his cousin and his letter. Thoroughly outraged at him and all Gerbersau, he was beginning to plot revenge when it gradually occurred to him how little he himself had thought of Frau Entriss in the last few weeks. While he had been making plans and enjoying himself, the poor dear woman had been going through hell and perhaps hoping for his help.

As he thought it over, he began to feel ashamed of himself. What was he to do now? In any case, he would go back at once. Without delay he summoned the landlord, arranged to leave the following morning, and informed Herr Trefz of his intentions. As he was packing his bag, his shame and anger and misgiving gave way to a cheerfulness that lasted all evening. It had become clear to him that the happenings in Gerbersau were so much grist for his mill. The sister-in-law was gone, thank goodness; Frau Entriss was eating her heart out with loneliness and probably had financial worries. In other words, it was time for him to go back to her good room and repeat his proposal in the glow of the evening sun. In high spirits he spent the evening with Herr Trefz, over an excellent bottle of Markgräfler wine. They drank to their next meeting and to a lasting friendship, the landlord joined them in a glass and expressed the hope of seeing both his honored guests the following year.

Early next morning Schlotterbeck was at the station, waiting for the train. The landlord, who had accompanied him, shook hands with him again, the hotel porter lifted his bag into the car and took his tip, and the train pulled out. After a few impatient hours the journey was over and Schlotterbeck, after an exchange of greetings with the stationmaster, made his way into town.

He took second breakfast at the Eagle, which was on his way, had his coat brushed, and went straight up to Frau Entriss. The door was locked and he had to wait a few minutes. Then with a questioning look—for she had not seen him coming—the lady of the house opened the door. When she recognized him, she blushed and tried to put on a look of severity, but he entered with an amiable greeting and she led him into the good room.

His coming had taken her by surprise. Though she had had little time to think of him, his return no longer frightened her but came as a consolation. This was plain to him for all her silence and affected coolness, and he made things easy for her and himself by taking her heartily by both shoulders, looking half-laughingly into her flushed face, and saying: "It's all right now, isn't it?"

She tried to smile and play coy and protest a little; but in spite of herself she was overcome by emotion, by the memory of all the trouble and bitterness of the last few weeks, which up to that moment she had borne bravely. Suddenly, to his consternation and her own, she burst into tears. But not long afterward, the timid glow of happiness which Herr Schlotterbeck remembered from his last visit reappeared on her cheeks, she pressed close to him and let him embrace her. After a gentle kiss her betrothed sat her down in a chair and said gaily: "Well, thank the Lord, that's that. But the house is being sold this fall, or do you absolutely insist on staying in this hole?"

The City

1910

NOW WE'RE GETTING SOMEWHERE," cried the engineer when the second train carrying people, coal, tools, and food arrived over the stretch of track that had been laid only the day before. The prairies glowed softly in the yellow sunlight, on the horizon the great wooded mountains were bathed in blue mist. Wild dogs and buffaloes looked on as work and bustle moved into the wilderness, as heaps of coal and ashes, paper and tin appeared on the green countryside. The first power saw sent its piercing scream through the terror-stricken wilds, the first gunshot burst like a thunderclap and rolled over the mountains, the first anvil rang under swift hammer blows. A tin-roofed shanty sprang up and next day a wooden house, and then others day after day, soon followed by stone buildings. The wild dogs and buffaloes kept their distance, the land was tilled and bore fruit. The very first spring the plains were covered with green grain; farms and stables and granaries were built; roads cut through the wilderness.

The railroad station was completed and inaugurated, soon followed by a government building, and a bank. Several sister cities, barely a few months younger, shot up nearby. Workers poured in from everywhere, peasants and city-dwellers; merchants and lawyers came, preachers and teachers. It was not long before the town could boast of a school, three religious congregations, and two newspapers. Oil was discovered in the west, prosperity came to the new city. Only a year later there were pickpockets, burglars, pimps, a department store, a temperance society, a tailor from Paris, a Bavarian beer hall. The competition of the neighboring towns acted as a goad. Nothing was lacking, from election campaigns to strikes, from movie houses to spiritualist séances. French wine, Norwegian herring, Italian sausage, English woolens, and Russian caviar all became available. Second-rate singers, dancers, and musicians came through on tour.

Little by little a culture grew up as well. The city, which had begun as a mere outpost, became a permanent dwelling place. There was a manner of greeting, of nodding to those one met, which differed ever so slightly from that prevailing in other towns. Men who had participated in founding the city came to be popular and respected; they were the nucleus of a small aristocracy. A young generation grew up, to whom the city seemed an old home that had been there just about forever. The days when the first hammer stroke had resounded, the first murder had been committed, the first divine services held, the first newspaper printed lay deep in the past and were looked upon as history.

The city had come to dominate the towns round about; it was now the capital of a large region. Where once the first shacks and shanties had bordered on ash heaps and puddles, now there were broad smiling avenues lined with imposing banks and public buildings, theaters and churches. Students sauntered through the streets on their way to the university or the library; ambulances threaded their way through the traffic; a congressman's limousine was sighted and cheered; in twenty large schoolhouses built of stone and iron the founding of the city was celebrated each year with songs and speeches. The former prairies were now covered with fields, factories, and villages and traversed by a dozen railroad lines; thanks to the railroad the mountains had come closer. There, or far away by the seashore, the wealthy had their summer houses.

A hundred years after its founding, the entire city was leveled by an earthquake. It rose again, but now wood

gave way to stone, small buildings to larger ones; narrow
streets were eliminated, and everything became more spacious. The railroad station and the stock exchange were
the biggest on the whole continent. Architects and artists
adorned the rejuvenated city with public buildings, parks,
fountains, and monuments. In the course of the new century, the city came to be known as the richest and most
beautiful in the whole country. Politicians and architects,
engineers and mayors came from all over the world to
study its buildings, waterworks, administration, and in-
stitutions. Work was begun on a new city hall, one of the
largest and most magnificent buildings in the world, and
since this period of rising prosperity and local pride coin-
cided happily with a general flowering of taste, particularly in architecture and sculpture, the rapidly growing
city became a miracle of pride and beauty. The midtown
section, whose buildings without exception were faced
with a noble light-gray stone, was surrounded by a broad
belt of splendid parks, beyond which long avenues, bordered by rows of houses, lost themselves in the open country. Much visited and admired was an immense museum,
whose hundred rooms, courtyards, and halls were devoted
to the history of the city from its founding. In the vast
courtyard models of the first wretched shacks and streets
were shown in their prairie setting, complete with vegeta-
tion and animal life. There the young people strolled
about, contemplating the course of their history from tent
and shanty, from the first straggling trail to the radiant
metropolis. Guided and instructed by their teachers, they
learned to understand the great laws of development and
progress: how the refined grows from the crude, man
from beast, civilization from barbarism, and abundance
from penury.

The city's wealth and luxury increased at a headlong
pace and attained their peak in the next century. Then a
bloody revolution of the lower classes put an end to this
development. The mob began by setting fire to many of

the large oil fields in the vicinity. A large part of the region, with its factories, farms, and villages, was burned or laid waste. Despite massacres and horrors of every kind, the city itself survived. In the quiet years that followed, it gradually recovered, but never again regained its old prosperity. There was no new building. During the troubled years a distant country beyond the seas had begun to flourish. It yielded grain and iron, silver and other treasures with the abundance of a generous, untired soil. The new country attracted the fallow energies, the strivings and ambitions of the old world, cities sprang from the ground overnight, forests disappeared, waterfalls were harnessed.

Little by little the beautiful city became impoverished. It ceased to be the heart and brain of a world, the market and stock exchange of many countries. The best it could do was continue to exist and preserve some shred of its fame amid the tumult of the new times. Those of its citizens who did not emigrate to the distant new world had nothing more to build or conquer; business was at a standstill and there was little money to be made. But now a spiritual life germinated in this cultural soil grown old, scholars and artists, painters and poets were born into the dying city. The descendants of those who had once built the first houses on this new ground spent their days smilingly amid a quiet late flowering of the arts. They painted the melancholy splendor of old moss-covered gardens with their weather-beaten statues and green ponds, or wrote sensitive verses about the remote tumult of the old heroic age or the silent dreams of tired men in old palaces.

Once again the city's name and fame resounded far and wide. Let the outside world be shaken with wars and busy with great projects—here men could live in peaceful seclusion and dream of ancient glories. Here there were silent streets arched over with flowering branches; here the weather-stained façades of vast buildings looked out on soundless squares and melodiously playing moss-encrusted fountains.

For a century or two the dreaming old city was loved

and revered by the young people of the world, celebrated by poets and visited by lovers. But life was shifting more and more to other continents. And in the city itself the descendants of the old native families began to die out or go to seed. The last cultural impulse had long since passed its prime and nothing remained of it but rotting vestiges. The small towns round about were dead, reduced to silent ruins, visited now and then by foreign painters and tourists and occasionally inhabited by gypsies and fugitive criminals.

An earthquake spared the city but changed the course of the river. Part of the devastated countryside was transformed into a swamp, the rest became a desert. And slowly the old forest crept down from the mountains, engulfing the crumbling remains of old country houses and stone bridges. It saw the vast region lying desolate and invaded it strip by strip, here covering a swamp with whispering green, there a rubble heap with hardy young conifers.

In the end the city was bereft of citizens; all that remained was a nondescript rabble, wild, unfriendly creatures who sought shelter in the crooked sinking palaces of days gone by and grazed their goats in the former gardens and streets. The whole region had been infested with fevers since the prairie had turned to swamp, and in time this population also died of disease and imbecility. After that, all was desolation.

The old city hall, once the pride of its time, was ruined but still standing; tall and stately, it continued to be celebrated in songs throughout the world and in innumerable legends of the neighboring peoples, whose cities had also fallen into neglect and whose civilization had degenerated. The names connected with the city and its former splendor still occurred in garbled forms in children's ghost stories and melancholy shepherds' tales, and occasionally the scholars of distant, now-flourishing peoples made long perilous journeys to visit the ruined sites, whose secrets were eagerly discussed by schoolboys of faraway lands.

There was talk of doors of pure gold, of tombs full of pre-cious stones. And it was said that the wild nomadic tribes of the region still preserved vestiges of an ancient magic dating back to the legendary past.

But the forest edged downward, from the mountains to the plain; lakes and rivers came into being and passed away, and the forest advanced, slowly cloaking the whole countryside, the remnants of old walls, palaces, temples, and museums. And fox and marten, wolf and bear in-habited the wilderness.

A young pine tree had taken root in the rubble of a fallen palace. Only a year ago it had been the first har-binger of the approaching forest. But now, as it looked about, it saw new saplings far and wide.

"Now we're getting somewhere!" cried a woodpecker who was hammering at the trunk, and looked with satis-faction at the spreading forest and the magnificent green progress that was covering the earth.

Robert Aghion

1913

IN THE COURSE of the eighteenth century a new type of Christianity and Christian endeavor grew up in England, expanding rather quickly from a negligible root into a large exotic tree. Today it is known to all as the Evangelical Mission to the Heathen.

On the surface there would seem to have been ample reason and justification for the missionary activity of the English Protestants. Since the glorious age of discovery, lands had been explored and conquered in every part of the earth. Scientific interest in the configuration of remote islands and mountain ranges as well as the heroism of navigators and adventurers had given way to a modern spirit, a new sort of interest in exotic regions, no longer hinging on adventurous exploits and experiences, strange animals and romantic palm forests, but on pepper and sugar, silks and furs, rice and sago, in short on the commodities with which traders make money. This commercial activity had often been pursued blindly and ruthlessly; certain rules having currency in Christian Europe had been forgotten and infringed upon. Terrified natives had been hunted like wild animals in America, Africa, and India; enlightened Christian Europeans had conducted themselves like foxes in a chicken coop, and one need not be oversqueamish to conclude that their behavior was monstrous, more like that of crude, swinish bandits than of Christians. Reactions of shame and indignation in their home countries led among other things to the missionary movement, springing from a laudable desire that the heathen peoples of the earth might receive something better and nobler from Europe than gunpowder and brandy.

In the latter half of the century it was not uncommon for high-minded private citizens to take an active interest in this missionary idea and to provide the wherewithal for its implementation. At that time, however, there were no regular missionary societies and organizations such as flourish today; each benefactor individually tried, so far as his resources permitted, to further the cause in his own way, and a man who in those days went to remote parts as a missionary did not, as he would now, cross the seas like a well-addressed piece of mail to embark on prearranged and well-organized activities, but, with little more than his trust in God to prepare himself for his task, flung himself headlong into a dubious adventure.

In the 1790s a London merchant, whose brother had grown wealthy in India and there died childless, decided to provide a sizable sum of money for the dissemination of the Gospel in that country. A member of the powerful East India Company and several clergymen were taken on as advisers and a plan was drawn up. As a first step three or four young men were to be provided with adequate equipment and travel money and sent out as missionaries.

The announcement of this undertaking quickly attracted any number of adventurous souls; unsuccessful actors and discharged barbers' apprentices felt that this journey was just what they needed, and the pious committee had the greatest difficulty in carrying on their search for worthy candidates over the heads of these undesirable applicants. Working through private channels, they addressed themselves chiefly to young theologians, but the English clergymen of the day were not at all weary of their homeland or eager for strenuous, not to say dangerous, undertakings; the search dragged out, and the donor began to be impatient.

At length the news of his intentions and difficulties reached a village parsonage in Lancashire, where it so happened that Robert Aghion, the parson's young nephew, was performing the duties of a curate in return for his board and lodging. Robert Aghion was the son of a sea captain and of a pious, hardworking Scotswoman; he had hardly known his father, who had died when he was very young, and his uncle, who thought well of his talents, had sent him to school and systematically prepared him for the ministry, in which he had made as much progress as could be expected of a candidate with good credentials but no private fortune. In the meantime he assisted his uncle and benefactor, during whose lifetime he could not hope for a parish of his own. And since the parson was still hale and hearty, the nephew's prospects were none too brilliant. As a poor young fellow with little hope of coming into a living before his middle years, he was not regarded as a desirable match, not at least by respectable girls, and he had never met any others.

Thanks to his deeply pious mother, he was animated by a simple Christian faith which he rejoiced in proclaiming from the pulpit. But his mind found its greatest pleasure in the observation of nature, for which he possessed a keen eye. A modest, unspoiled young man with capable eyes and hands, he found satisfaction in seeing and knowing, collecting and investigating the things of nature that came his way. As a boy he had grown flowers and studied botany, for a time he had taken a lively interest in stones and fossils, and recently, especially since he had been living in the country, he had developed a particular love for the colorful insect world. Most of all, he loved the butterflies; their dramatic transformation from the caterpillar and chrysalis state delighted him time and time again, while their colors and designs gave him the pure pleasure of which less gifted men are capable only in early childhood.

Such was the young theologian who was first to perk up his ears at the news of the mission. In his innermost soul it aroused a longing that pointed like a compass needle to India. His mother had died a few years before; he was not engaged, nor had he given any young girl his secret promise. He wrote to London, received an encouraging reply

and travel money, and set out at once with a small chest
of books and a bundle of clothes, regretting only that he
could not take his herbariums, fossils, and butterfly cases
with him.

Arrived in the somber, noisy city, the candidate went
to the pious merchant's tall, solemn house and entered
with beating heart. In the gloomy corridor an enormous
wall map of the eastern hemisphere and then in the first
room a large tiger skin spoke to him of the country he
longed for. Bewildered and uneasy, he followed the dis-
tinguished-looking servant to the room where the master
of the house was waiting. He was received by a tall, grave,
close-shaven old gentleman with sharp steely-blue eyes
and a look of severity, who, however, took a liking to the
timid young candidate after the first few words, bade him
be seated, and continued the interview with an air of
trusting benevolence. When it was completed the merchant asked for and received the applicant's credentials,
and rang for the servant, who silently led the young theologian to a guest room, where a moment later a second
servant appeared with tea, wine, ham, bread and butter.
Then Aghion was left alone with his collation. After still-
ing his hunger and thirst, he made himself comfortable
in a blue-velvet armchair, pondered his situation, and
looked idly about the room. After a short time he discovered two more messengers from the remote tropical country, a stuffed red-brown monkey in a corner beside the
fireplace, and above it, fastened to the blue-silk hangings,
the tanned skin of an enormous snake, whose eyeless
head hung down blind and limp. These were things he ap-
preciated and which he hastened to examine close at
hand and to feel. Though the thought of the living boa,
which he tried to substantiate by bending the glistening
silvery skin into a tube, was somewhat horrifying and re-
pugnant to him, the sight nevertheless fired his curiosity
about the mysterious far country. He was determined to
let himself be frightened neither by snakes nor by monkeys, and thought with delight of the fabulous flowers,

trees, birds, and butterflies there must be in those blessed climes.

By then it was coming on evening, and a silent servant brought in a lighted lamp. Outside the tall window it was foggy dusk. The silence of the distinguished house, the faint surge of the big city in the distance, the solitude of the tall, cool room in which he felt like a prisoner, the lack of anything to do, and the eerie uncertainty of his situation combined with the gathering darkness of the autumn night to subdue the young man's eager expectations. After two hours, which he spent listening and waiting in the armchair, he gave up all hope for the present day. Suddenly grown tired, he lay down on the excellent bed and soon fell asleep.

In the middle of the night, as it seemed to him, he was awakened by a servant, who announced that the young gentleman was expected for dinner and should please make haste. Barely awake, Aghion crawled into his clothes. Staggering and wild-eyed, he followed the servant through rooms and corridors and down a flight of stairs to the large dining room, where in the glare of the chandeliers the lady of the house, clad in velvet and sparkling with jewels, examined him through a lorgnette and the master introduced him to two clergymen, who during the meal subjected their young brother to a sharp examination, endeavoring in particular to satisfy themselves as to the genuineness of his Christian faith. The sleepy apostle had difficulty in understanding all the questions, not to say answering them; but his timidity became him, and the gentlemen, who had become accustomed to candidates of a very different stamp, were well disposed toward him. After dinner maps were spread out in the next room, and Aghion was shown a yellow spot, indicating the town where he was to proclaim the word of God.

The following day he was taken to see the venerable gentleman who was the merchant's chief ecclesiastical adviser. The old man was instantly won by Robert's candor. He was not long in fathoming his cast of mind and, perceiving little religious militancy, began to feel sorry for him. He proceeded to expatiate on the perils of the ocean voyage and the hardships of life in the tropics, for it struck him as absùrd that a young man should sacrifice and destroy himself in India when he seemed to have no special gifts or inclinations to prepare him for such a mission. Then he laid his hand on the candidate's shoulder, looked into his eyes with earnest kindness, and said: "What you say is all very well and I feel sure you are telling the truth; but I still fail to understand exactly what draws you to India. Be frank with me, my friend, and tell me without reservation: is it some worldly interest, or is it solely a heartfelt desire to carry our beloved Gospel to the poor heathen?" At this Robert Aghion blushed like a thief caught in the act. He cast down his eyes and said nothing for a time; then he admitted freely that though his pious intentions were quite sincere, it would never have occurred to him to apply for a post in India or to become a missionary altogether had he not been tempted by a longing for the rare plants and animals of that country, and in particular the butterflies. The old man saw that the youth had yielded up his ultimate secret and had nothing more to confess. He nodded and said with a friendly smile: "Well, that's a sin that you yourself will have to attend to. You shall go to India, my dear boy!" And growing grave again, he laid both hands on his head and solemnly blessed him in the words of the Bible.

Three weeks later the young missionary, well provided with chests and trunks, embarked as a passenger on a fine sailing vessel. He saw his native land sink into the gray sea, and in the very first week, before they had even sighted Spain, learned to know the moods and perils of the ocean. In those days it was not possible for a traveler to India to reach his goal as green and untried as today, when we board a comfortable steamer in Europe, avoid the circuit of Africa by passing through the Suez Canal, and reach our destination lethargic and befuddled by too much sleeping and eating. In those days sailing ships had to fight their way for months around the vastness of Africa, imperiled by storms and becalmed for days at a time. The passenger learned to bear heat and cold, to endure hunger and sleepless nights. A man who had such a journey behind him had long ceased to be an untried neophyte; he had learned to stand on his own feet more or less. And so it was with our missionary. The voyage from England to India took him 156 days, and the young man who landed in Bombay was a lean and weather-beaten mariner.

His enthusiasm and curiosity were still with him, though they had grown more serene. Whenever he had gone ashore in the course of his voyage, he had looked about him with the eyes of a naturalist; he had contemplated every tropical island with eagerness and awe. His courage and eagerness were undiminished as he set foot on the soil of India and made his way into the radiantly beautiful city.

He set out immediately to find the address he had been given; the house lay beneath tall coconut palms in a quiet suburban street. As he went in, his eyes grazed the small front garden, and though he had more important things to do and to look at just then, he found time to notice a bush with dark leaves and yellow flowers, around which a swarm of white butterflies were flitting merrily. With this image still in his slightly dazzled eyes, he climbed a few flat steps, crossed the wide, shady veranda, and passed through the house door, which was open. A white-clad Hindu servant with bare brown legs came running over the cool red-tile floor and made a deep bow. He said a few words of Hindustani in a nasal singsong, but soon noticed that the stranger did not understand him, and led him with supple bows and serpentine gestures of obeisance and invitation to a doorless doorway, covered with a loosely hanging bast mat. The mat was drawn aside from within, and out stepped a large, gaunt, domineering-looking man wearing a white tropical suit and straw sandals. In an incomprehensible Indian tongue he shot a few words of abuse at the servant, who made himself very small and slipped away. Then he turned to Aghion and bade him in English to come in.

The missionary tried to apologize for his unannounced arrival and to justify the unfortunate servant, who had done no wrong. But the other replied with a gesture of impatience: "You'll soon learn how to deal with the rascals. Come in. I've been expecting you."

"You must be Mr. Bradley," said the new arrival courteously, though he felt chilled and intimidated at this first step into the exotic household and at the sight of his future mentor.

"Yes, I'm Bradley, and you're Aghion, I presume. Well, don't stand there, come in! Have you had your lunch?"

With the curt, haughty manner of an experienced overseer and business agent, the big raw-boned man with the brown hairy hands took charge of his guest. He ordered him a meal of mutton, rice, and fiery curry, assigned him a room, showed him through the house, took his letters and instructions, answered his first eager questions, and supplied him with the most indispensable rules of life in India. The house resounded with his cold, irascible commands and vituperations as he set the four Hindu servants in motion. He sent for an Indian tailor and commanded him to supply Aghion immediately with a dozen appropriate garments. Grateful and somewhat abashed, Aghion took all this as it came, though he would have preferred a quieter, more peaceful introduction to India; he would have liked to spend a little time making himself at home and unburdening himself of his impressions and of the emotions of his journey in a friendly conversation. Six months at sea had taught him to adapt himself to any situation. Nevertheless, when late in the afternoon Mr. Bradley went to town on business, the young missionary gave a happy sigh of relief and decided to go out by himself and quietly pay his respects to the land of India.

Solemnly he left his airy room, which had neither door nor window but only large openings in every wall, and went outside. He was wearing a broad-brimmed hat with a long sun veil and holding a stout walking stick. At the first step into the garden he drew a deep breath and looked around him; with eager senses he drank in the air and the fragrances, lights and colors of the strange, legendary country, to whose conquest he was expected to make a modest contribution, and to which he was quite ready to abandon himself.

What he now saw and felt was very much to his liking and seemed to confirm his dreams and intimations a thousand times over. In the violent sunlight he saw tall dense bushes studded with large blossoms that struck him by the intensity of their color; he saw the smooth slender trunks of coconut trees culminating, at an amazing height, in the still, round crowns; behind the house there was a fan palm, stiffly holding out its astonishingly regular giant wheel of man-sized leaves. At the edge of the path his naturalist's eye perceived a little creature which he approached cautiously. It was a green chameleon with a small triangular head and malignant little eyes. As he bent down over it, he felt as happy as a small boy.

Strange music awakened him from his devout immersion. From the whispering stillness of the deep green wilderness of tree and garden there burst the rhythmic sound of trumpets and drums and piercingly high-pitched woodwinds. He listened in surprise, and since he could see nothing, started in the direction of the sound, curious to discover the nature and source of this festive barbaric music. He left the garden, whose gate was wide open, and followed the grassy road through a friendly landscape of gardens, palm groves, and smiling light-green rice fields, until, rounding the corner of a garden, he found himself in a villagelike alley bordered by Indian huts. The little houses were built of clay, or merely of bamboo poles, and roofed with dry palm leaves. In every doorway brown Hindu families were standing or squatting. He looked around him with curiosity; this was his first glimpse of the village life of these strange brown-skinned people;

their beautiful, childlike eyes were full of unconscious, unrelieved sadness, and from the very first he loved them. He saw lovely women with quiet, doelike eyes peering through masses of long deep-black plaited hair; they wore silver ornaments on their noses and on their wrists and ankles, and had rings on their toes. The children were naked except for silver or horn amulets hanging from their necks by thin strings of bast.

The wild music was still playing; it was now very near, and at the next street corner he found what he was look-ing for—a weird, fantastically shaped, frighteningly tall building with an enormous gate at the center. Looking up in amazement, he saw that the whole enormous façade, up to its fine, distant tip, was composed of stone figures representing fabulous animals, men, gods, and devils, a tangled forest of torsos, limbs, and heads. The terrifying stone colossus was a Hindu temple; as it lay gleaming in the level rays of the evening sun, it told the astonished newcomer very clearly that these half-naked people with their animallike gentleness were not the creatures of a primitive paradise, but had possessed ideas and gods, arts and religions for several thousand years.

The music fell silent, and from the temple emerged a throng of pious Indians in white and colored garments, led by a small group of grave Brahmans clearly set apart from the rest, the haughty bearers of an erudition and dignity that had frozen into set forms thousands of years before. They strode past the white man as nobles might stride past a common journeyman, and neither they nor the humble figures following them looked as if they had the slightest inclination to let a newly arrived foreigner instruct them in things divine or human.

When the crowd had dispersed and the street had grown quieter, Robert Aghion approached the temple and began with perplexed curiosity to study the figures of the façade, but soon gave up in dejection and terror, for the grotesque allegorical language of these sculptures con-fused and frightened him no less than the few shame-

lessly lewd scenes which he found naïvely depicted amid
the swarm of gods.

As he turned away and looked about him for the way
home, the temple and the street suddenly darkened; a
brief, quivering play of colors crossed the sky, and quickly
night fell. Though the young missionary had long been
familiar with this eerily sudden darkening, it sent a slight
shudder through him. With the deepening dusk thousands
of insects set up a strident singing and chirping in every
tree and bush round about, and in the distance he heard
the strange wild sound of an animal crying out with rage
or fear. Having luckily found the right way, Aghion hurried homeward. It was only a short distance, but by the
time he arrived the whole countryside was shrouded in
deep night and the high black sky was studded with stars.

Deep in thought he reached the house and made his
way to the first lighted room. Mr. Bradley was waiting for
him. "Ah," he said. "So there you are. You oughtn't to go
out so late in the evening. It's dangerous. Which reminds
me, can you handle a gun?"

"A gun? No. I've never learned to."

"Then you must learn soon . . . Where have you
been?"

Full of enthusiasm, Aghion told him what he had seen
and inquired eagerly to what religion this temple belonged,
what sort of gods or idols were worshiped there, what all
the carvings and the strange music meant, whether the
proud men in white garments were priests, and what gods
they served. But here he experienced his first disappointment. His mentor was not the least bit interested in such
things. No one, he said, could make head nor tail of these
idolatries, they were nothing but a hideous, obscene mud-
dle; the Brahmans were lazy, good-for-nothing exploiters,
the Indians in general were a swinish lot of beggars and
scoundrels, and if a self-respecting Englishman knew
what was good for him he would have nothing to do with
them.

"But," said Aghion uncertainly, "isn't it my mission to

show these misguided people the right way? If I'm to do that, mustn't I get acquainted with them and love them and know all about them—"

"You'll soon know more about them than you want to. Of course you must learn Hindustani and later on perhaps a few more of these beastly nigger languages. But when it comes to love, you won't get very far."

"But the people seemed inoffensive enough."

"Think so? Well, you'll see. I don't know what you're planning to do with the Hindus, and I can't judge. Our job is to bring this godless rabble a smattering of civilization and some conception of decency; I doubt if we ever get any further than that."

"But our morality, sir, or what you call decency, is the morality of Christ."

"You mean love? Well, just tell a Hindu you love him. Today he'll beg from you and tomorrow he'll steal your shirt out of your bedroom."

"Possibly."

"Definitely, my dear sir. The people you'll be dealing with here are irresponsible children; they still have no conception of honesty and right. They have nothing in common with our innocent English schoolchildren. No, they're a nation of sneaky brown brats, who are never happier than when they've committed some abomination. Mark my words!"

Sadly Aghion realized that further questioning would be useless; he resolved for the present to work hard, to do as he was told, and to learn as much as he could. But regardless of whether the stern Bradley was right or wrong, the mere sight of the prodigious temple and of the haughty, unapproachable Brahmans convinced Aghion that his work and mission in this country would be far more difficult than he had first thought.

Next morning the chests containing his belongings arrived. Carefully he unpacked, piling shirts on shirts and books on books. Some of the objects made him thoughtful: a small black-framed engraving—the glass had been

broken in transit—representing Mr. Defoe, the author of
Robinson Crusoe; his mother's old prayer book, familiar
to him since his earliest childhood; and encouraging tok-
ens of the future: a map of India given to him by his
uncle and two butterfly nets which he himself had had
made in London. One of these he set aside for use during
the next few days.

By evening his belongings had been sorted and stowed
away; he had hung the engraving over his bed, and the
whole room was in shipshape order. Following Bradley's
advice, he had set the legs of his table and bedstead in little earthenware bowls and filled the bowls with water as
a protection against ants. Mr. Bradley had been out on
business all day, and it seemed very strange to the young
man to be lured to meals by a sign from the servant and
to be waited on by this brown-skinned man with whom he
could not exchange a single word.

Next morning Aghion set to work. Bradley introduced
him to Vyardenya, the handsome dark-eyed young man
who was to teach him Hindustani. The smiling young Indian spoke English quite well and had the best of manners; but he shrank back in fright when the unsuspecting
Englishman held out his hand to him, and indeed avoided
all bodily contact with the white man, which would have
defiled him, since he was a member of a high caste. He
was even unwilling to sit on a chair that had been used by
a foreigner and each day brought with him, neatly rolled
under his arm, his own pretty bast mat, which he spread
out on the tile floor and sat on cross-legged and nobly
erect. His student, with whose zeal he had every reason to
be pleased, resolved to acquire this art, and during his
lessons sat beside him on a similar mat, though every
bone in his body ached until he had got used to it. Pa-
tiently and industriously, he learned word by word, beginning with the common formulas of greeting, which the
teacher smilingly repeated over and over again. Each day
Aghion flung himself with renewed courage into his struggle with the Indian palatals and gutturals, which at first

sounded to him like inarticulate gurgling but which he gradually learned to distinguish and imitate.

Interesting as the Hindustani language was and quickly as the morning hours passed with the courteous teacher, the afternoons and especially the evenings were long enough to make the ambitious young missionary aware of the solitude in which he was living. His host, whose relationship with him was ill-defined and whose manner toward him was half that of a patron and half that of a superior officer, was seldom at home; he usually came back from town at about noon, sometimes on foot and sometimes on horseback, and presided over the noonday meal, to which he occasionally invited an English clerk. Then he lay down on the veranda for two or three hours to smoke and to sleep. Toward evening he would go back to his office or warehouse for another few hours. From time to time he went off for several days to buy produce, which was no great blow to Aghion, who, try as he might, was unable to make friends with the gruff, taciturn businessman. Moreover, Bradley often conducted himself in a way that the missionary could not approve of, as for example when he would spend the evening drinking a mixture of water, rum, and lime juice with the clerk until they were both quite tipsy; at first he had invited the young clergyman to join them, but the answer had always been a gentle refusal.

Under these circumstances Aghion's daily life was not exactly amusing. In the long dreary afternoons when the wooden house was besieged by the searing heat, he had gone into the kitchen and tried to practice his first feeble knowledge of the language on the servants. The Moslem cook maintained a haughty silence and did not even seem to see Aghion, but the water carrier and the houseboy, who had nothing to do but squat idly on their mats chewing betel nuts, had no objection to amusing themselves over the young sahib's desperate efforts to make himself understood.

But one day Bradley appeared in the kitchen door just

as the two rascals were slapping their lean thighs with
pleasure at the missionary's mistakes. For a moment
Bradley looked on tight-lipped, then quick as a flash he
boxed the houseboy's ears, gave the water carrier a kick,
and without a word pulled the terrified Aghion into the
living room. "How often," he said angrily, "do I have to
tell you to keep away from the servants? You're spoiling
them, with the best of intentions, of course. Besides it
simply won't do for an Englishman to play the clown in
front of those brown scoundrels." And he left the room before Aghion could reply.

The only break in the missionary's solitude was on Sunday, when he went to church regularly; once he even de-
livered the sermon in place of the none too industrious
English parson. But though at home he had preached lovingly to the farm people and weavers, here, in a congrega-
tion of rich businessmen, tired sickly ladies, and gay
young clerks, he felt out of place, uninspired.

Often when he thought of his situation he felt depressed and sorry for himself, but there was one consolation that never failed him: his nature studies. He would
sling his specimen box over his shoulder and take his
butterfly net, which he had provided with a long, thin
bamboo pole. He delighted in the very things that most
Englishmen complained of most bitterly, the blazing hot
sun and the Indian climate in general, for he had kept
himself fresh in body and soul. To the naturalist this
country was an immeasurable treasure trove; at every
step unknown trees, flowers, birds, and insects caught his
attention, and he resolved that in time he would learn to
know them all by name. By then the strange lizards and
scorpions, the great centipedes and other monsters seldom frightened him, and since he had intrepidly killed a
fat snake in the bathroom with a wooden bucket, he felt
that he had little to fear from even the most forbidding of
animals.

When for the first time he swung his net at a magnificent large butterfly, when he saw he had captured it and

carefully took hold of the radiant proud creature, whose
broad wings glittered like alabaster beneath a vaporous
downy film of color, his heart beat with an impetuous joy
that he had not experienced since he had captured his
first swallow's nest as a boy. He cheerfully accepted the
hardships of the jungle; he did not lose heart when he
sank into hidden mud holes, when he was mocked by
howling troops of monkeys, or attacked by enraged
swarms of ants. Only once was he really afraid—when
with the sound of a storm or an earthquake a herd of elephants came rumbling through the dense woods, and he
cowered, trembling and praying, behind a great rubber
tree. In his airy bedroom he got used to the furious chat-
tering of the monkeys that woke him up in the morning
and to the howling of the jackals at night. His eyes shone
bright and alert in his sun-tanned face, which had grown
leaner and more manly.

He also explored the city, and especially the peaceful
gardenlike villages round about, and the more he saw of
the Hindus the better he liked them. The one thing that
distressed him was that the women of the lower castes
tended to go about naked from the waist up. Though it
was often a lovely sight, the missionary found it very hard
to get used to seeing women's bare throats, arms, and
breasts on the street.

Apart from this stumbling block nothing gave him so
much food for thought as the enigma of these people's
spiritual life. Wherever he looked, he saw religion. Assur-
edly one would not see so much piety in London on the
highest Church holiday as here on every weekday; on
every hand there were temples and sacred images, prayer
and sacrifices, processions and ceremonies, penitents and
priests. But how could anyone find his way in this tangle
of faiths? There were Brahmans and Moslems, fire worshipers and Buddhists, devotees of Shiva and of Krishna;
there were turbans and smooth-shaved heads, worshipers
of snakes and worshipers of holy tortoises. What god did
all these misguided souls serve? What sort of god was he,

and which of all these many cults was the oldest, holiest, and purest? No one knew, and especially to the Indians themselves it was a matter of total indifference; if a man was not satisfied with the faith of his fathers, he took up another, or went out as a penitent to find, if not to found, another religion. Food was offered up in little bowls to gods and spirits whose names no one knew, and all these hundreds of religions, temples, and priesthoods lived cheerfully side by side; never did it occur to the adherents of one faith to hate or kill those of another, as was customary in the Christian countries of Europe. Much of what he found was lovely and charming, the playing of flutes, for example, or the flower offerings, and on many pious faces there was a peace and a serene light that one would have sought in vain on English faces. Another thing that struck him as beautiful and holy was the commandment, strictly observed by the Hindus, not to kill any living thing, and sometimes he felt ashamed and in need of self-justification when he had mercilessly killed a beautiful butterfly or beetle and mounted it on a pin. Yet among these same peoples, who looked upon the lowliest worm as God's creature and therefore sacred, and who showed the most fervent devotion in their prayers and temple services, theft and falsehood, perjury and breach of trust were everyday matters that aroused no indignation or even surprise in anyone. The more the well-intentioned apostle pondered, the more these people struck him as an impenetrable riddle, defying all logic and theory. Despite Bradley's prohibition he had resumed his conversations with the houseboy. At one moment they had seemed the best of friends, but an hour later the boy had stolen one of his shirts. When earnestly and lovingly called to account, the servant first protested his innocence but soon smilingly confessed and brought back the shirt. There was a small hole in it, he explained, so he had felt sure that the sahib would not want to wear it.

On another occasion the water carrier filled him with astonishment. This man received board and wages for providing the kitchen and bathroom with water from the nearest cistern. He performed his daily task in the morning and in the evening; the rest of the day he sat in the kitchen or in the servants' hut, chewing betel or a stick of sugarcane. Once when the other servant had gone out, Aghion, whose trousers were covered with grass seed after one of his walks, asked the water carrier to brush them. The man only laughed and thrust his hands behind his back. The missionary became angry and ordered him to do as he was told. At that he complied, but grumbling and in tears; when he had finished he looked very unhappy and sat there muttering and expostulating for a whole hour. With great difficulty Aghion threaded his way through a series of misunderstandings and finally discovered that he had gravely offended the man by ordering him to do work incompatible with his position.

All these little experiences gradually condensed into an invisible wall that separated the missionary from his surroundings and left him more and more painfully alone. In his desperation he flung himself all the more eagerly into his language lessons and made good progress in the fervent hope of gaining access to this strange people. More and more often he ventured to speak to natives in the street; he went to the tailor's, the clothier's, the shoemaker's without an interpreter. Now and then he succeeded in striking up a conversation by such stratagems as complimenting a craftsman on his work or a mother on her baby; and often, through the words and glances of these heathen and in particular through their good, childlike laughter, their soul spoke to him so clearly and fraternally that for moments at a time all barriers vanished and he lost his feeling of strangeness.

After a while he gained the impression that most children and simple country people were accessible to him and that what came between him and the city people was the distrust and depravity they had acquired from contact with European sailors and businessmen. He began to venture farther and farther into the country, often

on horseback, taking with him copper coins and sometimes lumps of sugar for the children. Deep in the hills
he would hitch his horse to a palm tree, enter a peasant's
mud hut, and ask for a drink of water or coconut milk.
Almost always a friendly conversation ensued; men,
women, and children would join in, and he was not at all
displeased when they laughed merrily in their candid
amazement at his still imperfect knowledge of the language.

He made no attempt to speak of God. Not only did it
seem to him that there was no hurry; he also discovered
that it was a thorny, well-nigh impossible undertaking,
for he simply could find no words in Hindustani for the
most common Christian concepts. Moreover, he felt that
he would have no right to set himself up as these people's
teacher and bid them make important changes in their
way of life until he knew all about this way of life and
could live and speak with the Hindus on a more or less
equal footing.

This enlarged the sphere of his studies. He learned all
he could about the life and work of the natives; he asked
them about trees and fruits, domestic animals and implements and made a point of learning their names; little
by little he fathomed the secrets of wet and dry rice culture, of cotton growing and the preparation of bast; he
watched builders, potters, and straw plaiters at work, and
took a special interest in wool weaving, a craft with which
he was familiar at home. He looked on as the fat, rose-red
water buffaloes drew plows through muddy rice paddies,
he watched domesticated elephants at work, and saw tame
monkeys bring coconuts down from the trees for their
masters.

On one of his excursions, which took him to a peaceful
valley between high green hills, he was surprised by a
sudden downpour and sought shelter in the first hut he
could reach. In the small room with its mud-covered bamboo walls he found a little family, which greeted him with
awe-struck amazement. The mother had dyed her gray

hair a flaming red with henna, and as she turned to the stranger with the most hospitable of smiles she showed him a mouth full of equally red teeth, revealing her weakness for betel nuts. Her husband was a tall, grave-faced man whose long hair was still black. He rose from the ground, assumed a royally erect posture, exchanged greetings with the guest, and offered him a freshly opened coconut. The Englishman took a swallow of the sweetish milk. A little boy who had fled into the corner behind the stone fireplace peered out at him from under his glistening black hair with frightened, curious eyes; he was naked except for a glittering brass amulet on his dark chest. Several large bunches of bananas had been hung up over the door to ripen; what light there was in the hut came from the open doorway, but there was no sign of poverty, only an extreme simplicity and a pleasant order and cleanliness.

A quiet homelike feeling, rising from remote childhood memories—the kind of feeling that tends to come over a wanderer at the sight of a contented household and that he had never experienced in Mr. Bradley's bungalow—descended on the missionary. It almost seemed to him that in this house he had not only found refuge from the rain, but that, having been lost in the dark labyrinths of life, he had at last found the light and joy of an authentic, natural, self-sufficient way of life. The rain drummed furiously on the reed roof and in the doorway formed a sheet as thick and smooth as a glass wall.

The old people chatted with their unusual guest and when at length they politely asked the natural question—what had he come to this country for?—he felt uncomfortable and changed the subject. Once again it struck the modest young man as monstrously presumptuous that he should have come here as the envoy of a faraway nation to take away these people's faith and impose another upon them. He had always thought his misgivings would evaporate once he learned the language; but today it became clear to him beyond the shadow of a doubt that this had been a delusion and that the better he understood these brown people the less right and inclination he would feel to tell them how to live.

The rain abated and the water, turbid with red clay, drained from the sloping path; sunbeams forced their way between the glistening wet palm trunks and were reflected with dazzling brightness on the great shiny leaves of the pisang trees. The missionary thanked his hosts and was preparing to leave when a shadow fell across the floor and the room darkened. Quickly he turned around and saw a figure, a girl or young woman, step soundlessly through the doorway. Startled at the unexpected sight, she fled behind the fireplace, where the little boy was hiding.

"Bid the gentleman good day," her father called out to her. Shyly she took two steps forward, crossed her hands before her breasts, and bowed several times. Raindrops shimmered in her thick deep-black hair; embarrassed, the Englishman set his hand gently on her head and pronounced a greeting. He felt the soft, living hair in his fingers. A reddish-brown cloth was knotted below her breasts, otherwise she wore nothing except for a coral necklace and on one ankle a heavy gold bangle. Thus she stood in her beauty before the astonished stranger; the sun shone softly on her hair and on her smooth brown shoulders, and her teeth sparkled in her young mouth. Robert Aghion was enchanted at the sight: he tried to look deep into her gentle, quiet eyes, but then quickly he grew flustered; the moist fragrance of her hair and the sight of her bare shoulders and breasts confused him, and he cast down his eyes. He reached into his pocket, took out a pair of steel scissors which he used for his nails and beard and also for cutting plants, and gave them to the lovely girl, well aware that he was making her a sumptuous gift. Surprised and pleased, she took them shyly, while her parents poured forth thanks. When he left the hut after bidding the family goodbye, she followed him outside, took his left hand, and kissed it. The warm tender touch of her flowerlike lips sent his blood coursing, he would have liked to kiss her on the mouth. Instead he took both her hands in his right hand, looked into her eyes, and asked: "How old are you?"

"I don't know," she said.

"What's your name then?"

"Naissa."

"Goodbye, Naissa, and don't forget me."

"Naissa will not forget the gentleman."

Deep in thought, he set out for home. He arrived after dark. Only as he entered his room did it come to him that he had not brought home a single butterfly or beetle, a single leaf or flower. His lodgings, the gloomy bachelor's house with its idle servants and the cold morose Mr. Bradley, had never seemed so alien and dismal as in that evening hour when he sat at the wobbly table, trying to read the Bible by his little oil lamp.

That night, when he finally fell asleep despite the turmoil of his thoughts and the buzzing of the mosquitoes, the missionary was beset by strange dreams.

He was walking through a darkening palm grove. Yellow flecks of sunlight were playing over the red-brown ground. Parrots were crying out overhead; high, high up in the trees monkeys were performing intrepid gymnastic feats; little birds glittered like jewels, insects of every kind proclaimed their joy of life in sounds, colors, and movements. As he walked amid this splendor, the missionary was filled with happiness and gratitude; he called out to one of the simian acrobats, and lo and behold, the agile creature climbed obediently down to the ground, and stood before Aghion like a servant, making gestures of devotion. Aghion realized that all the creatures in this enchanted place were his to command. He summoned the birds and butterflies, and they came in great glittering swarms; he waved and beat time with his hands, nodded his head, gave orders by clicking his tongue and looking this way and that, and all the glorious creatures arranged themselves in the golden air into hovering rounds and processions; they piped and hummed, chirped and trilled

in delicate chorus, pursued and caught one another, described solemn circles and droll spirals in the air. It was
a magnificent ballet and concert, a paradise regained; yet
the dreamer's joy in this harmonious magical world, which
obeyed him and belonged to him, was tinged with pain.
Deep within his happiness there lurked a faint foreboding,
a suspicion that all this was undeserved and must pass
away, for how can a pious missionary feel otherwise in the
presence of sensuous pleasure?

Nor did his foreboding deceive him. Even as he was
reveling in the sight of a monkey quadrille and stroking
a great blue velvet butterfly, which had settled trustingly
on his left hand and was letting itself be caressed like a
dove, shadows of fear and desolation came fluttering
through the magic grove to darken the dreamer's soul. A
bird cried out in sudden terror, a fitful wind roared
through the treetops, the joyful warm sunlight grew dim
and pale. Soon all the birds darted off, the lovely great
butterflies, defenseless in their terror, were carried away
by the wind, and raindrops splashed angrily on the foliage. Faint thunder rumbled across the sky and died away
in the distance.

And then Mr. Bradley appeared. The last bright bird
had vanished. As gigantic and somber as the ghost of a
slain king, Bradley spat contemptuously and poured forth
a stream of angry, scornful, insulting words: Aghion was
a lazy scoundrel; his patron in London was paying him to
convert the heathen, and instead he loafed and roamed
about the country looking for bugs. Bowed with contrition,
Aghion was forced to admit that Bradley was right, that
he had neglected his duties.

Thereupon, the great rich patron from England, Aghion's employer, and several English clergymen appeared;
along with Bradley, they harried and drove the missionary
through thicket and brier, until they came to a bristling
street in the suburbs of Bombay, and there lay the towering, grotesque Hindu temple. A motley crowd poured in
and out, naked coolies and proud white-clad Brahmans.

But across from the temple the dreamer saw a Christian church, and above the door there was an immense stone carving of God, hovering in the clouds with a flowing beard and grave fatherly eyes.

The harried missionary climbed the steps of the church, held out his arms to the Hindus, and began to preach. In a loud voice he called upon them to look and compare, to observe how different the true God was from their wretched grimacing idols with all their countless arms and elephant trunks. He pointed a finger at the tangled figures on the façade of the Indian temple, and then with a gesture of invitation at the divine image on his church. But terror seized him when, following his own gesture, he looked up; for God had changed, he had acquired three heads and six arms, and in place of his rather idiotic and ineffectual solemnity, his faces had taken on the knowing smile that is often seen on the images of the Indian gods. Faltering, the preacher looked about him for Bradley, his patron, and the clergymen, but they had all vanished; he was alone and helpless on the church steps, and now God too forsook him, for he was waving his six arms in the direction of the temple and smiling at the Hindu gods with divine serenity.

Utterly forsaken and disgraced, Aghion stood on the church steps. He closed his eyes and held himself erect; all hope was gone; he waited with the calm of despair for the heathen to stone him. But after a few anguished moments, he felt himself thrust aside by a strong but gentle hand, and when he opened his eyes, he saw the great stone God striding down the steps with dignity, while across the way the divine figures descended in swarms from their places on the façade of the temple. After greeting them one and all, God entered the Hindu temple, where with a kindly gesture he received the homage of the white-clad Brahmans. Meanwhile the heathen gods with their trunks, ringlets, and slit eyes went into the church, where they found everything to their liking. Many of the devout folk followed them, and in the end gods and people were moving in pious procession from church to temple and from temple to church; gong and organ mingled fraternally, and dark, silent Indians offered up lotus blossoms on sober English-Christian altars.

In the midst of the festive crowd the dreamer saw the lovely Naissa with her smooth, glistening black hair and her childlike eyes. Surrounded by a throng of the faithful, she came from the temple, mounted the steps of the church, and stood before the missionary. She looked gravely and lovingly into his eyes, nodded to him, and held out a lotus blossom. In a surge of delight he bent down over her clear quiet face, kissed her on the lips, and enfolded her in his arms.

Before he had time to hear what Naissa might have to say about that, Aghion woke from his dream and found himself stretched out on his bed in deep darkness, exhausted and terrified. A painful confusion of all his feelings and impulses tormented him to the point of despair. His dream had laid bare his own self, his weakness and faintheartedness, his lack of faith in his mission, his love for the brown heathen girl, his un-Christian hatred of Bradley, and his guilty conscience toward his English patron.

For a time he lay forlornly in the darkness, overwrought and on the verge of tears. He tried to pray but couldn't; he tried to think of Naissa as a demon and of his love as a sin, but that too was impossible. At length, following a half-conscious impulse, still immersed in the shadows and terrors of his dream, he arose and went to Bradley's room, driven as much by an instinctive need for a human presence as by a pious wish to repent of his revulsion for this man, to speak frankly with him and make a friend of him.

He crept silently across the dark veranda on thin bast soles. The bamboo door to Bradley's room reached only halfway up the frame, and Aghion saw that the room was dimly lighted. Like many Europeans in India Bradley was in the habit of leaving a small oil lamp lighted all night. Cautiously Aghion pushed the flimsy door and went in.

The wick smoldered in an earthenware bowl on the floor, casting great dim shadows on the bare walls. A brown moth whirred around the flame. The mosquito net had been carefully drawn around the large bed. The missionary picked up the lamp, approached the bed, and opened the netting by a hand's breadth. He was just about to call the speaker by name when to his consternation he saw that Bradley was not alone. He was lying on his back in a thin silk nightdress, and his face with its jutting chin looked no softer or friendlier than by day. And beside him lay a second figure, a woman with long black hair. She was lying on her side, her face turned toward the missionary, and he recognized her; she was the big strapping girl who called for the washing each week.

Without stopping to close the netting, Aghion fled to his room. He tried to get back to sleep, but in vain; the day's experience, his dream, and finally the sight of the naked, sleeping woman had thoroughly roused him. His revulsion for Bradley had grown so strong that he dreaded the moment when he would have to see him and speak to him at breakfast. But what tormented him most was the question: was it his duty to reprimand Bradley for his conduct and try to reform him? Aghion's whole nature said no, but it seemed incumbent on him as a clergyman to overcome his cowardice and call the sinner to account. He lit his lamp and, plagued by the buzzing gnats, read the New Testament for several hours, but found no certainty or consolation. He was close to cursing all India, or at least his curiosity and spirit of adventure that had led him into this blind alley. Never had the future looked so dark and never had he felt so little cut out for an apostle and martyr.

His eyes were hollow and his features drawn when he went to breakfast. He stirred his fragrant tea morosely, broke off a banana and toyed with the peel until Mr. Bradley appeared. The master of the house muttered his usual "good morning," and set the houseboy and the water carrier in motion with loud commands. Slowly and circumspectly he picked the most perfect banana from the bunch and ate it quickly and haughtily, while the servant led his horse into the sunny yard.

"There's a matter I should like to discuss with you," said the missionary when Bradley was on the point of leaving. Bradley looked up suspiciously.

"I haven't much time. Does it have to be just now?"

"Yes, I believe so. I consider it my duty to tell you that I know of your illicit relations with a Hindu woman. You can imagine how painful it is for me—"

Bradley jumped up and burst into an angry laugh. "Painful!" he cried. "Aghion, you're a bigger fool than I thought. Obviously I don't give a damn what you think of me, but for you to nose around my house and spy on me is contemptible. I won't have it. I'll give you until Sunday. By then you'll kindly find yourself new lodgings. I won't keep you here a day longer."

Aghion had expected a sharp reply, but not this. Nevertheless, he was not to be intimidated.

"I shall be glad," he said with composure, "to relieve you of my burdensome presence. Good morning, Mr. Bradley!"

He walked out and Bradley looked after him, half-dismayed and half-amused. Then he stroked his stiff mustache, puckered up his mouth, whistled for his dog, and went down the wooden stairs to the yard, where his horse was waiting.

The brief, stormy exchange had come as a relief to both men; it cleared the air. Aghion, to be sure, found himself suddenly faced with problems which only a short while before had been pleasantly remote. But the more he pondered, the more clearly he saw that, though his quarrel with Bradley had been incidental, it had now become necessary for him to do something about the confusion of his affairs, and the thought cheered him. Life in this house, the empty hours, his unfilled desires, the want of an outlet for his energies, had become a torment which his simple, straightforward nature could not have borne much longer in any case.

It was still early in the morning, and a corner of the garden, his favorite spot, was still shady and cool. The branches of the untended bushes hung down over a small masonry pool which had originally been built for bathing but after long neglect had now become the home of a tribe of yellow turtles. He moved his bamboo reclining chair beside it, lay down, and watched the silent creatures swimming lazily about in the tepid green water, peering about them with their shrewd little eyes. In the yard nearby the stable boy was squatting idly in his corner, singing. The monotonous nasal song sounded like ripples ebbing away in the balmy air. Before he knew it, Aghion was overcome with weariness after his agitated, sleepless night; he closed his eyes, his arms drooped, and he fell asleep.

Awakened by the sting of a gnat, he saw to his shame that he had slept away most of the morning. But he felt refreshed and began at once to put his thoughts and desires in order, and calmly to unravel the tangled skein of his life. And now he knew, beyond any possible doubt, what had been paralyzing him and giving him anguished dreams: that though his coming to India had been a good and wise decision he lacked the inner vocation and drive to be a missionary. He was modest enough to regard this as a defeat and as a distressing shortcoming; but he saw no ground for despair. Quite to the contrary, now that he had made up his mind to find more suitable work, he was truly able to look upon India, with its immeasurable riches, as a promising haven and home. Unfortunate as it might be that all these natives had given themselves to false gods, it was not up to him to alter the fact. It was up to him to conquer this country for himself, to glean what was best in it for himself and others by bringing his practiced eye, his knowledge, and his youthful energy to bear, and by willingly accepting what hard work should present itself.

That very afternoon, after a brief interview, he was engaged by a Mr. Sturrock, a resident of Bombay, as secretary and overseer of a nearby coffee plantation. Aghion wrote a letter to his former patron, explaining his decision and undertaking to repay the money he had received, and Sturrock promised to forward it to London. When the new overseer returned home, he found Bradley alone at the dinner table, in his shirt sleeves. Before even sitting down, Aghion told him what he had done that day.

With his mouth full, Bradley nodded, poured a little whiskey into his drinking water, and said almost amiably: "Sit down and help yourself; the fish is cold. You could almost call us colleagues now. Well, I wish you luck. It's easier to raise coffee than to convert Hindus, no doubt about that, and for all I know it's just as useful. I wouldn't have given you credit for so much sense, Aghion."

The plantation that was to be his new home was two days' journey inland. Aghion was to set out in two days with a group of coolies, which left him only a day in which to attend to his affairs. Aghion asked leave to take a horse the following morning, and though surprised, Bradley asked no questions. After he had bidden the servant take away the lamp with its thousands of whirring insects, the two men sat facing each other in the warm balmy evening and felt closer to one another than they had in all their many months of forced cohabitation.

"Tell me something," Aghion began after a long silence. "Did you ever really believe in my plans to become a missionary?"

"Of course," said Bradley calmly. "I could see you were serious about it."

"But you must have seen how unfit I was for the work. Why didn't you tell me?"

"I had no instructions to do that. I don't like people meddling in my business, and I don't poke my nose into theirs. Besides, I've seen people do the craziest things here in India and succeed. Converting the heathen was your affair, not mine. And now you've seen your mistake all by yourself. In time you'll see others."

"For instance?"

"For instance, about that lecture you gave me this morning."

"Oh, the girl."

"Yes. You were a clergyman; but you'll have to admit that a normal man can't live and work and keep his health for years without having a woman now and then. Good God, there's nothing to blush about. Look: a white man in India, who hasn't brought a wife over with him from England, hasn't got much choice. There are no English girls. The ones that are born here are sent back to England when they're little. We can only choose between sailors' whores and Hindu women, and I prefer the Hindu women. What's so bad about that?"

"On that score we don't agree, Mr. Bradley. I stand with the Bible and our Church, which declare all relations with women out of wedlock to be evil and wrong."

"But if we can't get anything else?"

"Why not? If a man really loves a girl, he should marry her."

"A Hindu girl?"

"Why not?"

"Aghion, you're more broad-minded than I am. I'd sooner bite off my finger than marry a colored woman. And you'll feel the same way about it later on."

"Oh, no, I hope not. As long as we've got this far, I may as well tell you: I love a Hindu girl and I intend to make her my wife."

Bradley's face grew grave. "Don't do it," he said almost imploringly.

"But I will!" cried Aghion with enthusiasm. "We'll become engaged, and then I'll teach her and guide her until she can be baptized; and then we'll be married in the English church."

"What's her name?" Bradley asked thoughtfully.

"Naissa."

"And her father's?"

"I don't know."

"Well, it will take some time before she's ready for baptism; in the meanwhile think it over. Of course an Englishman can fall in love with an Indian girl, a lot of them are pretty enough. And they're said to be faithful and to make good wives. But I still can't help regarding them as animals, more like playful antelopes or pretty does than human beings."

"Isn't that a prejudice? All men are brothers, and the Indians are an old and noble people."

"You know more about that than I do, Aghion. But for my part, I have a good deal of respect for prejudices."

He stood up, said good night, and went to his bedroom, where the night before he had slept with the pretty laundry woman. "Animals," he had said, and as Aghion thought about it now, his heart rebelled.

Early next morning, before Bradley was up, Aghion sent for his horse and rode off. The monkeys were still screaming their morning concert in the treetops. The sun was still low in the sky as he neared the hut where he had met the pretty Naissa. He tied up his mount and approached on foot. The little boy was sitting naked on the threshold, playing with a young goat and laughing as it butted him in the chest.

Just as the visitor was turning off the path, a girl, whom he recognized immediately as Naissa, came from inside the hut and stepped over the little boy. Carrying a tall earthenware pitcher in her right hand, she passed Aghion without seeming to notice him, and he delightedly followed her. He quickly caught up with her and called out a greeting. She answered in a soft voice, raised her head, and looked at him calmly out of her lovely golden-brown eyes, giving no sign of recognition. When he took her hand, she withdrew as though frightened, and hurried on her way. He followed her to the brick basin fed by a meager spring, whose water came trickling over old, moss-

covered stones; he tried to help her fill the pitcher and lift
it up, but she silently resisted, and the look on her face
was cold and unfriendly. Surprised and disappointed at
so much coyness, he reached into his pocket for the gift
he had brought her, and all in all he felt rather hurt when
she immediately dropped her reserve and reached for it.
The gift was a small enameled box with flowers prettily
painted on it and a mirror on the inside of the round lid.
He showed her how to open it and put it into her hand.

"For me?" she asked, with great childlike eyes.

"For you," he said, and while she played with the box,
he stroked her velvet-soft arm and her long black hair.

She thanked him and with an uncertain gesture picked
up the pitcher. He tried to say something tender and loving, which apparently she only half understood. As he
stood beside her, groping helplessly for words, he was suddenly struck by the enormity of the gulf between them.
He reflected sadly on how little they had in common and
how very, very long it would be before she could ever be
his bride and companion, before she could understand his
language, know him for what he was, and share his
thoughts.

Meanwhile she had started slowly back to the hut, and
he walked beside her. The little boy was engaged in a
breathless game of tag with the goat; his black-brown back
shimmered like metal in the sun, and his rice-bloated belly
made his legs look scrawny. For a brief moment the Englishman was appalled when it came to him that if he married Naissa this child of nature would be his brother-in-
law. To divert his mind from such thoughts, he looked at
the girl again, at her entrancingly fine face with its great
eyes and cool childlike lips. And he could not help wondering whether he would succeed in obtaining a first kiss
from those lips that very day.

He was shaken out of his tender reverie by a figure
which suddenly emerged from the hut and stood like a
ghost before his incredulous eyes. The form that appeared
in the door frame, crossed the threshold, and stood be-

fore him was a second Naissa, a mirror image of the first. The mirror image smiled at him and greeted him, reached into her loincloth, and produced an object which she triumphantly raised over her head. It glistened in the sun and in a moment he recognized it. It was the little pair of scissors he had given Naissa, and the girl to whom he had just given the little box, into whose lovely eyes he had gazed and whose arm he had caressed, was not Naissa, but her sister. As the two girls stood side by side, still barely distinguishable, the lover felt infinitely cheated and lost. Two fawns could not have looked more alike, and if in that moment he had been left free to choose one of them and take her away with him and keep her forever, he would not have known which one he loved. He soon saw, to be sure, that the real Naissa was the older of the two, and somewhat smaller than her sister; but his love, which he had been so sure of only a few minutes past, had broken into two halves, just like his image of the girl, which had doubled so unexpectedly and eerily before his eyes.

Bradley learned nothing of this incident and asked no questions when Aghion returned home at noon and silently sat down at the table. Next morning Aghion's coolies came for his chests and sacks. When Aghion thanked Bradley for everything and held out his hand, Bradley shook it heartily and said: "Pleasant journey, my boy. A time will come when you will be sick of those sweet Hindu mugs and long for an honest, leathery face. When that happens, come and see me; we still disagree about a good many things, but then we'll see eye to eye."

The Cyclone

1913

I N THE MID-NINETIES I was doing volunteer work in a
small factory in my home town, which I was to leave
forever before the year was out. I was eighteen, I had no
suspicion of how wonderful my youth was, though I relished it each day and felt its touch as a bird feels the air.

Older people tend in their recollections to confuse one
year with another; I need only remind them that in the
year I am speaking of our region was struck by a cyclone
or hurricane, the like of which has never been seen in our
country before or since. It was that year. Two or three
days before, I had driven a chisel into my left hand. It
had left a deep cut and the wound was badly swollen; I
had to wear a bandage and was forbidden to go to work.

I can remember that throughout the late summer the
air in our narrow valley was incredibly sultry. For days
on end one storm followed another. All nature was restless with the heat; though I myself was affected only
dimly and unconsciously, I clearly recall the signs of this
restlessless around me. In the evening, for example, when
I went fishing, I found the fish strangely agitated by the
heaviness in the air; they knotted together in chaotic
swarms, often leaping out of the tepid water or flinging
themselves blindly at my hook. Then at last the weather
became somewhat cooler and more settled, the storms
were less frequent, and early in the morning there was a
faint smell of autumn.

One morning I left the house and went out in pursuit
of pleasure, with a book and a crust of bread in my pocket.
As I had done as a boy, I first went behind the house to

the garden, which was still in the shade. The fir trees which my father had planted and which I myself had known as frail saplings were now tall and sturdy; under them lay piles of light-brown needles, and for years nothing but evergreen had consented to grow there. But beside the garden my mother's shrubs grew lush and cheerful in a long narrow border, and every Sunday big bouquets were picked from them. One of these shrubs had clusters of small cinnabar-red flowers, it was called Cross of Jerusalem; there was a slender bush with innumerable heart-shaped red and white blossoms hanging on thin stems, these were called bleeding hearts; and another of the plants was known as stinking vainglory. Nearby there were long-stemmed asters, which were not yet in bloom, and crawling on the ground in between, fleshy white-thorned house leeks and droll purslane. That little bed was our favorite, our dream garden, because in it so many strange flowers, which struck our fancy more than the roses in the two round beds, grew side by side. When the sun glittered on the ivy-covered wall, every bush had its own special beauty; the bright-colored gladioli swaggered, the heliotropes stood gray as though enchanted, immersed in their sorrowful fragrance, the fading foxtail hung its head in resignation, but the columbine stood up on tiptoe, ringing its fourfold summer bells. The bees buzzed loudly in the goldenrod and blue phlox, and little brown spiders raced back and forth over the dense ivy; those quick, capriciously whirring butterflies with stout bodies and glassy wings, known as hawkmoths or swallowtails, quivered in midair over the gillyflowers.

In my holiday well-being I went from one flower to another, sniffed here and there at a fragrant cluster or opened a calyx with cautious fingers, so as to look into the mysterious, pale-colored depths at the quiet order of veins and pistils, soft threads and crystalline grooves. In between flowers I studied the cloudy morning sky with its strange confusion of fluffy clouds and tenuous wisps of mist. I expected a storm, and decided to go fishing for a few hours in the afternoon. In the hope of finding worms, I eagerly rolled a few stones away from the border of the path, but instead of worms swarms of gray, dry woodlice came scurrying out and fled frantically in all directions.

I cast about for something to do, and for the moment nothing occurred to me. A year before, on my previous vacation, I had still been a boy. My favorite occupations then had been shooting at a target with a hazel-wood bow, flying kites, and blowing up mouseholes in the fields with gunpowder. All that had lost its charm and glamour, as though a part of me had grown tired and no longer responded to the voices that had formerly been dear to me and given me pleasure.

Surprised and vaguely dejected, I looked about me in the old familiar precinct of my boyhood pleasures. The little garden, the flower-adorned balconies, and the damp sunless yard with its moss-green flagstones showed me a different face than before, and even the flowers had lost a little of their inexhaustible magic. The water barrel stood modest and uninteresting in a corner of the garden. Formerly, to my father's dismay, I had let the water run for hours at a time, operating wooden mill wheels and provoking great floods with the help of the canals and dams I had built on the garden path. The weather-beaten water barrel had been a loyal friend and entertainer, and when I looked at it now, an echo of my childhood joys stirred within me, but carried a note of sadness; the barrel had ceased to be a fountain, a river, a Niagara Falls.

Deep in thought, I climbed over the fence. A blue morning glory grazed my face; I snapped it off and took the stem between my teeth. I had decided to take a walk, to climb the mountain and look down at our town. Taking a walk was a mixed pleasure, the kind of undertaking that would never have entered my head in former days. A boy does not take a walk. He goes to the woods as a robber, a knight, or an Indian; he goes to the river as a raftsman or fisherman or builder of mills; he takes to the fields to hunt lizards or butterflies. My walk struck me as the dignified, rather tedious occupation of a grown-up who doesn't quite know what to do with himself.

My blue morning glory soon withered; I had thrown it away and now I was nibbling at a twig I had torn off a boxwood; it had a bitter, spicy taste. Near the tall broom bushes by the railroad tracks, a green lizard slipped away at my approach. At that the boy in me awakened; I ran and crept and lurked until I held the sun-warm, frightened creature in my hands. I looked into his little jewel-bright eyes and with a vestige of my old hunter's joy felt the supple, powerful body and the hard legs struggling between my fingers. But then my pleasure was exhausted and I could think of nothing more to do with the imprisoned animal. It meant nothing to me, there was no more happiness in it. I bent down and opened my hand. For a moment the lizard, surprised, lay still with heaving flanks, then it darted eagerly into the grass. A train came and went on the glittering steel rails. I looked after it. For a moment I saw clearly that this place held no more true pleasure for me, and I would have given anything to be on the train, riding out into the world.

I looked around to make sure no railroad guard was watching. Seeing and hearing nothing, I ran across the tracks. On the other side there was a high red sandstone cliff with blackened hollows where the rock had been blasted away by the railroad builders. I knew the way and started to climb, holding fast to tufts of broom, whose flowers were already fading. The red stone breathed a dry, sunny warmth, the hot sand dripped into my sleeves, and when I looked upward the warm, gleaming sky seemed astonishingly solid and close to the vertical stone wall. When I reached the top, I leaned forward, propping myself on the flat stone, and clutching the thin, thorny trunk of a locust tree, pulled my legs up after me. I was standing on a steep meadow.

This little wilderness high above the railroad tracks had always been one of my favorite retreats. In addition to the tough rank grass that could not be mowed, there were little rose bushes with fine thorns and a few stunted locust trees sown by the wind, through whose thin, transparent leaves the sun filtered. On this grassy island, bounded at the upper end by a chain of red cliffs, I had lived the life of Robinson Crusoe. This lonely spot belonged to no one but the adventurous spirit with the courage to conquer it by scaling the cliff. Here at the age of twelve I had incised my name in stone with a chisel; here I had read *Rosa von Tannenburg* and written a childish play about the brave chief of a dying Indian tribe.

On the steep slope the sun-parched grass hung down in pale strands, the sun-drenched broom smelled sharp and bitter in the still heat. I stretched out in the dry grass, looked up at the delicate, pedantically ordered leaves of the locust trees, sun-bright against the deep-blue sky, and pondered. It was time, I thought, to survey my life and my future.

But I could discover nothing new. I saw only the strange impoverishment that threatened me from all sides. In some mysterious way trusted pleasures and thoughts that had become dear to me were paling and fading. My profession could not make up for what I was reluctantly leaving behind, for all the lost joys of boyhood; it held no great appeal for me and I was to abandon it before long. It meant no more to me than a way into the world, which I felt sure would offer me new satisfactions. But what would they be?

I would be able to see the world and make money, I would be able to do as I pleased without consulting my father and mother, I would be able to bowl and drink beer on Sunday. But all these things, I was well aware, were secondary; they were not the meaning of the new life that awaited me. The meaning lay elsewhere, it was something more profound, more beautiful and mysterious, connected no doubt with girls and with love. A profound pleasure and satisfaction, I felt, must be hidden in that quarter; otherwise the sacrifice of my boyhood joys would be pointless.

I knew something about love, I had seen loving couples and read intoxicating love poems. I myself had fallen in love several times and in dreams experienced some notion of the bliss for which a man stakes his life and which becomes the goal of all his strivings. Some of my classmates were already going with girls, and at the factory I had friends who spoke unabashedly of their adventures at Sunday dances and of climbing into young ladies' windows at night. But for me love was still a closed garden, at whose gate I waited with timid longing.

The first clear call had come to me only the previous week, shortly before my accident with the chisel. Since then I had been going about in the restless, thoughtful state of one about to take leave; since then my old life had been transformed into the past and I had come to see what is meant by the future. One evening on my way home from the factory the second apprentice had joined me. As we were walking along, he had told me that he knew just the girl for me, that she still had no sweetheart and wanted none but me; she had embroidered a silk wallet as a present for me. He would not tell me her name, but said I would be able to guess it myself. After pressing him in vain, I affected indifference. Then—we were on the footbridge across the millrace—he stopped still and said in an undertone: "She's right behind us." I turned around in embarrassment, half hoping and half fearing that it was all a silly joke. A young girl was coming up the steps behind us—it was Berta Vögtlin; I remembered her from catechism class, and now she worked at the spinning mill. She stopped and smiled at me, and a blush spread over her cheeks until her whole face was aflame. I hurried on and went home.

Since then she had approached me twice, once at the spinning mill where we worked and once on my way home, but all she had said was *"Grüss Gott,"* followed by "Through for the day?"—meaning that she would welcome a chat; but I had only nodded and said yes and, feeling very frustrated, run along home.

My thoughts turned to this episode and I was utterly at a loss. I had often yearned to love a pretty girl. And here was one, pretty and blond and slightly taller than myself, who wanted me to kiss her and take her in my arms. She was strong and well-built, her face was pink and white and pretty, shadowy little curls hung down over the back of her neck, and her eyes were full of expectation and love. But I had never thought of her, I had never been in love with her, I had never pursued her in tender dreams, and had never trembled as I whispered her name into my pillow. If I liked I could fondle her and have her for my sweetheart, but I could not honor her, I could not kneel down and worship her. What would be the end of it? What should I do?

Thoroughly disgruntled, I arose from my bed of grass. Ah, it was a bad time. If only my year at the factory would be over tomorrow and I could go somewhere far away and start afresh and forget all this.

Just to be doing something and to feel alive, I decided to climb to the top of the mountain, though it would not be easy from where I was. Up there I would be high above the town with a view into the distance. I ran up the steep hill and climbed the rocky wall at the end. Then the mountain lay before me, an inhospitable expanse of branches and loose rock. The climb left me sweating and panting, but I breathed more freely in the gentle breeze of the sunny heights. Fading wild roses hung down from the tangled bushes, dropping pale weary petals as I grazed them. Wherever I looked there were little green blackberries, which only on the sunny side showed a first faint glimmer of metallic brown. Butterflies darted about in the still heat, creating flashes of color; innumerable red-and-black-spotted beetles had settled on a cluster of blue-tinged milfoil, a strange, silent assembly, and were moving their long thin legs like automatons. The last cloud had vanished from the sky, which was pure blue, pierced by the sharp black tops of the fir trees on the nearby wooded mountains.

On the topmost rock, where as schoolboys we had always made our autumn bonfires, I stopped and turned around. Deep in the half-shaded valley I saw the gleaming river and the flashing foamy millraces, and narrowly encased in the hills our old town with the smoke of its noonday stoves rising vertically into the still air. There was my father's house and the old bridge; there was our workshop with the little red forge fire, and farther down the river the spinning mill with grass growing on its flat roof. Behind its glittering windows Berta Vögtlin was at work, along with many others. Bah! I didn't want to think about her.

The town looked up at me with its old familiar face, with its gardens and playgrounds, its nooks and crannies; the golden numbers on the church clock sparkled knowingly, houses and trees were clearly reflected in the cool blackness of the shady canal. Only I myself had changed, and I was to blame for the ghostly veil of estrangement between this scene and myself. My life was no longer securely and contentedly embedded in this little precinct of walls, river, and woods; it was still bound by strong ties to these places, but it was no longer safely confined to them—waves of longing carried it beyond their narrow limits. As I looked sorrowfully down, all my secret hopes rose up solemnly in my mind, words spoken by my father and words of revered poets along with my own secret vows, and it struck me as a serious yet delightful thing to have become a man and to hold my destiny consciously in my own hands. This thought fell like a light upon the doubts that had been besetting me because of Berta Vögtlin. True, she was pretty and she liked me; but it was not my way to accept happiness ready-made and unearned from the hands of a girl.

It was almost noon. My desire to climb had seeped away. Thoughtfully I went down the footpath leading to town, under the railroad bridge where in former years I had caught fuzzy dark peacock-moth caterpillars amid the dense nettles, past the wall of the graveyard to the gate, where a moss-covered walnut tree cast deep shade. The gate was open, and I heard the fountain splashing inside. Beside the graveyard lay the town playground and fairground, where on May Day and Sedan Day the townspeople gathered to eat, drink, dance, and listen to speeches. Now it lay still and forgotten in the shade of the great ancient chestnut trees, interspersed here and there by garish flecks of sun on the reddish sand.

Here in the valley, on the sunny street along the river, the noonday heat was merciless. On the river bank, across from the sun-bright houses, the sparse foliage of the intermittent ash trees and maples had taken on the yellowish tinge of late summer. As usual, I walked on the river side, on the lookout for fish. In the limpid water dense bearded waterweeds swayed back and forth with long flowing movements. Here and there between the clumps, in dark gaps that were well known to me, a big solitary fish lurked motionless, its nose pointed into the current, and from time to time I saw a dark school of young bleaks dashing about nearer the surface. I saw that I had done well not to go fishing that morning, and the sight of a dark old barbel resting in the clear water told me that I would probably be able to catch something in the afternoon. After that observation I kept on going. It was with deep relief that I left the blinding street and passed through the doorway into our cellar-cool hall.

My father had a keen weather sense. "I think we're in for another storm," he said at table. I argued that there wasn't a cloud in the sky or any trace of a west wind, but he smiled and said: "Don't you feel the tension in the air? We'll see."

It was indeed very sultry, and the drainage canal gave off a strong smell as at the onset of the föhn. Feeling tired after my climb in the heat, I sat down on the veranda overlooking the garden. None too attentively, I read the story of General Gordon, the hero of Khartoum. Now and then I dozed off for a moment. I too began to feel that a storm was coming. The sky was still of the purest blue, but the air was growing more and more oppressive, as if the sun were swathed in overheated clouds, though actually it was shining clear and bright. At two o'clock I went back into the house to get my fishing tackle ready. While inspecting my hooks and lines, I anticipated the excitement of the chase, grateful for the feeling that I at least had this one profoundly passionate pleasure left.

I have never forgotten the sultry, strangely oppressive stillness of that afternoon. With my fish pail in hand I went down to the river to the lower footbridge, half of which was already in the shade of the large houses. From the nearby spinning mill I could hear the steady sleepy hum of the machines, like a swarm of bees, and from the upper mill at regular intervals the angry jagged scream of the buzz saw. Otherwise there was perfect silence; the artisans had retired to the shade of their workshops, and there was no one on the street. On Mill Island a little boy was wading about naked between the wet stones. Some rough planks leaning against the wall of the wagon-wright's workshop in the hot sun gave off a strong dry tang, which I could make out clearly through the rich, somewhat fishy smell of the water.

The fish were out of sorts, they too had noticed the unusual weather. In the first few minutes I caught several red bream, then a big fellow with magnificent red belly fins snapped my line when I had almost landed him. After that the fish took fright. The bream disappeared into the muck and lost interest in my bait. Above them whole schools of small fry, more and more of them, hove into view and hurried away downstream, as though in flight. Everything indicated a change in the weather, but the air was as still as glass and the sky was untroubled.

I suspected that the fish had been driven away by some noisome drainage. Still unwilling to give up, I decided to move and went to the spinning-mill canal. I had no sooner found a place near the storehouse, taken out my equipment, and settled on the low wall than Berta appeared at the staircase window of the mill. She looked down and

waved at me, but I bent over my fishing pole and pretended not to see her.

I saw myself in the dark water of the masonry canal, a
seated figure with waving outlines, my head between the
soles of my feet. The girl was still standing at the window.
She called out my name, but I went on staring motion-
lessly into the water and did not turn my head.

My fishing came to nothing, here too the fish were
racing about, as though on some pressing business. Exhausted by the oppressive heat, I just sat there, expecting
nothing more of this day and wishing it were over. Behind me in the spinning mill the machines hummed on
and on, the canal water lapped softly against the damp,
moss-covered walls. I felt sleepy and indifferent, and
stayed there only because I was too lazy to roll up my
tackle.

Perhaps half an hour later I suddenly awoke from my
lazy torpor with a feeling of intense uneasiness. A fitful
breeze was revolving slowly and reluctantly around an
unseen axis, the air was heavy and had a cloying taste, a
few frightened swallows flew past, skimming the surface
of the water. I felt dizzy—sunstroke, I thought—the smell
of the water seemed to have grown stronger, a sick feeling rose from my stomach to my head, and I broke out in
a sweat. I pulled in my line, the drops of water were cool
on my hands—and began to pack up my things.

When I stood up, I saw the little whirling dust clouds
on the yard outside the spinning mill. Suddenly they rose
up to form a single cloud; high in the air birds fled as
though under a whiplash, and a moment later, looking
down at the valley, I saw the air turn white as in a dense
snowfall. A sudden cold wind sprang at me like an enemy,
tore my fishing line out of the water, carried my cap away,
and battered my face as though with fists.

The whiteness, which a moment before had been a wall
of snow over distant roofs, was suddenly all around me,
cold and painful; the canal water splashed high as though
churned by powerful mill wheels. My fishing line was

gone, I was in the midst of a raging and fuming wilderness; blows struck my head and hands, pellets of earth spurted up beside me, sand and pieces of wood whirled through the air.

I understood nothing; I only knew that something terrible was happening and that I was in danger. With one leap I was in the storehouse, blind with fear and amazement. I steadied myself on an iron girder and for a few seconds stood numb and breathless, my head reeling in animal terror. Then I began to understand. This was a storm such as I had never seen or thought possible; above me I heard an angry or frightened clamor; big hailstones came pelting down, forming dense white heaps on the flat roof above me and on the ground outside; nuggets of ice were rolling at my feet. The din of the hail and wind was terrifying, the canal water frothed and foamed, dashing against the walls in furious waves.

I saw boards, shingles, and branches hurtling through the air; stones and chunks of mortar fell to the ground and were instantly covered over by a mass of hailstones; I heard tiles shatter and fall, glass break, and roof drains collapse as though under swift hammer blows.

Someone came running from the factory across the ice-covered ground, cutting across the storm. Battling the wind, her skirts fluttering wildly, she staggered on through the hideous deluge. Then she was in the storeroom, coming toward me. A known yet unknown face with great loving eyes and a sad smile was close to mine; warm, silent lips found mine in a long insatiable kiss, arms held me tight, and blond damp hair pressed against my cheeks. And while round about the hailstorm shook the world, I was shaken, more profoundly and more terribly, by a mute, anguished storm of love.

Closely enlaced, we sat on a pile of boards. Not a word was spoken. In timid wonderment I stroked Berta's hair and pressed my lips to her firm, full mouth. Her warmth encompassed me sweetly and painfully. I closed my eyes, she pressed my head to her throbbing heart, to her bosom, and stroked my head and face with gentle wandering hands.

When I opened my eyes, awakening from a fall into dizzy darkness, her strong grave face, sadly beautiful, was over me, and her eyes looked at me forlornly. From under her tousled hair a thin stream of bright red blood flowed over her clear forehead and down her face to her neck.

"What's the matter? What has happened?" I cried in alarm.

She looked deeper into my eyes and smiled feebly.

"I think the world's coming to an end," she said softly, and the roar of the storm swallowed up her words.

"You're bleeding," I said.

"That's from the hail. It's nothing. Are you afraid?"

"No," I said. "Are you?"

"I'm not afraid. Oh, darling, the whole town's being torn to pieces. Oh, darling, don't you love me at all?"

I said nothing, but looked spellbound into her large clear eyes. They were full of forlorn love, and as she bent over me, as her lips lay heavy and gluttonous on mine, I suddenly looked into her grave eyes. The little trickle of bright-red blood was flowing past her left eye over her white fresh skin. And while my senses reeled in drunkenness, my heart resisted, struggling desperately against being taken by storm, against its will. I sat up, and she read in my look that I was sorry for her.

She moved away from me and looked at me almost angrily. In an impulse of sympathy, I held out my hand. She took it in both of hers, buried her face in it, sank down on her knees, and began to cry. Her warm tears fell on my trembling hand. I looked down at her in embarrassment, her head was shaken with sobs, I looked at the soft shadowy little curls on her neck. If she were only someone else, I thought fiercely, someone I really loved, to whom I could give my heart, how happy I would be to fondle these sweet curls with loving fingers and kiss this white neck. But the tumult in my blood had died down and I suffered torments of shame that this girl, to whom I had no desire to devote my youth and my pride, should be kneeling at my feet.

I felt as if I had been under a spell for a whole year, and when I recollect this episode with all its impulses and gestures, I still see it as a long lapse of time. In reality only a few minutes had passed. Suddenly the room was filled with light, patches of damp blue sky emerged in smiling innocence. From one moment to the next, the uproar of the storm was gone, and an unbelievable stillness surrounded us.

As though from a fantastic dream cavern, I stepped out of the storehouse into the reborn light of day. The yard was a dismal sight, the ground furrowed and pitted as though trampled by horses; everywhere there were great heaps of hailstones. My fishing tackle was gone and my pail, too, had vanished. I looked through the shattered windows of the mill; people were rushing wildly about and shoving through all the doors. The yard was littered with glass and bricks; a long tin roof drain had been torn off and hung down on a slant, halfway to the ground.

I forgot everything else and felt nothing but a fevered, anguished curiosity to see what had actually happened and how much damage the storm had done. At first sight the mill with its gutted windows and smashed roof tiles was a picture of hopeless desolation, but on second thought all this was not so disastrous and hardly on a level with the nightmarish impression the cyclone had made on me. I felt relieved, but at the same time almost disappointed: the houses round about were still standing, and on both sides of the valley the mountains were still there. No, the world had not come to an end.

But when after leaving the factory yard I crossed the bridge and turned into the first street, things began to look worse again. The street was full of shards and broken shutters, chimneys had fallen, carrying pieces of roof with them; people were standing at every door, stricken and lamenting. I was reminded of pictures of besieged and invaded cities. Rubble and branches barred the way, gutted windows gaped. Garden fences lay flat on the ground or hung rattling from the tops of walls. Families were looking for missing children, a number of people were said to have been killed in the fields by the hail storm. Hailstones as big as silver talers, if not bigger, were being shown around.

I was still too excited to go home and face the damage in my own house and garden. It did not occur to me that I might be missed, for I was safe and sound. Instead of stumbling on through the rubble, I decided to go back to the outskirts. I was drawn to my favorite spot, the shady old fairground beside the graveyard, where I had celebrated all the great festive occasions of my boyhood years. I recollected to my astonishment that I had passed it only four or five hours ago on my way home from the mountain; it seemed to me that much more time had elapsed.

I went back down the street and across the lower bridge. On the way, through a gap between houses, I saw our red sandstone steeple intact, and the gymnasium as well had suffered little damage. Further along, there was a solitary old inn, I recognized its roof in the distance. It was still standing, but it seemed strangely changed, at first I did not know why. But when I concentrated, I remembered that there had been two tall poplars in front of the house. The poplars were gone. An old familiar sight was destroyed, a spot that had been dear to me desecrated.

A dark foreboding rose up in me that more and nobler things had been devastated. And my heart sank as I realized for the first time how much I loved my native town, how deeply dependent my heart and well-being were on these roofs and towers, bridges and streets, these trees, gardens, and woods. With renewed agitation and alarm I hurried on to the fairground.

There I stood still, viewing the nameless ruin that had struck the place of my fondest memories. The old chestnut trees in whose shade we had spent our holidays, whose trunks were so thick that three or four schoolboys in a circle could barely reach around them, lay shattered, torn out by the roots and overturned, leaving enormous holes in the ground. Not one was in its place, the grounds were a hideous battlefield, the lime trees and maples had also fallen, tree after tree. The broad expanse was a vast heap of broken branches, blasted trunks, roots, and clumps of earth. Here and there a great trunk was still standing, but branchless, broken and twisted, covered with naked white splinters.

It was impossible to go on, both the street and the fairground were blocked by enormous piles of tangled wreckage. Where since earliest childhood I had known only deep, holy shade and lofty tree temples, there was only devastation beneath an empty sky.

It seemed to me that I myself had been torn up with all my secret roots and vomited out into the merciless harsh daylight. For days I went about, finding no woodland path, no familiar shade tree, none of the oaks I had climbed as a child. Everywhere, for miles around, there were only ruins, holes, wooded hillsides mown like grass, tree corpses with naked roots turned mournfully to the sun. A chasm had burst open between me and my childhood. This was no longer my old home. The tenderness and folly of the years gone by fell away from me and soon afterward I left the town to become a man, to stand up against life, whose first shadows had grazed me in these days.

From the Childhood of
Saint Francis of Assisi

1919

"C esco!" cried his mother's voice from upstairs.
All was still and warm, a sleepy Italian afternoon.
Once again, playful and alluring: "Cesco!"

The twelve-year-old boy was sitting half-asleep on the dusty stones in the shady corner beside the front steps of the house. His lean hands were clasped over his bony knees, and a lock of brown hair hung down over his clear, delicately veined forehead.

How good it sounded! That gentle, light, birdlike, winged voice, as mild and friendly, as uniquely noble as his mother herself. Tenderly, Francesco's thoughts followed the vanishing tones. For a moment his legs tingled to jump up, but the feeble impulse quickly died down, and though he could still sense the resonance of the beloved voice, his mind was already far away.

There were wonderful things in the world. Everyone did not sit like this, tucked away in the shade outside his family's house, spoiled by his father and admonished by his mother, while from all sides the neighboring houses, the well, the cypress tree, and the mountains looked on, always the same. There were men who rode all over the world, through France and England and Spain, stopping at castles and cities, and wherever anything wicked was done, where a good pious man was led to his death or a beautiful unfortunate princess was under a spell, the hero, the knight, the savior appeared, drew his great sword, and set things right. There were knights who single-handed put whole armies of Moors to shameful flight. They sailed on ships to the ends of the earth, and the tempest blew their bold great names over land and sea. That was what Piero the hired man had told him about Orlando only yesterday.

Blinking, Francesco looked out from under his forelock into the gap to one side of a moss-covered roof. Between the stone pillars of a grape arbor there was a narrow space through which he could see into the distance, down into the Umbrian plain and across to the mountains beyond. Infinitely small and distant, a town with a white belfry clung to the mountain slope, and beyond lay blue air and an intimation of the colorful world. How beautiful it was, yet how painful to know that everything was out there behind the mountain, everything, rivers and bridges, cities and oceans, castles and army camps, squadrons of cavalry with music, heroes on horseback and beautiful noblewomen, tournaments and the plucking of strings, golden armor and rustling silk, all ready and waiting, a table set for him who would come, who would have the courage to make it his own.

Yes, one must have courage. If only to ride through a strange wilderness at night when the air was full of spooks and hostile magic and the path was bordered with caves full of dead men's bones. Would he, Francesco Bernardone, have courage enough? And suppose one were taken prisoner and led before an infuriated Moorish prince or shut up in a bewitched castle! It wasn't easy. It was almost unthinkable. It was terribly, terribly hard, and surely very few men were up to it. Had his father been up to it? Perhaps—who knows? But since there had been men capable of doing such things, since Orlando and Lancelot and all the rest had been capable of their exploits, what else could a young man do but try to become like them? Could he go on playing games for beans or planting pumpkin seeds, could he become an artisan or a merchant, or a priest or some such thing?

Deep creases formed in his white forehead; his eyes disappeared under his knitted brows. Lord, it was hard to decide. How many must have tried and perished at the very start—young squires and knights, whom no princess ever heard of, whom no songs were sung of, whom no stable boy told stories about in the evening. They were gone, struck down, poisoned, drowned, hurled from cliffs, devoured by dragons, immured in caves. They had ridden forth for nothing; in vain they had suffered hardships and torment!

Francesco shuddered. He looked down at his lean sunburned hands. One day perhaps they would be chopped off by Saracens, or nailed to a cross or eaten by vultures. Horrible. To think how many good things there were on earth, how much that was beautiful, pleasant, sweet to the taste. Oh, what good things! A hearth fire in the fall, with chestnuts roasting in it, or a flower carnival in the spring, with the daughters of the nobility all in white. Or a docile pony such as his father had promised him when he should be fourteen. But there were other things as well, much simpler things, hundreds and thousands of them, that were beautiful and precious. Such as sitting like this in the half-shade, with the sun on his toes and his back to the cool wall. Or lying abed in the evening, feeling nothing but the soft, gentle warmth and the mild twilight of his tiredness. Or to hear his mother's voice and feel her hand in his hair. And there were thousands of such things, waking and sleeping, evening and morning, so much fragrance and so many sweet sounds, so many colors, so much that was lovely and caressing.

Was it then necessary to make light of all that, to sacrifice and risk it? Just to slay a dragon (or to be torn to pieces by a dragon) or to be ennobled by a king? Did it have to be? Was it right?

It never entered the boy's head that no one in all the world, neither his father nor mother, demanded any such deeds of him, that only his own heart spoke of such things, dreamed of them and longed for them. He felt that such things were demanded of him. An ideal had taken form in his mind. A call had gone out to him, a flame had been kindled in him. But why was what seemed most beautiful, why was heroism so hard, so very hard? Why was it necessary to choose, to make sacrifices, to decide? Couldn't you simply do the things you liked? Yes, but what did he like? Everything and nothing, everything for a moment, nothing for always. Ah, the thirst! The consuming desire! And there was so much torment and secret fear in it!

Angrily he pressed his head against his knees. Very well; if he had to decide, he would be a knight. Let them strike him down, let him waste away in the desert—he would become a knight. They would all be amazed— Marietta and Piero, and his mother too, not to mention his idiotic Latin teacher! He would come riding home on a white stallion, wearing a golden helmet with Spanish plumes, and there would be a big scar on his forehead.

With a sigh he sank back and looked out between the pillars of the grape arbor into the reddish smoky distance, where every blue shadow was a dream and a promise. Inside, in the shop, he heard Piero bustling about with bolts of cloth. The strip of shade beside him had broadened and, clearly outlined, jutted out into the sunny street. Above the distant hills the hot sky was growing soft and golden.

Just then a little band of children came up the street, seven or eight little boys and girls. They came in pairs, playing "procession." They had twined garlands of leaves around their dusty necks and smocks, and in their hands they were carrying carelessly plucked meadow flowers, buttercups and daisies, cranesbill and salvia, intermingled with blades of grass and already half-faded. Their bare feet padded softly over the cobbles, and a larger boy clomped along beside them in wooden shoes, beating time. They were all singing a garbled little song, the mutilated echo of a hymn, with the refrain:

Mille fiori, mille fiori
A te, Santa Maria . . .

Up the hill came the little band of pilgrims, bringing sound and color into the lifeless street. A little girl came last; she was redoing one of her braids, meanwhile holding the other, flowers and all, in her mouth, but singing or humming all the while. A few lost flowers lay in the dust behind the procession.

Francesco had joined at once in humming the tune. He had played this game any number of times; it had long been a favorite with him. Now that he was a big boy and had participated more than once in the forbidden exploits of his contemporaries, he had lost the first innocence of childhood and had grown away from this pious amusement. Moreover, he was one of those hypersensitive children who in these earliest stirrings of the soul experience a sorrowful foreboding, a saddening intimation that all human joys are transient. And today more than ever, now that he had decided to become a hero, such childish doings were bound to strike him as worthless trumpery.

With haughty indifference he looked at the passing children. And beside the girl with the undone braid he saw a little boy, who might have been about six, holding a single bent flower and striding along with a solemn, almost waddling gait like a banner-bearer; and though his singing was very much out of tune, his round eyes gleamed with festive enthusiasm and religious fervor.

"Mille fiori," he sang, "mille fiori a te, Santa Maria."

Francesco was a creature of sudden moods; when he saw the little boy, he was overcome by the beauty and piety of this flowery procession, or rather by a surging memory of faded enthusiasms which he himself had known while playing the same game. With an ardent leap, he joined the children; he signaled them to gather round him and then commanded them to wait a moment here outside his house.

They obeyed—he was accustomed to leading, and be-

sides he was the son of a respected, well-to-do citizen—
and waited with their tattered flowers in their hands.
Their singing had ceased.

Francesco ran into his mother's garden, a tiny, well-
tended patch three or four paces long, where the ground
had been built up at the cost of great effort. There were
few flowers, the narcissi had faded and the wallflowers
had gone to seed. But there were two clumps of iris. They
belonged to his mother. It cost him a pang, but he broke
off nearly all the lovely large flowers. The fat juicy stalks
crunched in his hand. He looked at one flower, peering
into its calyx where the violet grew pale and the yellow
hairy stamens stood in precise order. He felt deeply that
it was a pity to ruin all these flowers.

Then he went back to the procession and gave each
child an iris to carry. He kept one for himself and took the
lead. Thus they marched into the adjoining street. The
lovely garden flowers and the example of the leader, who
was known to all, drew many other children after them.
With and without flowers they joined in, and in the next
street there were still more. When at length they arrived
singing on the cathedral square, and the mountains
glowed bluish red against the golden evening sky, they
were a large crowd. "Mille, mille fiori," they sang. Outside
the cathedral they began to dance, and Francesco, his
cheeks aflame with enthusiasm, led the dance. Evening
strollers and peasants returning from the fields stopped
to look on; the young girls praised Francesco, and in the
end one of them was bold enough to do what all had
thought of doing: she went up to the handsome boy, gave
him her hand, and danced along with him. Laughter mingled with applause, and for a moment the children's play-
procession became a joyful little festival, just as on the
lips of little girls child's laughter can turn to maiden's
smile.

By vespers it was all over and the children had run off.
Francesco came home excited and overheated. Only then
did he notice that he had been marching and dancing

barefoot and capless, something he had carefully avoided for some time, now that he frequented older boys and the sons of the nobility.

After supper, when despite a certain amount of resistance he had finally gone off to bed, he suddenly remembered the knighthood and the high manly duties he had taken upon himself and turned pale with anger and shame at having so forgotten himself. With closed eyes and compressed lips he bitterly reviled himself, as he had often done. A fine hero, a worthy Orlando, who broke off his mother's flowers and went playing and dancing with a horde of little children! A fine knight! A clown, that's what he was, a jester, a buffoon—how could the like of him have ever thought of becoming anything good and noble? Oh, how the evening sun and the fine gold of the hills in the distance had lighted up his heart even as he was dancing outside the cathedral! Did such things not speak, were they not a summons as noble and soul-stirring as the call of a herald? But he had danced and trifled, and in the end he had even let the peasant girl kiss him! Comedian! Buffoon! He dug his fingernails into his clenched fist and groaned for shame and humiliation. Oh, that was the way with everything he did. The intention was always good and proud and noble; he began well, but then came a mood, a wind, a smell, a temptation from heaven knew where, and the noble hero was a street urchin and a fool again. No, for him there could be no lofty dreams, no sacred vows and enthusiasms—all that was for others worthier than he. Oh, Lancelot! Oh, Orlando! Oh, heroic songs and holy fire on the distant mountains of Trasimeno!

In the failing light the door opened quietly and his mother came in. She slept in the same room when Francesco's father was away from home. On slippered feet she approached his bed.

"Aren't you asleep yet, Cesco?" she asked gently.

He thought of pretending to be asleep, but that was beyond his strength. Instead of answering, he reached for her hand and held it fast. He loved his beautiful mother's hands and voice with an almost love-sick tenderness. She kept her right hand in his and stroked his hair with her left.

"Is something wrong, child?"

He was silent for a time, then he said very softly: "I've done something wicked."

"Is it bad, Francesco? Tell me about it."

"I took almost all your flowers. You know, the big blue ones. They're not there any more."

"I know. I saw it. So it was you? I thought it must be Filippo or Graffe. You don't usually do wild things like that."

"I felt sorry the minute I'd done it. I gave them to the children."

"What children?"

"Some children came along. We played mille fiori."

"You too? You joined in?"

"Yes, all of a sudden I had to. They only had faded wild-flowers. I wanted to make it nice."

"Did you go to the cathedral?"

"Yes, to the cathedral, like we used to."

She laid her hand on his head.

"That wasn't bad, Cesco. Oh, if you had ruined the flowers out of sheer deviltry . . . but as it is, there's really no harm in it. You mustn't worry."

"It's not because of the flowers."

"No? What then?"

"I can't tell you."

"Of course you can. Is there something else on your conscience?"

"Mother, I want to be a knight."

"A knight? —Well, you can try . . . But what has that got to do with it?"

"Oh, a great deal. But you wouldn't understand! —Look, I want to be a knight. But I can't. I keep doing stupid things. It's so hard to be a knight, so hard—a real knight never does anything bad or stupid or silly, and that's how

I want to be, but I can't! I just ran off with the children and danced for them. Like a little boy!"

His mother made him lie back on the pillow.

"Don't be silly, Cesco. Dancing isn't a sin. Even a knight can dance now and then when he feels gay or wants to give other people pleasure. You're just making yourself unhappy about things that aren't at all as you think. You can't change everything from one minute to the next. Knights were little boys themselves once, they played and danced and all that. —But tell me, why do you want to be a knight? Because they're so pious and brave?"

"Oh, yes. But also—because then I can get to be a prince or a duke and everybody will talk about me."

"Oh. And must you have everybody talking about you?"

"Oh, yes, I want that very much."

"Then you must see to it that they have only good things to say! Otherwise it's bad to be talked about."

She had to sit there quite a while, holding his hand. It gave her a strange feeling to think that such childlike desires and projects could arouse so much passion and painful turmoil in his soul. This child would know great love, that much was certain, but also great disappointment. It was unlikely that he would ever become a knight, that was a dream. But his life would surely be out of the ordinary, for better or worse.

She made the sign of the cross over him in the darkness and in her heart called him by the name which he was later to give himself: Poverello.

Inside and Outside

1920

T HERE WAS A MAN by the name of Friedrich; he was
a thinker, and he knew a good deal. But to his mind
there was knowledge and knowledge, and thought and
thought; he loved a particular kind of thinking, but despised and detested the others. What he loved and honored was logic, that excellent method, and everything that
he termed "science."

"Two times two is four," he used to say. "In that I believe, and all man's thinking must be based on this truth."

It was not unknown to him that there are other kinds of
thought and knowledge, but these were not "science," and
he held them in low esteem. Though a freethinker, he was
not intolerant toward the religions. The reason for this
was a tacit agreement among scientists. For some centuries their science had concerned itself with almost everything worth knowing on earth, with one exception, the
human soul. In the course of time it had become customary among scientists to leave this one matter to religion
and to tolerate its speculations about the soul, though
without taking them seriously. Yet despite his indulgence
toward religion, Friedrich abominated everything that he
regarded as superstition. Such notions were all very well
for backward, illiterate peoples, and no one would deny
the existence of mystical, magical thinking in remote an-
tiquity—but now that science and logic had made their
appearance, there could be no point in such dubious, out-
moded conceptions.

So he said and so he thought, and when he discerned

traces of superstition in those about him, he grew angry
and felt as if a hostile hand had touched him.

What infuriated him most was to find such vestiges of
superstition among men of his own class, educated men
acquainted with the principles of scientific thought. And
nothing was more painful and intolerable to him than
the blasphemous idea, which he had recently heard expounded and discussed even among highly cultivated persons, the preposterous idea that scientific thought might
not be supreme, timeless, eternal, predestined and un-
shakable, but only one of many modes of thought, limited
in time and not immune to change or annihilation. This
disrespectful, destructive, poisonous idea was in the air,
even Friedrich would not deny that; a product of the suffering that war, revolution, and hunger had brought into
the world, it had sprung up here and there like a warning,
a ghostly maxim written by a white hand on a white wall.

The more Friedrich suffered from the existence of this
idea and from its power to trouble him so deeply, the more
passionately he hated it and all those whom he suspected
of secretly holding it. Thus far only a very few of those
who could properly be termed educated openly professed
this doctrine, which, if it were to spread and to gain
power, seemed destined to destroy the reign of the intel-
lect on earth and to usher in chaos. But things had not
yet come to such a pass, and the avowed adherents of the
idea were still so few that one could set them down as
mere cranks and eccentrics. Still, a drop of the poison,
an offshoot of the idea, was here and there discernible.
Among the common people and the half-educated, in any
case, all sorts of new doctrines, occult teachings, sects,
and cults had sprung up. The world was full of them; on
all sides one perceived superstition, mysticism, spiritism,
and other sinister influences. Of course these ought to
have been combated, but for the present, science, as
though from a sense of secret weakness, passed them over
in silence.

One day Friedrich went to the house of a friend with whom he had engaged in various studies. It so happened that he had not seen this friend for some time. As he was climbing the stairs, he tried to recall when and where he had last seen him. But much as he prided himself on his memory, he could not remember. This annoyed him and put him in a bad humor, and it cost him some effort to pull himself together when he reached his friend's door.

No sooner had he greeted Erwin, his friend, than he was struck by an indulgent smile on his friendly face. It seemed to him that he had never noticed that smile, which for all its friendliness seemed somehow mocking or hostile, and the moment he saw it, the memory for which he had been searching in vain came to him, the memory of his last meeting with Erwin. Now he recalled that they had parted without a quarrel, but with a sense of inner disharmony, because Erwin, so it seemed to him, had not supported his attacks on superstition with sufficient vigor.

Strange! How could he have forgotten that? He suddenly realized that if he had not called on his friend for so long, it was solely because of the resentment he had felt at the time, and it also came to him that he had known this all along, though he had given himself any number of other reasons for postponing his visit.

Now they stood face to face, and it seemed to Friedrich that in the meantime the gap between them had increased alarmingly. He felt instinctively that in that moment something was lacking between him and Erwin, something that had always been present, a sense of complicity, of immediate understanding, one might have called it affection. In its place there was a void, a gulf, an estrangement. They exchanged greetings, spoke of the weather, of friends, of their health—and heaven knows why, at every word Friedrich had the oppressive feeling that he did not fully understand his friend, that Erwin did not really know him, that they were not reaching each other with their words and could find no proper ground for a true conversation. And on Erwin's face there was still that friendly smile, which Friedrich almost began to hate.

In a pause in the awkward conversation, Friedrich looked about the familiar study and saw a sheet of paper pinned loosely to the wall. The sight affected him strangely and awakened old memories, for he remembered that long ago, during his student years, it had been a habit with Erwin to remind himself in this way of a passage from a philosopher or poet. He arose and went over to the wall to read what was written on the paper.

In his neat, elegant hand Erwin had written: "Nothing is outside, nothing is inside, for that which is outside is inside."

Friedrich turned pale and stood there for a moment motionless. There it was! This was what he had dreaded. At any other time he would have made nothing of it. He would have passed it off indulgently as a mood, as a harmless and perfectly permissible amusement, perhaps as a bit of sentimentality, to be treated with forbearance. But now it was different. He felt that these words had not been written in a passing poetic mood, that no mere whim had driven Erwin back to a habit of his younger years. —These words were an avowal of his friend's new preoccupation: mysticism! Erwin was a renegade.

Slowly he turned toward him. Again he saw that radiant smile.

"Explain this to me," he demanded.

All friendliness, Erwin nodded.

"Haven't you ever read that saying?"

"Yes, of course," cried Friedrich. "Of course I know it. It's mysticism, Gnosticism. Poetic perhaps, but . . . Now please, explain it to me, and tell me why it's hanging on your wall."

"Gladly," said Erwin. "It's a first introduction to a theory of knowledge in which I am interested at present and to which I owe a great deal of happiness."

Friedrich fought down his irritation and asked: "A new theory of knowledge? Is there such a thing? What is it called?"

"Oh," said Erwin, "it's new only for me. It's old and venerable. It's called magic."

The word had been spoken. Filled with consternation by so open an avowal, Friedrich felt that he was face to face with the archenemy in the person of his friend. He was silent. He did not know whether he was closer to anger or tears; he had a bitter sense of irretrievable loss. For a long while he was silent. Then in a tone of affected mockery he said: "So now you want to be a magician?"

"Yes," said Erwin without hesitation.

"Kind of a sorcerer's apprentice, eh?"

"That's it."

Again Friedrich was silent. It was so still that the ticking of a clock could be heard from the next room.

Then he said: "You realize, I suppose, that you are breaking your ties with serious science—and consequently with me?"

"I hope not," Erwin replied. "But if that's how it has to be . . . what else can I do?"

Friedrich exploded. "What else can you do?" he screamed. "Give up this nonsense, this dismal, degrading hocus-pocus, give it up once and for all. That's what you can do if you want to keep my respect."

Erwin smiled a little, but his serenity seemed to have left him.

"You speak—" he said so softly that Friedrich's angry voice still seemed to echo through the room, "you speak as if it were a matter of will, as though I had a choice. No, Friedrich, that is not so. I have no choice. I did not choose magic. Magic chose me."

Friedrich heaved a deep sigh. "Then goodbye," he said painfully, and stood up without proffering his hand.

"No!" Erwin cried. "No, you mustn't leave me like this. Suppose one of us were dying—and that's how it is!—and we had to take our leave of one another."

"But which one of us is dying, Erwin?"

"My friend, today it is undoubtedly myself. A man in search of rebirth must be prepared to die."

Again Friedrich went over to the wall and read the maxim.

"Very well," he said finally. "You're right. It won't help us any to part in anger. I'll do as you say and assume that one of us is dying. It could be me. But before I leave you, I want to ask a last favor."

"I'm glad of that," said Erwin. "Tell me, what can I do for you in parting?"

"I should simply like to repeat my first question, that is my favor: explain these words to me as well as you can."

Erwin thought for a moment. Then he spoke.

"Nothing is outside, nothing is inside. The religious meaning is well known: God is everywhere. He is in the mind and He is also in nature. All things are divine, because God is the All. We used to call that pantheism. And the philosophical meaning: the distinction between inside and outside is habitual to our thinking, but not necessary. Our mind is capable of passing beyond the dividing line we have drawn for it. Beyond the pairs of opposites of which the world consists, other, new insights begin. —Ah, my dear friend, I must own to you that since my manner of thinking changed, no word or maxim has a single meaning for me; every word has ten, twenty, a hundred meanings. And that, precisely, is the beginning of what you are so much afraid of: magic."

Friedrich frowned and started to interrupt him, but Erwin looked at him reassuringly and continued in a louder voice: "Let me give you an example to take home with you. Take something of mine, anything, observe it a little from time to time, and soon the maxim of inside and outside will reveal one of its many meanings to you."

He looked around him, took a small clay figure with a glazed surface from a ledge on the wall, and gave it to Friedrich.

"Take this as my parting gift," he said. "When this ob-

ject I am putting into your hands ceases to be outside you
and is inside you, come back to me. But if it remains forever outside you as it is now, then let our parting also be
forever."

Friedrich would have had a good deal more to say, but
Erwin pressed his hand and said goodbye in a tone that
did not admit of another word.

Friedrich left him and went down the stairs (how in-
conceivably long it was since he had climbed them!); he
passed through the streets and went home with the little
clay figure in his hand, feeling perplexed and thoroughly
unhappy. Outside his house he stopped, shook his fist
angrily for a moment, and felt very much like dashing
the ridiculous little object to the ground. He did not do
so. He bit his lips and went in. He had never been so agitated, so tormented by conflicting emotions.

He looked about for a place in which to put his friend's
gift and finally chose the upper shelf of a bookcase. And
there for the time being he left it.

As the days passed, he looked at it now and then, wondering where it came from and wondering what meaning
this absurd object was expected to have for him. It was
a small figure of a man, god, or idol with two faces like
the Roman god Janus, rather clumsily modeled of clay,
and covered with a fired glaze that had cracked in several
places. The little thing looked crude and insignificant; it
was surely not the work of a Greek or Roman, but more
likely of some backward African or South Sea Island people. On both faces, which were identical, there was a
stupid, lazy smile, one might have said a grin—it was
positively disgusting how the little goblin kept dispensing
that silly smile.

Friedrich could not get used to the figurine. It repelled
him, it was in his way, it annoyed him. The very next day
he took it down and put it on the stove, and a few days
later he moved it to the top of a cupboard. Time and time
again it caught his eye as though thrusting itself forward,
and smiled at him coldly and stupidly, making itself im-

portant, demanding attention. Two or three weeks later he moved it out to the vestibule, in among the photographs from Italy and the whimsical little souvenirs that no one ever looked at. Now at least he saw the idol only on his way in or out; he passed quickly, never stopping to look at it more closely. But even here, though he would not admit it to himself, the thing upset him.

This lump of clay, this two-faced monster, had brought trouble and torment into his life.

One day, months later, he returned home from a short journey—a kind of restlessness had come over him and he had taken to going off on such trips now and then. He opened the door, passed through the vestibule, exchanged a few words with the maid, and read some letters that had come during his absence. But he was restless and distraught, as though he had forgotten something important; none of his books attracted him, he felt at ease in none of the chairs. He began to examine himself, trying to remember: what had caused this sudden change in his mood? Had he failed to do something important? Had something irritated him? Had he eaten something that disagreed with him? He pondered and searched; it occurred to him that this unpleasant feeling had come to him the moment he got home, in the doorway. He went out to the vestibule, and the first thing he looked for, quite involuntarily, was the clay figure.

A strange shudder passed through him when he failed to see the idol. It had vanished. It was not there. Had it run off on its little clay legs? Flown away? Had a magic spell wafted it away to wherever it came from?

Friedrich pulled himself together, smiled, and shook his head in self-reproof at his fears. Then he searched the whole room systematically. When he failed to find the idol, he called the maid. She came, she wrung her hands, and admitted at once that she had dropped the little thing while dusting it.

"Where is it?"

It no longer existed. It had seemed so solid, she had

often held it in her hand, but it had smashed into tiny
bits and splinters and could not be mended; she had
shown the shards to the glazier, who had laughed at her;
then she had thrown them away.

When the maid had gone, Friedrich smiled. He was not
displeased. God knows the idol was no loss. Now the monster was gone and he would have peace. If he had only
smashed the thing to bits the very first day! How he had
suffered all this time! The lazy, strange, sly, evil, diabolical way that goblin had smiled at him! Well, now that the
idol was gone, he could own it to himself: he had feared
it, he had honestly and truly been afraid of that clay god!
Was it not a sign and symbol of everything that was loathsome and intolerable to Friedrich, everything he had always regarded as harmful, hostile, and to be combated, all
superstition, all darkness, everything that hampered the
free workings of the mind? Did it not represent that
dreaded subterranean power whose rumblings he sometimes heard, that distant earthquake which would destroy
civilization and usher in chaos? Had this contemptible
figure not robbed him of his best friend—no, not only
taken him away, but turned him into an enemy! Well,
now the thing was gone. Gone. Smashed. Finished. And
that was perfect, much better than if he himself had
smashed it.

So he thought, or said, and went about his occupations
as usual.

But it was as though a curse had been put upon him.
Now that he had more or less got used to the absurd figure, now that the sight of it in its accustomed place on the
vestibule table had little by little become familiar and almost a matter of indifference to him, now its absence be- .
gan to torment him. Yes, he missed it. Whenever he
passed through the vestibule, he saw nothing but the
empty space where it had been, and that space emanated
an emptiness that made the whole room cold and alien.

Bad days and worse nights began for Friedrich. He
could no longer pass through the vestibule without think-

ing of the two-faced idol, without missing it, without a feeling that his thoughts were tied to it. It was torture to think of it, but he couldn't help himself. And it was not only in the moments spent passing through the vestibule that the compulsion seized hold of him. Far from it. Just as an emptiness and desolation emanated from the empty space on the table, so this compulsion emanated from deep within him, gradually crowding out everything else, corroding all other thoughts and leaving a chilling void in his soul.

Time and again he recalled the figurine clearly to mind, if only to prove to himself how absurd it was to grieve over its loss. He visualized it in all its stupid barbaric ugliness, with its empty or crafty smile and its two faces. Sometimes he even found himself curling his lips as though moved by some outside force, in an attempt to imitate that hateful smile. A question pursued him: had the two faces really been identical? Didn't some slight roughness or a crack in the glaze give one of them a somewhat different expression? A questioning look? Something sphinxlike? And how uncanny, or at least strange, the color of the glaze had been! There had been green and blue and gray in it, but also red; and now he began to see that glaze in other objects, in a windowpane glistening in the sun, in the sheen of a wet pavement.

He thought a good deal about this glaze, by day and night. *Glasur*—what a strange, foreign, unpleasant-sounding word it was! He dissected the word; consumed with hate, he split it apart, and once he reversed it. Then it became *Rusalg*. That too had a forbidding ring to it. *Rusalg*—he knew that word, he definitely knew it, a hostile, unpleasant word with ugly and upsetting overtones. For a long time he racked his brains; then finally it came to him that *Rusalg* reminded him of a book he had bought and read while traveling years before, *Princess Russalka* was the title. That book had horrified, tormented, and yet secretly fascinated him. Surely there was a curse on that figurine; everything connected with it—the glaze, the blue, the green, the smile—had hostile implications, each one of them a cruel poisoned barb. And how very strangely Erwin, his former friend, had smiled while putting the idol into his hands! How very strange, how significant and hostile that smile had been!

For many days Friedrich fought bravely, and not altogether unsuccessfully, against the thoughts that forced themselves upon him. He was well aware of the danger—he did not want to go mad. No, sooner die. Reason was a necessity. Life was not. And it occurred to him that perhaps just this was magic, that perhaps Erwin had cast a spell on him with the help of this figurine, and that he was going under—a victim of the war for reason and science and against these dark powers. But if this were so, if he could even conceive of it as a possibility, then magic must exist! No, he would rather die!

A doctor recommended walks and cold baths; and sometimes in the evening he sought distraction in a tavern. But none of this helped much. He cursed Erwin. He cursed himself.

One night he woke up in terror, as he often did at that time, and could not get back to sleep. He felt thoroughly anguished and ill at ease. He tried to think, to find some consolation. He looked for words to say to himself, comforting, reassuring words full of soothing peace and clarity, such as "Two times two is four." Nothing occurred to him, but in a half-maddened state he began to mumble sounds and syllables. Little by little, words formed on his lips and several times, without grasping the meaning, he repeated a short sentence that had somehow taken form within him. He mumbled it over and over as though to deaden his mind, as though to grope his way back to his lost sleep, on a narrow path skirting the abyss.

Suddenly his voice grew somewhat louder and the mumbled words penetrated his consciousness. He knew these words. They were: "Now you are inside me!" And all at once he knew what they meant, he knew that they re-

ferred to the clay idol and that now, in this gray hour of
night, he had fulfilled, exactly and to the letter, the pre-
diction that Erwin had made on that awful day. The figurine, which he had then held contemptuously in his fingers, was no longer outside him but within him! "For that
which is outside is inside."

Leaping out of bed, he felt ice and flame in his veins.
The world was spinning, the planets were staring madly
at him. He lit the lamp, hurried into his clothes, and went
out. Regardless of the hour, he had to see Erwin. There
was light in the old familiar window of his friend's study,
the door was unlocked, everything seemed to be waiting
for him. He staggered into the bedroom and propped his
trembling hands on the table. His friend was sitting in the
soft lamplight, smiling thoughtfully.

Erwin arose to welcome him. "You have come. I am
glad."

"Were you expecting me?" Friedrich whispered.

"As you know, I have been expecting you since the day
you left me with my little gift. Has what I told you then
happened?"

In little more than a whisper Friedrich said: "It has
happened. The idol is inside me. I can't bear it any
longer."

"Can I help you?" Erwin asked.

"I don't know. Do what you think best. Tell me more
about your magic. Tell me how to get this idol out of me."

Erwin laid his hand on his friend's shoulder. He led
him to an easy chair and made him sit down.

Then he smiled and said in a warm, almost motherly
tone: "The idol will come out. Trust me. Trust yourself.
You have learned to believe in him. Now learn to love
him. He is inside you, but he is still dead, he is still a ghost
to you. Wake him, speak to him, question him! For he is
yourself! Stop hating him, stop fearing him and torturing
him—oh, how you have tortured your poor idol, who was
only yourself! How you have tortured yourself!"

"Is this the way to magic?" Friedrich asked. He sat slumped in his chair, as though aged; his voice was gentle.

Erwin said: "This is the way. And perhaps you have already taken the hardest step. You have learned by your own experience that outside can become inside. You have been beyond the pairs of opposites. It seemed a hell to you: learn, my friend, that it is heaven! For it is heaven that lies ahead of you. Magic, you see, is this: to exchange inside and outside, not under compulsion, not passively as you have done, but freely, of your own volition. Summon up the past, summon up the future: they are both within you! Up until now you have been the slave of what is inside you. Learn to master it. That is magic."

Tragic

1923

WHEN THE EDITOR-IN-CHIEF was told that Johannes the compositor had been waiting for an hour in the anteroom and would on no account be turned away or put off, he nodded with a smile of melancholy resignation and swung around in his office chair to meet his silently entering visitor. He knew in advance what sort of request had brought the faithful, white-bearded compositor to see him, knew the request was a hopeless one, both sentimental and boring, and knew that he could not meet this man's wishes or do him any other service except to listen courteously to what he had to say. Since the petitioner, who had served the newspaper as typesetter for many years, was not only a sympathetic and worthy human being but an educated man as well, an author in fact, who had been highly esteemed in the pre-modern period, had been indeed almost famous, the editor experienced on the occasions of his visits, which took place customarily once or twice a year and always had the same purpose and the same success or rather lack of it, a feeling compounded of sympathy and embarrassment. Now the feeling rose to active discomfort as his caller quietly entered, closing the doors behind him with meticulous courtesy and absolute soundlessness.

"Sit down, Johannes," the editor-in-chief said in an encouraging tone (almost the same tone he had once employed toward young writers when he had been editor of the book section and now employed toward young politicians). "How goes it? Any complaints?"

Johannes regarded him timidly and sadly out of eyes

that were surrounded by thousands of tiny wrinkles, child's eyes in the face of an ancient.

"It's always the same thing," he said in a soft, sad voice. "And it's getting steadily worse, it's rapidly approaching complete ruin. I have recently noticed dreadful symptoms. Things that ten years ago would have made even the average reader's hair stand on end are not only willingly accepted by today's readers in the news notes and the sports section, not to mention the advertisements— no, they have even invaded the book section, even the lead editorials. Even with good, established authors these mistakes, these monstrosities and evidences of degeneration have today become a matter of course, they have become the rule. Even with you, sir, the editor-in-chief, forgive me, even with you! I have long ago given up mentioning the fact that our written language is now no better than a beggar's jargon, destitute and louse-infested, that all beautiful, rich, rare, highly evolved forms have disappeared, that for years now I have failed to find a single future perfect in any lead article, let alone a rich, deep-breathed, nobly constructed, elastic-paced sentence, a true period, aware of its own structure, beautifully rising and gracefully dying away. That, I know, is gone. Just as in Borneo and all those other islands they have extirpated the bird of paradise, the elephant, and the king tiger, they have destroyed and abolished all the lovely sentences, all the inversions, all the delicate play and shading of our dear language. I know there's nothing left to be saved there. But the absolute errors, the uncorrected slips, the complete irresponsibility toward even the first principles of grammatical logic! Alas, Herr Doktor, out of habit they will begin a sentence with 'Although' or with 'On the one hand,' and will forget within two lines the not very complicated obligation that such an opening entails; they suppress the independent clause, switch to a new construction, and it is only the best of them who attempt to hide the scandal behind a dash or to attenuate it through the connecting link of a series of dots. You know, sir, that this

dash is a part of your armory too. Once, years ago, it was
poison to me, I hated it, but things have now come to such
a pass that today I greet it with emotion whenever it appears; I am deeply grateful to you for every one of these
dashes, for after all they are a remnant of former times,
an evidence of culture, of bad conscience, they are abbre-
viated, coded confessions on the writer's part that he is
aware of a certain obligation toward the laws of language,
that he is in some measure repentant and regretful when,
as too often happens, he is compelled by harsh necessity
to sin against the holy spirit of our tongue."

The editor, who had closed his eyes during this dis-
sertation and had gone on with the calculations which his
caller had interrupted, now opened his eyes, allowed them
to rest brightly on Johannes, smiled benignly, and said,
slowly, ingratiatingly, visibly at pains to formulate his
thoughts properly out of consideration for the old man:

"Look here, Johannes, you are absolutely right; I've always gladly admitted that to you before. You are right:
that language of a bygone time, that cultivated, beautifully groomed language which two or three decades ago
was still practiced or at least approximated by a number
of writers, that language has perished. It perished as the
monuments of the Egyptians and the systems of the Gnos-
tics perished, as Athens and Byzantium had to perish.
That is sad, dear friend, it is tragic"—at this word the
compositor winced and opened his lips as though to cry
out, but controlled himself and sank resignedly back into
his former posture—"but it is our destiny and must be our
endeavor, don't you think, to accept what fate brings to
pass, however sad that may be. As I have said to you before, it is a fine thing to preserve a certain loyalty toward
the past, and in your case I not only understand this loyalty, I am compelled to admire it. But this clinging to
things and circumstances that are once and for all doomed
to destruction must be kept within bounds. Life itself im-
poses those bounds, and when we transgress them, when
we attach ourselves too firmly to the old, we come into

conflict with life, which is stronger than we are. I understand you very well, please believe that. You, the accom-
plished master of that language, to whom that fine, inherited tradition is intimately known, you, the former
poet, must naturally suffer more than others at the degen-
erative, transitional state in which our language, our
whole former culture, finds itself. The fact that as a compositor you are compelled to be a daily witness of this de-
terioration, to participate in it indeed and in some measure to collaborate, has something bitter, something trag—"
(at this word Johannes winced again so that the editor
automatically chose another phrase), "something of the
irony of fate about it. But I can do as little to remedy this
as you yourself or anybody else. We must let things go
their way and resign ourselves."

The editor looked sympathetically at the old typesetter's
face, which wore an expression at once childlike and troubled. One had to admit there was something to be said for
these gradually disappearing representatives of the old
world, of the pre-modern, so-called sentimental epoch;
they were agreeable folk despite their mournfulness. In a
kindly tone he went on:

"You know, dear friend, about twenty years ago the last
poetical works were printed in our country, some in book
form, although that had already become very rare at that
time, and partly in the literary supplements of the papers.
Then quite suddenly the realization struck us all that
there was something amiss about these poetical works,
that they were unnecessary, that actually they were silly.
At that time we became aware of something, something
thrust itself on our attention that for a long time had been
quietly ripening and now all at once confronted us as an
acknowledged fact: the time of art was over, art and
poetry in our world had died, and it was better to say goodbye to them for good, dead as they were, than to go on
dragging them about with us. For all of us, and for me
too, that was a bitter realization at the time. And yet we
were right in acting upon it. Whoever wants to read

Goethe or anything of that sort can do it just as well as before; he loses nothing simply because there is no longer
day by day a mountainous aftergrowth of new, feeble, en-
ervated verse. We all adapted ourselves. You did, too, Johannes, by giving up your vocation of poet and seeking
the simple post of a wage earner. And if today in your old
age you suffer too much from the fact that as typesetter
you come so often into conflict with the tradition and
practice of language, which are still holy in your eyes,
then I have a proposal to make: Give up this irksome and
thankless work. —Wait a moment, let me finish. You're
afraid you'll lose your daily bread? Not at all, that would
make us barbarians! No, there's no question of going hungry. You have old-age insurance, and over and above that
our company—I give you my word—will grant you a lifetime pension so that you can be permanently sure of the
same income you have now." He was pleased with himself. This solution, of granting a pension, had only occurred to him while he was talking.

"Well, what do you say to that?" he asked smiling.

Johannes could not reply immediately. During the kind
gentleman's last words his aged child's face had taken on
an expression of dreadful apprehensiveness, his faded
lips had gone completely white, his eyes stared, fixed and
helpless. Only gradually did he regain control of himself.
His chief regarded him with disappointment. And so the
old man began to speak, he spoke very quietly but with
tremendous and anxious urgency, passionately striving to
give the right, the persuasive, the irresistible expression
of his cause. Little red spots appeared and disappeared on
his forehead and cheeks; there was a desperate plea in his
eyes, in the crooked angle of his head, for a hearing, for
mercy; his wrinkled neck twisted, long, beseeching, and
ardent, out of the wide collar of his shirt. Johannes said:

"Please forgive me, sir, for having troubled you. I will
not do it again, never again. It was done in a good cause,
but I realize now that I have been a bother to you. I realize
too that you cannot help me, the wheel runs over us all.

But for God's sake don't take away my work! You reassure me on the subject of going hungry—but that's something I have never feared! I will even be glad to work for smaller wages; no doubt I am no longer very efficient. But leave me my work, leave me my chance to serve, otherwise you kill me!" And very softly, with glowing eyes, hoarse and intense, he went on: "I have nothing at all but this service, it is the one thing that makes me want to live! Oh, Herr Doktor, how could you make this dreadful proposal, you the only one left who knows me, who still knows who I once was!"

The editor endeavored to quiet the man's alarming excitement by patting him repeatedly on the shoulder to the accompaniment of kindly growls. Not because he was calmed but because he sensed the other's good will and sympathy, Johannes began again after a short pause:

"I know, sir, that once in your youth you read Nietzsche's works. Well, I read him too. One evening in my beloved attic study when I was seventeen years old I came upon those pages in *Zarathustra* that contain the Night Song. Never in these almost sixty years have I forgotten that hour, when for the first time I read the words: Night has come; clearer now is the voice of every gushing spring—! For it was at that hour that my life acquired its meaning, that I entered upon that service in which I persevere today, in that hour the marvel of language struck me like sheet lightning, the unspeakable magic of the word; dazzled I looked into an immortal eye, felt a divine presence, and surrendered myself to it as to my fate, my love, my happiness, and my destiny. Then I read other poets, found nobler, more holy words than those of the Night Song, found, as though drawn by a magnet, our great poets, whom no one now knows, found the dream-sweet, dream-heavy Novalis, whose magic words all taste of wine and blood, and the fiery young Goethe, and the old Goethe with his secret smile, I found the dark, hurrying, breathless Brentano, the quick, palpitant Hoffmann, the noble Mörike, the slow, painstaking Stifter, and all, all

the lordly ones: Jean Paul! Arnim! Büchner! Eichendorff!
Heine! I clung to them; my longing was to be their
younger brother, to quaff their words, my sacrament; the
high, holy wood of this poetry became my temple. In this
world I lived; for a time I considered myself almost one of
them; I knew the marvelous delight of running my hands
through the pliant stuff of words like the wind in the tender foliage of summer, of making words ring, dance,
crackle, shudder, snap, sing, shout, freeze, tremble, leap,
congeal. There were people who recognized in me a poet,
in whose hearts my melodies dwelt like harps. Well,
enough of that, enough. There came that time of which
you were pleased to speak, the time when our whole race
turned away from poetry, when all of us as though with
an autumnal pang recognized the fact: Now the temple
doors are closed, now it is evening and the high, wild
woods of poetry are darkened, no man of today can find
the magic path to the inner sanctuary. Quiet had descended and quietly we poets disappeared into the sober
land for which great Pan had died."

The editor squared his shoulders with a feeling of profound unease, an ambiguous and tormenting feeling. To
what mad lengths was this poor old man going? He threw
him a covert glance which clearly said: "All right, all
right, let's drop the subject, we know all about it!" But Johannes had not finished.

"At that time," he went on softly, speaking with difficulty, "at that time I too took leave of poetry, whose heart
had ceased to beat. For a while I lived a lamed and
thoughtless existence until the diminution and finally the
drying up of my customary income from my writings
forced me to seek other means of livelihood. I became a
typesetter because I had by accident learned this trade as
a volunteer at a publisher's. And I have never regretted it
although in the first years this day labor tasted very bitter.
But I found in it what I needed, what every man needs to
be able to live: a task, a meaning for my life. Even a typesetter, honored sir, serves in the temple of language, his

handiwork too is done in the service of the word. I dare
admit this to you today, now that I am an old man: in
lead articles, in the supplements, in the parliamentary de-
bates, in the courtroom notices, in the notes on local
events, and in the advertisements I have quietly corrected
many thousands and tens of thousands of linguistic sins,
I have reset and put on their feet many thousands of crip-
pled sentences. Oh, what joy that gave me! How fine it
was when out of the dictation tossed off by an overworked
editor, out of a garbled quotation by some half-educated
politician, out of the deformed, paralytic syntax of some
reporter, after a few magical touches and alterations, the
pure language looked back at me with sound and undis-
torted features! But as time passed this became constantly
harder, the difference between my language and that of
the fashionable writers grew constantly greater, the cracks
in the structure constantly wider. A lead article that I
could have completely healed twenty years ago by means
of ten or twelve little services of love, today would require
hundreds and thousands of corrections in order to be in
my sense readable. It would no longer work, more and
more often I had to give up. Well yes, you see, even I am
not wholly stiff and reactionary, even I learned, alas, to
make concessions and no longer to oppose the great evil.

"But there is still the other, which I used to consider my
minor service and which for a long time now has been my
only one. Herr Doktor, compare a column I have set with
one in any other paper; the difference will strike you in
the eye. Today's compositors, all of them without exception, have long since acquiesced in linguistic depravity, in
fact they approve it and hasten it on. There is hardly a
single one of them who still knows there is a delicate,
inner law, an unwritten law of art, that governs the position of commas, colons, and semicolons. And how dreadful, how murderous indeed, is the treatment, first in the
typed manuscript and then at the hands of the typesetters,
given to those words that stand at the end of a line and
have the unmerited misfortune to be too long and must

be chopped in two! It is horrible. In our own paper I have
had to witness with increasing frequency as the years
pass hundreds of thousands of such poor words, strangled, falsely divided, dismembered and dishonored words:
circ-umference, reg-ards—yes, once there was withdrawn! Here then is a field where even now I can fight my
daily battle, do my small service in the cause. And you,
sir, do not know, you cannot imagine, how fine it is, what
good it does one, when a word released from the rack, a
sentence clarified by proper punctuation looks gratefully
up at the compositor! No, please never again ask me to
abandon all this and leave it defenseless!"

Although the editor had known Johannes for years he
had never before heard him speak in so animated and personal a way, and while he maintained an attitude of cool
detachment toward what was foolish and exaggerated in
his harangue, nevertheless he felt too there was some
small, hidden value in this confession. Nor was he unaware how highly such conscientiousness and devotion in
a compositor were to be prized. Once more he made his
intelligent face assume an expression of friendliness and
said:

"Well, all right, Johannes, you convinced me some time
ago. Under the circumstances my proposal—it was well
meant, you know—shall be withdrawn. Go on setting
type, keep up the good work! And if there's any other
small favor I can do you, just tell me." He rose, stretching
out his hand to the compositor, convinced that the latter
would now finally go.

But Johannes, seizing the proffered hand with ardor,
opened his heart again, saying: "Thank you, sir, from the
bottom of my heart. How kind you are! Oh, as a matter of
fact, I do have a request, a small request. If you would
only be willing to help me with it!"

Without sitting down again the editor urged him, with
a rather impatient glance, to speak.

"It's about," Johannes said, "once more it's about
'tragic,' Herr Doktor. You know about it, of course; we

have discussed it several times before. You are familiar with the reporters' wretched habit of calling every accident tragic, whereas the proper use—well, I must be brief, enough of that. And so every bicyclist who has tumbled off his machine, every child with a burned finger, every cherry picker who has fallen from his ladder is qualified with the desecrated word 'tragic.' I had almost broken our former reporter of that habit, I gave him no peace, at least once a week I went to see him, and he was a kind man, he laughed and often gave in, possibly he even understood, at least in part, what it meant to me. But now the new editor in charge of local items—I'll say nothing about him in other respects, but I am hardly exaggerating when I state: every chicken that is run over provides him with a welcome opportunity to misuse that sacred word. If you could arrange an opportunity for me to talk seriously to him, if you would ask him for once at least really to listen to me—" The editor stepped to the switchboard, depressed a key, and spoke a few words into the mouthpiece.

"Herr Stettiner will be in his office at two o'clock and will spare you a few minutes. I'll speak to him about it. But be brief when you're talking to him!"

With expressions of thanks the old typesetter took his leave. The editor watched him move gently through the door, saw his thin, white hair straggling down over his funny old linen coat, saw the bent back of the faithful servant, and was no longer sorry he had failed to entice the old man into retirement. Let him stay! Let him go on repeating these audiences once or twice a year. He was not angry. He could quite easily put himself in his place.

That, however, was precisely what Herr Stettiner could not do when Johannes turned up in his office at two o'clock (in the press of business the editor-in-chief had, to be sure, forgotten to inform him).

Herr Stettiner, an extremely useful junior member of the staff who had rapidly swung himself up from district reporter to editorial rank, was by no means a monster; moreover as a reporter he had learned to get along with all sorts of people. But confronted by the phenomenon of Johannes this knowledgeable man was wholly at a loss; he had not in fact known, he had never dreamed, that this sort of human being exists, or existed. Also as an editor he felt, understandably enough, no obligation to accept advice and admonition from a typesetter, even though the latter might be a hundred years old and even though he might in an earlier, sentimental age have been a celebrity, yes, even if he had been Aristotle himself. And so the inevitable happened; after a few minutes Johannes was hastily escorted to the door by an angry, red-faced editor and forced to leave the office. It happened further that a half hour later in the composing room old Johannes, after setting up a quarter column full of unheard-of errors, uttered a plaintive whimper and collapsed over his manuscript. An hour later he was dead.

The people in the composing room, so suddenly robbed of their senior member, agreed after a brief, whispered conference to take up a collection for a wreath to be placed on his coffin. To Herr Stettiner, however, fell the task of composing a small notice of the death, for after all Johannes had been, thirty or forty years before, a kind of celebrity.

He wrote "Tragic End of a Poet"—then he remembered that Johannes had had an odd prejudice against the word "tragic." The strange figure of the ancient and his sudden death shortly after their conversation had, after all, made enough impression on him to make him feel obliged to pay the dead man some honor. Accordingly he struck out the headline and replaced it with the words "Regrettable Demise," suddenly found this, too, empty and inadequate, became annoyed, pulled himself together, and wrote over his notice the final headline "One of the Old Guard."

Dream Journeys

1927

H E WAS A MAN who followed the not very highly regarded profession of popular writer but who belonged, nevertheless, to that smaller circle of authors who
take their profession with the greatest seriousness and are
honored by certain enthusiasts just as true poets used to
be honored in earlier times when poets and poetry still
existed. This man of letters wrote all sorts of pleasant
things; he wrote novels, stories, and even poems, and he
took the greatest pains to do his work well. Seldom, however, did he succeed in satisfying his ambition, for he
made the mistake, although he considered himself a modest man, of presumptuously comparing himself with and
measuring himself against not his colleagues and contemporaries, the other writers of light literature, but the poets
of the past—those, that is, who have survived for generations. And so, to his distress, he had to recognize again
and again that the most successful page he had ever written still fell far short of the most wayward sentence or
verse of those true poets. Thus he grew constantly more
dispirited and lost all joy in his work, and if now and
again he still wrote some trifle, he did so only to give vent
and expression to this dissatisfaction and inner aridity in
bitter criticism of his times and of himself, and naturally
nothing was thereby improved. Sometimes, too, he tried
to find his way back into the enchanted gardens of pure
poetry and praised beauty in pretty word pictures, in
which he paid conscientious tribute to Nature, Women,
and Friendship. These verses did in fact possess a certain
music and some similarity to the true poetry of true poets,

of which they reminded one in much the same way that a passing infatuation or flutter of the emotions may on occasion remind a businessman or worldling of his lost soul.

One day in the season between winter and spring, this author, who would so dearly have loved to be a poet and was even taken for one by some people, was once again sitting at his desk. As usual he had got up late, not until nearly twelve, after having read half the night. Now he was sitting and staring at the place on the page where he had stopped writing the day before. There were clever things on that page, expressed in smooth and cultivated language, delicate conceits, artful descriptions; many a pretty rocket and star shell rose from these lines and pages, many a tender sentiment found expression there— and yet the writer was disillusioned by what he read; sobered, he sat in front of what he had begun the preceding evening with a certain joy and enthusiasm, what for the space of an evening hour had looked like poetry and had now overnight simply turned into literature, into miserable scribbled pages that were really a waste of paper.

And once again in this rather pitiful noonday hour he felt and pondered something he had already felt and pondered many times, namely the odd tragicomedy of his position, the stupidity of his secret pretensions to true poetry (since after all in the real world of today true poetry did not exist and could not exist), and the childishness and silly futility of his efforts, prompted by his love of the old poetry and aided by his fine ear for the words of the true poets, to try to breed something that would be equivalent to true poetry or at any rate would look enough like it to be mistaken for it (since he knew quite well that from education and imitation nothing whatever can be bred).

He was also partially aware that the hopeless striving and childish illusion of all his efforts were by no means an isolated and personal phenomenon, but that every man, even the apparently normal, even the apparently happy and successful, nourishes within himself exactly the same foolish and hopeless self-deception, that every man strives constantly and incessantly after something impossible, that even the most ill-favored carries within him the ideal of Adonis; the most stupid, the ideal of the sage; the poorest, the aspiration to be Croesus. Yes, he actually half knew that even the so greatly venerated ideal of "pure poetry" amounted to nothing, that Goethe had looked up to Homer and Shakespeare just as hopelessly as a writer of today might perhaps look up to Goethe, and that the conception of "poet" was only a lovely abstraction, that even Homer and Shakespeare had been only men of letters, gifted specialists who had succeeded in giving their works an appearance of the impersonal and the eternal. He half knew all this in the way that clever men accustomed to ideas know these obvious and terrifying things. He even knew or surmised that some part of his own attempts at writing would perhaps impress the readers of a later time as "true poetry," that future men of letters would perhaps look back with yearning to him and to his times as though to a golden age in which real poets, real feelings, real human beings, a real nature, and a real soul had still existed. The comfortable philistine of the Biedermeier period and the fat philistine of some small medieval city had, he knew, contrasted their own refined and decadent times in just the same critical and sentimental fashion with an innocent, naïve, blessed yesterday and had regarded their own grandfathers and their way of life with just the same mixture of envy and sympathy with which the men of today regard the blessed time before the invention of the steam engine.

All these thoughts were familiar to the writer, all these truths were known to him. He knew: the same game, the same eager, noble, hopeless striving for something valid, enduring, valuable in itself that impelled him to cover sheets of paper with words, actuated all others as well: the general, the ambassador, the senator, the woman of fashion, the merchant's apprentice. All human beings were striving in some fashion, however cleverly or stupidly, to transcend themselves and the possible, fired by secret desires, dazzled by models, enticed by ideals. No lieutenant who did· not bear within him the idea of Napoleon—and no Napoleon who had not at times felt himself an ape, his triumphs false coin, his goals illusory. No one who had not joined in this dance. No one, either, who had not at some time, through some crevice, perceived the truth about this illusion. To be sure, there were some who were perfect, there were the men-gods, there was a Buddha, there was a Jesus, there was a Socrates. But even they were made perfect, were penetrated through and through by omniscience, only at a single instant, at the instant of their deaths. Indeed, their deaths had been nothing but the last state of transfused understanding, the last, finally successful surrender. And conceivably every death had this significance, conceivably everyone at the point of death was at the point of perfection, having put aside the error of striving, having surrendered himself and no longer desiring to be.

Thoughts of this sort, uncomplicated though they are, seriously disturb a man's efforts, his activity, the continued playing of the game. And so in this hour the work of the aspiring poet did not advance. There was no word worthy of being set down, there was no thought whose communication was really necessary. No, it was a pity to waste paper, better to leave it unmarred.

With this feeling, the writer put away his pen and pushed the sheets of paper into a drawer; had there been a fire, he would have pushed them into that. His state of mind was not new; it was an oft-experienced and by now tamed and gentled despair. He washed his hands, put on his hat and coat, and went out. Change of place was one of his well-tried remedies; he knew it was not good, in such a mood, to stay too long in the same room with all those blank and all those bescribbled sheets of paper. Better to go out, and feel the air and busy one's eyes with the changing spectacle of the streets. Beautiful women might greet him or he might meet a friend; a crowd of schoolchildren or some droll toy in a shopwindow might change the tenor of his thoughts; the automobile of one of the lords of his world, a newspaper publisher or a rich banker, might run over him at a crossing; all sorts of chances for a change of circumstance, for the creation of a new situation.

He wandered slowly through the early spring, looked at the nodding clusters of snowbells in the sad little patches of grass in front of the boarding houses, breathed the soft, moist March air, and was enticed by it into entering a park. There he sat down on a sunny bench between the bare trees, closed his eyes, and gave himself up to the play of the senses in this hour of premature spring sunshine: how softly the air touched his cheeks, with what hidden ardor the sun already seethed, how tart and anxious the earth smelled, with what engaging playfulness the little shoes of children pattered, from time to time, over the gravel of the road, how charmingly and all too sweetly somewhere in the naked copse a blackbird was singing. Yes, all this was very beautiful, and since the spring, the sun, the children, the blackbird were all age-old things in which man had rejoiced for thousands and thousands of years, it was really incomprehensible that one should not be able to make a beautiful spring poem this very day just as well as fifty or a hundred years ago. And yet it was useless. The briefest recollection of Uhland's "Spring Song" (with the Schubert music, to be sure, whose prelude tastes so penetratingly and excitingly of early spring) was sufficient to show a present-day poet most conclusively that those enchanting things were, for the time being, exhausted as subjects for poetry and that there was no sense in attempting to imitate in any way those inexhaustibly full, blessedly living creations.

At this instant, as the poet's thoughts were on the point of slipping back into their old, unfruitful groove, he peeped out from beneath lowered eyelids and perceived, not with his eyes alone, a luminous fluttering and twinkling, islands of sunshine, reflected light, shadowy hol-

lows, blue sky touched with white, a flickering round of
dancing lights such as anyone sees when squinting at the
sun, only somehow significant, in some fashion valuable
and unique, transformed through some secret content
from simple perception into an experience. What flashed
out here in prismatic hues, fluctuating, receding, undulat-
ing, and pulsing, was not just a storm of light from outside, whose theater was simply the eye; it was at the same
time life, the impulse surging up from within, and its
theater was the soul, was his own fate. This is the way the
poets see, the "seers"; this is the enchanting and shatter-
ing fashion in which those who have been touched by
Eros feel. Gone was all thought of Uhland and Schubert
and spring songs; there no longer was an Uhland, a
poetry, a past; everything was the eternal instant, was experience, was profoundest reality.

In complete submission to this miracle—which he had
experienced before, but for which he thought he had long
since forfeited the capacity and grace—he hovered for unending instants in timelessness, in a harmony of world
and soul, he felt his breath waft the clouds, he felt the
warm sun revolving in his breast.

But while he remained surrendered to this strange experience, his eyes narrowed and all the gates of sense half
closed—for he knew the propitious current came from
within—he became aware of something close to him on
the ground that riveted his attention. It was, as he realized
only slowly and by degrees, a girl's foot, a child's; it was
in a low, brown shoe and it moved firmly and gaily upon
the sand of the walk with the weight on the heel. This little girl's shoe, the brown of the leather, the childish happy
lifting of the little sole, the span of silk stocking over a
delicate ankle, reminded the poet of something, overwhelmed his heart suddenly and urgently like the recollection of a profound experience, but he could not find the
thread. A child's shoe, a child's foot, a child's stocking—

what connection could they have with him? Where was
the key? Where was the spring in his soul that responded
to just this image among millions, loved it, drew it close,
perceived it as precious and important? For an instant he
opened his eyes wide, saw for the space of half a heartbeat
the whole figure of the child, a pretty child, but he realized at once that this was no longer the image that concerned him, that was important to him, and with involuntary speed he closed his eyes again to the point where he
could just see, for the remnant of an instant, the child's
disappearing foot. Then he shut his eyes completely, med-
itating on the foot, feeling its significance, yet not understanding it, tormented by his fruitless searching, enraptured by the power of the image in his soul. Somewhere,
sometime this little image, this delicate foot in its brown
shoe, had been perceived by him and had become infused
with the value of experience. When had that happened?
Oh, it must have been a long time ago, ages ago, so far
away did it seem to lie, from such a long way off, from
such unthinkable depths of space did it look up at him, so
deep was it sunk in the well of his memory. Perhaps he
had been carrying it within him, lost and never regained
until today, since the very beginnings of childhood, since
that fabulous time whose memories are all so indistinct
and formless, so hard to recall, and yet are more colorful,
warmer, fuller, than all later memories. For a long time
with closed eyes he rocked his head, lost in reflection, seeing now this, now that clue light up, this series, that chain
of experiences, but nowhere was the child with the brown
shoe at home. No, she was not to be found, it was hopeless
to continue the search.

His experience in this memory quest was like that of a
man who cannot recognize something directly in front of
him because he thinks of it as far away and therefore mis-
interprets all its features. But then at the moment when
he abandoned his efforts and was ready to forget this ridiculous little squint-eyed incident, the thing twisted around
and the child's shoe fell into place. With a deep sigh the

man suddenly realized that in the crowded storeroom of
his inner life the child's shoe did not lie at the bottom,
did not belong among his ancient possessions, but was
quite fresh and new. Only recently had he been concerned
with this child, only recently, so it seemed to him, had he
seen that shoe running off.

And now all of a sudden he had it. Yes, oh yes, there it
was, there stood the child whose shoe it was, part of a
dream the writer had dreamed the night before. Dear God,
how was such forgetfulness possible? During the night he
had awakened, enchanted and shaken by the mysterious
power of his dream, had awakened with the feeling of
having had a significant and splendid experience—and
then he had presently gone to sleep again, and a single
hour of morning sleep had sufficed to wipe out the whole
splendid experience so that only at this second, wakened
by the fleeting sight of the child's foot, had he thought of
it again. So fleeting, so transitory, so completely subject to
chance were the deepest, the most wonderful experiences
of the soul! And look, even now he was not successful in
building up in his mind the whole of last night's dream.
Only isolated pictures, some of them unconnected, were
still to be found, some fresh and full of living radiance,
others already gray and dusty, already on the point of
fading away. And yet what a beautiful, profound, life-
giving dream it had been! How his heart had beaten when
he first awoke in the night, enchanted and afraid like a
child on a holiday! How completely filled he had been with
the lively assurance that this dream was a noble, profound, unforgettable, never-to-be-lost experience! And
now, only a few hours later, all that was left was these
fragments, these few fading pictures, this faint echo in
his heart—all the rest was lost, gone, no longer alive!

All the same, these few bits at least had been rescued.
The writer immediately decided to search about in his
memory for whatever was left of the dream and to write
it down as truly and accurately as possible. At once he
took his notebook out of his pocket and made the first en-

tries in catch-words, with the intention of establishing if possible the structure and outline, the general shape of the dream. But in this too he was unsuccessful. Neither beginning nor end could now be distinguished, and he did not know where most of the remaining fragments fitted into the dream story. No, he would have to set about it differently. He must, first of all, rescue what was within reach, must at once fix firmly the few unfaded images, above all the child's shoe, before they too, those timid magic birds, had fled.

Like an archaeologist attempting to decipher a new-found inscription, starting with the few still-recognizable letters or pictograms, so our man sought to read his dream by putting it together piece by piece.

In the dream he had had something to do with a girl, a strange, perhaps not really beautiful but somehow fascinating girl, who was perhaps thirteen or fourteen years old but small for her age. Her face was tanned. Her eyes? No, he did not see them. Her name? Unknown. Her relationship to him, the dreamer? Stop, there was the brown shoe! He saw it move together with its twin, saw it dancing, saw it take a dance step, a step in the Boston. Oh yes, now one knew a lot. He must begin all over again.

Well then: In the dream he had danced with a strange, marvelous little girl, a child with a tanned face and brown shoes—had not everything about her been brown? Her hair too? And her eyes? No, he could no longer be sure—it was reasonable, it seemed possible, but it was not certain. He must stick to certainties, to what had firm support in his memory, otherwise he would be lost. Already he was beginning to suspect that this dream search would lead him far afield, that he had set out upon a long, an unending road. And at that very instant he found another piece.

Yes, he had danced with the little one, or had wanted to dance, or had been supposed to dance, and she had taken a series of gay, buoyant, enchantingly formal dance steps all by herself. Or had he danced with her after all, had she in fact not been alone? No. No, he had not

danced, he had only wanted to, or rather it had been
agreed, by him and by someone else, that he was to dance
with the little brown girl. But then the little one had begun
to dance alone, without him, and he had been somehow
afraid of the dance or embarrassed; it was the Boston, a
dance he did not know well. But she had begun to dance
by herself, playfully, with marvelous rhythm, her little
brown shoes carefully describing the figures of the dance
on the rug. But why hadn't he danced? Or why had he
originally wanted to dance? What sort of agreement had
there been? He could not discover.

Another question presented itself: Whom had the precious child resembled, of whom had she reminded him?
For a long time he searched in vain; again everything
seemed hopeless, and for a moment he became really impatient and irritated, again he was almost ready to give
up. But once more there came a flash, a new clue blazed
up. The little one had resembled his beloved—oh no, resemblance was not it, he had even been surprised that she
was so little like her, although she was her sister. Stop!
Her sister? Oh now the whole search was illuminated,
took on meaning; everything was there again. He began
once more to make notes, overcome by the suddenly
emerging inscription, deeply delighted by the return of
the pictures he had thought lost.

Thus it had been: Magda, his beloved, had been present
in the dream; moreover she had not been quarrelsome
and ill-disposed as of late but altogether friendly, rather
quiet but contented and beautiful. Magda had greeted
him with a strange, calm tenderness, had given him her
hand without kissing him, and had explained that now at
last she was going to introduce him to her mother and
that there at her mother's he would meet her younger sister, who was destined later to become his beloved and his
wife. Her sister was much younger than she and very fond
of dancing, he would win her quickest by taking her dancing.

How beautiful Magda had been in that dream! How all

that was distinctive, lovable, soulful, and tender in her
being, as those qualities had existed in his mind at the
time of his greatest love for her, had shone forth from her
cool eyes, her clear brow, her heavy, fragrant hair!

And then in the dream she had led him into a house,
her mother's house, the house of her childhood, the house
of her soul, so that she might show him her mother and
her small, prettier sister, for it was she who was destined
to be his beloved. He could not, however, any longer remember the house. Only the empty entrance hall in which
he had to wait, nor could he any longer recall the mother;
only an old woman, a *bonne* or nurse, dressed in gray or
black had been visible in the background. But then the little one had come, the sister, an enchanting child, a girl of
perhaps ten or twelve but in manner like one of fourteen.
In particular her foot in its brown shoe had been so childlike, so wholly innocent, laughing, and unaware, not yet
entirely ladylike and yet so womanly! She had received his
greeting gaily, and from that moment on Magda had disappeared, only the little one was there. Remembering
Magda's advice, he had proposed a dance. And at once she
had nodded, beaming, and without hesitation had begun
to dance, alone, and he had not even ventured to put his
arm around her and dance with her because she was so
beautiful and so perfect in her childish dance, and then
too because what she was dancing was the Boston, a
dance in which he did not feel sure of himself.

In the midst of his struggle to recapture the dream pictures, the writer had to smile at himself for a moment.
He realized that he had just been thinking how profitless
it was to worry about a new poem to spring, since it
had all long ago been said unsurpassably—but when he
thought about the foot of the dancing child, the light,
charming movement of the brown shoes, the neatness of
the dance figure they described on the carpet, and how,
nevertheless, over all this pretty grace and assurance
hung a trace of embarrassment, a fragrance of maidenly

shyness, then it was clear to him that one need only sing a song to that childish foot in order to surpass all that earlier poets had said about spring and youth and the presentiment of love. But his thoughts had barely strayed into this field, he had barely begun to toy with the idea of a poem "To a Foot in a Brown Shoe," when he realized with horror that the whole dream was beginning to slip from him again, that the blissful pictures were growing insubstantial and melting away. Alarmed, he forcibly controlled his thoughts, and yet he realized that at this moment, although he had written down the content of the dream, it did not any longer belong to him completely, that it was beginning to grow alien and old. And he immediately realized, too, that this would always be so: that these enchanting pictures would only belong to him and fill his soul with their fragrance as long as he dwelt upon them wholeheartedly, without ulterior thought, without design, without anxiety.

Thoughtfully the poet started on his way home, carrying the dream before him like an infinitely complex, infinitely fragile toy of thinnest glass. He was full of concern about his dream. Oh, if he could only succeed in reconstructing completely within himself the figure of his dream beloved! To restore the whole from the brown shoe, the dancing figure, the shimmer of brown in the little one's face, from these few, precious fragments, seemed more important to him than anything else in the world. And was it not in fact infinitely important to him? Had not this charming spring figure been promised to him as his beloved, had she not been born out of the deepest and best springs of his soul, had she not come to meet him as a symbol of his future, as a presentiment of what fate held in store for him? —And while he was filled with concern, he was nevertheless infinitely happy in the depths of his being. Was it not marvelous that one could dream such things, that one bore within oneself this world of airiest magic stuff, that inside our souls where we have so often sought in vain, as though in a refuse heap, some remnant of faith, of joy, of life, that inside these souls such flowers could spring up?

Arrived home, the writer shut the door behind him and lay back in his easy chair. Notebook in hand, he read through his jottings attentively and found that they were worthless, that they contributed nothing, that they only hindered and obstructed. He tore out the pages and carefully destroyed them and decided not to write down anything more. In agitation he lay there seeking composure, and suddenly another piece of the dream emerged. All at once he saw himself again in the unfamiliar house, waiting in the bare entrance hall, saw in the background an anxious old lady in a dark dress moving back and forth, felt once more the moment of fate: that now Magda had gone to bring him his new, younger, fairer, his true and eternal beloved. Kindly and anxiously the old woman looked over at him—and behind her features and behind her gray clothes other features and other clothes were discernible, faces of attendants and nurses out of his own childhood, the face and gray housedress of his mother. And so from this layer of memories, from this motherly, sisterly circle of pictures, he felt the future, the beloved, growing to meet him. Behind this empty entrance hall, under the eyes of anxious, sweet, devoted mothers and maids, had grown the child, whose love was to bless him, whose possession was to be his happiness and whose future was to be his own.

Magda, too, he now saw again; how she greeted him without a kiss so tenderly and earnestly, how her face had once more contained, as though in the golden light of evening, all the magic it had once held for him, how at the moment of renunciation and parting she once more shone with all the amiability of their happiest times, how her thoughtful, serious countenance heralded in advance the younger, fairer one, the true, the only one, whom she had come to bring him and to help him win. She seemed to be a symbol of love itself, her humility, her pliability, her half-maternal, half-childlike magic power. All that he had ever read into this woman, all that he had dreamed and wished and invented for her, all the glorification and worship he had offered her in the high time of his love was concentrated in her face, her whole soul and his own love shone visibly from her serious, lovely features, smiled sadly and kindly from her eyes. Was it possible to take leave of such a beloved? But her glance said: Parting must be, the new must take place.

And on the nimble feet of a little child in came the new, in came her sister, but her face was not to be seen, nothing of her was clearly to be seen except that she was small and delicate, had on brown shoes, was brown in face and brown in dress, and that she could dance with enchanting perfection. And, moreover, the Boston—the dance her future lover did not know by any means well. Nothing could have better expressed the superiority of the child over the grown, experienced, often disillusioned man than that she danced so freely, lithely, faultlessly, and in particular the dance in which he was weak, in which he was hopelessly inferior to her!

All day the writer remained absorbed in his dream, and the deeper he penetrated into it the more beautiful it appeared to him and the more it seemed to excel all the poems of the best poets. For a long time, for many days, he cherished the desire to record this dream so that it would have, not for the dreamer alone but for others as well, this unspeakable beauty, depth, and intensity. Only at long last he abandoned these wishes and efforts and realized that he must content himself with being a true poet, a dreamer, a seer, only in his soul, and that his handiwork must remain that of a simple man of letters.

Harry, the Steppenwolf

1928

THE ENTERPRISING OWNER of a small menagerie had succeeded in signing up Harry, the famous Steppenwolf, for a short engagement. He had posters put up all over town, confident that they would draw a large crowd, and in this expectation he was not disappointed. Everyone had heard of the Steppenwolf, his legend had become a favorite topic of conversation in cultivated society; everyone had his bit of information to contribute, and opinions were very much divided. Some held that such an animal was under all circumstances a dangerous, unwholesome phenomenon; nothing was sacred to him, he scoffed at respectability, ripped the portraits of the great off the walls of the temples of culture and went so far as to ridicule Johann Wolfgang von Goethe; he was infecting the young with his asocial attitude, and the only solution was for all respectable citizens to band together and do away with him, for until he was dead and buried he would give the community no peace. But this simple, straightforward, and probably sound opinion was far from universal. There was a second party, which held an entirely different view, namely, that though the Steppenwolf was indeed a dangerous animal, he not only had a right to live, but also performed an ethical and social function. Each one of us, said the adherents of this party, who for the most part were highly educated, each one of us secretly and unbeknownst even to himself nurtures a Steppenwolf in his bosom. The bosoms referred to by the speakers of these words were the highly respectable bosoms of the best society, of lawyers and manufacturers, and these bosoms were covered with silk shirts and vests of the most modern cut. Deep within him, said these liberal-minded persons, each one of us has the feelings, instincts, and sufferings of the Steppenwolf; we must all come to grips with such instincts, for at heart each one of us is a poor, howling, hungry Steppenwolf. So they spoke when under cover of their silk shirts and fashionable vests they discussed the Steppenwolf, and many who publicly criticized him assented. Then the gentlemen put on their fine felt hats and sumptuous fur coats, got into their sumptuous motor cars, and rode back to their work, to their offices, editorial rooms, and factories. One evening, as a group of these eminent citizens gathered over their whiskey, one of them even suggested that they start an association of Steppenwolves.

On the day when the menagerie opened its new attraction, many curious persons came to see the notorious animal. A visit to his cage cost an extra groschen. It was a small cage, formerly inhabited by a panther who had regrettably died before his time. The enterprising owner had done his best to furnish it for the occasion, something of a problem, for this Steppenwolf was undoubtedly a rather unusual animal. Just as our friends and lawyers and industrialists allegedly had a wolf concealed beneath their shirts and frock coats, so in his hairy breast this wolf allegedly concealed a complex human soul, Mozart arias, and so on. To do justice to the unusual circumstances and the expectations of the public, the shrewd entrepreneur (who had known for years that the wildest animals are not so capricious, dangerous, and incalculable as the public) had resorted to rather startling accessories, emblems as it were of the wolf-man. It was an ordinary cage, with iron bars and a bit of straw on the floor, but on one wall hung a handsome Empire mirror and in the middle of the cage there was an open small piano, a pianette. On top of this rather wobbly piece of furniture stood a plaster bust of Goethe, the prince of poets.

As for the animal himself, who had aroused so much

curiosity, there seemed to be nothing in the least remarkable about him. He looked exactly as a Steppenwolf, *Lupus campestris*, cannot help looking. Most of the time he lay motionless in a corner, as far as possible from the visitors, gnawing on his forepaws and staring into space as though he had before him not bars but the endless steppe. Now and then he stood up and strode back and forth a few times; then the piano wobbled on the uneven floor and the plaster Olympian also wobbled alarmingly. The animal paid little attention to the visitors, and most of them were rather disappointed in his looks. But here again there were divergent opinions. Many declared that he was a perfectly ordinary animal, without expression, a common dull-witted beast, and that was that; and furthermore, "Steppenwolf" was not a biological term. Others maintained on the contrary that the animal had beautiful eyes and that his whole being expressed such soulfulness that one's heart went out to him in sympathy. Only a handful of intelligent visitors realized that the remarks of both camps would have applied equally well to any other animal in the menagerie.

Early in the afternoon two children accompanied by their governess entered the room with the wolf's cage in it and stood for a long time watching him. One of the children was a pretty, rather quiet eight-year-old girl, the other a sturdy boy of about twelve. The Steppenwolf liked them both, their skin smelled young and healthy; he kept eyeing the little girl's firm, well-shaped legs. The governess, well, that was something else again; he thought it preferable to pay her as little attention as possible.

In order to be near the pretty little girl Harry lay down just behind the bars of his cage. While enjoying the children's scent, he listened to the three of them and was rather bored by their conversation. They were talking about Harry, in whom they all seemed to take a lively interest. But their attitudes were very different. The boy, a healthy, active young fellow, staunchly supported the opinion he had heard from his father at home. A cage in

a menagerie, he said, was just the right place for such a[n]
animal; to let him run around loose would be irresponsibl[e]
foolishness. In a pinch they could try to train him, mayb[e]
he could be taught to pull sleds like a husky, but it pro[b-]
ably wouldn't work. No, if young Gustav were to com[e]
across this wolf, no matter where, he would not hesita[te]
to shoot him down.

The Steppenwolf listened and licked his chops amiab[ly].
He liked the boy. "I only hope," he thought, "that if [we]
should suddenly meet, you'll have a gun. And I hop[e I]
meet you out in the steppe, rather than surprise you [by]
stepping out of your mirror." Yes, the boy appealed to h[im].
He would grow up to be a spirited young man, a con[ten-]
tent and successful engineer or manufacturer or offi[cer,]
and Harry would have no objection to measuring [his]
strength with him now and then and, if the worst cam[e to]
the worst, to being shot by him.

It would have been harder to say how the pretty [little]
girl felt about the Steppenwolf. At first she just lo[oked]
at him, but much more carefully and with much [more]
curiosity than the two others, who thought they alr[eady]
knew all about him. The little girl discovered that she [liked]
Harry's tongue and teeth; she liked his eyes too, bu[t she]
had misgivings about his rather unkempt coat, an[d his]
pungent animal smell aroused a strange feeling of e[xcite-]
ment, in which revulsion, disgust, and prurient cu[riosity]
were mingled. All in all, she liked him and it di[dn't]
escape her that Harry was very fond of her, that h[e was]
looking at her with admiration and desire. She bre[athed]
in his admiration with visible pleasure and from t[ime to]
time asked a question.

"Fräulein, why has this wolf got a piano in his [cage?]"
she asked. "Wouldn't he rather have something t[o eat?]"

"He's not an ordinary wolf," said the governess[, "he's]
a musical wolf. But you're too young to understan[d that.]"

The little girl frowned and said: "There seem t[o be a lot]
of things that I'm too young to understand. If the [wolf is]
musical, of course he should have a piano, two [if he]

care. But that statue on top of the piano—I do think it's funny. What is he supposed to do with it?"

"It's a symbol." The governess was about to launch into an explanation, but the wolf came to the little girl's help. With a loving look at her, he jumped up so suddenly that for a moment all three were afraid, stretched voluptuously, went over to the wobbly piano, and began to rub and scrape against it. He went on rubbing more and more violently, until the wobbly bust lost its balance and fell. The floor resounded, and Goethe, like the Goethe of certain learned professors, broke into three pieces. The wolf sniffed for a moment at each of the three fragments, then turned his back on them with indifference, and went back to the vicinity of the little girl.

At this point the governess took the center of the stage. She was one of those who despite sports clothes and bobbed hair felt certain that they had discovered wolves in their bosoms. She was one of Harry's readers and admirers and regarded herself as his soul sister, for deep down inside her she too had all sorts of complicated feelings and conflicts. A faint voice told her, to be sure, that her sheltered middle-class life was not really a steppe or a wilderness, that she would never summon up the courage or despair to break out of it and like Harry to take a desperate leap into chaos. No, of course she would never do any such thing. But she would always have sympathy and understanding for the Steppenwolf, and she wished she could let him see it. The next time this Harry reverted to human form and put on a dinner jacket, she had a good mind to invite him to tea or to play Mozart with her four-handed. Yes, indeed, she would try.

Meanwhile the little eight-year-old had been giving the wolf her undivided attention. She was delighted with his cleverness in toppling the bust. She knew he had done it for her benefit; he had understood her words and clearly sided with her against her governess. Would he demolish the silly piano too? Oh, he was marvelous, she just loved him.

But Harry had lost interest in the piano. He crouched down as near as he could get to the child, and lay there like a fawning dog with his head on the floor and his muzzle thrust forward between the bars, looking up at her with rapture in his eyes. The child could not resist. Spellbound and trusting, she put out her little hand and stroked his dark nose. Harry ogled at her encouragingly and gently licked her little hand with his warm tongue.

When the governess saw this, her mind was made up. She too wanted to make herself known to Harry as an understanding sister; she too wanted to establish a bond with him. Quickly she untied the gold string on the elegant little package she was holding, unwrapped it, and peeled the silver paper from a pretty chocolate heart. Then with a glance full of deep meaning she held it out to the wolf.

Harry blinked and quietly went on licking the little girl's hand, but at the same time he kept a close eye on the governess's movements. And the instant the hand with the chocolate heart was close enough, he snapped like a flash, closing his teeth on heart and hand. The three visitors screamed in unison and recoiled, but the governess was unable to get away, for her brother wolf held her fast, and it was several anguished moments before she was able to pull back her bleeding hand and look at it. It had been bitten to the bone.

The poor young lady let out another piercing scream. But in that moment she was fully cured of her inner conflict. No, she was not a she-wolf, she had nothing in common with this loathsome brute, who was now sniffing with interest at the bloody chocolate heart. And then and there she declared war.

A bewildered group formed around the governess and she found herself face to face with the livid menagerie owner. Standing straight and firm, holding out her bleeding hand for fear of soiling her dress, she declared with breathtaking eloquence that she would not rest until this brutal assault had been avenged, and the guilty parties would be amazed to hear the amount of damages she would demand for the disfiguring of her shapely pianist's hand. And the wolf had to be killed, she wouldn't settle for less, they would see.

Quickly recovering his composure, the owner called her attention to the chocolate heart, which was still lying in front of Harry. There were signs all about, saying that it was strictly forbidden to feed the animals. Which relieved him of all responsibility. Let her sue him, no court in the world would take her part. Moreover, he had liability insurance. But right now, if the young lady knew what was good for her, she would see a doctor.

And so she did; but no sooner had the doctor dressed her wounds than she went on to see a lawyer. The next day people flocked to Harry's cage by the hundreds.

Since then the whole town has been talking about the lawsuit between the lady and the Steppenwolf. For the plaintiff is taking the position that Harry the wolf is primarily responsible and the owner of the menagerie a mere accessory. For, as the complaint explains at great length, this Harry cannot be regarded as an irresponsible animal; he is a citizen with a first and last name, he has been employed only temporarily as a wolf, and has published his memoirs. Regardless of what the lower court may decide, the case is sure to make its way through all the echelons of justice and ultimately to be set before the Reich Court.

Accordingly, the highest judicial authority in the land can be expected in the foreseeable future to provide us with a definitive decision on the question: Is the Steppenwolf, in the last analysis, an animal or a man?

An Evening with Dr. Faust

1929

D R. FAUST WAS SITTING at his dining table with his friend Dr. Eisenbart (the great-grandfather, it might be said, of the physician who was later to become so famous*). The sumptuous dinner was over, the heavy gilded goblets were filled with fragrant Rhine wine, and the musicians, a flutist and a lutenist, who had played during the meal, had just vanished.

"Now," said Dr. Faust, taking a swallow of the old wine, "I shall give you the promised demonstration." He was no longer a young man and had grown somewhat heavy about the jowls. This was two or three years before his terrible end.

"I have already told you that my famulus sometimes makes odd contrivances that enable us to see and hear far into the past and future. And now the fellow has invented something most curious and amusing. He has often shown us the heroes and fair ladies of the past in magical mirrors. But now he has devised something for the ear, a kind of horn through which we can hear the sounds that some day in the distant future will occur in the spot where this mechanism is placed."

"But, my good friend, might your retainer not be hoodwinking you a little?"

"I don't believe so," said Faust. "The future is by no means inaccessible to black magic. As you know, we have always gone by the assumption that all happenings on earth, without exception, are subject to the law of cause

---

* Dr. Johannes Andreas Eisenbart (1661–1727). His name has become proverbial for a crude, brutal physician, a quack.—Ed.

and effect. Accordingly, the future can be modified no more than the past; it too is determined by the law of causality. Consequently every future occurrence is already present, though we are not yet able to see and to taste it. Just as a mathematician and astronomer can predict the exact time of an eclipse far in advance, so it would be possible, if we had devised a method, to render any other portion of the future visible and audible. And now Mephistopheles has invented a sort of auditory divining rod; he has built a trap in which to catch the sounds that will occur here in this room several hundred years hence. We have tried it a number of times. Sometimes, of course, there is no sound, but that only means that we have struck a vacuum in the future, a moment in which nothing audible is happening here. On other occasions we have heard all sorts of things; once, for instance, we heard a group of people who will live in the remote future talking about a poem in which the exploits of Dr. Faustus—*my* exploits— are related. But enough, suppose we try it."

In answer to his call, the famulus appeared in his customary gray friar's robe. He was carrying a small contrivance equipped with a horn, which he set down on the table. Having impressed it on the gentlemen that they must be absolutely silent during the whole performance, he turned a crank, and the machine began to hum softly.

For quite some time there was nothing to be heard but this humming, to which both doctors listened in tense anticipation. Then suddenly there came a sound such as they had never heard before: a wild, evil, diabolical howling. Was it some unknown monster, or was it an infuriated demon? Impatient, angry, menacing, it recurred in short violent outbursts suggesting nothing so much as the hissing of a hunted dragon. Dr. Eisenbart went pale, and heaved a sigh of relief when finally, after many repetitions, the hideous screams lost themselves in the distance.

A silence followed, but then came a new sound: a man's voice as though from far away, speaking in insistent, didactic tones. The listeners were able to hear snatches of

what was said, and jot down the words on the writing pads
that had been placed in readiness. Such sentences as:

". . . and so, in emulation of America's shining example, the ideal of industrial progress is moving irresistibly toward its victorious realization and completion . . .
While on the one hand the comfort of the working class
has achieved unprecedented levels . . . and we can say
without presumption that thanks to modern techniques of
production our ancestors' childlike dreams of paradise
have been more than . . ."

Again silence. Then came a new voice, deep and solemn, saying: "Ladies and gentlemen, may I now ask
you to lend ear to a poem by the great Nicholas Under-
wrought, who, I may say without exaggeration, is without
equal when it comes to baring the innermost essence of
our times and penetrating the sense and non-sense of our
existence.

> *"He holds a chimney in his hands*
> *On either cheek he bears a bladder*
> *And when the pressure gauge demands*
> *He climbs a rungless ladder.*
>
> *And so he climbs up ladders long*
> *As clouds about his shirttails blow,*
> *And fearing lest his life go wrong*
> *He's overcome by vertigo."*

Dr. Faust was able to copy the greater part of this
poem, and Eisenbart was also hard at work.

A sleepy voice, undoubtedly that of an elderly woman,
was heard. She said: Boring program. Is that what they
invented the radio for? But never mind. Now we'll have
some music at least."

And a moment later there was indeed an eruption of
music, wild, sensual, strongly rhythmical, jangling and
languid by turns, an utterly unfamiliar, strangely indecent, malignant music, played by howling, croaking, cack-

ling wind instruments, punctuated by gongs, through which one could occasionally hear a howling voice singing words in an unknown language.

At regular intervals a mysterious couplet rang out:

> *Googoo, if applied each night,*
> *Will make your tresses smooth and bright.*

And intermittently the first malignant, menacing sound, the howl of an angry tormented dragon, was repeated.

When the famulus smilingly stopped his machine, the two scholars exchanged looks of shame and embarrassment, as though they had been involuntary witnesses to an indecent, forbidden incident. They read through their notes and showed them to one another.

"What do you think of it?" Faust asked at length.

Dr. Eisenbart took a long swallow from his beaker; he looked at the floor and remained for a long while thoughtful and silent. Finally he said, more to himself than to his friend: "It's horrible. It cannot be doubted that mankind, of whose life we have just heard a sampling, is mad. It is our descendants, the sons of our sons, the great-grandchildren of our great-grandchildren, that we have heard saying such dismal, distressing, confused things, uttering such horrifying screams, and singing those incomprehensible, idiotic verses. Our descendants, friend Faust, will end in madness."

"I wouldn't be so sure of that," said Faust. "Your opinion is not unplausible, but it is more pessimistic than need be. The occurrence of such wild, desperate, indecent, and undoubtedly insane sounds in one little corner of the earth does not necessarily mean that all mankind has gone mad. Perhaps in a few hundred years an insane asylum will be built on this particular spot, and we have been listening to a sampling of its daily life. Or possibly the people we have been listening to were dead drunk. Think of the merrymakers at carnival time, and how they roar. It sounds very much the same. But what alarms me is those other sounds, those screams that can have been produced neither by human voices nor by musical instruments. They strike me as absolutely diabolical. Only demons can make such sounds."

He turned to Mephistopheles. "Do you happen to know anything about it? Can you tell us what manner of sounds we have been listening to?"

"Indeed," said the famulus, smiling, "we have heard demonic sounds. A time will come when the earth, a good half of which is the devil's property even now, will belong to him entirely; it will form a part, a province, of hell. You have spoken rather harshly and disparagingly of the word-and-sound language of this earthly hell, gentlemen. In my opinion it is pleasant and not without interest to observe that there will be music and poetry even in hell. Belial is in charge of that department. I should say that he handles it very nicely."

Edmund

1934

EDMUND WAS a gifted young man of good family. For several years he had been the favorite student of the then widely known Professor Zerkel.

The so-called postwar period was drawing to a close. The great wars, overpopulation, and the total disappearance of morality and religion had given Europe the despairing face that we see in nearly all the portraits of representative figures of that age. The period known as the "Rebirth of the Middle Ages" had not yet actually begun, but the ideas and values which had enjoyed universal validity and esteem for more than a hundred years had been shaken, and dissatisfaction with those branches of knowledge and activity which had been most favored since the beginning of the nineteenth century was becoming more and more widespread. People had had their fill of analytical methods, of technology as an end in itself, of logical explanations, of the shallow rationalistic world view, associated with such names as Darwin, Marx, and Haeckel, which had dominated European culture only a few decades before. In advanced circles such as that to which Edmund belonged, the prevailing attitude was one of weariness, reflected in a skeptical, disillusioned self-criticism, not entirely free from vanity. These intellectuals went so far as to cultivate a contempt for themselves and their habitual methods. They took a fanatical interest in the study of religions, which at that time was highly developed. They no longer, as in times gone by, considered the records of past religions primarily from a historical, sociological, or philosophical point of view, but tried to penetrate their immediate reality, the psychological and magical workings of their forms, images, and usages. The older men and teachers, to be sure, continued to be motivated largely by the somewhat disabused curiosity of the pure scientist, by a certain pleasure in collecting, comparing, explaining, classifying, and knowing best; but the younger men pursued these studies in a new spirit. They not only revered, but actually envied the manifestations of religious life. They thirsted to know the inner meanings of the cults and formulas that history has transmitted to us, and were animated by a secret desire—half weariness with life, half readiness to believe—to get to the heart of religion, to achieve a faith and state of mind which would enable them, as it had their remote ancestors, to live with the freshness and intensity that emanate from religious cults and the art works of the early world.

The story of the young *privatdozent* in Marburg, who had set out to write a paper on the life and death of the pious poet Novalis, was much talked of. As we know, this Novalis decided, after the death of his fiancée, to follow her into death. Pious poet that he was, he did not to this end resort to mechanical means such as poison or firearms, but slowly induced death by purely psychic and magical methods. And he died very young. Falling under the spell of this extraordinary life and death, the *privatdozent* conceived the desire to do as the poet had done and to die by pure psychic imitation and attunement. He was motivated not so much by weariness with life as by the desire for a miracle, that is, the desire to influence and govern physical life through the powers of the soul. And indeed he lived in imitation of the poet and like him died before attaining the age of thirty. The case attracted attention and the *privatdozent* was violently condemned by all the older conservatives and by those among the young who found contentment in sports and in the material enjoyment of life. But enough of that; our aim is not to analyze the period, but solely to give an idea of the mood and state of mind prevailing in the circles to which young Edmund belonged.

He was studying the science of religions under Professor Zerkel. He was interested almost exclusively in those partly religious, partly magical exercises in which the people of former times tried to achieve spiritual mastery of their lives and to fortify the human soul against nature and fate. He was not, like his teacher, concerned with the intellectual and literary aspect of the religions, with their so-called philosophies. What he tried to fathom and to understand was the rites, exercises, and formulas that acted directly upon life: the secret power of symbols and sacraments, the techniques of psychic concentration, the means of provoking creative states. The superficial way in which a whole century had explained such phenomena as asceticism, exorcism, monasticism, and anchoritism had long since given way to serious study. At the moment Edmund was attending an exclusive seminar under Zerkel. Apart from him there was only one student. This seminar was devoted to the study of certain magic formulas and tantras that had recently been discovered in northern India. The professor's interest in the matter was purely scientific; he collected and classified such phenomena as another man might collect insects. But he was well aware that his student Edmund had been brought to these formulas of magic and prayer by a very different impulse, and he had also noticed that thanks to the greater piety of his approach the student had penetrated certain secrets which had evaded the teacher. He hoped to keep this good student with him for years and to make him his associate.

They were engaged in deciphering, translating, and interpreting the texts of these Indic tantras, and Edmund had just translated one of the texts as follows:

"If you find yourself in a situation where your soul falls sick and forgets what it needs for life, and you wish to know what it is that your soul needs and that you must give it: then make your heart empty, limit your breathing to a minimum, perceive the center of your head as an empty cave, direct your gaze upon this cave, and concentrate on the contemplation of it. Then the cave will suddenly cease to be empty and will show you an image of what your soul needs in order to go on living."

"Excellent," said the professor, nodding. "But where you say 'forget' I believe it would be somewhat more accurate to say 'lose.' And have you noticed that the word for 'cave' is the same as that which those shrewd priests or doctors of magic employ for womb? Those fellows actually succeeded in transforming a set of rather dry instructions for the cure of melancholia into a complicated magic formula. This *mar pegil trafu gnoki* with its reminiscences of the great snake-magic formula must have sounded quite eerie and terrifying to the poor Bengalis they were hoodwinking! Of course, there is nothing new in the instructions themselves: to empty the heart, to limit the breathing, and to direct the gaze inward. All that is formulated elsewhere with greater precision, in text no. 83, for example. Well, Edmund, I trust that your opinion will as usual be entirely different. What do you think?"

"Herr Professor," said Edmund in a low voice, "I believe that in this case you very much underestimate the value of the formula itself; the essential here is not our cheap interpretations of the words, but the words themselves. Apart from the bare meaning of the text, there must be something else, the sound, the choice of rare and archaic words, the associations aroused by the reminiscence of the snake magic—it was all this together that gave the text its magical power."

"If it actually had any," said the professor, laughing. "It's a pity you were not alive then, when these texts were still living. You would have been wonderfully amenable to the magical arts of the men who wrote these texts. But unfortunately you have come along several thousand years too late, and I am willing to bet that however hard you may try to carry out the instructions you have just read, you will never get the slightest result."

In excellent spirits he turned to the other student and went on with his interesting explanations.

Meanwhile Edmund reread his text several times; the opening words had made a particular impression on him, for they seemed to apply to himself and his situation. Word for word, he recited the formula inwardly, trying at the same time to carry out its instructions:

"If you find yourself in a situation where your soul falls sick and forgets what it needs for life, and you wish to know what it is that your soul needs and that you must give it: then make your heart empty, limit your breathing, etc."

He was able to concentrate much more fully than at the first attempt. He followed the instructions; his feeling told him that this was indeed the right moment, that his soul was in danger and had forgotten something important.

Soon after beginning the simple breathing yoga, which he had often practiced, he felt something happening within him. Then he felt a small hollow in the middle of his head. It was small and dark; he could see it. With mounting passion he directed his attention to the nut-sized cave, or "womb." And hesitantly the cave began to light up from within. The brightness gradually increased, and within the cave he perceived more and more clearly the image of what he had to do in order to go on living. The image did not frighten him; not for a moment did he doubt its authenticity; he felt in his innermost soul that the image was right, that it revealed nothing other than the "forgotten" need of his soul, its profoundest need.

Drawing from the image strength such as he had never known, he obeyed its command with joyful certainty and did the deed whose model he had glimpsed in the cave. He opened his eyes, which he had closed during the exercise, arose from his chair, took a step forward, stretched out his hands, put them around the professor's neck, and

squeezed it until he felt that it was enough. He let the
strangled man sink to the floor, turned away, and was
only then reminded that he was not alone: his fellow student was sitting there deathly pale, his forehead beaded
with sweat, staring at him in horror.

"It has all been fulfilled to the letter!" Edmund cried
out with enthusiasm. "I made my heart empty, I reduced
my breathing, I thought of the cave in my head, I directed
my gaze toward it until it really penetrated. And then I
saw the image; I saw the professor and I saw myself, I saw
my hands on his throat. Automatically, I obeyed the
image, no strength was needed, no decision. And now I
feel as wonderfully happy as never before in my life!"

"Get hold of yourself and think!" cried the other. "You've
killed a man! You're a murderer! You'll be executed!"

Edmund was not listening. For the moment these words
did not reach him. He mumbled the words of the magic
formula—*mar pegil trafu gnoki*—and saw neither living
nor dead professors, but the limitless expanse of the world
and of life, which lay open before him.

The Interrupted Class
1948

I T SEEMS AS THOUGH I were under the necessity in my late years not only of turning back to my childhood memories as all old people do, but also, by way of atonement as it were, of resuming the questionable art of storytelling under radically different conditions. Storytelling presupposes listeners and demands of the storyteller a courage which he can summon up only when he and his listeners have a setting, a society, an ethic, a language, and a manner of thinking in common. The models I revered in my youth (and whom I still revere and love), especially the teller of the *Seldwyla Tales*,* long supported me in those days in the pious belief that I too had been born into a community of this kind, that when I told stories I too had a home in common with my readers, that when I played for them it was on an instrument and with a system of notation which were equally familiar and self-evident to them and to myself. Light and dark, joy and grief, good and evil, action and suffering, piety and godlessness were, to be sure, not as categorically and glaringly distinguished as in the moralistic tales to be found in schoolbooks; there were shadings, there was psychology, above all there was humor, but I had no serious doubt either in the understanding of my readers or in the narrative quality of my stories, most of which, indeed, had solidly constructed plots, developing, as a well-behaved story should, from preparation to conflict to solution. I had no doubt that they gave my readers and myself

---

* Gottfried Keller, 1819–1890.—Ed.

almost as much pleasure as his stories had given the great
master of Seldwyla and his readers. Only very slowly and
reluctantly did I perceive in the course of the years that
my way of living did not correspond to my way of telling
stories, that for the sake of a good story I had more or less
distorted most of my experiences, and that I must either
give up storytelling or make up my mind to become a poor
storyteller rather than a good one. My attempts in this
direction, roughly from *Demian* to *The Journey to the
East,* led me further and further away from the good old
tradition of storytelling. And when today I try to record
an experience, be it ever so insignificant and ever so well
insulated, all my art seeps away and the substance of my
experience becomes almost uncannily polyphonic, am-
bivalent, complex, and opaque. To this I must resign myself; in the course of the last decades greater and older
values and treasures than the mere art of storytelling have
become questionable.

One morning we were sitting over a written exercise in
our none too well loved classroom at the Calw Latin
School. Only a few days before, we had returned to school
from a long vacation and handed in our blue report cards,
which our fathers had been obliged to sign. We were more
keenly aware of our imprisonment and boredom than
usual, because we hadn't had time to get used to them
again. The teacher, who though only in his mid-thirties
seemed as old as the hills to us eleven- and twelve-year-
olds, was also out of sorts, not hostile but dejected. There
was a look of suffering on his sallow features as he sat on
his raised throne, bent over a pile of report cards. Since
the death of his young wife he had been living alone with
his only son, a pale little boy with a high forehead and
watery blue eyes. The grave man looked strained and unhappy in his august loneliness; he was respected, but also
feared. Sometimes when he was annoyed, not to say angry, a flash of diabolical savagery burst through and mo-
mentarily belied his classical, humanistic countenance.

The room smelled of ink, boys, and shoe leather; the stillness was relieved only very rarely by a sound: the thud of
a dropped book on the dusty pinewood floor, a whispered
conversation, the spluttering wheeze of a repressed laugh,
which made it impossible not to turn around. The teacher
heard each one of these sounds and instantly quelled it,
usually with a mere glance, a finger upraised in warning
or a slight thrust of the chin; in extreme cases he would
clear his throat or say a word or two. The atmosphere was
not exactly electric, but between class and teacher there
was the sort of mild tension that can give rise to surprising
and often unpleasant incidents. It is quite possible that
this suited me better than perfect peace and harmony.
Maybe there was danger in the air, maybe something dis-
agreeable would happen, but especially during one of
these written exercises we longed for nothing so much as
some interruption or surprise, regardless of its nature. We
were very bored and restless, we had been sitting still too
long.

I no longer remember what sort of exercise our teacher
had given us to do while he, entrenched behind his desk,
busied himself with routine duties. It cannot have been
Greek, for the whole class was present, and in Greek the
teacher presided over only four or five "humanists," including myself. It was our first year of Greek, and the
separation of us "Greeks" or "humanists" from the rest of
the class had given our whole life in school a new note.
On the one hand we few Greeks, future pastors and aca-
demicians, found ourselves set apart from the great mass
of future tanners, clothiers, merchants, and brewers. This
was an honor, a challenge, and a goad, for we were the
élite, those destined to higher things than manual work
and moneymaking, but this honor, as is only fitting, also
had its troublesome and dangerous aspect. We knew that
in the distant future, examinations, whose difficulty was
legendary, lay in wait for us, in particular the dreaded
Landexamen—a competitive exam held in Stuttgart, to
which the humanistic students of all Swabia were con-

voked; it went on for several days and its purpose was to sift out the true élite; the entire future of many of the candidates depended on the outcome, for most of those who did not pass through this strait gate were condemned to abandon their studies. Since I myself was among the humanists, among those under consideration for membership in the élite, the thought had several times come to me, suggested no doubt by talks with my elder brother, that it must be extremely bitter and unpleasant for a humanist, for one who had been called but not yet by any means chosen, to be stripped of his title to honor and reduced to sitting out the final year of our school as a philistine among philistines.

Since the beginning of this school year, we few Greeks had been treading the narrow path to glory, and this had brought us into a new, far more intimate, and consequently more delicate relationship with our class teacher. For it was he who taught us Greek, and in Greek class we were no longer part of a large body that had at least its numbers to oppose to the teacher's power, but were individually at the mercy of this man who soon came to know each one of us better than he did anyone else in the class. In these often inspiring and more often terrifying hours, he imparted his knowledge and guidance, his ambition and love without stint, but also his moods, his suspicions and susceptibilities; we were the elect, we were his future colleagues, we were the small group of the more gifted or more ambitious destined for higher things; to us he gave more care and devotion than to all the rest of the class, but from us he demanded far more attention, industry, and interest, and also far more understanding for himself and his mission. We humanists were expected to be not run-of-the-mill students who willy-nilly let their teacher bludgeon the prescribed minimum of education into them, but ambitious and grateful companions on the narrow path, conscious of the high obligation flowing from our distinguished position. He would have liked to see humanists who made it necessary for him to rein in their burning ambition and thirst for knowledge, students who anticipated and received every morsel of spiritual food with avid hunger and converted it forthwith into new spiritual energies. I do not know in what degree my fellow Greeks were willing or able to live up to this ideal, but I imagine that they were all pretty much like myself, deriving a certain pride and feeling of class superiority from their humanism, regarding themselves as something rather nobler and more precious than the average, and I also believe that in their better moments this arrogance helped them to develop a certain sense of obligation and responsibility. But all in all we remained eleven- or twelve-year-old schoolboys, scarcely distinguishable from our non-humanist brethren, and none of us Greeks if offered the choice between an afternoon off and an extra Greek lesson would have hesitated for a moment, but would have delightedly picked the afternoon off. Of that there can be no doubt; and yet there was something else in our young minds, some glimmer of what our teacher expected and demanded of us so passionately and often so impatiently. As for me, I was no more intelligent than the others, nor was I mature beyond my years; I could have been lured away from Koch's *Grammar* and my humanistic dignity with far less than the paradise of an afternoon off. And yet, at times, in certain parts of my being, I was already a Journeyer to the East and a child of the Muses, unconsciously preparing myself to become a member and historian of all Platonic academies. Sometimes at the sound of a Greek word, or while shaping Greek letters in my copybook plowed through with the teacher's peevish corrections, I experienced the magic of a spiritual home; I was prepared, without reservation or competing desires, to follow the call of the spirit and the master's guidance. And so our fatuous pride at being an élite, our isolation, and our feeling of being at the mercy of our often-dreaded scholarch, were actually illumined by a ray of true light, a sense of mission, a breath of the sublime.

At the moment to be sure, in that tedious and dismal

morning hour, as I was sitting over my long-finished exercise, listening to the subdued sounds in the room and the distant, joyful notes of freedom from the outside world— the whirring wings of a flight of pigeons, the crowing of a cock, or the crack of a coachman's whip—it did not seem to me that noble spirits had ever dwelt in this low-ceilinged room. A trace of nobility, a ray of spirituality was discernible only on the rather tired, careworn face of the teacher, whom I secretly observed with a mixture of sympathy and guilty conscience, ready at any moment to avert my gaze should he look up. Thinking of nothing in particular, with no intentions of any kind, I was totally preoccupied with looking, with incorporating this face, which though unbeautiful was not without nobility, in my collection of images, and there it has been preserved for more than sixty years: the thin strands of hair over the sallow, angular forehead, the rather faded eyelids with their sparse lashes, the yellowish-pale, haggard face with its highly expressive mouth, which had the gift of articulating so clearly and of smiling with such mocking resignation, and the forceful, smoothly shaven chin. That image has remained imprinted on my mind—one of many; for years it lay unused in its spaceless archives, but whenever its time came, when it was summoned; it was always perfectly present and fresh, as though I had seen the original only a moment before. And as I watched the man on the platform, making a note of his unhappy face with its barely discernible tremors of passion repressed by discipline and mental effort, and inwardly converting it into a lasting image, the gloomy schoolroom was not so dismal after all and the seemingly so empty and tedious hour was not so empty and tedious. The teacher has been dead and buried for many years; of that batch of humanists I am probably the only one still alive, and with my death his portrait will be extinguished forever. None of my fellow Greeks became my close friend, we were not together long enough. All I know of one is that he has long been dead; of another that he was killed in the war in 1914. A third, whom I was very fond of, actually attained what was then our goal, becoming a clergyman and theologian. Fragments of his strange, undeviating career became known to me from time to time. He was a man who preferred idleness to any form of work and was very much given to life's little sensual enjoyments. At the university his fraternity brothers nicknamed him "Fleshpots." He remained single, studied theology, became a village pastor, traveled a good deal, was frequently reprimanded for shortcomings in the performance of his duties, retired while still in the prime of life, and had a long-drawn-out lawsuit with the church authorities over his pension claims. In his retirement he soon fell prey to boredom (even as a boy he had been uncommonly restless), which he combated partly by traveling and partly by spending several hours a day as a listener at courthouses. At the age of sixty, the emptiness and boredom became intolerable and he drowned himself in the Neckar.

My eyes were riveted to the top of the teacher's head. When he looked up and surveyed the class, I took fright as though caught in the act and lowered them.

"Weller," we heard him call out. Obediently Otto Weller stood up from one of the last benches. His big red face hovered like a mask over the heads of the others.

The teacher called him to his desk, held a little blue folder up to his face, and asked him a few questions in an undertone. Weller answered in a whisper, slightly averting his eyes, which gave him an anxious look that we were not accustomed to seeing in him. He was an easygoing sort, things that tormented the rest of us seemed to make no impression on him. It was an odd and unmistakable face that he turned toward the equally unforgettable face of my Greek teacher. Some of my classmates' faces, and even their names, left no trace in my memory, for the very next year I was sent to another school in another town. But I can still see Otto Weller's face clearly. It attracted attention, at that time at least, chiefly by its size; it was enlarged at the sides and bottom, for the parts below the cheekbone were conspicuously swollen, and this swelling made the face much broader than it would otherwise have been. Alarmed at this phenomenon, I once asked him what was the matter with his face. I remember his answer: "It's the glands. You see, I've got glands." Even apart from these glands, Weller's face was picturesque enough; it was full and vividly red; his hair was dark, his eyes good-natured, and the movements of his eyeballs very slow. His lips, despite their redness, resembled those of an old woman. Probably because of his glands, he held his chin somewhat upraised, so that one could see his whole throat; this posture helped to make the upper part of his face pass almost unnoticed, whereas despite its excess flesh, the lower, enlarged part had a benevolent, congenial look and, though rather vegetative and uninspired, was not without charm. I liked him, with his broad dialect and easygoing ways, but we did not see very much of each other. We lived in different spheres: in school I belonged to the humanist group and had my seat near the teacher's desk, while Weller sat in the back rows with the cheerful idlers, who seldom knew the answer to the teacher's questions, spent half their time munching nuts, dried pears, and the like that they dug out of their trouser pockets, and gave the teacher a good deal of trouble with their passivity and their uncontrolled talking and giggling. Outside of school Otto Weller also belonged to a different world; he lived out near the railroad station, far from my neighborhood, his father worked on the railroad and I had never so much as laid eyes on him.

After brief whispering Otto Weller was sent back to his place. He seemed unhappy. The teacher stood up, holding the little dark-blue folder, and peered out over the class, as though looking for something. His eyes finally lit on me; he stepped down, took my copybook, looked at it, and asked: "Have you finished?" When I said yes, he motioned me to follow him, went to the door, opened it to my surprise, led me out, and closed it behind him.

"There's something you can do for me," he said, hand-ing me the blue folder. "This is Weller's report card; I want you to take it to his parents. Tell them I should like to know whether the signature under Weller's report is really in his father's hand."

I slipped back into the classroom, took my cap from the wooden rack, put the folder in my pocket, and started out.

A miracle had happened. In the middle of the tedious class, the teacher had taken it into his head to send me out for a walk into the beautiful bright morning. I was overcome with surprise and happiness, I could not have conceived of anything more wonderful. As I leapt down the two flights of worn pinewood stairs, I could hear the monotonous drone of a teacher dictating in one of the other classrooms. I ran out the front door and down the flat sandstone steps, and sauntered happily and gratefully out into the lovely morning, which only a moment before had seemed so infinitely long and empty. Out here it was nothing of the sort; here there was no trace of the dullness or the hidden tensions that in the classroom sucked the life out of the hours and stretched them to such unbelievable length. Here the wind was blowing; the shadows of hurried clouds were passing over the cobbles of the big marketplace, flocks of pigeons were frightening little dogs and making them bark, horses harnessed to peasants' carts were eating hay out of a wooden crib, artisans were at work or chatting with their neighbors through their low-lying windows. The sturdy little pistol with the blue steel barrel was still on display in the little window of the hardware store. It was said to cost two and a half marks and I had been coveting it for weeks. Frau Haas's fruit stand in the market and Herr Jenisch's tiny toy shop were beautiful and tempting; and from the open workshop window nearby, the white-bearded, resplendently red face of the coppersmith was looking out, vying in brilliance and redness with the polished metal of the cooking pot on which he was hammering. This always cheerful and always inquisitive man seldom let anyone pass his window without talking to him or at least exchanging greetings. And now he spoke to me. "School out so soon?" he asked. And when I had explained that I was running an errand for my teacher, he said sympathetically: "Well, in that case don't be in too much of a hurry. The morning still has a long way to go." I took his advice and stood for a long while on the old bridge. Leaning against a parapet, I looked down into the quietly flowing water and watched a school of perch deep down, close to the bottom. They seemed to be asleep, lying motionless in one place, but in reality they were changing places. Mouths pointed downward, they were searching the bottom, but from time to time when they straightened out and could be seen without fore-shortening, I recognized the striped light-and-dark pattern. The water flowed over the nearby weir with a soft, high-pitched gurgling. Far downstream on the island, flocks of wild ducks were clamoring; at that distance their quack-ing and screaming also had a soft, monotonous sound and merged with the flowing of the water over the weir to pro-duce that magical murmur of eternity into which one can sink, lulled and blanketed as by the sound of rain on a summer night or by softly falling snow. I stood and looked, stood and listened, and for the first time that day I had a brief taste of the sweet eternity in which one knows nothing of time.

Aroused by the striking of the church clock, I came to myself with a start. Afraid that I had been there a long time, I remembered my errand. Only then did the errand and everything connected with it capture my attention. As I directed my steps without further delay to the railroad station district, I remembered Weller's unhappy face as he was exchanging whispers with the teacher, the way he had averted his eyes, and the expression of his back as he returned slowly, as though beaten, to his bench.

I had long known that a person is not the same at all times, that everyone can take on very different expressions and attitudes; I had observed this in myself and in others. What came as a surprise to me was that such transforma-tions, such strange, disconcerting shifts between courage

and fear, joy and misery could occur in him, in good old
Weller with the glandular face and the trouser pockets
full of edibles, in one of those boys in the back rows, who
seemed to have no worries at all about school and nothing
to fear but boredom, to whom study meant nothing, who
knew so little about books, but who, when it came to fruit
and bread, business, money, and other grown-up matters,
were so far ahead of the rest of us and indeed were almost
grown-ups themselves. I found this very upsetting.

I remembered a brief, matter-of-fact statement Weller
had made recently, which so startled me that I was almost
at a loss for an answer. We were on the way to the brook,
walking side by side in the midst of our schoolmates. His
rolled towel and swimming trunks wedged under his arm,
he was sauntering along beside me in his carefree way.
Suddenly he stopped still for a moment, turned his big
face toward me, and said: "My father makes seven marks
a day."

Up until then, I had never known how much anyone
made, nor did I have any very precise idea what seven
marks actually amounted to. Still, it struck me as a tidy
enough sum, and he had spoken in a tone of satisfaction
and pride. But since boasting with figures and magnitudes
was part of the conversational tone prevailing among us
boys, I refused to be impressed, though presumably he had
told the truth. As though returning a ball, I flung back my
answer, informing him that my father made twelve marks
a day. This was a lie, pure invention, but I had no scru-
ples, for the whole exchange was a rhetorical exercise.
Weller pondered a moment, and when he said "Twelve?"
his tone and expression left room for doubt whether he
had taken my figure seriously or not. He did not bother to
unmask me, he let well enough alone. I had said something that might be open to doubt, but never mind, it
wasn't worth arguing about, and that made him superior
again; he was experienced in practical matters, almost a
grown-up, and this I recognized without opposition. It was

like a man of twenty talking to an eleven-year-old. But weren't we both eleven-year-olds?

And then I remembered another speech of his, which he had tossed off in his grown-up, matter-of-fact way and which had amazed and shaken me even more than the first. It concerned a locksmith whose workshop was not far from the house where we were living with my grandfather. One day, as I had heard to my horror from the neighbors, this man had committed suicide, something which had not happened in our town for years and which to me seemed utterly unthinkable, at least so near us, amid the beloved scenes of my childhood life. The story was that he had hanged himself, but about this there was some argument; such an event was too big and unusual to be shelved from one day to the next; the neighbors were determined to get their share of gooseflesh out of it, and so no sooner was the poor man dead than the neighbor women, servantgirls, and postmen began to weave a cycle of legends around him, a few strands of which reached my ears. The next day Weller met me on the street as I was glancing furtively at the locksmith's house with its closed and silent workshop, and asked if I wanted to know how the locksmith had done it. Whereupon he proceeded, amiably and with a convincing air of absolute certainty, to enlighten me: "Well, you see, being a locksmith, he didn't want to use rope, so he did it with a wire. He took wire and nails and a hammer and pliers, and went into the woods; he went almost as far as the mill. Then he fastened the wire to the trees good, he even snipped off the loose ends with his pliers, and then he hung himself with the wire. But usually, you know, when somebody hangs himself, he does it by the neck, and that makes the tongue stick out and it looks terrible. He didn't want that. So what does he do? He didn't put the wire down around his neck, but right under his chin. That way his tongue didn't hang out. But his face was all blue."

And now it was plain that this Weller, who knew so

much about the world and troubled himself so little about school, was gravely worried. The teacher had doubted that the signature on his last report card was really his father's. And since Weller had looked so dejected, since his expression as he was going back to his seat had been so woebegone, it looked as if the teacher's doubts were justified. In that case it was more than a doubt, it was a suspicion, an accusation; Otto Weller was accused of trying to imitate his father's signature. Only then, when after my brief intoxication with the joys of freedom I woke up and was capable of thinking again, did I begin to understand the tortured look in my friend's averted eyes; only then did I realize that this was an ugly, serious business and begin to wish that I had not been the lucky boy chosen to go for a walk during school hours. The smiling morning with its wind and its racing cloud shadows and the beautiful smiling world through which I had passed had changed; my joy gave way to thoughts about Weller and his situation, unpleasant, saddening thoughts. Though without knowledge of the world and a child beside Weller with his practical experience, I knew from pious, moralistic tales for children of a certain age that forging a signature was something very bad, a criminal act, one of the stages on the sinner's path to prison and the gallows. But I liked Otto, he was a friendly, good-natured fellow, whom I could not regard as a profligate, headed for the gallows. I would have given a good deal for it to turn out that the signature was genuine and the suspicion unfounded. But hadn't I seen his worried, frightened face; hadn't he shown clearly that he was afraid, and what could that mean but a guilty conscience?

Again walking very slowly, I was approaching the building where the railroad workers lived, when I began to wonder if there was anything I could do for Otto. What, I thought, if I didn't go to the house at all, but went back to school and told the teacher the signature was all right? No sooner had the thought come to me than I was filled with anguish: now I had involved myself in this bad business;

if I followed my idea, I would no longer be a mere messenger and minor character, I would become a protagonist and accomplice. Walking more and more slowly, I finally passed the house and kept going; I needed time to think. But when I imagined that the noble, saving lie, to which I was already half resolved, had already been spoken and lost myself in its tangled consequences, I realized that it was beyond my strength. It was not intelligence, but fear of the consequences that made me renounce the role of helper and savior. A second, less drastic solution occurred to me. I could simply go back and report that no one had been home at the Wellers'. But even for that lie I had not enough courage. The teacher would believe me, but he would ask what had kept me so long. Feeling guilty and dejected, I finally went into the house and asked for Herr Weller. A woman told me that he lived on the top floor but had gone out to work and that I would find only his wife. I climbed the stairs; it was a bare, unfriendly kind of place, with a smell of cooking and of lye or soap. Frau Weller was home; she appeared from the kitchen, she was in a hurry and asked curtly what I wanted. But when I told her the class teacher had sent me, that it was about Otto's report card, she dried her hands on her apron and led me into the front room. She offered me a chair and even asked if I would like something to eat, maybe a sandwich or an apple. But I had already taken the folder out of my pocket. I held it out to her, explaining that the teacher wished to know if the signature was really Otto's father's. At first she did not understand, I had to say it again. She listened with a strained look, then held the open folder up to her eyes. I had time to watch her; for a long while she sat silent and motionless, staring at the folder. It seemed to me that she looked very much like her son, all except the glands. She had the same fresh red face, but as she sat there, saying nothing and holding the folder in her hands, I saw it slowly slacken and grow tired, faded, and old. Several minutes passed, and when she finally let the folder sink to her knees and looked at me again, or tried to, big tears were flowing from her wide-open eyes. While she had held the folder, pretending to herself to be studying it, I felt certain that the very same visions that had haunted me must be passing in a maca-bre, terrifying procession before her inner eye, visions of the sinner's path to the courtroom, prison, and gallows.

With my heart in my mouth I sat facing my friend's mother, who to my child's eyes was an old woman; I saw the tears flowing down her red cheeks and waited for her to say something. The long silence was hard to bear. But she said nothing. She sat there and wept. And when, un-able to endure it any longer, I finally broke the silence my-self and asked her once again if Herr Weller himself had signed the report card, her face became more forlorn and anguished than ever, and she shook her head several times. I stood up, she too stood up, and when I held out my hand, she held it a little while in her strong warm hands. Then she took the wretched blue folder, wiped a few tears off it, went to a chest, took out a newspaper, tore it into two pieces, put one back in the chest, and with the other neatly covered the folder. I did not dare to put it back in my pocket, but went away carrying it carefully in my hands.

On my way back I saw neither weir nor fish, neither shopwindows nor coppersmith. I told the teacher what he had wanted to know. He did not scold me for staying out so long, and to tell the truth I was disappointed. I was entitled to a reprimand, and it would have been a kind of consolation, for then I too would have had a small share in the punishment.

I never found out whether or how my classmate was punished. We never exchanged a word about the incident. Once on the street, when I saw his mother in the distance, I made a long detour—no detour could have been too long —to avoid meeting her.